WOLE SOYINKA

Six Plays

The Trials of Brother Jero
Jero's Metamorphosis
Camwood on the Leaves
Death and the King's Horseman
Madmen and Specialists
Opera Wonyosi

METHUEN DRAMA

METHUEN WORLD CLASSICS

First published in this edition in 1984 by Methuen London Ltd.
Reprinted in 1992 by Methuen Drama
an imprint of Reed Consumer Books Limited
Michelin House, 81 Fulham Road, London SW3 6RB
and Auckland, Melbourne, Singapore and Toronto
Reissued with a new cover design 1994

The Trials of Brother Jero first published in Great Britain in 1964 by Oxford
University Press, and in 1973 by Eyre Methuen Ltd. Copyright © 1964, 1973,
1984 by Wole Soyinka

Jero's Metamorphosis first published in Great Britain in 1973 by Eyre Methuen
Ltd. Copyright © 1973, 1984 by Wole Soyinka

Camwood on the Leaves first published in Great Britain in 1973 by Eyre Methuen
Ltd. Copyright © 1973, 1984 by Wole Soyinka

Death and the King's Horseman first published in Great Britain in 1975 by Eyre
Methuen Ltd. Copyright © 1975, 1984 by Wole Soyinka

Madmen and Specialists first published in Great Britain in 1971 by Methuen and
Co Ltd. Copyright © 1971, 1984 by Wole Soyinka

Opera Wonyosi first published in Great Britain in 1981 by Rex Collings Ltd.
Copyright © 1981, 1984 by Wole Soyinka

British Library Cataloguing in Publication Data

Soyinka, Wole
  Six plays.——(The Master playwrights)
  I. Title   II. Series
  822   PR9387.9.S6

ISBN 0–413–55350–7

Front cover: Soyinka & the Dance of the Gods by Gift Orakpo.

CAUTION

Printed in Great Britain by Cox & Wyman Ltd, Reading, Berkshire

Contents

Wole Soyinka : A Chronology

Note: Only first or specially notable productions of plays are given.

1934   Born in Abeokuta, of Ijegba parentage.

1938–43 Primary education – St Peter's School, Ake, Abeokuta.

1944–45 Abeokuta Grammar School.

1946–50 Government College, Ibadan.

1952–54 University College, Ibadan (now University of Ibadan).

1954–57 University of Leeds, obtained degree in English. Short stories published: *Madame Etienne's Establishment* and *A Tale of Two Cities*. Another story similarly titled in what was to be a series of that title.

1957–59 Attached to the Royal Court Theatre, London, as Play Reader. *The Invention* (never published) performed at the theatre in November 1959. On the programme were poems from the play in progress *A Dance of the Forests*, and other poems.

1959   *The Swamp Dwellers* produced for the *Sunday Times* Student Drama Festival. *The Swamp Dwellers* and *The Lion and the Jewel* (first version) produced in Ibadan, Nigeria.

1960   Langston Hughes' *African Treasury* published, containing Soyinka's poems.

     Back in Nigeria, Soyinka formed the 1960 Masks drama company. *A Dance of the Forests* produced with that company, the play winning the *Encounter* award.

1961–62 Rockerfeller Research Fellow in Drama, University of Ibadan.

1962   Frances Ademola's *Reflections* published, containing pieces by Soyinka.

1962–64   Lecturer in English, University of Ife.

1963   Satirical revue, *The Republican* performed by the 1960 Masks. Later in the same year, *The New Republican* performed. *The Lion and the Jewel* and *A Dance of the Forests* published. *Modern Poetry from Africa* (ed. Gerald Moore and Ulli Beier, Penguin) published, containing Soyinka's poems.

1964   Orisun Theatre (drama group) formed. March: twenty-five minute adaptation of *The Strong Breed* filmed in Nigeria for American Television (Esso World Theatre). *The Strong Breed* and *The Trials of Brother Jero* produced at Greenwich Mews Theatre, New York.

1964   *Five Plays* published (OUP).

1965   *Before the Blackout*, satirical revue, produced, Lagos and Ibadan, September. *The Road* directed by David Thompson at Theatre Royal, Stratford, East London. October: Soyinka arrested in connection with a 'pirate' broadcast made from the Western Region studios of the Nigerian Broadcasting Corporation, following disputed election results. Charged with Armed Robbery of two tapes from studios. December: acquitted. *The Road* published (OUP). *Camwood on the Leaves* (radio play) broadcast BBC, London. *The Interpreters* published. *Kongi's Harvest* directed by the author, Lagos.

1965–67   Senior Lecturer in English, University of Lagos and Acting Head of Department.

1966   *Kongi's Harvest* performed at the Dakar Festival of Negro Arts. *Rites of the Harmattan Solstice* (unpublished) celebrated at University of Lagos. June: *The Trials of Brother Jero* produced at Hampstead Theatre, London. December; *The Lion and the Jewel* produced at Royal Court Theatre, London.

1967   *Kongi's Harvest* published. *Idanre and Other Poems*

(Methuen) published. Awarded the John Whiting Drama prize. Appointed Head of Department of Theatre Arts, University of Ibadan. August: Detained by the Federal Military Government of Nigeria.

1968   Awarded the Jock Campbell *New Statesman* Literary Award. *The Forest of a Thousand Daemons*, Soyinka's translation of D. O. Fagunwa's novel *Ogboju Ode Ninu Igbo Irunmale* published (Nelson).

1969   *Three Short Plays* published. *Poems from Prison* published. October: released from detention. Assumed position as Head of Department of Theatre Arts, University of Ibadan.

1970   *Madmen and Specialists* (early version) produced at the Eugene O'Neil Theatre Center, Waterford, USA.

1971   January: complete version of *Madmen and Specialists* directed by the author in Ibadan and Ife. *Before the Blackout* published (Orisun Editions).

1972   *The Man Died* (prison notes) and *A Shuttle in the Crypt* (poems) published (Rex Collings).

1973   *The Jero Plays*, including *The Trials of Brother Jero* and *Jero's Metamorphosis*, and *Camwood on the Leaves* published (Methuen). *Collected Plays I* published (Oxford University Press). *Season of Anomy* published (Rex Collings). *The Bacchae of Euripides* performed at the National Theatre, London.

1973–74 Visiting Fellow, Churchill College, Cambridge.

1974   *Poems from Black Africa* (Soyinka ed.) published by Secker and Warburg.

1974–75 Visiting Professor, University of Ghana, Legon. Editor of *Transition* (later *Ch'Indaba*).

1975   Elected Secretary-General of the Union of Writers of the African Peoples, newly formed. *Collected Plays II* published (Oxford University Press). *Jero's Metamorphosis* performed Lagos. *The Detainee* (radio play) broadcast by BBC, London. Returned to Nigeria to take up appointment as Professor of Comparative Literature, University of Ife.

1976   *Death and the King's Horseman* performed in Ife. *Ogun Abibiman* (long poem) published (Rex Collings). *Myth, Literature and the African World* (essays) published (Cambridge University (Press).

1977   *Opera Wonyosi* (adaptation of *The Threepenny Opera*) performed in Ife, directed by author.

1978   Head, Department of Dramatic Arts, University of Ife. Created the Unife Guerilla Theatre, performing satirical revues.

1979   *Death and the King's Horseman* performed at the Goodman Theatre, Chicago and J. F. Kennedy Center, Washington, the author directing.

1979–80 Visiting Professor, Yale University.

1980   *Rice Unlimited* (satirical revues) performed Ife, Ibadan, Lagos.

1981   *Ake, The Years of Childhood* published (Rex Collings). *The Critic and Society* (essay) published (University of Ife Press).

1982   *Die Still, Dr Godspeak* (radio play) broadcast BBC, London. *Priority Projects* (satirical revue) toured in Nigeria.

1983   *Requiem for a Futurologist* performed in Ife and on tour.

1984   *A Play of Giants* published (Methuen). *Requiem for a Futurologist* published (Rex Collings). April: *The Road* directed by author, Goodman Theatre, Chicago.

INTRODUCTION

This article is based on edited extracts from an interview with Wole Soyinka by Dr Biodun Jeyifo, a lecturer in English Literature at the University of Ife, Nigeria, conducted on behalf of a Nigerian magazine in July 1983.

JEYIFO: You have been writing for more than two decades now. During this same period you have been very active in cultural movements and institutions both in Nigeria and the continent at large. Moreover, your international contacts as Secretary-General of the Union of Writers of African Peoples, the production of your plays around the world, all these have placed you in a rather privileged position to see literature and art in terms of broad social and historical forces. Has the situation of the African writer changed in the period of more than two decades that you have been writing? Can one in fact generalise about the situation of the African or Third World writer?

SOYINKA: I do not believe that one can generalise ... Obviously there are important, even critical differences in the situation of the Nigerian writer and that of – for example – Mobutu's Zaire, even though the politics of these two countries do not differ ideologically. I cannot imagine, for example, the Zairean writer being passionately concerned with thoughts on how to stop the recent South African raids into Angola ... he's far too immediately involved with that 'throwback' whose continued hold on power in his own country threatens his very existence, should he step out of line.

By contrast, the Nigerian writer can actually afford to be positive in his concern with the movement of worldwide forces, such as are gathering around Southern Africa or even Latin America, and the Middle East of course, even as he attempts to utilise his craft in the immediate context of desired changes within his society. We are of course speaking in general terms.

Twenty-five years ago, to use me as an example, I was almost exclusively concerned with the problem of black liberation from the settler-colonial and apartheid obscenities. As a student just beginning to write seriously, I saw the political battleground in Africa as being situated in Southern Africa, nowhere else. You see, in West Africa, for instance, we were thrown right in the midst of the nationalism of people like Enahoro, Oged Macauley, Azikiwe, Nduka Eze, etc, right from the very beginning, from childhood. So colonialism, for me, was already dead ... I was already thinking of it in the past tense, as something already dealt with. It was just a matter of time; obviously it could not last.

Perhaps that's why my political attention centred so squarely on Southern Africa at the time ... My first two 'serious' plays were on Southern Africa. One of them was a melodramatic piece which, after about six versions, I realised was just 'wrong' and I destroyed it in a sober moment. The other was *The Invention*, which marked my debut on the professional stage in London. Neither of course was very satisfactory to me and, later on, I understood why. The passion was there, it was 'correct' and genuine and honest, but I was experiencing the situation vicariously. I also threw myself frenetically into the collective production of *Eleven Men Dead at Hola* also at the Royal Court Theatre, which was a sort of haven for a number of aspiring writers at the time. This was a dramatisation of the scandalous beating and stamping to death of eleven suspected 'Mau-Mau' detainees in Kenya, and I remember contributing quite extensively to the writing and even to the music. I acted in it also. Well, there were other things I did in preparation for the 'day of liberation'. Now the change, when it came, was an abrupt change, a total change. I took one look at our first set of legislators – you know, partial self-government at the time – when they visited the UK and talked to students, and I listened to them, watched them, and I *knew* . . . That instant, I think I received what the Japanese might term 'political satori', you know, instant illumination. I realised that the first enemy was within. If there was any shadow of doubt left, it was soon removed by the pattern of thought which developed among my erstwhile 'comrades' for whom all thought of liberation in Southern Africa, etc, also suddenly disappeared, but for very different reasons. They could not wait to return home and get a slice of 'independence cake', because that was all independence meant to them: step fast into the shoes of the departing whites before other people got there. It was then that I began to write *A Dance of the Forests*, which takes a jaundiced view of the much-vaunted glorious past of Africa. And I suppose since then I've been doing nothing but the *danse macabre* in this political jungle of ours.

JEYIFO: Has your conception of your audience changed from what you once described as minds out there in the world with whom you can communicate? At any rate, what views can you offer now as to who the writer's audience is or ought to be?

SOYINKA: No, my conception has not changed about this belief in the fact that I cannot write for myself, that it is impossible for me to write something that is entirely and solely for myself. But I think there is a lot of mystique about this business of whom one reaches in one's writing and whom one *ought* to reach. It's a mystique because, whenever one has to speak to a specific issue, and to a specific situation and people, anytime, anybody who is as socially and politically committed as I think I am, one will always find the means for it. It won't always be a *tome* – I consider literature, all writing, all creative work, a joint social operation. There are various media of expression and one can employ any of these media at any time to reach a public. In the early sixties, for instance, and in Ife in recent times, whenever I've been able to gather groups together, we've been experimenting, indulging in what we call the guerilla theatre – the political and social sketches are very different in content, in tone and style from, for instance, a novel like *The Interpreters*. And the purposes are different. *The Interpreters* was an attempt to capture a particular moment in the lives of a generation which was trying to find its feet after independence. By contrast, all those sketches, Orisun Theatre Sketches, the recent 'Ethical Revolution' sketches and so on, are an attempt to reach a much larger audience and make certain statements which are pertinent and even crucial to the ongoing economic and political situation within the country. It's a kind of sensitizing of the political and social conscience and consciousness of the people. And at the same time, the idea even of putting the songs on record also came into being because of the approaching elections, which I consider very critical to the remote possibility of a future for this country.

Well, a desperate consciousness of the critical moment in which we are gave me the idea, for the first time, of actually making a record out of some of the songs in our sketches of political commentary, and even writing a totally new one for the other side of the record. So you see, returning to this business of whom one is addressing at any given time, I believe there is a lot of *angst* about it because as I said, writing, creativity in general, is a *social* phenomenon, and therefore, somewhere, at any given time, what needs to be said has a way of coming to be said in whatever form ... It's a combination of various pressures, of learning to think slightly out of your normal routine and finding a new form of expression which says very desperately and urgently what *needs* to be said in that particular form ...

JEYIFO: You once expressed – in a private conversation – your admiration of Shakespeare, Beethoven and Picasso above all others in Western culture and art, for their protean range and mastery of diverse styles, forms and subjects. But Proteus, as a metaphor of the creative principle, comes from Western culture while you have also adopted Ogun as an essence of the creative artist. Similarly, in your important essay, 'The Fourth Stage', you conjoin classical Greek and traditional Yoruba deities and idealities as expressive paradigms of the psychic aspects of art in general and tragedy in particular. Such procedures have drawn a label of 'Europhile' intellectualism from certain African critics. What is your reaction to this?

SOYINKA: Well, 'Europhile' criticism used to be the favourite terminology of certain groups, and there's so much nonsense in this accusation that I don't think it's even worth replying to. For a start, many of these people are not even critics, they're merely 'throwback activists' – the kind of criticism which they make about literature they also make about the bearing of foreign names, as if this is what the radicalisation of society is all about. That pattern is not my conception of what the African heritage is. If I want to name my son after Fidel Castro, *nobody* is going to stop me – if I want to name him after Lenin, after Garibaldi, for reasons of sentiment or political optimism, whatever, nobody is going to stop me ... because I don't think *that* constitutes a betrayal of my African resources. These throwbacks – I call them 'Neo-Tarzanists' – lack the intellectual capacity first of all even to appreciate the kind of exploration which I am making into points of departure as well as meeting points between African and European literary and artistic traditions, quite unabashedly exploiting these various complementarities, or singularities, or contradictions, in my own work. So these throwbacks are missing out on a lot that can be enjoyed intellectually and creatively in the entire creative corpus of man. There's no way at all that I will ever preach the cutting off of *any* source of knowledge: Oriental, European, African, Polynesian, or whatever. There's no way anyone can ever legislate that, once knowledge comes to one, that knowledge should be forever excised as if it never existed ...

JEYIFO: Still on this issue of points of departure and convergence between Western and African traditions: there's the case of Christianity and its historic contact with African art and culture. Do you think Christianity can inspire significant artistic or literary expression? You have spoken very strongly on Christianity as a force that is inimical to the creative roots of our culture.

SOYINKA: This relates to the former question. Of course Christianity can inspire, and *has* inspired, significant artistic expressions. You see, a work of art very often leaves its moorings, its sources of inspiration, and becomes an object of admiration in itself. So it doesn't matter that it started out in Bhuddism, or Islam, like the work of Skunder Boghossian and Ibrahim el-Salahi. They began by attempting to stay within the Islamic culture which sort of frowns on direct human representation, so that Salahi began working within calligraphic motifs, the calligraphic idiom, and created the most incredible and beautiful works of art. Boghossian moved in a different direction and started by exploring the symbols of productivity, procreation in general. So these were people who were *conditioned*, at least at the beginning, by a religious point of view and then either deviated or exploited the *very* constrictions within those religions. And the same thing goes of course for Indian Tantric art, medieval architecture, medieval 'naive' painting, which are admired today. I derive great aesthetic pleasure out of my encounters with such works, so I can never rule out any religion ... To do that is to say that in my own society our religions have not produced, have not inspired great works of art – and we do know that they have. The artefacts, the objects themselves, are all around us, magnificent carvings which have also inspired European artists like Picasso and Modigliani. The entire Cubist and Expressionist movements owe much to the encounter of these artists with works which were inspired by our traditional religions. So how can we preach a kind of 'valve system' of artistic contact? Of course it must open both ways. Yes, it is true that I have stated that the Christian faith has been inimical to, and even destructive of, the creative roots of our cultures and sensibilities. But this is a *historic* fact. I've documented it in some of my essays. We know how the early missionaries – but you see they were philistines, *they* were barbarians – used to go out and literally create bonfires out of our works of art, how they banned traditional music and instruments in the churches of their religions. Now in fact we lost quite a sizeable heritage of skills because they were not satisfied with merely converting our forefathers, they actually *warned* them that their cultural activities, their habits of thought and so on, were works of the devil. The same thing with Islam – these two religions have, for me, been very, very destructive of a number of aspects of our traditional cultures. These are historical facts.

JEYIFO: To take the whole texture or *oeuvre* of your literary work, one is struck by certain all but irreconcilable antinomies – a constant evocation of a communal ethos, a communal spirit side by side with an implacable affirmation of individualism – a strong celebration of *joie de vivre* almost amounting to literary hedonism, side by side with a deeply and profoundly tragic and pessimistic outlook. How do you react to the observation that these antinomic tensions are barely contained or integrated or resolved in your works?

SOYINKA: Yes, the 'antinomies' in my writings. But are these not a reflection of the human condition? Nobody can say that he's never been through moments of intense pain or pessimism, whether on a very private level, or even of viewing what I've termed a 'recurrent cycle of stupidities', an expression which distresses those who want human existence to be so obviously and patently, without any qualifications, optimistic. But what Nigerian today, *what* thinking or feeling Nigerian this very moment that I'm talking, looks at his country and does not experience absolute despondency? Well, is one to pretend that such gloom does not exist? When Fidel Castro's comrades were destroyed during the very first attempt to liberate Cuba, you see, I try to get into the heart of a man like that, at the moment when he was the *sole* survivor of a band of revolutionaries who tried to overthrow Batista, and the rest perished in the swamps or were shot down by Batista's goons; what did he experience? This is the *moment* of tragedy. But the human spirit constantly overrides the *negative* side of it, not always, but those who inspire us ultimately are those who succeed in overcoming the moment of despair, those who arise from the total fragmentation of the psyche, the annihilation of even their ego, and yet succeed in piecing them together, *piece* the rubble together to emerge and enrich us by that example.

But how can we ever be enriched by that example if we do not recognise the *tragic prelude* to the moment of triumph? It's there, tragedy exists in human life and I do not believe that the function of the writer is to ignore the tragic aspect of human experience, that tragic face of truth. That would be just to write propaganda, to write one-dimensional works, and even to ask ourselves what was all the victory about if it was so obvious anyway. And it's true that one can get seduced by the poetry of tragedy, but why not? If tragedy enforces its own music, its own poetry, if this *tragic grandeur* can be expressed only in beautiful tomes or sublime music, or the particular sound and orchestration of words which we call poetic, what is wrong with that? That is part of the property of the experience, and that is part of the richness of art and literature. When the moments of celebration come, you are quite right, I do experience my 'joie de vivre', but it is beyond mere sensual existence, no, the kind of 'joie de vivre' which I'm referring to is the kind which is experienced at the moment of the acceptance of a challenge. That's why, for instance, I was able to write *Ogun Abibiman*, which I called a 'revolutionary joie de vivre'. For me, that moment when Samora Machel accepted the challenge of South Africa – and remember what I said at the beginning: that this sore, this festering toe of the continent of Africa, has always been my petty obsession, even though since my early days I've re-defined my immediate constituency – was not a tragic moment at all, even though I know it predicates loss. Suddenly there's a statement to the people of a continent, to myself personally, that somebody thousands of miles away has finally rejected further dialogue or compromise with an uncompromisable situation; for me it's the same kind of *joie de vivre* that I experience in *that* moment as I experience when I drink a good, heady glass of wine. There's no difference! So this antinomic tension is not something to be contained; in fact it's at the very heart of my creative existence, the acceptance of the tragic face of life, the tragic face inherent even in the joyous acceptance of responsibility, because the acceptance of responsibility or commitment is, unless one is an out-and-out unreflective optimist, even the acceptance of commitment cannot escape the historic experience in other areas by other people, and the simultaneous awareness of the history of others of similar undertakings gives it a tragic tinge. The history of betrayals is constantly at the back of one's mind, the knowledge of the constant possibility of betrayals[1] in the whole history of political movements in the world, yet the knowledge that one must go on, which you might describe as fatalism but which I consider the very essence of life, of existence, of change, of progress within society. So is there a tension in my work? Yes, but the tension has sort of become the reality, the very material on which I work.

JEYIFO: On the psycho-affective level, how do you write? What sparks off or ignites the creative urge? Is this even an appropriate metaphor to use for the subjective aspects of the creative process?

SOYINKA: How do I write? What sparks off or ignites the urge to write? I do not know. I refer to myself often as being basically lazy in the sense that I would rather not write. I suppose recollection sometimes, a sort of intense recollection of a former experience can trigger off the need to write. And of course there's the other kind of writing when writing is *merely* a medium for expressing what *needs* to be expressed, like an urgent political situation for instance, so you address yourself to that instant and that one is plain enough; that's why journalists write, columnists write, that's why our troubadours sing. But in general, what ignites the creative spark, I honestly do not know.

JEYIFO: You have called for the adoption of one single language for the entirety of black Africa and have translated from Yoruba to English. Yet you continue to use English and are uncontestably entirely self-assured in that language. Are we now beyond the 'Prospero-Caliban' syndrome of the complexes which attend the adoption of a language of colonial imposition?

SOYINKA: Yes, I have called for the adoption of one single language for the whole of Africa – Kiswahili – and I believe very much in it. I do not believe that I will ever write in Kiswahili, although I will write a few poems in it, a few *careful* verses, you know. I will set up the machinery, assist and participate in setting up a machinery for translating works, including mine, into Kiswahili. And that comes to the same thing. A lot of works come to us in translation, what's wrong in that? They lose something, but they also gain in other respects. I have said, I consider, very seriously consider, literature as a *very* social activity, even though very often it takes place in the privacy of one's creative space. But it *is* a social activity and so the continuity of it, even the criticism is part of the social continuity of a work of literature. So translation occupies its own place within the overall social activity. English of course continues to be my medium of expression as it is the medium of expression for millions of people in Nigeria, Ghana, Sierra Leone, Gambia, Kenya, who I want to talk to, if possible. And I want to talk also to our black brothers in the United States, in the West Indies. I want to talk *also* even to Europeans, if they are interested in listening. But *they* are at the very periphery of my concerns. I do know that I enjoy works of literature from the European world – I'd be a liar if I said I didn't. And I also enjoy literary works from the Asian world, Chinese literature, Japanese literature – I teach Japanese drama. I've taught Chinese poetry, when I was still in the Literature Department. I always interjected translations of poetry from the Asiatic world because I wanted to open up that vast area to our students. I enjoy the works of Tolstoy, Turgenev, Gogol, etc. So, I find no contradiction, no sense of guilt, in the fact that I write and communicate in English. And I'll tell you something. I receive letters from totally unknown people, *totally* unknown, from the Soviet Union, from the United States, from Cuba, from Asia,

Japan, from the Arab world, who were only able to read my work because it's in English and other foreign tongues — I've received a hundred letters from all corners of the world since *Ake* came out, for instance, from people, from some school-children, and to say that this does not give me joy, some kind of very special pleasure, is to lie. I'm glad that I'm reaching all these people.

But that should not prevent us adopting some means of reaching, first, our own people on this continent. I would like everybody on this continent to be able to read works of Kole Omotoso, Odia Ofeimun, Iroh, Sowande, Iyayi, as well as the works of our comrades in Ghana, Kenya, and so on. The 'Prospero-Caliban' syndrome, I think, is dead.[2]

---

[1] 'Remember dreams that *will* go sour, ideals
Afloat upon the cesspools of our time.'

Just in time for proofs of this collection, the same Mozambican leader, with the full approval of all the 'front-line states' signs a non-agression pact with South Africa. The ANC has bewailed its sense of 'betrayal' and vowed to continue the struggle.

Does that make 'Ogun Abibiman' a tragic poem? Is Busia (one of the early proponents of 'dialogue' with South Africa) chuckling in his grave? Is Banda smarming under his bowler-hat? Is Houphouet-Boigny toasting with champagne flown in specially for the occasion? Only one thing is certain: this poet is still grateful that the War Muse seized upon him the moment that earlier uncompromising declaration emerged from an African leader, but acknowledges also that even while celebrating, the possibility of 'loss', 'betrayals', remained stubbornly entwined in the euphoria.

[2] It occurs to me — not for the first time — but prompted this time by the Nigerian Military coup of December 1983, that this question should be extended to the real 'moulders' of society whose impact on their society is always of a far more critical and profound effect than the writer's. The first and succeeding announcements of that coup (as always) took place in English. All the interviews by the coup-leaders, both local and international, took place in English. Now I did not hear one questioner — Nigerian or foreign — agonise over the fact that an event of such magnitude, affecting over eighty million Nigerians directly and crucially, was not communicated in a Nigerian language. Elaboration of this theme is unending for all ex-colonial peoples — the judiciary, the legislatures, commerce, pop culture, the media, bureaucracy, public services etc, etc. Is the writer somehow mystically situated outside this comprehensive communication territory?

THE TRIALS
OF BROTHER JERO

CAST

JEROBOAM, *a Beach Divine*
OLD PROPHET, *his mentor*
CHUME, *assistant to Jeroboam*
AMOPE, *his wife*
A TRADER
MEMBER OF PARLIAMENT
THE PENITENT, *a woman*
THE ANGRY WOMAN, *a tough mamma*
A YOUNG GIRL
A DRUMMER BOY
A MAN AND AN OLD COUPLE (*worshippers*)

SCENE ONE

The stage is completely dark. A spotlight reveals the PROPHET, *a heavily but neatly bearded man; his hair is thick and high, but well-combed, unlike that of most prophets. Suave is the word for him. He carries a canvas pouch and a divine rod.* He speaks directly and with his accustomed loftiness to the audience.*

JERO. I am a prophet. A prophet by birth and by inclination. You have probably seen many of us on the streets, many with their own churches, many inland, many on the coast, many leading processions, many looking for processions to lead, many curing the deaf, many raising the dead. In fact, there are eggs and there are eggs. Same thing with prophets. I was born a prophet. I think my parents found that I was born with rather thick and long hair. It was said to come right down to my eyes and down to my neck. For them, this was a certain sign that I was born a natural prophet. And I grew to love the trade. It used to be a very respectable one in those days and competition was dignified. But in the last few years, the beach has become fashionable, and the struggle for land has turned the profession into a thing of ridicule. Some prophets I could name gained their present beaches by getting women penitents to shake their bosoms in spiritual ecstasy. This prejudiced the councillors who came to divide the beach among us. Yes, it did come to the point where it became necessary for the Town Council to come to the beach and settle the prophets' territorial warfare once and for all. My Master, the same one who brought me up

* A metal rod about eighteen inches long, tapered, bent into a ring at the thick end.

in prophetic ways staked his claim and won a grant of land . . . I helped him, with a campaign led by six dancing girls from the French territory, all dressed as Jehovah's Witnesses. What my old Master did not realize was that I was really helping myself. Mind you, the beach is hardly worth having these days. The worshippers have dwindled to a mere trickle and we really have to fight for every new convert. They all prefer High Life to the rhythm of celestial hymns. And television too is keeping our wealthier patrons at home. They used to come in the evening when they would not easily be recognized. Now they stay at home and watch television. However, my whole purpose in coming here is to show you one rather eventful day in my life, a day when I thought for a moment that the curse of my old Master was about to be fulfilled. It shook me quite a bit, but . . . the Lord protects his own . . .

Enter OLD PROPHET *shaking his fist.*

OLD PROPHET. Ungrateful wretch! Is this how you repay the long years of training I have given you? To drive me, your old Tutor, off my piece of land . . . telling me I have lived beyond my time. Ha! May you be rewarded in the same manner. May the wheel come right round and find you just as helpless as you make me now . . .

He continues to mouth curses, but inaudibly.

JERO (*ignoring him*). He didn't move me one bit. The old dodderer had been foolish enough to imagine that when I organized the campaign to acquire his land in competition with (*Ticking them off on his fingers.*) – The Brotherhood of Jehu, the Cherubims and Seraphims, the Sisters of Judgement Day, the Heavenly Cowboys, not to mention the Jehovah's Witnesses whom the French girls impersonated – well, he must have been pretty conceited to think that I did it all for him.

OLD PROPHET. Ingrate! Monster! I curse you with the curse of the Daughters of Discord. May they be your downfall. May the Daughters of Eve bring ruin down on your head!

OLD PROPHET *goes off, shaking his fist.*

JERO. Actually that was a very cheap curse. He knew very well that I had one weakness – women. Not my fault, mind you. You must admit that I am rather good-looking . . . no, don't be misled, I am not at all vain. Nevertheless, I decided to be on my guard. The call of prophecy is in my blood and I would not risk my calling with the fickleness of women. So I kept away from them. I am still single and since that day when I came into my own, no scandal has ever touched my name. And it was a sad day indeed when I woke up one morning and the first thing to meet my eyes was a daughter of Eve. You may compare that feeling with waking up and finding a vulture crouched on your bedpost.

Blackout.

SCENE TWO

Early morning.

A few poles with nets and other litter denote a fishing village. Downstage right is the corner of a hut, window on one side, door on the other.

A cycle bell is heard ringing. Seconds after, a cycle is ridden on stage towards the hut. The rider is a shortish man; his feet barely touch the pedals. On the cross-bar is a woman; the cross-bar itself is wound round with a mat, and on the carrier is a large travelling sack, with a woman's household stool hanging from a corner of it.

AMOPE. Stop here. Stop here. That's his house.

The man applies the brakes too suddenly. The weight leans towards the woman's side, with the result that she props up the bicycle with her feet, rather jerkily. It is in fact no worse than any ordinary landing, but it is enough to bring out her sense of aggrievement.

AMOPE (*her tone of martyrdom is easy, accustomed to use*). I suppose we all do our best, but after all these years one would think you could set me down a little more gently.

CHUME. You didn't give me much notice. I had to brake suddenly.

AMOPE. The way you complain – anybody who didn't see what happened would think you were the one who broke an ankle. (*She has already begun to limp.*)

CHUME. Don't tell me that was enough to break your ankle.

AMOPE. Break? You didn't hear me complain. You did your best, but if my toes are to be broken one by one just because I have to monkey on your bicycle, you must admit it's a tough life for a woman.

CHUME. I did my . . .

AMOPE. Yes, you did your best. I know. Didn't I admit it? Please . . . give me that stool . . . You know yourself that I'm not the one to make much of a little thing like that, but I haven't been too well. If anyone knows that, it's you. Thank you (*Taking the stool.*) . . . I haven't been well, that's all. Otherwise I wouldn't have said a thing.

She sits down near the door of the hut, sighing heavily, and begins to nurse her feet.

CHUME. Do you want me to bandage it for you?

AMOPE. No, no. What for?

CHUME *hesitates, then begins to unload the bundle.*

CHUME. You're sure you don't want me to take you back? If it swells after I've gone . . .

AMOPE. I can look after myself. I've always done, and looked after you too. Just help me unload the things and place them against the wall . . . you know I wouldn't ask if it wasn't for the ankle.

CHUME *had placed the bag next to her, thinking that was all. He returns now to unpack the bundle. Brings out a small brazier covered with paper which is tied down, two small saucepans . . .*

AMOPE. You haven't let the soup pour out, have you?

CHUME (*with some show of exasperation*). Do you see oil on the wrapper? (*Throws down the wrapper.*)

AMOPE. Abuse me. All right, go on, begin to abuse me. You know that all I asked was if the soup had poured away, and it isn't as if that was something no one ever asked before. I would do it all myself if it wasn't for my ankle – anyone would think it was my fault . . . careful . . . careful now . . . the cork nearly came off that bottle. You know how difficult it is to get any clean water in this place . . .

CHUME *unloads two bottles filled with water, two little parcels wrapped in paper, another tied in a knot, a box of matches, a piece of yam, two tins, one probably an Ovaltine tin but containing something else of course, a cheap breakable spoon, a knife, while* AMOPE *keeps up her patient monologue, spoken almost with indifference.*

AMOPE. Do, I beg you, take better care of that jar . . . I know you didn't want to bring me, but it wasn't the fault of the jar, was it?

CHUME. Who said I didn't want to bring you?

AMOPE. You said it was too far away for you to bring me on your
bicycle . . . I suppose you really wanted me to walk . . .

CHUME. I . . .

AMOPE. And after you'd broken my foot, the first thing you asked
was if you should take me home. You were only too glad it
happened . . . in fact if I wasn't the kind of person who would
never think evil of anyone – even you – I would have said that
you did it on purpose.

The unloading is over. CHUME *shakes out the bag.*

AMOPE. Just leave the bag here. I can use it for a pillow.

CHUME. Is there anything else before I go?

AMOPE. You've forgotten the mat. I know it's not much, but I
would like something to sleep on. There are women who sleep
in beds of course, but I'm not complaining . . . They are just
lucky with their husbands, and we can't all be lucky I suppose.

CHUME. You've got a bed at home.

He unties the mat which is wound round the cross-bar.

AMOPE. And so I'm to leave my work undone. My trade is to
suffer because I have a bed at home? Thank God I am not the
kind of woman who . . .

CHUME. I am nearly late for work.

AMOPE. I know you can't wait to get away. You only use your
work as an excuse. A Chief Messenger in the Local Government Office – do you call that work? Your old school friends
are now Ministers, riding in long cars . . .

CHUME *gets on his bike and flees.* AMOPE *shouts after him,
craning her neck in his direction.*

AMOPE. Don't forget to bring some more water when you're

returning from work. (*She relapses and sighs heavily.*) He doesn't realize it is all for his own good. He's no worse than other men, but he won't make the effort to become something in life. A Chief Messenger. Am I to go to my grave as the wife of a Chief Messenger?

> *She is seated so that the* PROPHET *does not immediately see her when he opens the window to breathe some fresh air. He stares straight out for a few moments, then shuts his eyes tightly, clasps his hands together above his chest, chin uplifted for a few moments' meditation. He relaxes and is about to go in when he sees* AMOPE's *back. He leans out to try and take in the rest of her, but this proves impossible. Puzzled, he leaves the window and goes round to the door which is then seen to open about a foot and shut rapidly.*
>
> AMOPE *is calmly chewing kola. As the door shuts she takes out a notebook and a pencil and checks some figures.*
>
> PROPHET JEROBOAM, *known to his congregation as* BROTHER JERO, *is seen again at the window, this time with his canvas pouch and divine stick. He lowers the bag to the ground, eases one leg over the window.*

AMOPE (*without looking back*). Where do you think you're going?

> BROTHER JERO *practically flings himself back into the house.*

AMOPE. One pound, eight shillings and ninepence for three months. And he calls himself a man of God.

> *She puts the notebook away, unwraps the brazier and proceeds to light it preparatory to getting breakfast.*
> *The door opens another foot.*

JERO (*coughs*). Sister . . . my dear sister in Christ . . .
AMOPE. I hope you slept well, Brother Jero . . .

JERO. Yes, thanks be to God. (*Hems and coughs.*) I – er – I hope you have not come to stand in the way of Christ and his work.

AMOPE. If Christ doesn't stand in the way of me and my work.

JERO. Beware of pride, sister. That was a sinful way to talk.

AMOPE. Listen, you bearded debtor. You owe me one pound, eight and nine. You promised you would pay me three months ago but of course you have been too busy doing the work of God. Well, let me tell you that you are not going anywhere until you do a bit of my own work.

JERO. But the money is not in the house. I must get it from the post office before I can pay you.

AMOPE (*fanning the brazier*). You'll have to think of something else before you call me a fool.

> BROTHER JEROBOAM *shuts the door.*
> A woman TRADER *goes past with a deep calabash bowl on her head.*

AMOPE. Ei, what are you selling?

> *The* TRADER *hesitates, decides to continue on her way.*

AMOPE. Isn't it you I'm calling? What have you got there?

TRADER (*stops without turning round*). Are you buying for trade or just for yourself?

AMOPE. It might help if you first told me what you have.

TRADER. Smoked fish.

AMOPE. Well, let's see it.

TRADER (*hesitates*). All right, help me to set it down. But I don't usually stop on the way.

AMOPE. Isn't it money you are going to the market for, and isn't it money I'm going to pay you?

TRADER (*as* AMOPE *gets up and unloads her*). Well, just remember it is early in the morning. Don't start me off wrong by haggling.

AMOPE. All right, all right. (*Looks at the fish.*) How much a dozen?

TRADER. One and three, and I'm not taking a penny less.

AMOPE. It is last week's, isn't it?

TRADER. I've told you, you're my first customer, so don't ruin my trade with the ill-luck of the morning.

AMOPE (*holding one up to her nose*). Well, it does smell a bit, doesn't it?

TRADER (*putting back the wrappings*). Maybe it is you who haven't had a bath for a week.

AMOPE. Yeh! All right, go on. Abuse me. Go on and abuse me when all I wanted was a few of your miserable fish. I deserve it for trying to be neighbourly with a cross-eyed wretch, pauper that you are . . .

TRADER. It is early in the morning. I am not going to let you infect my luck with your foul tongue by answering you back. And just you keep your cursed fingers from my goods because that is where you'll meet with the father of all devils if you don't.

She lifts the load to her head all by herself.

AMOPE. Yes, go on. Carry the burden of your crimes and take your beggar's rags out of my sight . . .

TRADER. I leave you in the hands of your flatulent belly, you barren sinner. May you never do good in all your life.

AMOPE. You're cursing me now, are you?

She leaps up just in time to see BROTHER JERO *escape through the window.*

Help! Thief! Thief! You bearded rogue. Call yourself a prophet? But you'll find it is easier to get out than to get in. You'll find that out or my name isn't Amope . . .

She turns on the TRADER *who has already disappeared.*

Do you see what you have done, you spindle-leg toad? Receiver of stolen goods, just wait until the police catch up with you . . .

> *Towards the end of this speech the sound of gangan drums is heard, coming from the side opposite the hut. A* BOY *enters carrying a drum on each shoulder. He walks towards her, drumming. She turns almost at once.*

AMOPE. Take yourself off, you dirty beggar. Do you think my money is for the likes of you?

> *The* BOY *flees, turns suddenly and beats a parting abuse on the drums.**

AMOPE. I don't know what the world is coming to. A thief of a prophet, a swindler of a fish-seller and now that thing with lice on his head comes begging for money. He and the prophet ought to get together with the fish-seller their mother.

> *Lights fade.*

SCENE THREE

A short while later. The Beach. A few stakes and palm leaves denote the territory of Brother Jeroboam's church. To one side is a palm tree, and in the centre is a heap of sand with assorted empty bottles, a small mirror, and hanging from one of the bottles is a rosary and cross. BROTHER JERO *is standing as he was last seen when he made his escape – white flowing gown and a very fine velvet cape, white also.*

---

* Urchins often go through the streets with a drum, begging for alms. But their skill is used also for insults even without provocation.

Stands upright, divine rod in hand, while the other caresses the velvet cape.

JERO. I don't know how she found out my house. When I bought the goods off her, she did not even ask any questions. My calling was enough to guarantee payment. It is not as if this was a well-paid job. And it is not what I would call a luxury, this velvet cape which I bought from her. It would not have been necessary if one were not forced to distinguish himself more and more from these scum who degrade the calling of the prophet. It becomes important to stand out, to be distinctive. I have set my heart after a particular name. They will look at my velvet cape and they will think of my goodness. Inevitably they must begin to call me . . . the Velvet-hearted Jeroboam. (*Straightens himself.*) Immaculate Jero, Articulate Hero of Christ's Crusade . . . Well, it is out. I have not breathed it to a single soul, but that has been my ambition. You've got to have a name that appeals to the imagination – because the imagination is a thing of the spirit – it must catch the imagination of the crowd. Yes, one must move with modern times. Lack of colour gets one nowhere even in the prophet's business.

  Looks all round him.

Charlatans! If only I had this beach to myself. (*With sudden violence.*) But how does one maintain his dignity when the daughter of Eve forces him to leave his own house through a window? God curse that woman! I never thought she would dare affront the presence of a man of God. One pound eight for this little cape. It is sheer robbery.

  He surveys the scene again. A YOUNG GIRL *passes, sleepily, clothed only in her wrapper.*

JERO. She passes here every morning, on her way to take a swim. Dirty-looking thing.

He yawns.

I am glad I got here before any customers – I mean worshippers – well, customers if you like. I always get that feeling every morning that I am a shop-keeper waiting for customers. The regular ones come at definite times. Strange, dissatisfied people. I know they are dissatisfied because I keep them dissatisfied. Once they are full, they won't come again. Like my good apprentice, Brother Chume. He wants to beat his wife, but I won't let him. If I do, he will become contented, and then that's another of my flock gone for ever. As long as he doesn't beat her, he comes here feeling helpless, and so there is no chance of his rebelling against me. Everything, in fact, is planned.

The YOUNG GIRL *crosses the stage again. She has just had her swim and the difference is remarkable. Clean, wet, shiny face and hair. She continues to wipe herself with her wrapper as she walks.*

JERO (*following her all the way with his eyes*). Every morning, every day I witness this divine transformation, O Lord.

He shakes his head suddenly and bellows.

Pray Brother Jeroboam, pray! Pray for strength against temptation.

He falls on his knees, face squeezed in agony and hands clasped. CHUME *enters, wheeling his bike. He leans it against the palm tree.*

JERO (*not opening his eyes*). Pray with me, brother. Pray with me. Pray for me against this one weakness ... against this one weakness, O Lord ...

CHUME (*falling down at once*). Help him, Lord. Help him, Lord.

JERO. Against this one weakness, this weakness, O Abraham ...

CHUME. Help him, Lord. Help him, Lord.

JERO. Against this one weakness David, David, Samuel, Samuel.

CHUME. Help him. Help him. Help 'am. Help 'am.

JERO. Job Job, Elijah Elijah.

CHUME (*getting more worked up*). Help 'am God. Help' am God. I say make you help 'am. Help 'am quick quick.

JERO. Tear the image from my heart. Tear this love for the daughters of Eve ...

CHUME. Adam, help 'am. Na your son, help 'am. Help this your son.

JERO. Burn out this lust for the daughters of Eve.

CHUME. Je-e-esu, J-e-esu, Je-e-esu. Help 'am one time Je-e-e-e-su.

JERO. Abraka, Abraka, Abraka.

CHUME *joins in.*

Abraka, Abraka, Hebra, Hebra, Hebra, Hebra, Hebra, Hebra, Hebra ...

JERO (*rising*). God bless you, brother. (*Turns around.*) Chume!

CHUME. Good morning, Brother Jeroboam.

JERO. Chume, you are not at work. You've never come before in the morning.

CHUME. No. I went to work but I had to report sick.

JERO. Why, are you unwell, brother?

CHUME. No, Brother Jero ... I ...

JERO. A-ah, you have troubles and you could not wait to get them to God. We shall pray together.

CHUME. Brother Jero ... I ... I. (*He stops altogether.*)

JERO. Is it difficult? Then let us commune silently for a while.

CHUME *folds his arms, raises his eyes to heaven.*

JERO. I wonder what is the matter with him. Actually I knew it was he the moment he opened his mouth. Only Brother Chume reverts to that animal jabber when he gets his spiritual excitement. And that is much too often for my liking. He is too crude, but then that is to my advantage. It means he would never think of setting himself up as my equal.

He joins CHUME *in his meditative attitude, but almost immediately discards it, as if he has just remembered something.*

Christ my Protector! It is a good job I got away from that wretched woman as soon as I did. My disciple believes that I sleep on the beach, that is, if he thinks I sleep at all. Most of them believe the same, but, for myself, I prefer my bed. Much more comfortable. And it gets rather cold on the beach at nights. Still, it does them good to believe that I am something of an ascetic . . .

He resumes his meditative pose for a couple of moments.

(*Gently.*) Open your mind to God, brother. This is the tabernacle of Christ. Open your mind to God.

CHUME *is silent for a while, then bursts out suddenly.*

CHUME. Brother Jero, you must let me beat her!
JERO. What!
CHUME (*desperately*). Just once, Prophet. Just once.
JERO. Brother Chume!
CHUME. Just once. Just one sound beating, and I swear not to ask again.
JERO. Apostate. Have I not told you the will of God in this matter?
CHUME. But I've got to beat her, Prophet. You must save me from madness.

JERO. I will. But only if you obey me.

CHUME. In anything else, Prophet. But for this one, make you let me just beat 'am once.

JERO. Apostate!

CHUME. I no go beat 'am too hard. Jus' once, small small.

JERO. Traitor!

CHUME. Jus' this one time. I no' go ask again. Jus' do me this one favour, make a beat 'am today.

JERO. Brother Chume, what were you before you came to me?

CHUME. Prophet . . .

JERO (*sternly*). What were you before the grace of God?

CHUME. A labourer, Prophet. A common labourer.

JERO. And did I not prophesy you would become an office boy?

CHUME. You do 'am, brother. Na so.

JERO. And then a messenger?

CHUME. Na you do' am, brother, na you.

JERO. And then quick promotion? Did I not prophesy it?

CHUME. Na true, Prophet. Na true.

JERO. And what are you now? What are you?

CHUME. Chief Messenger.

JERO. By the grace of God! And by the grace of God, have I not seen you at the table of the Chief Clerk? And you behind the desk, giving orders?

CHUME. Yes, Prophet . . . but . . .

JERO. With a telephone and a table bell for calling the Messenger?

CHUME. Very true, Prophet, but . . .

JERO. But? But? Kneel! (*Pointing to the ground.*) Kneel!

CHUME (*wringing his hands*). Prophet!

JERO. Kneel, sinner, kneel. Hardener of heart, harbourer of Ashtoreth, Protector of Baal, kneel, kneel.

CHUME *falls on his knees.*

CHUME. My life is a hell . . .

JERO. Forgive him, Father, forgive him.

CHUME. This woman will kill me . . .

JERO. Forgive him, Father, forgive him.

CHUME. Only this morning I . . .

JERO. Forgive him, Father, forgive him.

CHUME. All the way on my bicycle . . .

JERO. Forgive . . .

CHUME. And not a word of thanks . . .

JERO. Out Ashtoreth. Out Baal . . .

CHUME. All she gave me was abuse, abuse, abuse . . .

JERO. Hardener of the heart . . .

CHUME. Nothing but abuse . . .

JERO. Petrifier of the soul . . .

CHUME. If I could only beat her once, only once . . .

JERO (*shouting him down*). Forgive this sinner, Father. Forgive him by day, forgive him by night, forgive him in the morning, forgive him at noon . . .

    A MAN *enters. Kneels at once and begins to chorus 'Amen', or 'Forgive him, Lord', or 'In the name of Jesus' (pronounced Je-e-e-sus). Those who follow later do the same.*

. . . This is the son whom you appointed to follow in my footsteps. Soften his heart. Brother Chume, this woman whom you so desire to beat is your cross – bear it well. She is your heaven-sent trial – lay not your hands on her. I command you to speak no harsh word to her. Pray, Brother Chume, for strength in this hour of your trial. Pray for strength and fortitude.

    JEROBOAM *leaves them to continue their chorus,* CHUME *chanting 'Mercy, Mercy' while he makes his next remarks.*

They begin to arrive. As usual in the same order. This one who always comes earliest, I have prophesied that he will be made a chief in his home town. That is a very safe prophecy. As safe as our most popular prophecy, that a man will live to be eighty. If it doesn't come true . . .

Enter an OLD COUPLE, *joining chorus as before.*

that man doesn't find out until he's on the other side. So every-body is quite happy. One of my most faithful adherents – unfortunately, he can only be present at weekends – firmly believes that he is going to be the first Prime Minister of the new Mid-North-East State – when it is created. That was a risky prophecy of mine, but I badly needed more worshippers around that time.

He looks at his watch.

The next one to arrive is my most faithful penitent. She wants children, so she is quite a sad case. Or you would think so. But even in the midst of her most self-abasing convulsions, she manages to notice everything that goes on around her. In fact, I had better get back to the service. She is always the one to tell me that my mind is not on the service . . .

Altering his manner –

Rise, Brother Chume. Rise and let the Lord enter into you. Apprentice of the Lord, are you not he upon whose shoulders my mantle must descend?

A woman (the PENITENT*) enters and kneels at once in an attitude of prayer.*

CHUME. It is so, Brother Jero.

JERO. Then why do you harden your heart? The Lord says that you may not beat the good woman whom he has chosen to be your wife, to be your cross in your period of trial, and will you disobey him?

CHUME. No, Brother Jero.

JERO. Will you?

CHUME. No, Brother Jero.
JERO. Praise be to God.
CONGREGATION. Praise be to God.
JERO. Allelu ...
CONGREGATION. Alleluia.

*To the clapping of hands, they sing 'I will follow Jesus',
swaying and then dancing as they get warmer.* BROTHER JERO,
as the singing starts, hands two empty bottles to CHUME *who
goes to fill them with water from the sea.* CHUME *has hardly
gone out when the* DRUMMER BOY *enters from upstage,
running. He is rather weighed down by two gangan drums, and
darts fearful glances back in mortal terror of whatever it is that
is chasing him. This turns out, some ten or so yards later, to be
a* WOMAN, *sash tightened around her waist, wrapper pulled so
high up that half the length of her thigh is exposed. Her sleeves
are rolled above the shoulder and she is striding after the* DRUM-
MER *in an unmistakable manner.* JEROBOAM, *who has followed
the* WOMAN's *exposed limbs with quite distressed concentration,
comes suddenly to himself and kneels sharply, muttering. Again
the* DRUMMER *appears, going across the stage in a different
direction, running still. The* WOMAN *follows, distance un-
diminished, the same set pace.* JEROBOAM *calls to him.*

JERO. What did you do to her?
DRUMMER (*without stopping*). Nothing. I was only drumming and
then she said I was using it to abuse her father.
JERO (*as the* WOMAN *comes into sight*). Woman!

She continues out. CHUME *enters with filled bottles.*

JERO (*shaking his head*). I know her very well. She's my neighbour.
But she ignored me ...

JEROBOAM *prepares to bless the water when once again the
procession appears,* DRUMMER *first and the* WOMAN *after.*

JERO. Come here. She wouldn't dare touch you.
DRUMMER (*increasing his pace*). You don't know her . . .

The WOMAN *comes in sight.*

JERO. Neighbour, neighbour. My dear sister in Moses . . .

She continues her pursuit off-stage. JERO *hesitates, then hands over his rod to* CHUME *and goes after them.*

CHUME (*suddenly remembering*). You haven't blessed the water, Brother Jeroboam.

JERO *is already out of hearing.* CHUME *is obviously bewildered by the new responsibility. He fiddles around with the rod and eventually uses it to conduct the singing, which has gone on all this time, flagging when the two contestants came in view, and reviving again after they had passed.*
CHUME *has hardly begun to conduct his band when a woman detaches herself from the crowd in the expected penitent's paroxysm.*

PENITENT. Echa, echa, echa, echa, echa . . . eei, eei, eei, eei.
CHUME (*taken aback*). Ngh? What's the matter?
PENITENT. Efie, efie, efie, efie, enh, enh, enh, enh . . .
CHUME (*dashing off*). Brother Jeroboam, Brother Jeroboam . . .

CHUME *shouts in all directions, returning confusedly each time in an attempt to minister to the* PENITENT. *As* JEROBOAM *is not forthcoming, he begins very uncertainly, to sprinkle some of the water on the* PENITENT, *crossing her on the forehead. This has to be achieved very rapidly in the brief moment when the* PENITENT'S *head is lifted from beating on the ground.*

CHUME (*stammering*). Father . . . forgive her.

CONGREGATION (*strongly*). Amen.

The unexpectedness of the response nearly throws CHUME, *but then it also serves to bolster him up, receiving such support.*

CHUME. Father, forgive her.
CONGREGATION. Amen.

The PENITENT *continues to moan.*

CHUME. Father, forgive her.
CONGREGATION. Amen.
CHUME. Father, forgive 'am.
CONGREGATION. Amen.
CHUME (*warming up to the task*). Make you forgive 'am. Father.
CONGREGATION. Amen.

They rapidly gain pace, CHUME *getting quite carried away.*

CHUME. I say make you forgive 'am.
CONGREGATION. Amen.
CHUME. Forgive 'am one time.
CONGREGATION. Amen.
CHUME. Forgive 'am quick, quick.
CONGREGATION. Amen.
CHUME. Forgive 'am, Father.
CONGREGATION. Amen.
CHUME. Forgive us all.
CONGREGATION. Amen.
CHUME. Forgive us all.

And then, punctuated regularly with Amens . . .

Yes, Father, make you forgive us all. Make you save us from palaver. Save us from trouble at home. Tell our wives not to give us trouble . . .

The PENITENT *has become placid. She is stretched out flat on the ground.*

... Tell our wives not to give us trouble. And give us money to have a happy home. Give us money to satisfy our daily necessities. Make you no forget those of us who dey struggle daily. Those who be clerk today, make them Chief Clerk tomorrow. Those who are Messenger today, make them Senior Service tomorrow. Yes Father, those who are Messenger today, make them Senior Service tomorrow.

The Amens grow more and more ecstatic.

Those who are petty trader today, make them big contractor tomorrow. Those who dey sweep street today, give them their own big office tomorrow. If we dey walka today, give us our own bicycle tomorrow. I say those who dey walka today, give them their own bicycle tomorrow. Those who have bicycle today, they will ride their own car tomorrow.

The enthusiasm of the response becomes, at this point quite overpowering.

I say those who dey push bicycle, give them big car tomorrow. Give them big car tomorrow. Give them big car tomorrow, give them big car tomorrow.

The angry WOMAN *comes again in view, striding with the same gait as before, but now in possession of the drums. A few yards behind, the* DRUMMER *jog-trots wretchedly, pleading.*

DRUMMER. I beg you, give me my drums. I take God's name beg you, I was not abusing your father ... For God's sake I beg you ... I was not abusing your father. I was only drumming ... I swear to God I was only drumming ...

They pass through.

PENITENT (*who has become much alive from the latter part of the prayers, pointing . . .*). Brother Jeroboam!

BROTHER JERO *has just come in view. They all rush to help him back into the circle. He is a much altered man, his clothes torn and his face bleeding.*

JERO (*slowly and painfully*). Thank you, brother, sisters. Brother Chume, kindly tell these friends to leave me. I must pray for the soul of that sinful woman. I must say a personal prayer for her.

CHUME *ushers them off. They go reluctantly, chattering excitedly.*

JERO. Prayers this evening, as usual. Late afternoon.
CHUME (*shouting after*). Prayers late afternoon as always. Brother Jeroboam says God keep you till then. Are you all right, Brother Jero?
JERO. Who would have thought that she would dare lift her hand against a prophet of God!
CHUME. Women are a plague, brother.
JERO. I had a premonition this morning that women would be my downfall today. But I thought of it only in the spiritual sense.
CHUME. Now you see how it is, Brother Jero.
JERO. From the moment I looked out of my window this morning I have been tormented one way or another by the Daughters of Discord.
CHUME (*eagerly*). That is how it is with me, Brother. Every day. Every morning and night. Only this morning she made me take her to the house of some poor man whom she says owes her money. She loaded enough on my bicycle to lay a siege for a week, and all the thanks I got was abuse.

JERO. Indeed, it must be a trial, Brother Chume ... and it requires great ...

He becomes suddenly suspicious.

Brother Chume, did you say that your wife went to make camp only this morning at the house of a ... of someone who owes her money?

CHUME. Yes, I took her there myself.

JERO. Er ... indeed, indeed. (*Coughs.*) Is ... your wife a trader?

CHUME. Yes, petty trading, you know. Wool, silk, cloth and all that stuff.

JERO. Indeed. Quite an enterprising woman. (*Hems.*) Er ... where was the house of this man ... I mean, this man who owes her money?

CHUME. Not very far from here. Ajete settlement, a mile or so from here. I did not even know the place existed until today.

JERO (*to himself*). So that is your wife ...

CHUME. Did you speak, Prophet?

JERO. No, no. I was only thinking how little women have changed since Eve, since Delilah, since Jezebel. But we must be strong of heart. I have my own cross too, Brother Chume. This morning alone I have been thrice in conflict with the daughters of discord. First there was ... no, never mind that. There is another who crosses my path every day. Goes to swim just over there and then waits for me to be in the midst of my meditation before she swings her hips across here, flaunting her near nakedness before my eyes ...

CHUME (*to himself with deep feeling*). I'd willingly change crosses with you.

JERO. What, Brother Chume?

CHUME. I was only praying.

JERO. Ah. That is the only way. But er ... I wonder really what the will of God would be in this matter. After all, Christ himself was not averse to using the whip when occasion demanded it.

CHUME (*eagerly*). No, he did not hesitate.

JERO. In that case, since, Brother Chume, your wife seems such a wicked, wilful sinner, I think . . .

CHUME. Yes, Holy One . . .?

JERO. You must take her home tonight . . .

CHUME. Yes . . .

JERO. And beat her.

CHUME (*kneeling, clasps* JERO's *hand in his*). Prophet!

JERO. Remember, it must be done in your own house. Never show the discord within your family to the world. Take her home and beat her.

> CHUME *leaps up and gets his bike.*

JERO. And Brother Chume . . .

CHUME. Yes, Prophet . . .

JERO. The Son of God appeared to me again this morning, robed just as he was when he named you my successor. And he placed his burning sword on my shoulder and called me his knight. He gave me a new title . . . but you must tell it to no one – yet.

CHUME. I swear, Brother Jero.

JERO (*staring into space*). He named me the Immaculate Jero, Articulate Hero of Christ's Crusade. (*Pauses, then, with a regal dismissal* –) You may go, Brother Chume.

CHUME. God keep you, Brother Jero – the Immaculate.

JERO. God keep you, brother. (*He sadly fingers the velvet cape.*)

> *Lights fade.*

SCENE FOUR

As Scene Two, i.e. in front of the prophet's home. Later that day.
CHUME *is just wiping off the last crumbs of yams on his plate.* AMOPE
watches him.

AMOPE. You can't say I don't try. Hounded out of house by
debtors, I still manage to make you a meal.

CHUME (*sucking his fingers, sets down his plate*). It was a good
meal, too.

AMOPE. I do my share as I've always done. I cooked you your
meal. But when I ask you to bring me some clean water, you
forget.

CHUME. I did not forget.

AMOPE. You keep saying that. Where is it then? Or perhaps the
bottles fell off your bicycle on the way and got broken.

CHUME. That's a child's lie, Amope. You are talking to a man.

AMOPE. A fine man you are then, when you can't remember a
simple thing like a bottle of clean water.

CHUME. I remembered. I just did not bring it. So that is that.
And now pack up your things because we're going home.

AMOPE *stares at him unbelieving.*

CHUME. Pack up your things; you heard what I said.

AMOPE (*scrutinizing*). I thought you were a bit early to get back.
You haven't been to work at all. You've been drinking all day.

CHUME. You may think what suits you. You know I never touch
any liquor.

AMOPE. You needn't say it as if it was a virtue. You don't drink
only because you cannot afford to. That is all the reason there is.

CHUME. Hurry. I have certain work to do when I get home and I
don't want you delaying me.

AMOPE. Go then. I am not budging from here till I get my money.

> CHUME *leaps up, begins to throw her things into the bag.* BROTHER JERO *enters, hides and observes them.*

AMOPE (*quietly*). I hope you have ropes to tie me on the bicycle, because I don't intend to leave this place unless I am carried out. One pound eight shillings is no child's play. And it is my money, not yours.

> CHUME *has finished packing the bag and is now tying it on to the carrier.*

AMOPE. A messenger's pay isn't that much, you know – just in case you've forgotten you're not drawing a Minister's pay. So you better think again if you think I am letting my hard-earned money stay in the hands of that good-for-nothing. Just think, only this morning while I sat here, a Sanitary Inspector came along. He looked me all over and he made some notes in his book. Then he said, I suppose, woman, you realize that this place is marked down for slum clearance. This to me, as if I lived here. But you sit down and let your wife be exposed to such insults. And the Sanitary Inspector had a motor-cycle too, which is one better than a bicycle.

CHUME. You'd better be ready soon.

AMOPE. A Sanitary Inspector is a better job anyway. You can make something of yourself one way or another. They all do. A little here and a little there, call it bribery if you like, but see where *you've* got even though you don't drink or smoke or take bribes. He's got a motor-bike . . . anyway, who would want to offer kola to a Chief Messenger?

CHUME. Shut your big mouth!

AMOPE (*aghast*). What did you say?

CHUME. I said shut your big mouth.

AMOPE. To me?

CHUME. Shut your big mouth before I shut it for you. (*Ties the mat round the cross-bar.*) And you'd better start to watch your step from now on. My period of abstinence is over. My cross has been lifted off my shoulders by the prophet.

AMOPE (*genuinely distressed*). He's mad.

CHUME (*viciously tying up the mat*). My period of trial is over. (*Practically strangling the mat.*) If you so much as open your mouth now . . . (*Gives a further twist to the string.*)

AMOPE. God help me. He's gone mad.

CHUME (*imperiously*). Get on the bike.

AMOPE (*backing away*). I'm not coming with you.

CHUME. I said get on the bike!

AMOPE. Not with you. I'll find my own way home.

> CHUME *advances on her.* AMOPE *screams for help.* BROTHER JERO *crosses himself.* CHUME *catches her by the arm but she escapes, runs to the side of the house and beats on the door.*

AMOPE. Help! Open the door for God's sake. Let me in. Let me in . . .

> BROTHER JERO *grimaces.*

Is anyone in? Let me in for God's sake! Let me in or God will punish you!

JERO (*sticking his fingers in his ears*). Blasphemy!

AMOPE. Prophet! Where's the prophet?

> CHUME *lifts her bodily.*

AMOPE. Let me down! Police! Police!

CHUME (*setting her down*). If you shout just once more I'll . . . (*He raises a huge fist.*)

> BROTHER JERO *gasps in mock-horror, tut-tuts, covers his eyes with both hands and departs.*

AMOPE. Ho! You're mad. You're mad.

CHUME. Get on the bike.

AMOPE. Kill me! Kill me!

CHUME. Don't tempt me, woman!

AMOPE. I won't get on that thing unless you kill me first.

CHUME. Woman!

Two or three NEIGHBOURS *arrive, but keep a respectful distance.*

AMOPE. Kill me. You'll have to kill me. Everybody come and bear witness. He's going to kill me so come and bear witness. I forgive everyone who has ever done me evil. I forgive all my debtors especially the prophet who has got me into all this trouble. Prophet Jeroboam, I hope you will pray for my soul in heaven . . .

CHUME. You have no soul, wicked woman.

AMOPE. Brother Jeroboam, curse this man for me. You may keep the velvet cape if you curse this foolish man. I forgive you your debt. Go on, foolish man, kill me. If you don't kill me you won't do well in life.

CHUME (*suddenly*). Shut up!

AMOPE (*warming up as more people arrive*). Bear witness all of you. Tell the prophet I forgive him his debt but he must curse this foolish man to hell. Go on, kill me!

CHUME (*who has turned away, forehead knotted in confusion*). Can't you shut up, woman!

AMOPE. No, you must kill me . . .

The CROWD *hub bubs all the time, scared as always at the prospect of interfering in man-wife palaver, but throwing in half-hearted tokens of concern –*

'What's the matter, eh?' 'You too keep quiet.' 'Who are they?' 'Where is Brother Jero?' 'Do you think we ought to send for the

Prophet?' 'These women are so troublesome! Somebody go and call Brother Jero.'

CHUME (*lifting* AMOPE's *head. She has, in the tradition of the 'Kill me' woman, shut her eyes tightly and continued to beat her fists on the prophet's door-step*). Shut up and listen. Did I hear you say Prophet Jeroboam?

AMOPE. See him now. Let you bear witness. He's going to kill me . . .

CHUME. I'm not touching you, but I will if you don't answer my question.

AMOPE. Kill me . . . Kill me . . .

CHUME. Woman, did you say it was the prophet who owed you money?

AMOPE. Kill me . . .

CHUME. Is this his house? (*Gives her head a shake.*) Does he live here. . .?

AMOPE. Kill me . . . Kill me . . .

CHUME (*pushing her away in disgust and turning to the* CROWD. *They retreat instinctively*). Is Brother Jeroboam . . .?

NEAREST ONE (*hastily*). No, no. I'm not Brother Jero. It's not me.

CHUME. Who said you were? Does the prophet live here?

SAME MAN. Yes. Over there. That house.

CHUME (*turns round and stands stock still. Stares at the house for quite some time*). So . . . so . . . so . . . so . . .

The CROWD *is puzzled over his change of mood. Even* AMOPE *looks up wonderingly.* CHUME *walks towards his bicycle, muttering to himself.*

So . . . so . . . Suddenly he decides I may beat my wife, eh? For his own convenience. At his own convenience.

He releases the bundle from the carrier, pushing it down carelessly. He unties the mat also.

BYSTANDER. What next is he doing now?

CHUME (*mounting his bicycle*). You stay here and don't move. If I don't find you here when I get back . . .

He rides off. They all stare at him in bewilderment.

AMOPE. He is quite mad. I have never seen him behave like that.

BYSTANDER. You are sure?

AMOPE. Am I sure? I'm his wife, so I ought to know, shouldn't I?

A WOMAN BYSTANDER. Then you ought to let the prophet see to him. I had a brother once who had the fits and foamed at the mouth every other week. But the prophet cured him. Drove the devils out of him, he did.

AMOPE. This one can't do anything. He's a debtor and that's all he knows. How to dodge his creditors.

She prepares to unpack her bundle.

Lights fade.

SCENE FIVE

The Beach. Nightfall.
A MAN *in an elaborate 'agbada' outfit, with long train and a cap is standing right, downstage, with a sheaf of notes in his hand. He is delivering a speech, but we don't hear it. It is undoubtedly a fire-breathing speech.*

The PROPHET JEROBOAM *stands bolt upright as always, surveying him with lofty compassion.*

JERO. I could teach him a trick or two about speech-making. He's a member of the Federal House, a back-bencher but with one eye on a ministerial post. Comes here every day to rehearse his speeches. But he never makes them. Too scared.

Pause. The PROPHET *continues to study the* MEMBER.

Poor fish. (*Chuckles and looks away.*) Oho, I had almost forgotten Brother Chume. By now he ought to have beaten his wife senseless. Pity! That means I've lost him. He is fulfilled and no longer needs me. True, he still has to become a Chief Clerk. But I have lost him as the one who was most dependent on me ... Never mind, it was a good price to pay for getting rid of my creditor ...

Goes back to the MEMBER.

Now he ... he is already a member of my flock. He does not know it of course, but he is a follower. All I need do is claim him. Call him and say to him, My dear Member of the House, your place awaits you ... Or do you doubt it? Watch me go to work on him. (*Raises his voice.*) My dear brother in Jesus!

The MEMBER *stops, looks round, resumes his speech.*

Dear brother, do I not know you?

MEMBER *stops, looks round again.*

Yes, you. In God's name, do I not know you?

MEMBER *approaches slowly.*

Yes indeed. It is you. And you come as it was predicted. Do you not perhaps remember me?

MEMBER *looks at him scornfully.*

Then you cannot be of the Lord. In another world, in another body, we met, and my message was for you . . .

The MEMBER *turns his back impatiently.*

MEMBER (*with great pomposity*). Go and practise your fraudulences on another person of greater gullibility.

JERO (*very kindly, smiling*). Indeed the matter is quite plain. You are not of the Lord. And yet such is the mystery of God's ways that his favour has lighted upon you . . . Minister . . . Minister by the grace of God . . .

The MEMBER *stops dead.*

Yes, brother, we have met. I saw this country plunged into strife. I saw the mustering of men, gathered in the name of peace through strength. And at a desk, in a large gilt room, great men of the land awaited your decision. Emissaries of foreign nations hung on your word, and on the door leading into your office, I read the words, Minister for War . . .

The MEMBER *turns round slowly.*

. . . It is a position of power. But are you of the Lord? Are you in fact worthy? Must I, when I have looked into your soul, as the Lord has commanded me to do, must I pray to the Lord to remove this mantle from your shoulders and place it on a more God-fearing man?

The MEMBER *moves forward unconsciously. The* PROPHET *gestures him to stay where he is. Slowly –*

Yes . . . I think I see Satan in your eyes. I see him entrenched in your eyes . . .

The MEMBER *grows fearful, raises his arms in half-supplication.*

The Minister for War would be the most powerful position in
the Land. The Lord knows best, but he has empowered his
lieutenants on earth to intercede where necessary. We can reach
him by fasting and by prayer ... we can make recommenda-
tions ... Brother, are you of God or are you ranged among his
enemies ...?

JEROBOAM's *voice fades away and the light also dims on him as
another voice – * CHUME's *– is heard long before he is seen.*
CHUME *enters from left, downstage, agitated and talking to
himself.*

CHUME. .... What for ... why, why, why, why 'e do 'am? For
two years 'e no let me beat that woman. Why? No because
God no like 'am. That one no fool me any more. 'E no be man
of God. 'E say 'in sleep for beach whether 'e rain or cold but
that one too na big lie. The man get house and 'e sleep there
every night. But 'in get peace for 'in house, why 'e no let me
get peace for mine? Wetin I do for 'am? Anyway, how they
come meet? Where? When? What time 'e know say na my
wife? Why 'e dey protect 'am from me? Perhaps na my woman
dey give 'am chop and in return he promise to see say 'in
husband no beat 'am. A-a-a-ah, give 'am clothes, give 'am food
and all comforts and necessities, and for exchange, 'in go see
that 'in husband no beat 'am ... Mmmmmm.

He shakes his head.

No, is not possible. I no believe that. If na so, how they come
quarrel then. Why she go sit for front of 'in house demand all
'in money. I no beat 'am yet ...

He stops suddenly. His eyes slowly distend.

Almighty! Chume, fool! O God, my life done spoil. My life done spoil finish. O God a no' get eyes for my head. Na lie. Na big lie. Na pretence 'e de pretend that wicked woman! She no' go collect nutin! She no' mean to sleep for outside house. The Prophet na 'in lover. As soon as 'e dark, she go in go meet 'in man. O God, wetin a do for you wey you go spoil my life so? Wetin make you vex for me so? I offend you? Chume, foolish man, your life done spoil. Your life done spoil. Yeah, ye . . . ah ah, ye-e-ah, they done ruin Chume for life . . . ye-e-ah, ye-e-ah . . .

He goes off, his cries dying off-stage.
Light up slowly on JERO. *The* MEMBER *is seen kneeling now at* BROTHER JERO's *feet, hands clasped and shut eyes raised to heaven. . .*

JERO (*his voice gaining volume*). Protect him therefore. Protect him when he must lead this country as his great ancestors have done. He comes from the great warriors of the land. In his innocence he was not aware of this heritage. But you know everything and you plan it all. There is no end, no beginning . . .

CHUME *rushes in, brandishing a cutlass.*

CHUME. Adulterer! Woman-thief! Na today a go finish you!

JERO *looks round.*

JERO. God save us! (*Flees.*)
MEMBER (*unaware of what is happening*). Amen.

CHUME *follows out* JERO, *murder-bent.*

MEMBER. Amen. Amen. (*Opens his eyes.*) Thank you, proph . . .

He looks right, left, back, front, but he finds the PROPHET *has really disappeared.*

Prophet! Prophet! (*Turns sharply and rapidly in every direction, shouting.*) Prophet, where are you? Where have you gone? Prophet! Don't leave me, Prophet, don't leave me!

He looks up slowly, with awe.

Vanished. Transported. Utterly transmuted. I knew it. I knew I stood in the presence of God . . .

He bows his head, standing. JEROBOAM *enters quite collected, and points to the convert.*

JERO. You heard him. With your own ears you heard him. By tomorrow, the whole town will have heard about the miraculous disappearance of Brother Jeroboam. Testified to and witnessed by no less a person than one of the elected rulers of the country . . .

MEMBER (*goes to sit on the mound*). I must await his return. If I show faith, he will show himself again to me . . . (*Leaps up as he is about to sit.*) This is holy ground. (*Takes off his shoes and sits.*) I must hear further from him. Perhaps he has gone to learn more about this ministerial post . . . (*Sits.*)

JERO. I have already sent for the police. It is a pity about Chume. But he has given me a fright, and no prophet likes to be frightened. With the influence of that nincompoop I should succeed in getting him certified with ease. A year in the lunatic asylum would do him good anyway.

The MEMBER *is already nodding.*

Good . . . He is falling asleep. When I appear again to him he'll think I have just fallen from the sky. Then I'll tell him that

Satan just sent one of his emissaries into the world under the
name of Chume, and that he had better put him in a strait-
jacket at once . . . And so the day is saved. The police will call
on me here as soon as they catch Chume. And it looks as if it is
not quite time for the fulfilment of that spiteful man's prophecy.

He picks up a pebble and throws it at the MEMBER. *At the
same time a ring of red or some equally startling colour plays on
his head, forming a sort of halo. The* MEMBER *wakes with a
start, stares open-mouthed, and falls flat on his face, whispering
in rapt awe –*

MEMBER. 'Master!'

Blackout.

THE END

JERO'S METAMORPHOSIS

CAST

BROTHER JEROBOAM

SISTER REBECCA

ANANAIAS

CHIEF EXECUTIVE OFFICER

CLERK TO THE TOURIST BOARD

CHUME

MAJOR SILVA

SHADRACH

CALEB *and other Beach Prophets*

ISAAC

MATTHEW

A POLICEWOMAN

SCENE ONE

BROTHER JERO's *office. It is no longer his rent-troubled shack of* The Trials *but a modest white-washed room, quite comfortable. A 'surplus-store' steel cabinet is tucked in a corner. On a cloth-covered table is an ancient beat-up typewriter of the oldest imaginable model but functioning. A vase of flowers, the usual assortment of professional paraphernalia – bible, prayer-book, chasuble, etc. etc.*
On the wall, a large framed picture of a uniformed figure at a battery of microphones indicates that JERO's *diocese is no longer governed by his old friends the civilian politicians. As* JERO *dictates, striding up and down the room, it is obvious that he has his mind very much on this photograph. A demure young woman, quite attractive, is seated at a table taking the dictation.*

JERO. . . . in time of trouble it behoves us to come together, to forget old enmities and bury the hatchet in the head of a common enemy . . . no, better take that out. It sounds a little unchristian wouldn't you say?

REBECCA (*her voice and manner are of unqualified admiration*). Not if you don't think it, Brother Jeroboam.

JERO. Well, we have to be careful about our brother prophets. Some of them might just take it literally. The mere appearance of the majority of them, not to mention their secret past and even secret present . . . ah well, stop at 'bury the hatchet'.

REBECCA. Whatever you say, Brother Jeroboam.

JERO. Not that I would regret it. We could do with the elevation to eternity of some of our dearly beloved brother prophets on this beach, and if they choose the way of the hangman's noose or elect to take the latest short cut to heaven facing a firing squad at the Bar Beach Show,* who are we to dispute such a divine solution? Only trouble is, it might give the rest of us a bad name.

REBECCA. Nothing could give you a bad name, Brother Jero. You stand apart from the others. Nothing can tarnish your image, I know that.

JERO. You are indeed kind, Sister Rebecca. I don't know what I would do without you.

REBECCA. You won't ever have to do without me, Brother Jero. As long as you need me, I'll be here.

JERO. Hm, yes, hm. (*The prospect makes him nervous.*) I thank you, Sister. Now we must get back to work. Read me the last thing I dictated.

REBECCA. . . . in time of trouble it behoves us to get together, to forget old enemies and bury the hatchet in the head . . . no, we stop at 'hatchet'.

JERO. Good. I have therefore decided to summon – no, invite is better wouldn't you say? The more miserable they are the more touchy and proud you'll find them. The monster of pride feeds upon vermin, Sister Rebecca. The hole in a poor man's garment is soon filled with the patchwork of pride, so resolutely does Nature abhor a vacuum.

REBECCA. Oh Brother Jero, you say such wise things.

JERO. I have but little gifts, Sister Rebecca, but I make the most of them. Yes, let the phrase read – after much prayer for guidance, I am inspired to invite you all to a meeting where we shall all, as equals before God and servants of his will, deliberate and find a way to stop this threat to our vocation. In our own mutual interest – underline that heavily – in our own mutual interest, I trust that all shepherds of the Lord whose pastures are upon this sandy though arable beach will make it their duty to be present.

* Popular expression for the new fashion of public executions in Lagos, capital of Nigeria.

He shakes his head as if to clear it, goes to a small cupboard and brings out a bottle. Pouring a drink.

The gall is bitter, Sister Rebecca. The burden is heavy upon me.

REBECCA. It has to be done, Brother Jero. The end will justify the means.

JERO. To fraternize with those cut-throats, dope-pedlars, smugglers and stolen goods receivers? Some of them are ex-convicts do you know that? Some of them are long overdue for the Bar Beach Spectacular.

REBECCA. The more noble of you in sinking your pride and meeting with them in the service of God.

JERO (*offering a glass*). You will join me, Sister Rebecca?

REBECCA. No, Brother Jero, but you must have one.

JERO. You are sure it is not wrong?

REBECCA. All things are God's gifts. It is not wrong to use them wisely.

JERO. You comfort me greatly, Sister Rebecca. The times are indeed trying. Believe me, it is no time for half-measures.

REBECCA. Brother Jero, you promised . . .

JERO. Oh I didn't mean this half-measure. (*Tosses down drink.*)

REBECCA. Forgive me, I . . .

JERO. A natural error. No, I was referring to our present predicament. To survive, we need full-bodied tactics.

REBECCA. I know you will find a way.

JERO. It seems to me that in our upward look to heaven for a solution we have neglected what inspiration is afforded us below. Yes, indeed we have.

REBECCA. Has earth anything to offer the true Christian, Brother Jero? How often have you said yourself . . .

JERO. That was before I read this precious file which you brought to Christ as your dowry. An unparalleled dowry in the history of spiritual marriages Sister Rebecca. And before . . . (*He takes down the picture on the wall, inspects it at arm's length nodding with satisfaction.*) ... yes, I think we have neglected our earthly inspirations.

REBECCA. But Brother Jero ...

JERO. Trust me, Sister Rebecca.

REBECCA. I do, Brother Jero, I do.

JERO. The voice of the people is the voice of God, did you know that Sister?

REBECCA. I trust you. I follow wherever you lead me, Brother Jeroboam.

JERO. I shall lead you to safety, you and all who put their faith in me.

REBECCA. Instruct me, Brother Jero.

JERO (*hanging up the picture*). Distribute those invitations at once. Go to my tailor and ask him to deliver my order tonight. Prepare everything for the spiritual assembly. When the moment comes, all shall be made plain.

REBECCA. I am with you to the end.

JERO. When the tailor delivers the order, you will understand.

REBECCA (*looking at the notes*). You did not fix a time for the meeting.

JERO. Tonight, Sister, at eight. We have no time to lose.

> *He picks up his chasuble, drapes it round his neck, his holy rod, bible etc. Then he picks up the file again, opens it at a page and smiles, nodding with satisfaction, pats the file tenderly.*

Our secret weapon, Sister Rebecca. We must take good care of it.

> *Locks it up in a cabinet.*

REBECCA. You are going out Brother Jero?

JERO. Preparations, Sister, preparations. If we must fight this battle well, there is a certain ally we cannot do without. I must go and seek him.

He stops. Benevolent smile.

But we shall win, Sister Rebecca, we shall win. Because I have already the best ally on my side. Here, in this room.

Going, hesitates, moves towards the vase of flowers and raises it to his face, sniffing delicately with his eyes shut.

And I thank you for brightening up my humble shack with these flowers, even as you have lightened my life with your spiritual lamp.

Goes out rapidly, leaving SISTER REBECCA *coy, enraptured, confused and overwhelmed all at once.*
Once outdoors BROTHER JERO *slips round the side and observes her through a window. The woman's condition obviously uplifts him for he moves off with even jauntier step and a light adjustment to his chasuble. He is immediately confronted by a fellow prophet,* ANANAIAS, *one of the poorer specimens of the brotherhood but built like a barrel.*

ANANAIAS. What are you up to now, Jero? Spying on your own little nest?

JERO (*clamps his hand on* ANANAIAS *and drags him off*). S-sh.

ANANAIAS. Take your hands off me. (*Shakes him off easily but follows him.*) So who have you got in there? The bailiffs?

JERO. Bailiffs like all sinners are welcome in my church, Brother Ananaias. But I do not welcome them in my humble abode.

ANANAIAS. That's enough of that pious nonsense. I know you.

JERO. Just what do you know of me, Brother?

ANANAIAS. Eh, come off it. If it's bailiffs . . .

JERO. Bailiffs do not even know my dwelling Ananaias.

ANANAIAS. That's because you're a clever man, Jero. Not even your worst enemy will deny you that.

JERO. Will you kindly say what business brought you here? I'm a busy man.

ANANAIAS. All right, then. I came to tell you you're going to need all that cunning of yours very soon. The City Council have taken a final decision. They're going to chuck us out. Every last hypocritical son of the devil.

JERO. That is old news, Ananaias. And for some of us it doesn't matter of course. The Lord will provide. But for those with no true vocation . . .

ANANAIAS. Like you.

JERO. I said vocation. You wouldn't know what that is. The beach for you is just a living, nothing else.

ANANAIAS. You haven't done badly out of it yourself I notice.

JERO. It is written that the good Lord shall feed his true servants. What are you going to do when you wake up one morning and find yourself face to face with a bulldozer?

ANANAIAS (*flexing his muscles*). Let them try that's all, let them try.

JERO. Wrestling is one thing but a bulldozer is another. Not even you can wrestle a bulldozer. And let me tell you, you are getting no younger.

ANANAIAS. Am I a born fool? There's a man drives those clumsy beasts isn't there? I leave the machine alone and drag him out by the scruff of his neck. When I've dipped him in the sea a few times he will emerge a good Christian and learn how to leave holy prophets alone.

JERO. That's not the way to fight them.

ANANAIAS. What's the way then? Stand by? Let them run me out of this land of milk and honey? I was doing quite well as a wrestler before I got the call and came into the service of the Lord. Gave all that up for this barren waste and now I can't even call it my own?

JERO. A moment ago it was a land of milk and honey.

ANANAIAS. Spiritual milk and honey of course. Otherwise barren waste. Look at it yourself.

JERO. Violence will not help us. I am calling a meeting tonight at which all these matters will be discussed. The good Lord shall help us find a way.

ANANAIAS. Calling a meeting? You already have something up your sleeve or you wouldn't be calling a meeting. Come on, let's have it. Let's be partners, you and me.

JERO. Tonight.

ANANAIAS. Now. Or I'll go in that room and tell whoever is there you were hiding and spying on them. I'll shout and tell them you're right here.

JERO (*folding his arms*). Go ahead, then.

ANANAIAS. Hey?

JERO. I said go ahead.

ANANAIAS. You're bluffing you know.

JERO. Call my bluff then. And by the way, when the battle is over and we have won our rights, I shall run you off this beach without lifting a finger.

ANANAIAS. You can't do that to me. I've got as much right as you to be here.

JERO. Not you.

ANANAIAS. You can't do it. I'm a holy man same as you.

JERO (*contemptuously*). Wrestling. Were you also wrestling in Kiri-kiri Prisons?

ANANAIAS (*clamping his hand over JERO's mouth in turn, and staring wildly round*). You're the devil himself you are. How come you know that?

JERO. I know.

ANANAIAS (*suddenly*). What of it? So I did a bit of thieving before and got nabbed. But I've been straight ever since. Earned my living wrestling for pick-ups clean and honest. And then I got the call. I'm reformed. What's wrong with a reformed sinner?

JERO. Reformed sinner? Hm. You didn't by any chance thug for a certain businessman just this last week did you? A little trade war over the monopoly of the whisky retail trade. Whisky Ananaias, whisky!

ANANAIAS (*dignified*). I beg your pardon, Brother Jero. I never was no thug in all my life. Bodyguard, yes. Bodyguard I was, and whoever says that is not a respectable position, internationally recognized, I'd just like to meet him that's all.

JERO. The police still have the fingerprints of the man who set fire to the store of one of the trade rivals. Bottles of spirits exploding all night and injuring innocent people. And the dumb, gross, incompetent all-muscle-and-no-brain petty criminal left a hefty thumbprint on the kerosene tin and then threw the kerosene tin on a refuse heap near by. They also know that that dirty great print matches the thumbprint of a certain ex-convict. The only thing they don't know is where he is hiding out after crimes of arson, unlawful wounding, attempted murder . . .

ANANAIAS (*swallowing hard*). Brother Jero . . .

JERO. Even the tin of kerosene was stolen from a near-by shop . . . that was robbery. Did you also use violence, Ananaias?

ANANAIAS. I swear to God, Brother Jero . . .

JERO. You are known to be a violent man. The Prosecutor can make it robbery with violence. And you know what that means.

ANANAIAS. I mean to say, Brother Jero, you are pretty hard on a man. You know yourself business is slow . . . A man must eat . . .

JERO *lets him squirm a little.*

JERO. Tonight at the meeting I shall put forward certain plans . . .

ANANAIAS. I'll support you, Brother, depend on my vote any time. (*Getting warmer.*) And if there's anyone you'd prefer to take a walk outside on his head for making trouble . . .

JERO. I don't need your violence thank you. (*Going.*) And keep away from this place until meeting time.

ANANAIAS (*running after him*). I say Brother, Brother . . .

JERO. Well?

ANANAIAS. Brother Jero. Could you lend me a shilling or two till the meeting? You know I wouldn't ask if . . . you . . . well you see how it is yourself. Things haven't been going well lately. No contribution, nothing at all. The congregation have shrunk

to nothing and even them as comes, all I get is the story of their
family troubles. They no longer pay tithes.

JERO. You were greedy, Brother Ananaias. If every man of a
hundred congregation paid a tithe at the end of every month he
is going to notice very soon that a tithe from everyone means
several times what each man is earning. And all that for one
man – you – alone! That's why they stopped coming.

ANANAIAS. Heh?

JERO. Yes, that's how you lost your little flock.

ANANAIAS. From a hundred to nothing!

JERO. From a hundred to nothing, except those who come to
borrow money.

ANANAIAS. But how come such an idea enter their head? I would
never have thought of it.

JERO (*handing him a shilling*). Perhaps *somebody* put it in their
head. Good day, Ananaias.

ANANAIAS. Heh? (*Stands open-mouthed, gaping at the retreating*
JERO.)

From the opposite side, the CHIEF EXECUTIVE OFFICER *of the*
Tourist Board of the City Council emerges, rumpled and dusty
from his hiding place. He is followed by the CLERK *to the*
Board and a POLICEWOMAN. ANANAIAS *hides and observes.*

CLERK. This is the place, sir.

EXECUTIVE (*angrily brushing his bowler hat and suit. The* CLERK
helps him). About time too. I shall deal very rigorously with all
of you who subjected me to this most humiliating adventure.
Come all this way to lose not only a confidential file but a
Confidential Secretary. Why I should be the one to be saddled
with their recovery . . .

CLERK. Sir, it is the only way . . .

EXECUTIVE. Nothing unbecoming to a man's dignity is ever the
only way. Bear that in mind.

CLERK. To achieve results sir . . .

EXECUTIVE. Kindly stop arguing with me. It is not in my character to skulk and hide until a mere charlatan is out of the way. I prefer to confront him squarely even if he's the devil himself.

CLERK. Sir, please let's enter and get the business over. He may return any time.

EXECUTIVE. If you are planning for me to escape through the window if he returns suddenly . . .

CLERK. Nothing of the sort, sir, nothing of the sort. I only say time is money, sir. Let's go in.

He knocks on the door but the CHIEF EXECUTIVE *barges in.* REBECCA *looks startled at their entrance.* ANANAIAS *creeps closer. The* POLICEWOMAN *waits by the door.*

EXECUTIVE. Is this the woman?

CLERK. Yes, sir. Miss Denton, this is the Chief Executive Officer of the Tourist Board of the City Council. Miss Denton, sir.

EXECUTIVE. Miss Denton . . .

REBECCA. My name is Rebecca.

EXECUTIVE. I do not believe, young lady, that we are on Christian name terms.

REBECCA. I do not believe that you are on Christian terms at all, sir. Your soul is in danger.

EXECUTIVE (*splutters badly and explodes*). My religious state is no concern of yours, young woman.

REBECCA. But it is, sir, it is. I am my brother's keeper. The state of your soul distresses me, sir.

CLERK. That's how it started, sir. That's how it started.

EXECUTIVE. That is how what started?

CLERK. That was how the prophet got her. He wasn't even addressing her at all but the C.E.O. who came to serve him notice. He kept preaching at him all the time but she was the one who got the message. Christ sir, you should have seen her convulsions!

EXECUTIVE. Why the hell did he bring her in the first place?

REBECCA. Hell is true sir. I was living in hell but did not know it until Brother Jero pointed the path of God to me.

EXECUTIVE. I was not addressing you, woman.

CLERK. She was his private secretary . . .

EXECUTIVE. I know she was his private secretary, damn you . . .

REBECCA. He will not be damned sir, the Lord is merciful . . .

EXECUTIVE. Can't anyone shut up this religious maniac? I asked, why bring her along? Do you see me here with my private secretary?

REBECCA. I shall answer that question. When you are saved, you are no longer afraid to tell the truth. My boss asked me to come with him to take notes, but in my heart I knew that he was planning to seduce me.

EXECUTIVE. What! You dare slander a senior government official of my department in my presence? I shall order an investigation and have you charged with . . .

CLERK. Don't, sir. It's the truth. The C.E.O. has had his eye on her a long time. Wouldn't let her alone in the office, making her do overtime even if there was no work to do, just to try and . . .

EXECUTIVE. That's enough thank you. I don't need the whole picture painted in bold and dirty colours.

CLERK. Yes, sir, I mean, no, sir.

REBECCA. Do not distress yourself for that poor sinner. I pray for the salvation of his soul every day.

EXECUTIVE. And we are praying for you to come to your senses. And for a start just hand me the file you had with you. And be thankful I am not having you charged for keeping an official file after office hours.

CLERK. And a confidential file don't forget that, sir. Very confidential.

EXECUTIVE. Quite right. The file, young lady. We will overlook the offence since you weren't really in possession of your senses.

REBECCA. I was never more clearly within my senses as now.

EXECUTIVE. You call this a sensible action? You, an intelligent young girl, a fully trained Confidential Secretary . . .

CLERK. Eighty words per minute, sir, one hundred and twenty
   shorthand . . .

EXECUTIVE. Did I ask you to supply me statistics?

CLERK. Beg pardon, sir. Just saying what a waste it is.

EXECUTIVE. Of course it's a bloody waste. Eighty words per
   minute and a hundred and twenty shorthand. You had enough
   will-power to resist the revolting advances of a lecherous Chief
   Eviction Officer on the rampage, you are trusted sufficiently to
   be assigned an official duty which is most essential to our
   national economy and what happens – you permit yourself to
   be bamboozled by a fake prophet, a transparent charlatan . . .

REBECCA (*pitying*). It is the devil which speaks in you sir, it's the
   devil which makes you call Prophet Jeroboam all those bad
   names.

EXECUTIVE. He deserves more than a bad name. He deserves a
   bad end and he will come to it yet.

REBECCA. Fight the devil in you, sir, let us help you fight and
   conquer him.

EXECUTIVE. Can't you see Jeroboam is the devil, damn you? All
   the prophets on this beach are devils . . .

REBECCA. The devil is in you, sir, I can see him.

EXECUTIVE. They have to be evicted. They stand in the way of
   progress. They clutter up the beach and prevent decent men
   from coming here and paying to enjoy themselves. They are
   holding up a big tourist business. You know yourself how
   the land value has doubled since we started public executions
   on this beach.

REBECCA. Shameless sinners who acquire wealth from the mis-
   fortunes of others? Will you make money off sin and iniquity?
   Oh sir, you must let Brother Jero talk to you about the evil in
   your plans. To make money out of sin is to bring sin upon the
   dwellers of your city. Not Sodom nor Gomorrah shall suffer as
   this city of yours when the wrath of the Lord descends upon it
   and the walls are wiped off the surface of the earth. The Lord
   speaks in me. I am the mouthpiece of his will. Give up this

plan and let the prophets continue the blessed task of turning
men back to the path of goodness and decency . . .

EXECUTIVE. Shut her up. For God's sake shut her up.

REBECCA (*sudden joy*). Praise the Lord! A change has begun in
you already. When you first came in you called on hell and you
damned your fellow man. Now you call out in God's name.
Hallelujah! Hallelujah! Hallelujah! Come to me, said the Lord.
Call my name and I shall answer. Hallelujah! Hallelujah! Call
his name and he shall heed you. Come to me, said the Lord,
come to me. Come to me, said the Lord, come to me. Come to
me, said the Lord, come to me. Call my name, and I shall heed
you. Turn from sin and I shall feed you. Turn from filth and I
shall cleanse you. Turn from filth and I shall cleanse you.

She approaches the EXECUTIVE OFFICER *with outstretched
arms as if to embrace him. He retreats round the room but she
follows him. She gets progressively 'inspired'.*

Give up the plan, said the Lord, give up the plan. What avails all
the wealth of the world, if your soul is lost. What avails your
cars and houses if you'll burn in hell. Save this sinner, Lord
save his soul. Burn out the greed of his heart, burn out the
greed.

The CHIEF EXECUTIVE *makes the door but* ANANAIAS, *with
a roar of 'Hallelujah' steps out and blocks it. The* CHIEF
EXECUTIVE *flings himself back into the room, bang into the
arms of* REBECCA *who with a shout of 'Hallelujah' holds him
in an unbreakable embrace. His bowler hat is knocked off and he
soon parts company with his umbrella. The* CLERK *retreats to
the corner of the room on seeing* ANANAIAS, *while the* POLICE-
WOMAN *who tries to squeeze past* ANANAIAS *is herself swept
up with one arm and held there by* ANANAIAS.

ANANAIAS. And this sinner, lord, and this sinner!

REBECCA. Hallelujah!

ANANAIAS. From her labour of sin, oh Lord, from her labour of sin.

REBECCA. Hallelujah!

ANANAIAS. Policework is evil, oh lord, policework is evil.

REBECCA. Halle-Halle-Hallelujah. (*And continues the chorus.*)

ANANAIAS. Save this sinner, Lord, save this sinner. Protect her from bribery, oh Lord! Protect her from corruption! Protect her from iniquities known and unknown, from practices unmentionable in thy hearing. Protect her from greed for promotion, from hunger for stripes, from chasing after citations with actions over and beyond the call of duty. Save her from harassing the innocent and molesting the tempted, from prying into the affairs of men and nosing out their innocent practices. Take out the beam in thine own eye, said the Lord.

REBECCA. Hallelujah!

ANANAIAS. Take out the beam in thine own eye!

REBECCA. Hallelujah!

ANANAIAS. Take out the beam in thine own eye, for who shall cast the first stone sayeth the Lord! Let him that hath no sin cast the first stone! Let him that hath no sin make the first arrest! Vengeance is mine saith the Lord, I shall recompense. Vengeance is mine, take not the law into your own hands! Verily I say unto you it is easier for a camel to pass through a needle's eye than for a police man or woman to enter the kingdom of heaven. We pray you bring them into the kingdom of heaven Lord. Bring them into the kingdom of heaven Lord. Bring them into the kingdom of heaven Lord. Bring them all into the kingdom of heaven. Save them from this hatred of their fellow men, from this hatred of poor weak vessels who merely seek a modest living. Oh bring them into the kingdom of heaven Lord. Right up to the kingdom of heaven Lord. Right into the kingdom of heaven. . .

    REBECCA's *ecstasy has reached such proportions that she is*

trembling from head to foot. Suddenly she flings out her arms,
knocking off the glasses of the EXECUTIVE OFFICER.

REBECCA. Into the kingdom of heaven Lord, into the kingdom of
heaven. . .

EXECUTIVE OFFICER *seizes his freedom on the instant, dives*
through the window headfirst. The CLERK *is about to help him*
pick up his fallen bowler and umbrella but changes his mind as
ANANAIAS *steps forward. He follows his master through the*
window. ANANAIAS *in making for the fallen trophy lets go the*
POLICEWOMAN *who makes for safety through the door.*
REBECCA *is completely oblivious to all the goings-on, only*
gyrating and repeating 'into the kingdom of heaven . . .'
ANANAIAS *picks up the umbrella and bowler, looks in the*
cupboard and pockets a piece of bread he finds there, sniffs the
bottle and downs the contents. Finding nothing else that can be
lifted, he shrugs and starts to leave. Stops, takes another look at
the yet ecstatic REBECCA, *goes over to a corner of the room and*
lifts up a bucket of water, throws it on SISTER REBECCA. *She*
is stopped cold and shudders. Exit ANANAIAS, *taking the*
bucket with him.

SCENE TWO

A portrait of the uniformed figure, in a different pose, hangs over the
veranda of the house where CHUME *lives in rented rooms. He is*
practising on a trumpet, trying out the notes of 'What a friend we
have in Jesus'. His Salvation Army uniform is laid out carefully on
a chair, stiffly starched and newly ironed. Enter MAJOR SILVA, *also*
of the Salvation Army.

SILVA (*his accent is perfect RP plus a blend of Oxford*). Good day, Corporal Chummy. I'm afraid the Captain could not come today, but I will do my humble best to deputize for him. (*Points to the trumpet and the sheet music.*) I am glad to notice that you at least do some homework.

CHUME *looks at him with a mixture of suspicion and hostility.*

CHUME. How can? You don't yourself blow trumpet.

SILVA. That indeed is true, but I do understand music and that really is what I intend to teach. Well, shall we begin?

CHUME. Where is Captain Winston?

SILVA. I have told you, he is unable to come. Now, if you will just tell me how far you have progressed with him we shall er, see what we can do eh?

CHUME (*obviously dissatisfied*). It is much better for man to have only one teacher. I begin get used to Captain Winston and then somebody else comes. Captain Winston understand how to teach me.

SILVA. Well, if you gave me a chance, Chummy, I think I may be able to fill Captain Winston's shoes for a lesson at least, with God's help. Well now . . .

CHUME. I think . . . well, we can wait. I mean I can just practise by myself until . . .

SILVA. Now now, Chummy, we haven't got all day you know. Here, let's start with this shall we? Let's hear you play this piece, enh. (*Selecting a sheet from the pile.*) Then I can form some sort of idea. Right? Just play it once through.

CHUME. No, I don't want to play that one.

SILVA. Oh? All right. What do you wish to play? Pick out another one . . . anything you like. What hymn did you last practise with the Captain?

CHUME. I don't know. We just dey practise that's all.

SILVA. Well, play me what you last practised then.

CHUME. We practise hymn upon hymn. Er – one hymn like that, but I don't remember the name.

SILVA. Well, give me the first few bars and we will go from there. Right?

CHUME, *obviously still uncomfortable, lifts the trumpet to his lips.*

Good. After four. One – Two – Three – Four.

CHUME *sets upon 'What a friend we have in Jesus', SILVA listens, registers mild surprise and shrugs. He waits for CHUME to finish a verse.*

But that is the music I picked for you. I thought you said you didn't want to play it.

CHUME. En-hen? I change my mind.

SILVA. All right. Now, Chummy, this time try and play what is written down here. Stick it on your trumpet please. You see, you cannot give church hymns your own rhythm. You have to play what has been put down, so please read the score and play.

CHUME. I no talk so? I say is better to wait for Captain Winston. You can't understand how to teach me properly.

SILVA. Now, now, let's stop all this silliness. Here, let's have another go. It's all a matter of tempo, Chummy, tempo – Tam. ta. ra. ta. ra. ta. tam . . . tam . . . tam . . . ta. ra. ta. ra. ta. tam . . . Sharp and precise, Chummy, not like high life or juju music. Now shall we try again? This time, follow the score.

He hands the sheet to CHUME who sticks it on his trumpet.

Now, are we ready? One – Two – Three . . . Tam . . . ta. ra . . .

CHUME *plays the tune in the same swingy beat and SILVA stops him.*

SILVA. No, no, tempo, Chummy, tempo . . . good God! (*Coming round to point out the score.*) Corporal, do you always read music upside down?

CHUME. Hm? (*Guiltily begins to re-set the card,* SILVA *looks at him with increasing suspicion.*) No wonder . . . en-hen, that's better.

SILVA (*severely.*) Corporal Chummy, can you read music notation at all?

CHUME (*angrily*). I no talk so? You done come with your trouble. I say I go wait for Captain Winston you say you go fit teach me. Now you come dey bother me with music notation. Na paper man dey take trumpet play abi na music?

SILVA. Can you read music or not, Brother Chummy?

CHUME. Can you play trumpet or not, Major Silva?

SILVA. Really this is too much. How can Captain Winston expect me to teach you anything when you are musically illiterate.

CHUME. So I am illiterate now? I am illiterate? You are illiterate yourself. Illiterate man yourself.

SILVA. What! All right let us keep our temper.

CHUME. I have not lost my temper, it is you who don't know where you leave your own. You no even sabbe call my name correct and you dey call man illiterate. My name na Chume, no to Chummy.

SILVA (*with superhuman effort*). Anger, the Christian soldier's anger must be reserved only for the enemies of God and righteousness. It has no place within the army of God itself. Please bow your head, Corporal Chummy. I beg your pardon – Choo-may.

He strikes an attitude of prayer and CHUME *obediently does likewise. They remain silent for several moments.*

May God give us strength against the sin of false pride and the devil of wrath, Amen.

CHUME. Amen.

SILVA. And now we shall begin all over again. (*Taking off the music card.*) We will forget all about this for the moment shall we? Captain Winston said that you were a natural on the trumpet and I suppose he is right. But there are certain things still to be learnt otherwise you will be like a lone voice crying in the wilderness. Now, shall we try again? I want you to watch me and try and follow the er, the movement of my hands – like this. Watch, watch ... Tam ... ta. ra. ta. tam. ta. ra ... tam and so on. Got it?

CHUME (*assertively*). Yes, yes. That is how Captain Winston is teaching me.

SILVA. Good. Now are we ready? One – Two – Three ...

Continues to talk as he plays.

That's better. Always remember that the tunes of the Army must be martial in colour and tempo. We march to it remember, not dance. No, no. Stop. No flourishes please, no flourishes. Especially not with a march. Most especially not with a march.

CHUME. Which one be flourish again?

SILVA. Beg your pardon?

CHUME. I say which one be flourish?

SILVA. Oh, flourish. Well, flourish is er ... extra, you know, frills, decoration. What we want is pure notes, pure crystal clear notes. (CHUME *looks blank.*) Look, just play the first bar again will you.

CHUME (*more mystified still*). Bar?

SILVA. Yes, the first ... all right, start from the beginning again will you and I will stop you when you come to the flourish ...

CHUME plays. SILVA stops him after a few notes.

That's it. You played that bit Ta-a-ta instead of ta-ta.

CHUME. Oh you mean the pepper.

SILVA. Pepper?

CHUME. Enh, pepper. When you cook soup you go put small pepper. Otherwise the thing no go taste. I mean to say, 'e go taste like something, After all, even sand-sand get in own taste. But who dey satisfy with sand-sand? If they give you sand-sand to chop you go chop?

SILVA (*beginning to doubt his senses*). Mr Chume, if I tell you I understand one word of what you're saying I commit the sin of mendacity.

CHUME. What! You no know wetin pepper be? Captain Winston, as soon as I say pepper 'e know wetin I mean one time.

SILVA. I do not know, to use your own quaint expression, wetin musical pepper be, Mr Chume.

CHUME. And condiments? Iru? Salt? Ogiri? Kaun? And so on and so forth?

SILVA. Mr Chume, I'm afraid I don't quite see the relevance.

CHUME. No no, no try for *see* am. Make you just *hear* am. (*Blows a straight note.*) Dat na plain soup. (*Blows again, slurring into a higher note.*) Dat one na soup and pepper. (*Gives a new twist.*) Dat time I put extra flavour. Now, if you like we fit lef' am like that. But suppose I put stockfish, smoke-fish, ngwam-ngwam ...

SILVA. If you don't mind I would just as soon have a straightforward rehearsal. We have no time for all this nonsense.

CHUME. Wait small, you no like ngwam-ngwam or na wetin? Na my traditional food you dey call nonsense?

SILVA. I had no intention whatsoever to insult you, Mr Chume.

CHUME. If nonsense no to big insult for man of my calibre, den I no know wetin be insult again.

SILVA. Brother Chume, please. Do remember we have an important date at tomorrow's executions We must rehearse!

CHUME (*blasts an aggressive note on the trumpet*). Stockfish! (*Another.*) Bitter-leaf! I done tire for your nonsense. (*Throws down cap, blows more notes.*) Locust bean and red pepper! (*Kicks off shoes.*) If you still dey here when I put the ngwam-ngwam you go sorry for your head.

Throws himself into the music now, turning the tune into a traditional beat and warming up progressively. His legs begin to slice into the rhythm and before long his entire body is caught up with it. He dances aggressively towards SILVA *who backs away but cannot immediately escape as* CHUME's *dance controls the exit. Finally when* CHUME *leaps to one side he seizes his chance and takes to his heels.* CHUME *continues dancing and does not notice* BROTHER JERO *who enters and, after a despairing shake of his head, with his usual calculating gesture, steps into the dance with him.* CHUME *becomes slowly aware that other legs have joined his, his movement peters to a stop and he follows the legs up to the smiling, benevolent face of* BROTHER JERO. CHUME *backs off.*

JERO (*holds out his arms*). It is no ghost, Brother Chume. It is no apparition that stands before you. Assure yourself that you are well again and suffer no more from hallucinations. It is I, your old beloved master the Prophet Jeroboam. Immaculate Jero. Articulate Hero of Christ's Crusade.

CHUME (*he stands stock still*). Commot here before I break your head.

JERO. Break my head? What good will my broken head do you?

CHUME. It will make compensation for all de ting I done suffer for your hand. I dey warn you now, commot.

JERO. Suffer at my hands? You, Brother Chume? Suffer at my hands.

CHUME. You tell the police say I craze. Because God expose you and your cunny-cunny and I shout 'am for the whole world ...

JERO. Brother Chume ...

CHUME. I no be your Brother, no call me your brother. De kin' brother wey you fit be na the brotherhood of Cain and Abel. The brotherhood of Jacob and Esau. Eat my meat and tief my patrimony ...

JERO. You do me great injustice, Brother Chume.

CHUME. Na so? And de one you do me na justice? To lock man

inside lunatic asylum because you wan' cover up your wayo. You be wayo man plain and simple. Wayo prophet! (*Warming up.*) Look, I dey warn you, commot here if you like your head! (*Advancing.*)

JERO. You raised your hand once against the anointed of the Lord, remember what it cost you.

CHUME. Which anointed of the Lord? You?

JERO. You raised a cutlass against me Brother Chume, but I forgave you.

CHUME. Dat na forgiveness? Three month inside lunatic asylum! Na dat den dey call forgiveness for your bible?

JERO. Was that not better than a life sentence for attempted murder?

CHUME. If to say I get my cutlass inside your head that time this world for done become better place. They can hang me but I for become saint and martyr. I for die but de whole world go call me Saint Chume.

JERO. But look round you, Brother Chume, look around you. You want to make this world a better place? Good! But to get hanged in the process? And perhaps in public? For whom? For the sake of people like Major Silva? People who don't even understand the musical soul which the Lord has given you? Are they worth it, Brother Chume? Oh I was watching you for some time you know – that man is an enemy believe me. An enemy. He does not understand you. I am sure they are all like that.

CHUME. They are not all like that. Captain Winston . . .

JERO. A white man. He is not one of us. And you know yourself he's a hypocrite. All white men are hypocrites.

CHUME. Na him come save me from that lunatic asylum, not so? If dat na hympocrisy then thank God for hympocrites.

JERO. He needed a trumpeter.

CHUME. Before that time I no fit play trumpet. I no sabbe hol' am self.

JERO. But you were playing on a penny flute and he heard you. I know the whole story, Brother Chume. He and his band came round to comfort you unfortunate inmates ...

CHUME (*violently*). I am not unfortunate inmate. Na you tell them to lock me inside dat place with crazemen. The day I fust meet you, dat day na my unfortunate.

JERO (*going progressively into a 'sermonic' chanting style*). Brother Chume, you should thank the good Lord, not blame him for the situation in which you found yourself. When he, in his wisdom saw fit to place wings on my feet and make me fly upon the deserted beach away from your flaming cutlass of wrath, it was not, be assured, my life upon which he set such value. No, Brother Chume, it was yours. Yours! Consider, if you had indeed achieved your nefarious intention and martyred me upon the sands, would not your soul be damned for ever? Picture my blood sinking into the sand and mingling with the foam, your feet sinking into the gruesome mixture and growing heavy with the knowledge of eternal damnation. What man, be he so swift of foot can run unaided upon a sandy shore? Could you think to escape the hounds of God's judgement and the law? See yourself as you would be, a fugitive from man and God, a dark soul lost and howling in the knowledge of damnation. Or would you fling yourself upon the waves and seek to drown yourself? If you succeeded, you were doubly damned. If you failed and the sea rejected you, flung your tainted body back upon the shore, think what a life of rejection yours would be, unable to seek solace even in death! Did you not yourself mention the moral tale of Cain and Abel only this minute? Was Cain not damned for ever? Was he not cursed by the Almighty himself? But I knew it was not in you to perform such an evil act. It was, obviously, the work of the devil. Your mind was turned away from the light of reason and your judgement clouded for a while. Was it then wrong of me to protect you the only way I could? For three months you received tender care and treatment. Your good woman, Amope, seeing her husband in danger of losing his reason proved once again that a heart of gold beat beneath her shrewish nature. For the first time since your marriage, Brother Chume, you saw that a voice of honey may lurk beneath the sandy tongue of a termagant. She showed you the care and love which she had denied you these many years. And so at last, seeing that you had recovered your reason, the good Lord sent unto you a deliverer just as he did deliver Nebuchadnessar of old from the horror of darkness and insanity. Oh, Brother Chume, Brother Chume, great is the Lord and full of kindness. Let us kneel down and praise his name. Praise the Lord, Brother Chume, praise the Lord. Praise the Lord for the gift of reason and the gift of life. Then praise him also for your coming promotion, yes, your coming promotion for this is the glad tidings of which I am the humble bearer.

CHUME (*hesitant*). Promotion?

JERO. Of whose glad tidings I am made humble bearer. I send *you*, Prophet Jero, said the Lord. Blessed are the peacemakers for they shall inherit the kingdom. Make your peace with Brother Chume and take with you this peace-offering, the good tidings of his coming promotion.

CHUME. Promotion? How can?

JERO (*sternly*). Do you doubt, Brother Chume? Do you doubt my prophecy? Has your sojourn among lunatics made you forget who prophesied war and have we not lived to see it come to pass? Do you trust in me and praise the Lord or do you confess yourself a waverer at this hour of trial.

CHUME. Praise the Lord.

JERO. In his new image, brother, sing his praise.

CHUME. Sing his praise.

JERO. Through blood has he purged us, as prophesied by me.

CHUME. Sing his praise.

JERO. Sing his praise, hallelujah, sing his praise.

CHUME. Hallelujah!

JERO. Out of the dark he brought you, into the light.

CHUME. Hallelujah!

JERO (*going all out to truly arouse* CHUME's '*rhythmic rapport*'). Out of the dark he brought you, into the light!

CHUME. Hallelujah!

JERO. Never again to stumble, never again.

CHUME. Hallelujah!

JERO. Sent him off howling, praise Him, fire in his tail.

CHUME. Hallelujah!

JERO. Praise the Lord Hallelujah praise the Lord.

CHUME. Hallelujah!

JERO. Praise the Lord, Brother, praise the Lord.

CHUME. Praise the Lord, Brother, praise the Lord.

JERO. Praise the Lord, Brother, praise the Lord.

CHUME. Hallelujah! Hallelujah, praise the Lord, Hallelujah! Praise the Lord. Hallelujah, praise the Lord, Hallelujah! Praise the Lord . . .

With JERO *clapping in rhythm and* BROTHER CHUME *swaying and chanting on his knees.*

JERO (*moves aside and detachedly observes* CHUME *in ecstasy*). I had my doubts for a while but I should have known better. These Salvation Army brothers may be washed in the red blood of the Lord, but the black blood of the Bar Beach brotherhood proves stronger every time. (*Sudden shout, turning to* CHUME.) Hallelujah, Brother, Hallelujah!

He joins CHUME *for a few more moments, then taps him on the shoulder.*

JERO. Brother Chume. Brother Chume. (*He shakes him a little.*) Brother Chume. Brother Chume!

Picks up the trumpet and blows a blast in CHUME's *ear.*

CHUME (*starts out of his ecstasy*). Here, Brother Jero.

JERO (*with excitement*). The trumpet of the Lord, Chume! It sounds the clarion to duty. There is a time for everything, so says the Lord. A time for laughing and time for crying; a time for waking and a time for sleeping; a time for praying and a time for action. This is a time for action.

CHUME. Action?

JERO. Yes, action. Rise, Brother Chume, and follow me. The Lord hath need of thee.

CHUME (*getting up, hastily pulls himself together*). Of me, Brother Jero?

JERO. Yes, of you. You have stayed too long among the opposition. Cheated. Humiliated. Scorned. It is time for your elevation. Pick up your trumpet and follow me. I shall explain it all on our way to meet your – (*He pauses for deliberate emphasis.*) – Brother *Prophets*.

CHUME (*open-mouthed*). Brother Prophets, Brother Jero? But me na . . .

JERO. Not any longer, Chume. From now you are a holy prophet in your own light. No, no, that is *not* the promotion. It is only the first taste. Your full elevation takes place tonight, before the assembled brotherhood of the beach. You have gone through the fires of hell and emerged a strong servant of the Lord. You are saved, redeemed, inspired and re-dedicated. From now on, a true brother, an equal; no longer a servant of mine. Kneel, Brother Chume.

CHUME (*kneeling groggily*). But prophet . . . me na only poor . . .

JERO. I perform only the good Lord's commands, nothing more. (*With his holy rod he taps him on both shoulders.*) Arise Prophet Chume, serve the Lord and fight his cause till eternity. (*Turns the rod round and offers him the 'hilt'.*) Until you obtain yours and it is consecrated you may use mine.

CHUME (*overwhelmed*). Dis kindness too much, Brother Jero.

JERO. I am only the instrument of the Lord's will. (*Briskly.*) Now get up and let's go. The others are awaiting and we have much to do.

Blackout.

SCENE THREE

The front space of BROTHER JERO'S *headquarters. Loud chatter among a most bizarre collection of prophets.* SISTER REBECCA *emerges from the house carrying the portrait from the office and hangs it against the outer wall. The desk and chair have already been moved out of the office for the meeting. Rebecca takes a chair to a most unbending individual who stares straight ahead and keeps his arms folded. He is the only one who seems to abstain from the free-flowing drinks, the effect of which is already apparent on one or two.*

SHADRACH. No, Sister, we refuse to sit down. We refuse to sit down. We have been slighted and we make known our protest. We have been treated with less courtesy than becomes the leader of a denomination twenty thousand strong. Brother Jero, at whose behest we have presented ourselves here at great inconvenience, is not himself here to welcome us. We protest his discourtesy.

CALEB. Hear hear. (*Hiccups.*) Hardly the conduct of a gentleman prophet.

REBECCA. Brother Shadrach, I assure you he was held up by matters which concern this very affair you have come to discuss.

ISAAC. He is very long about it then.

SHADRACH. Much much too long, Sister Rebecca. To make us wait is an act of indignity thrust upon us.

ANANAIAS. Oh sit down, you fatuous old hypocrite.

SHADRACH (*turns to go*). We take our leave.

CALEB. Hear hear. (*Hiccup.*) Let's all stage a dignified walk-out. Nobody walks out these days. Not since the parliamentarians vanished.

ISAAC. Good old days those. Good for the profession.

CALEB. Come on, old Shad, give us a walk-out. (*With much difficulty on the word.*) An ecclesiastically dignified walk-out.

REBECCA. Brother Shadrach, please . . .

SHADRACH. No, we take our leave. For the third time tonight we have been insulted by a common riff-raff of the calling. We take our leave.

CALEB. Hear hear. The honourable member for . . .

REBECCA. Pay no attention Brother. I apologize on their behalf. Forgive us all for being remiss.

SHADRACH. I forgive you, Sister. (*Sits down.*)

ANANAIAS (*leans over the back of his chair*). You will burst, Shadrach, you will burst like the frog in the swamp.

CALEB. Like the frog in the adage, Brother. (*Hiccup.*) Frog in the adage.

SHADRACH (*without losing his poise, whips his hand round and seizes that of* ANANAIAS *by the wrist and brings it round front. The hand is seen to contain a purse*). Mine, I believe, Ananaias?

ANANAIAS. It dropped on the ground. Is that the thanks I get for helping you pick it up.

SHADRACH. I accuse no one, Ananaias. (*Returning wallet into the recesses of his robes.*) We are all met, I hope, in a spirit of brotherhood. The lesson reads, I am my brother's keeper Ananaias, not, I am my brother's pursekeeper.

ANANAIAS (*turns away*). Lay not your treasures upon earth says the good book. Verily verily I say unto you, it is easier for a camel and so on and so forth.

CALEB (*raising his mug*). Sister Rebecca, my spirits are low.

REBECCA (*rushing to fill it*). Forgive me, Brother Caleb.

CALEB. Upliftment is in order, God bless you.

ISAAC. So where is this Jeroboam fellow? When is he coming to tell us why he has made us forsake our stations to wait on his lordship?

REBECCA. In a moment, Brother Matthew. (*Going to fill his mug.*)

ISAAC. I am not Brother Matthew . . .

REBECCA. I beg your pardon, Brother.

CALEB. A clear case of mistaken identity, Sister Rebecca.

ISAAC. I am not Brother Matthew, sister, and I beg you to note that fact.

MATTHEW (*nettled*). May one ask just what you have against being Brother Matthew?

ISAAC. I know all about Brother Matthew, and that should be enough answer for anyone with a sense of shame.

REBECCA. Forgive my unfortunate error. Don't start a quarrel on that account.

ISAAC. And to think he has the nerve to show his face here. Some people are utterly without shame.

CALEB. Hear hear.

MATTHEW. And others are poor imitation Pharisees.

CALEB. Hear hear.

ISAAC. Better an imitation Pharisee than a sex maniac.

MATTHEW. I take exception to that!

ISAAC. Very good. Take exception.

MATTHEW. Dare repeat that and see if it doesn't land you in court for slander. Go on, we are all listening. I have witnesses. Come on I dare you.

ISAAC. I don't have to. We all know the truth. You may have been acquitted but we know the truth.

MATTHEW. Coward!

ISAAC. Fornicator.

MATTHEW. Drunkard, con-man. Forger.

CALEB. Three to one. Foul play.

REBECCA (*getting between them as they head for a clash*). Brothers, in the name of our common calling I beg of you . . .

JERO *and* CHUME *enter.* REBECCA *sighs with relief.*

Oh, Brother Jero, you are truly an answer to prayer.

JERO. Welcome, Brothers, welcome all of you and forgive me for arriving late at my own meeting. (*Hands* REBECCA *a key.*) Unlock the safe and bring out our secret weapon, Sister.

ISAAC. We have waited two hours, Brother.

ANANAIAS. You have not been here a half-hour Isaac. I saw you come in.

JERO. A-ah, I see empty mugs. No wonder our brothers are offended. Sister Rebecca, we require better hospitality.

REBECCA (*emerging with the file*). Do you think that wise, Brother Jero? They are already quite . . .

JERO. Trust me, I know what I am doing Sister. (*Loudly.*) More drinks for our brothers. Fill up the cups Sister Rebecca.

SHADRACH. We do not drink. We came here for a serious discussion, so we were informed. We have not come here to wine and dine.

JERO. We will not quarrel. I admit the fault is mine. Sister Rebecca, some snuff for Brother Shadrach.

REBECCA. I shall get it at once, Brother Jero.

JERO (*turns and beams on the gathering*). And now, dear brother shepherds of the flock, let us waste no more time. We are mostly known to one another so I shall not waste your time on introductions. The subject is progress. Progress has caught up with us. Like the oceantide it is battering on our shore-line, the door-step of our tabernacle. Projects everywhere! Fun fairs! Gambling! Casinos! The servants of Mammon have had their heads turned by those foreign fleshpots to which they are drawn whenever they travel on their so-called economic

missions. And our mission, the mission of the good Lord
Jehovah shall be the sacrificial lamb, on the altar of Mammon.
Oh when you see smoke rising on that grievous day, know that
it rises from these shacks of devotion which we have raised to
shelter the son of God on his Visitation on that long-awaited
day. And shall he find? What shall he find when he comes over
the water, that great fisherman among men, thinking to step on
to the open tabernacle which we, you and I, have founded here
to await his glorious coming? *THIS!* (*With a flourish he pulls
out a sheaf of photographs from his bag.*) This, my brothers!

JERO *observes their reactions as the photos of luscious scantily-
clad bathers are circulated. Reactions vary from* SHADRACH
who turns away in calculated disgust to ANANAIAS *who finds
them lewdly hilarious and* MATTHEW *who literally drools.*

SHADRACH. It must never happen here!

ISAAC. Never. We must organize.

CALEB. I concur. Rally the union. No business sharks in our
spirituous waters.

ISAAC. All legitimate avenues of protest must be explored.

MATTHEW. What for?

ANANAIAS. What do you mean, what for?

MATTHEW. I said what for? These photos reveal strayed souls in
need of salvation. Must we turn away from suchlike? Only the
sick have need of the physician.

ISAAC. Not your kind of physic, Brother Matthew.

SHADRACH. If we take Brother Jeroboam's meaning correctly,
and we think we do, the intention is to exclude ... er ... us,
the physicians from this so-called resort is it not, Brother?

MATTHEW. We don't know that for certain.

JERO (*hands him the file at an open page*). Read this, Brother
Matthew. These are the minutes of the meeting of Cabinet at
which certain decisions were taken.

MATTHEW (*shrinks away*). What file is that?

JERO. Read it.

MATTHEW. It says Confidential on that paper. I don't want any government trouble.

ISAAC. Very wise of you, Brother Matthew. Mustn't risk your parole. (*Takes the file.*) I'll read it. (*At the first glance he whistles.*) How did you get hold of this, Jero?

JERO. The Lord moves in mysterious ways . . .

ANANAIAS. . . . His wonders to perform. Amen.

ISAAC (*reading*). 'Memorandum of the Cabinet Office to the Board of Tourism. Proposals to turn the Bar Beach into an a National Public Execution Amphitheatre.' Whew! You hadn't mentioned that.

JERO. I was saving it for a surprise. It is the heart of the whole business enterprise.

SHADRACH. We don't understand. Does this mean . . .?

JERO. Business, Brother Shadrach, big business.

MATTHEW. Where do we come in in all this?

JERO. Patience, we're coming to it. Brother Isaac, do read on. Go down to the section titled Slum Clearance.

ISAAC (*his expression clouds in fury*). Hn? Hn? Hng!!!

MATTHEW. What is it? What is it?

ISAAC. Riff-raff! They call us riff-raff!

JERO. Read it out, Brother Isaac.

ISAAC. 'Unfortunately the beach is at present cluttered up with riff-raff of all sorts who dupe the citizenry and make the beach unattractive to decent and respectable people. Chiefest among these are the so-called . . .' Oh may the wrath of Jehovah smite them on their blasphemous mouths!

JERO (*taking back the file*). Time is short, Brothers. We cannot afford to be over-sensitive. (*Reads.*) '. . . the so-called prophets and evangelists. All these are not only to be immediately expelled but steps must be taken to ensure that they never at any time find their way back to the execution stadium.'

SHADRACH. Fire and brimstone! Sodom and Gomorrah!

JERO. Patience Brothers, patience. 'It is proposed however, that since the purpose of public execution is for the moral edification and spiritual upliftment of the people, one respectable religious denomination be licensed to operate on the Bar Beach. Such a body will say prayers before and after each execution, and where appropriate will administer the last rites to the condemned. They will be provided a point of vantage where they will preach to the public on the evil of crime and the morals to be drawn from the miserable end of the felons. After which their brass band shall provide religious music.'

ISAAC. A brass band? That means . . .

JERO. Yes, the Salvation Army.

SHADRACH. Enough. We have heard all we need to know of the conspiracy against us. The question now is, what do we do to foil them?

JERO. Organize. Band together. Brother Matthew is right: the sick have need of healing. We must not desert the iniquitous in their greatest hour of need.

SHADRACH (looking towards CALEB, then ANANAIAS). We foresee problems in banding together with certain members of the calling.

JERO. All problems can be overcome. The stakes are high, Brother Shadrach.

SHADRACH. The price is also high.

ANANAIAS. Oh shut up, you fatuous hypocrite!

SHADRACH. Ananaias!

JERO. Peace, Brothers, peace. Ananaias, I shall require greater decorum from you.

ANANAIAS. You have it before you ask, Brother Jero. Anything you say.

MATTHEW. What does Jeroboam have in mind, exactly? You didn't call us together without some idea in your head.

JERO. Quite correct, Brother Matthew. I have outlined certain plans of action and have even begun to pursue them. The time is short, in fact, the moment is now upon us. The Bar Beach becomes the single execution arena, the sole amphitheatre of death in the entire nation. Where at the moment we have spectators in thousands, the proposed stadium will seat hundreds of thousands. We must acquire the spiritual monopoly of such a captive congregation.

CALEB. Hear, hear!

ISAAC (*impatiently*). Yes, but how?

JERO. We form ONE body. Acquire a new image. Let the actuality of power see itself reflected in that image, reflected and complemented. We shall prophesy with one voice, not as lone voices crying in the wilderness, but as the united oracle of the spiritual profession.

CALEB. Brother Jero, I hand it to you. I couldn't have phrased it better and I pride myself on being a bookish sort of fellow.

MATTHEW. What image then?

JERO. Such an image as will make our outward colours one with theirs.

CALEB. Show them up in their true colours you mean. (*He splutters with laughter until he is coughing helplessly, near-choking.*)

JERO. Brother Caleb, I think that remark was in very bad taste.

MATTHEW (*wildly*). And dangerous. Very dangerous. I refuse to remain one moment longer if such remarks are permitted. We are not here to look for trouble. I dissociate myself from that remark.

ISAAC. Still watching your parole, Brother Matthew?

CALEB (*leans over drunkenly*). Psst. Is it true the magistrate was a sideman in your church?

JERO. Brothers, Brothers, this is no time for our private little quarrels. We must not envy Brother Matthew his spiritual influence in er . . . certain fortunate quarters when we are on the threshold of bringing the highest and the mightiest under our spiritual guidance.

SHADRACH. Are you day-dreaming? In a day or two you will not even have a roof over your head and you speak of . . .

JERO. Yes Brother Shad, the highest and mightiest, I assure you, will come under our spiritual guidance.

SHADRACH. Success has swelled your head, Brother Jero.

CALEB. That's why he thinks big. (*Roars off alone into laughter.*)

JERO. Suppose I tell you, Shadrach, that it has come to the ears of the rulers that a certain new-formed religious body has prophesied a long life to the regime? That this mysterious body has declared that the Lord is so pleased with their er . . . spectacular efforts to stamp out armed robbery, with the speed of the trials, the refusal of the right to appeal, the rejection of silly legal technicalities and the high rate of executions, that all these things are so pleasing to the Lord that he has granted eternal life to their regime?

SHADRACH. They won't believe you.

JERO. They have already. The seed was well planted and it has taken root. Tomorrow the Tourist Board shall propose a certain religious body for the new amphitheatre. The Cabinet will be informed that it is the same body which has made the prophecy. Our spiritual monopoly shall be approved without debate – Does anyone doubt me?

SHADRACH. The Shadrach-Medrach-Abednego Apostolic Trinity has a twenty-thousand strong congregation all over the country. These include men from all walks of life including very high ranks within the uniformed profession. We propose therefore that our Apostolic Trinity absorb all other denominations into its spiritual bosom. . .

The proposal is greeted with instant howls of rejection.

JERO. No, Brother Shadrach. As you see, it just will not do. Are there any other proposals?

They all shrug at one another.

ISAAC. All right Jero, let's have your proposal.

JERO. You all know Brother Chume. Prophet Chume I ought to say.

MATTHEW. But he's the one who went off his head.

ANANAIAS. Looks saner than you or me. Cleaner anyway.

JERO. Prophet Chume has left the ranks of the enemy and cast his lot among us. With his help, with the intimate knowledge which he has acquired of the workings of that foreign body to which he once belonged we shall recreate ourselves in the required image. We shall manifest our united spiritual essence in the very form and shape of the rulers of the land. Nothing, you will agree could be more respectable than that. (*Rises.*) Sister Rebecca, bring out the banner!

REBECCA (*runs out with the flag, flushed with excitement*). Is this the moment, Brother Jero?

JERO. The moment is now, Sister. Witness now the birth of the first Church of the Apostolic Salvation Army of the Lord!

CHUME *begins the tune of 'Are you washed in the Blood of the Lamb'.* REBECCA *sings lustily, deaf to the world.*

Behold the new body of the Lord! Forward into battle, Brothers!

ISAAC. Against what?

JERO. Precisely.

SHADRACH (*disdainfully*). Precisely what? He asks, against what? You say, precisely.

JERO. Precisely. Against what? We don't know any more than our secular models. They await a miracle, we will provide it.

SHADRACH (*indicating* CHUME). With lunatics like him. You fancy yourself an empire-builder.

JERO. A spiritual empire builder, Brother Shadrach. Those who are not with us, are against us. This is the Salvation Army with a difference. With pepper and ogiri. With ngwam-ngwan. Right, Brother Chume?

CHUME *nods vigorously without stopping the music.*

ISAAC. Hey, you haven't said who is to be head of this Army.

CALEB. Good point. Very good point.

JERO. We come in as equals. We form a syndicate.

SHADRACH. Everybody needs a head.

CALEB (*solemnly*). Old Shad is de-ee-eep. (*Hiccups.*)

JERO. A titular head. He gives the orders and keeps close watch on the church treasury. Purely ceremonial.

ISAAC. Yes, but who? Who do you have in mind for Captain?

JERO. Captain, Brother Isaac? No, no, not captain. We must not cut our image small in the eyes of the world. General, at least.

SHADRACH. And who would that be, you still haven't said.

JERO. Whoever has the secrets of the Tourist Board in his hands. Whoever can guarantee that the new body does obtain nomination from the Tourist Board.

ANANAIAS. I knew it. I knew he was keeping something to himself.

ISAAC. You have thought of everything, haven't you?

JERO. You may say I am divinely inspired, Brother Isaac.

SHADRACH. And you, we presume, are in possession of the aforesaid secrets?

JERO. Have we a united body or not?

ANANAIAS. Christ! Those fat pockets begging to be picked while their owners are laughing at the poor devil at the stake. It's a sin to be missing from this garden of Eden. (*Throws* JERO *a salute.*) General! Reporting for duty, sir.

JERO (*saluting in turn*). Sergeant-major! Go in the room and find a uniform that fits you.

ISAAC. Millionaire businessmen! Expensive sinners coming to enjoy the Bar Beach show.

JERO. Who else is for the Army of the Lord?

ISAAC. It's Sodom and Gomorrah. The milk is sour and the honey is foul.

JERO. Who is for the Army of the Lord?

ISAAC. What rank do you have in mind for me?

JERO. Major. (*Gestures.*) In there. You'll find a uniform that fits you.

> *As he goes in* ANANAIAS *returns singing lustily and banging a tambourine. He is uniformed in what looks like a Salvation Army outfit except for the cap which is the 'indigenous' touch, made in local material and 'abetiaja' style. The combination is ludicrous.*

MATTHEW (*takes another look at the picture of a curvaceous bathing belle and decides*). I used to play the flute a little, Brother Jer . . . I mean General Jeroboam. In fact I was once in my school band.

JERO. You'll find a uniform in there, Captain.

SHADRACH. The uniform will not change you. You will still be the same Bar Beach riff-raff no matter what you wear. Nobody will give you a monopoly.

CALEB. Wrong on all counts, Brother Shad. By the cut of his tailor shall a man be known. Uniform maketh man.

JERO. Very soon the syndicate will be closed. The Army hierarchy is for foundation members only. We hold office by divine grace, in perpetuity. Join now or quit.

SHADRACH. Overreacher. We know your kind, Jeroboam. Continue to count your chickens.

CALEB. Wrong again, Shad. You don't know the worthy Jero it seems. If he says he'll get the monopoly, he will. A thorough methodical man, very much after my heart.

JERO. What rank do you want, Caleb?

CALEB. I'll stick out for Colonel. I may be slightly (*Hiccups.*) see what I mean, but I know what's what. I'm an educated man and that's a rare commodity in this outfit. Present company naturally excepted, General.

JERO. Lieutenant-Colonel.

CALEB. General, I'm thinking that instead of merely preaching at the assembly we could do a morality play, you know, something

like our Easter and Christmas Cantata. I'm quite nifty at things
like that – The Rewards of Sin, The Terrible End of the
Desperado . . . and so on. Well er . . . that sort of specialized
duties deserves a higher rank don't you think, mon General?

JERO (*firmly*). Lieutenant - Colonel.

CALEB (*throws a drunken salute*). So be it, mon General.

Goes in. The others are coming out, uniformed.

JERO. You are alone, Shadrach.

SHADRACH. We are never alone. We proceed this minute to the
Chairman of the Tourist Board, there to put an end to our
ambitions. The much-respected aunt of the Chairman is a
devout member of our flock.

JERO (*looks at his watch*). If you wish to see the Chief Executive
Officer in person he will arrive in a few minutes. He was invited
to this meeting.

SHADRACH. Here?

JERO. He will negotiate for the other side.

SHADRACH. Bluff! The only officer you'll see here is the Eviction
Officer.

ANANAIAS (*looking out*). My General, the enemy is without!

JERO. Let him pass freely.

ANANAIAS. What do they want? (*Going to the door.*) You're
back are you? Lucky for you the General gives you safe
conduct.

EXECUTIVE. You have a nerve summoning us here at this time of
night. (*Blocking his ears.*) Will you tell them to stop that lunatic
din!

JERO. Colonel Chume . . .

ANANAIAS. He won't hear. I'll stop him for you.

Goes over, salutes and takes the trumpet from his mouth.

JERO. Sit down.

EXECUTIVE. I demand . . .

JERO. Seat him down Sergeant-Major.

ANANAIAS. My pleasure, General, sir.

Forces down the CHIEF EXECUTIVE *into a chair. The* CLERK *quickly scurries into a seat.*

JERO. Excuse me while I get ready for the negotiations.

He picks the file off the table with deliberate movements. The EXECUTIVE OFFICER *stares at the file fascinated. He exchanges looks with the* CLERK *who quickly looks down.*
JERO *goes into the room.*

SHADRACH. We are, we presume, in the presence of the Chief Eviction Officer of the Tourist Board.

CLERK. No, that's C.E.O. II. This is C.E.O. I, Chief Executive Officer. C.E.O. III is still to be appointed – that's the Chief Execution Officer, a new post.

EXECUTIVE (*turns to inspect* SHADRACH *slowly, like a strange insect*). And who might you be?

SHADRACH. Leader of the Shadrach-Medrach-Abednego Apostolic flock, twenty thousand strong.

EXECUTIVE (*wearily*). Another fanatic.

SHADRACH. It is our hope that you have come here to put an end to the schemes of this rapacious trader on piety who calls himself . . .

EXECUTIVE. Oh Christ!

Enter JERO, *resplendent in a Salvation Army General uniform.* CHUME *blares a fanfare on the trumpet.*

JERO. The file, Sister Rebecca.

EXECUTIVE. And now I hope you will . . .

JERO. You came, I trust, alone as requested.

EXECUTIVE. Yes I foolishly risked my life coming without protection to this haunt of cut-throats.

JERO. It was entirely in your own interests.

EXECUTIVE. So you said. And now perhaps you will kindly tell me what my interests are.

JERO. They are such as might be unsuitable for the ears of a policeman. That is why I suggested that you leave your escort behind.

EXECUTIVE. Come to the point.

JERO (*takes a seat, carefully brushing his creases*). You will remember that when the Chief Eviction Officer was compelled, as a result of the violent spiritual conversion of Colonel Rebecca . . .

EXECUTIVE. Colonel who?

JERO. Colonel Rebecca of the Church of the Apostolic Salvation Army. CASA for short. Do you know that Casa means home? In this case, spiritual home. I am sure you approve our new image.

Enter REBECCA *with file. She is now in uniform.*

EXECUTIVE. Your image does not interest me in the slightest.

JERO. And your own image Chief Executive Officer?

Hands him two sheets of paper from the file.

Great is the Lord and Mighty in his ways. He led your Chief Eviction Officer to my door in the company of one He had marked down for salvation, overwhelmed him with the onslaught of such hot holiness that he fled leaving his documents in the possession of a woman possessed.

EXECUTIVE. What do you want? Just say what you want?

JERO. Monopoly is the subject of your file No. I.B.P. stroke 537 stroke 72A. Beauty parlours, supermarkets, restaurants, cafés and ice-cream kiosks, fair-grounds, construction and hiring of beach huts, amusement gadgets, gambling machines and dodgems and roundabouts and parking facilities – for the new National Amphitheatre to be built on the Bar Beach. Mr Executive Officer, the list is endless, but what is of interest to the good Lord whose interests I represent is the method of awarding these very superabundant contracts.

EXECUTIVE. No need to talk so loud. (*Looks round nervously.*) Just say what you want.

JERO. Render unto Caesar what is Caesar's, and unto God what is God's.

EXECUTIVE. What does that mean in plain Caesar's language?

JERO. A monopoly on spirituality.

EXECUTIVE. What's that?

JERO. Made out to the Church of the Apostolic Salvation Army. CASA.

SHADRACH. We on this side place our trust in your integrity not to accede to any such request.

EXECUTIVE. Will someone tell me who this fellow is?

JERO. Colonel Rebecca has been kind enough to prepare the letter. It requires only your signature she tells me.

EXECUTIVE (*taking the letter, incredulous*). Is that all? Just a monopoly on the rights to hold religious rallies here?

JERO. It's enough.

EXECUTIVE. Not even a monopoly on some small business enterprise?

JERO. We are already in business. Of course we expect you to declare that all land actually occupied as of now by the various religious bodies would from now on be held in trust, managed and developed by the newly approved representative body of all apostolic bodies, CASA. . .

EXECUTIVE. What!

SHADRACH. Mr Executive Officer . . .

EXECUTIVE. What has that to do with monopoly on spirituality?

JERO. Spirituality, to take root, must have land to take root in.

EXECUTIVE. Yes, yes, of course, I – er – see your point.

JERO. Our image also conforms on all levels. We are not fanatics.

Our symbol is blood. It washes all sins away. *All* sins, Mr Tourist Board.

EXECUTIVE. Yes, indeed. A point decidedly in your favour.

SHADRACH. We protest, sir. We strongly protest!

EXECUTIVE. Who is this man?

JERO. An apostate. Ignore him. (SHADRACH *splutters speechlessly.* JERO *pushes a piece of paper to the official.*) The declaration. It says nothing but the truth You are present at the meeting for apostolic union. You see yourself the new body which has emerged, fully representative.

SHADRACH. Thieves! Robbers! Rapists and cut-throats!

JERO. We did not include you, Brother Shadrach.

The EXECUTIVE OFFICER *signs, then* JERO *pushes it to the* CLERK.

Witness it. (*The* CLERK *looks at* EXECUTIVE OFFICER.)

EXECUTIVE. Sign the damn thing and let's get out of here.

JERO (*hands the paper to* REBECCA). Are those their genuine signatures, Colonel?

EXECUTIVE (*offended*). I don't double-deal. I am a man of my word.

JERO. It isn't that I don't trust you.

REBECCA. It is their signatures, my General.

EXECUTIVE. And now may I have . . .

JERO. Your list of contracts? Just one more paper to be signed. The attachment. The survey map which indicates what portions of the beach are referred to as trust property of CASA.

EXECUTIVE. This is impossible. We have allocated some of the land squatted on by your . . .

JERO. Please give me the credit of having done my home-work. You forget we have had a formidable ally in the person of Colonel Rebecca, your former Confidential Secretary. And we have drawn on that precious file which your Eviction Officer so generously loaned us. There is no duplication, check it if you wish.

EXECUTIVE. All right, all right. (*About to sign.*)

SHADRACH. Don't sign your soul away to the devil, sir!

EXECUTIVE. Can't you shut him up?

JERO. Sergeant-major!

ANANAIAS. My pleasure sir. Come on, Shad.

Holds him expertly by the elbow and ejects him.

SHADRACH. We protest most strenuously at this barefaced conspiracy. We shall pursue it to the highest level. The leader of a flock twenty thousand strong is not to be taken lightly we promise you . . .

EXECUTIVE. Are you sure he won't make trouble later? (*He signs.*)

JERO. Leave him to us. The testimony of the Salvation Army will weigh against that of a disgruntled charlatan anywhere. (*Takes the map and returns the incriminating papers.*) Your documents, sir. I hope you take better care of them next time.

EXECUTIVE (*grabs them quickly, glances through and stuffs them in his pockets*). And now to go and deal with that stupid Eviction Officer.

JERO. Blame him not. The power of the spirit on murky souls overcomes the strictest civil service discipline.

EXECUTIVE. Don't preach at me, humbug.

JERO. On the contrary we will preach at you. Every Tuesday at twelve o'clock the Church of Apostolic Salvation Army will preach outside your office. The subject of our sermons shall be, the evils of corruption – of the soul. We intend to restrict ourselves to spiritual matters. We will not contradict the secular image.

The CLERK *bursts out laughing. The* EXECUTIVE *eyes him balefully and the laughter dries on his face.*

EXECUTIVE. You report to me in my office first thing tomorrow morning. You and the Eviction Officer. (*Storms out.*)

ANANAIAS (*as the* CHIEF CLERK *hesitates*). Hey you, follow your master.

CLERK. Er . . . Brother . . . I mean . . . er – General, you wouldn't . . . I mean . . . by any chance . . . what I mean to say is . . . even a Lance-Corporal would do me.

REBECCA. Glory be! (*Rushes forward to embrace him.*) I think there is a uniform just his size, my General.

JERO. As you wish Colonel, Lance-Corporal it is then.

ANANAIAS. What next, my General?

JERO. No time like the present. We march this moment and show the flag. Brother Chume, kneel for your second christening. Or third. I'm beginning to lose count. (CHUME *kneels.* JERO *anoints his head.*) Go down, Brother Chume, rise Brigadier Joshua!

SEVERALLY (*amidst embraces*). God bless you, Joshua. God bless Brigadier Joshua.

CHUME (*overwhelmed*). Oh Brother – sorry General – Jero. I am so unworthy . . .

JERO. Nonsense, Chume, you are the very ornament of your rank. Stand to action Brigade. Brigadier Joshua will lead, blowing the trumpet. Sergeant Ananaias!

ANANAIAS. My General?

JERO. When Joshua blows the trumpet, it will be your duty to make the miracle happen. The walls shall come tumbling down or you will have some explaining to do.

ANANAIAS. Leave it to me, my General.

JERO. Just lean on the rotting walls Ananaias and the Lord will do the rest. By dawn the entire beach must be cleansed of all pestilential separatist shacks which infest the holy atmosphere of the united apostolate of the Lord. Beginning naturally with Apostate Shadrach's unholy den. The fire and the sword, Ananaias, the fire and the sword. Light up the night of evil with

the flames of holiness! Consecrate the grounds for the Bar
Beach Spectacular!

ANANAIAS. Apostolic Army of the Lord, Atten ... tion! Forward,
Banner of the Lord! (REBECCA *takes up position.*) Forward,
Trumpet of the Lord! (CHUME *positions himself.*) Sound the
Trumpet! By the left, Quick ... Swing against Corrup ...
tion!

> CHUME *blasts the first bar of 'Joshua Fit the Battle of Jericho'*
> *in strict tempo, then swings elated into a brisk indigenous rhythm*
> *to which the Army march–dance out into the night.* JERO, *with*
> *maximum condescension acknowledges the salute of the army.*
> *As the last man disappears, he takes a last look at the framed*
> *photo, takes it down and places it face towards the wall, takes*
> *from a drawer in the table an even larger photo of himself in his*
> *present uniform and mounts it on the wall. He then seats himself*
> *at the table and pulls towards him a file or two, as if to start*
> *work. Looks up suddenly and on his face is the amiable-charlatan*
> *grin.*

JERO. After all, it is the fashion these days to be a desk General.

Blackout.

THE END

CAMWOOD
ON THE LEAVES

CAST

MOJI, *the mother*
REVEREND ERINJOBI, *the father*
ISOLA, *their son*
MOROUNKE, *daughter to the* OLUMORIN
MR OLUMORIN
MRS OLUMORIN
CHILDREN, MEN, CROWD, VOICES, *etc.*

Setting: a small Yoruba town in West Africa.

Camwood On The Leaves was first broadcast by the Nigeria Broadcasting Corporation in November 1960.

Song. Agbe to'romo re d'aro o . . . Olenle
Aluko t'or'omo re g'osun o . . . Olenle
Baba iyoku t'or'omo re p'agogo ide o
Awa o le taro iwon yen
K'ama a b'olu s'ere imoran . . .

Olenle

Fade into urgent knocking

MOJI. Open the door! Isola, open the door!

She bangs again on the door.

Isola, for your mother's sake. I beg you, my son, open the door to me. Let me talk to you, please . . . my son . . . open this door. (*More desperately.*) Isola, what have *I* done to you? Why do you shut me out? My son, open the door before the wrath of God descends upon my house.

Her pounding becomes frantic, a baby begins to cry, timid footsteps of children shuffling nearby, one of them tries to shush the baby.

Isola, can't you hear me? Do you want to shame me this day? My son, think of your brothers and sisters . . . Isola, can't you see me? I'm on my knees. Your brothers and sisters are all pleading with you. Open this door if you care for me. Open the door, my son . . . Isola, do you want to shame me? Do you want to drive me into the grave before my time? Isola, even the baby is unhappy . . . please have pity on us all. Come out, please, I shall plead with your father, I promise you, I will plead with him.

Only the sound of the baby crying.

(With sudden shrillness.) Isola!
In the distance, a door is opened suddenly. MOJI *gasps.*

God help me now, he's here.

Sobbing, she pleads earnestly, trying not to be overheard.

My son, before he gets here. Isola, my lord, my lord and master,
my son, my favoured one of heaven, come out, come out, please.
I will talk to him. But open the door. Don't let him think you are
unrepentant. Please, please . . . open the door . . .

ERINJOBI *(from below).* Where is he? Moji! Where is he?
MOJI. S-sh . . . take that child away. Quickly . . . take him to the
next room and lock the door . . . quickly . . . my God, what must
I do . . . what must I do now . . .

Heavy footsteps begin to ascend the stairs.

MOJI *(whispering desperately).* Isola, he is not yet here. He is not
yet here, my son . . . you can still come out . . . ask anything . . .
anything at all . . . I'll be your slave, but open this door, my
son . . .
ERINJOBI *(on his way up).* Moji!
MOJI. I am lost . . . oh God, I am lost.
ERINJOBI. Moji, go downstairs.
MOJI. Reverend . . .
ERINJOBI. Go downstairs, Mother.
MOJI. Reverend, he is your son . . . whatever he's done he is your
son . . .
ERINJOBI. Downstairs. Downstairs! And take the children with
you.
MOJI. He is not being stubborn, Reverend. You mustn't think he is

not repentant. He is merely praying in his room. Praying for forgiveness.

ERINJOBI *moves, opens the adjoining door, the baby's distressed cry issues forth suddenly.*

ERINJOBI. Go downstairs, all of you. Go to your mother's room and shut the door. I don't want a sound from any of you, is that clear? Not a sound.

Children's footsteps hurry downstairs. MOJI *continues to sob and mumble softly.*

MOJI. That I should live to see this day . . . it is a punishment for my sins, but good Lord, could you not have punished me another way? Oh, not through my children, Lord, not through my children . . .

A door is shut downstairs.

ERINJOBI. Moji!
MOJI. It is too great a trial, Lord . . . I have not the strength . . . I have not the strength to bear it . . . punish me for my sins . . . but not this way . . . not this way . . .
ERINJOBI. Moji! I order you to stop this behaviour.
MOJI. Reverend, I am a weak woman. I have not your strength.
ERINJOBI. Then pray for strength. But there must be no moaning in my hearing.
MOJI. He is your son, Reverend . . .
ERINJOBI. My son? I disown him. He is no son of mine – nor yours!
MOJI. No, let me claim him. Let me talk to him. I am his mother.
ERINJOBI. Are you afraid to do God's bidding? I say leave this creature to his fate.
MOJI. How can I? Reverend, I cannot. God is merciful. He is my

son . . .

ERINJOBI. I say he is no son of yours . . . He has dishonoured the
daughter of Olumorin . . . he has shamed me . . . He is no son of
yours.

MOJI. Ah, but he is. I cannot disown him. He is your own, too,
Reverend, you cannot shut him out.

ERINJOBI. Moji! From now on you commit a sin against God
every time you call that creation of the devil your son.

MOJI. Reverend!

ERINJOBI. And I call upon God to witness the justice of my
sentence.

Silence.

Go down now, Mother. If your heart dictates it, pray for him.
But I fear he is past salvation.

MOJI (*an effort to be dispassionate*). I leave him in your hands,
Reverend, and in the hands of God. Reverend, if you looked
now, you would find him on his knees. He knows he has sinned,
he knows that, and he is praying that the Lord should soften his
heart. Give him a little time, Reverend. Give him a little time.

ERINJOBI. I will wait. The judgement of God is not to be hurried.

MOJI. Be merciful.

ERINJOBI. God is merciful. Go down to the children, wife. And
lock the door.

MOJI's *tired steps die slowly downstairs. A door is opened,
shut gently, and a key turned in the lock.* REVEREND
ERINJOBI *draws a chair, sits.*

ERINJOBI. I shall wait.

Silence. Then song.

Mo le j'iyan yo bi ara oko
Mo le j'amala bi onisango
Mo le gbo'omo pon bi ab'ejire
Omo yin-in o, ara yin o
Taiwo yin-in o, ara yin o
Kehinde yin-in o, ara yin – o

Fade to dusk sounds. Fade to night-owls, frogs, crickets etc. Two people swishing through bushes.

MOROUNKE. Isn't the torch much better? Hm? Isola!

ISOLA. Yes, what is it?

MOROUNKE. You didn't hear me. You weren't listening.

ISOLA. I was.

MOROUNKE. You were not. Are you still thinking of your father? About what happened today?

ISOLA. No, no. I have put that from my mind. Now what was it you said?

MOROUNKE. I said isn't the torch better?

ISOLA. We have always managed with the lantern.

MOROUNKE. Yes, but aren't you glad now that I stole the torch. You were angry with me, but don't you think this is more useful?

ISOLA. I preferred the lantern. I admit this is easier to handle. But . . . well, what about you? Don't you notice a change?

MOROUNKE. What change?

ISOLA. Look on the ground. We have no shadows tonight. Neither have the trees.

MOROUNKE. Oh, I don't like shadows. This is less frightening.

ISOLA. Tell the truth, you enjoy being frightened. And you preferred it when we had shadows. You were always trying to run after them.

MOROUNKE (*laughing*). The legs were funny. They would climb halfway up every time and wobble over the bushes . . .

langa-langa . . . langa-langa . . . like Agere.

ISOLA. Agere with legs of jelly. (MOROUNKE *laughs*.) You see, you preferred the lantern yourself.

MOROUNKE. No, no. A torch is more sensible.

ISOLA. Oh, here's a big one. I've got it. Open the bag for me.

Sound of snail hitting the others.

How many have we got now?

MOROUNKE. No, we mustn't count them. Bimpe says it's unlucky to count snails.

ISOLA. Hm. That maid of yours. The things she tells you.

MOROUNKE. She is a very wise person. It's good to take her advice.

ISOLA. Well, if she doesn't count the snails, how does she manage to sell them for us.

MOROUNKE. Oh she says it's all right to count them in the market.

ISOLA. But not when you're hunting them? Here are two more . . .

MOROUNKE. You see, it's the torch that brings them out.

ISOLA. All right, I give in. I *am* glad you brought the torch. But you shouldn't have taken it. It belongs to your father.

Brief silence except for the swishing of bushes.

Morounke.

MOROUNKE. Yes.

ISOLA. I didn't think you would come tonight.

MOROUNKE. But why not?

ISOLA. I thought you might be afraid to come.

MOROUNKE. Of what? Oh, I see. No, I came prepared.

ISOLA. Prepared? What for?

MOROUNKE. Look. Point your torch this way.

ISOLA. What is it? A knitting pin?

MOROUNKE. Yes. And I have a small stone . . . here it is.

ISOLA. What are you talking about?

MOROUNKE. For protection against night spirits.

ISOLA. What!

MOROUNKE. Bimpe told me. When she heard I was pregnant, she came and warned me never to go out without taking a stone and a sharp object. Especially at night. (ISOLA *bursts out laughing*.) It's true. I asked my uncle and he confirmed it.

ISOLA. All right. I think I ought to take lessons from Bimpe myself. She seems the most knowledgeable housemaid in the world.

MOROUNKE. She is.

ISOLA. Anyway, she gets a good price for my snails . . . but that wasn't really what I meant. I thought after all the battle of the afternoon, you wouldn't dare come out.

MOROUNKE. But it didn't really affect me.

ISOLA. No, and just as well it didn't. Somehow I could bear it that your parents and the minister joined hands to try and murder me. You were more or less forgotten. Were you frightened?

MOROUNKE. No, I couldn't understand most of it. Why did your father curse you?

ISOLA. I don't know. Perhaps he doesn't know himself. Shall we pick mushrooms too?

MOROUNKE. No, not at night.

ISOLA. There seems to be plenty here. Look . . . look at all that.

MOROUNKE. We'll come early in the morning and pick them. Bimpe says morning is the time to do it. First thing in the morning. That is when they are really big because they have been drinking the dew all night.

ISOLA. Is there anything your housemaid does not profess to know?

MOROUNKE. Not many.

ISOLA. And has she any other warnings on snail-hunting?

MOROUNKE. Only that midnight is the best time to get them. That is the time they go to market.

ISOLA. Better bring her with you next time, then we won't do anything wrong.

Sounds of searching in the undergrowth.

MOROUNKE. I wish you would use a stick, Isola. You can't go on sticking your arms into the bush like that. Suppose there are snakes in it?

ISOLA. Very likely there are snakes.

MOROUNKE. There are? Suppose they bite you?

ISOLA. They won't.

MOROUNKE. Oh? I suppose you are their friend?

ISOLA. Not really. But they won't bite me. They know I will bite them harder.

MOROUNKE. But you haven't poison in your mouth. Like they have.

ISOLA. How do you know? I even have fangs . . . Don't you know I am the pastor's son?

MOROUNKE. It's all very well for you. I can't bite snakes. Suppose I get bitten?

ISOLA. Well, you can call Bimpe to bite them for you.

MOROUNKE. A-ah, I'll tell Bimpe you don't like her.

ISOLA. She won't believe you.

Brief pause.

MOROUNKE. Does that hurt?

ISOLA. What?

MOROUNKE. My hand. It's on your back. Does it hurt?

ISOLA. No. Why?

She hits him.

MOROUNKE. Now. Did it hurt then?

ISOLA. Why? (*She hits him again.*) Stop hitting me.

MOROUNKE. I wanted to see if your back hurt. Didn't he beat you? Your father?

ISOLA. No.

MOROUNKE. Are you telling the truth? Did he beat you? What happened when you got home? What did your mother say? You haven't told me anything.

ISOLA. There isn't much to tell. I went and locked myself in my room. Then when he came home, I escaped through the window.

MOROUNKE. From your room, Isola? But that is upstairs.

ISOLA. He was guarding the door. I jumped through the window.

MOROUNKE. You might have killed yourself.

ISOLA. No, I couldn't. Anyway, I did it, and I'm not dead.

MOROUNKE. But you mustn't do it again. Promise.

ISOLA. Don't worry. I won't ever again need to.

MOROUNKE. But what will he say when he finds you gone?

ISOLA. I expect he will curse me again. He'll curse me again because he has to.

MOROUNKE. Why? Why does he have to? My parents didn't curse me, did they? I don't understand. Why was everyone shouting? And your father. He was going to beat you with his walking-stick. Does he hate you?

ISOLA (*brusquely*). I don't know ... Come on now. I think we've caught enough. There is still the surprise I have for you.

MOROUNKE. Where is it?

ISOLA. Follow me.

MOROUNKE. Is it very far?

ISOLA. Somewhat.

MOROUNKE. Suppose we get lost?

ISOLA. We won't. By the way, remember to tell Bimpe that she must charge a little more for these. I shall need more money for myself from now on. There are a few things I must have.

MOROUNKE. Isola, won't you let me take it for you. They will never find out. Father leaves his money all over the place.

ISOLA. I've told you, No. I don't want your parents' money.

MOROUNKE. But it's mine too, isn't it?

Brief pause.

Isola, are you angry again?

ISOLA. No. But you promised not to mention that again.

MOROUNKE. I am sorry. Please, don't be angry.

ISOLA. I'm not . . . Do you remember this place?

MOROUNKE. No, I'm quite lost.

ISOLA. Careful now. Hold on to my shirt. The path stops here.

MOROUNKE. Where are we going?

ISOLA. To the chapel. Don't you remember it? The chapel.

MOROUNKE. The chapel?

ISOLA. I took you there a long time ago. The place by the big rocks. It's a long time now . . . we were very little then. In fact, it was you who called it a chapel.

MOROUNKE. Was . . . there . . . a rock?

ISOLA. Yes, with clusters of bamboo.

MOROUNKE. And there was a little stream, wasn't there?

ISOLA. It's not so little now. And there is a clear pool of water which I made myself. But wait till you see it.

MOROUNKE. Are you sure we are not lost? I can't see a path.

ISOLA. I've been careful not to make one. Careful. We're nearly there.

MOROUNKE (*excitedly*). That's the rock.

ISOLA. Yes. But it's on the other side, what I want to show you. Now, shut your eyes . . . it's all right, I'll hold you.

MOROUNKE. Oh . . .

ISOLA. You're all right. We are merely going through the cleft in the rock. Do you remember it?

MOROUNKE. Yes. But we were smaller then.

ISOLA (*laughing*). You are not so big now, don't worry. Even I can get through without squeezing. Right. No ... not yet. Just wait until I light the lamp.

A match is struck.

All right, you may open your eyes now.

MOROUNKE. Isola ... You built it!

ISOLA. Look ... come here ... that's your little stream. Do you remember now? It was this bamboo clump ... right here, in fact. That was where we found the eggs of the tortoise.

MOROUNKE. Yes, I remember. And we came back and watched them until they were all hatched.

ISOLA. Watch now ... watch. Moji ... Moji ...

MOROUNKE. Moji? Is your mother here? Isola, there is something in there! Something moved!

ISOLA. Of course there is something there. Now be careful not to frighten her ... here she comes ... can you still remember her?

MOROUNKE (*excitedly*). She's still here! The mother, she's still here ... (*Gets more and more excited.*) Isola, it's the same one, isn't it? The same mother. You mean she's never gone away? All that time?

ISOLA. Now you've scared her back into the hole.

MOROUNKE. I am sorry. Oh dear, won't she come out again?

ISOLA. Later perhaps. She's not used to strangers and she's forgotten you by now. She's used to me only. As soon as she hears my voice, she comes out.

MOROUNKE. Try again. Call her, perhaps she's no longer frightened.

ISOLA. I'll try. Moji ... Moji ...

MOROUNKE. Is that her name?

ISOLA. Have you forgotten? I gave her that name when we first found her.

MOROUNKE. But that is your mother's name.

ISOLA. She wouldn't mind. They remind me of each other . . . they look so burdened and I cannot tell their age.

MOROUNKE. Moji . . . Moji . . . come out, it's me. Come out please.

ISOLA. No good.

MOROUNKE. Oh, Isola, why did you ever show me this place. I want to live here for ever.

ISOLA. You'll do nothing of the sort. Come on, it's time you went back home. I only hope your mother hasn't missed you.

MOROUNKE. Why should she? She never pays me any attention.

ISOLA. But she has good reason now not to let you out of her sight.

MOROUNKE. She locked me in my room before she went to bed. So she won't be worrying her head at all. (*They enter the hut.*) What is that?

ISOLA. Where?

MOROUNKE. That. Is it a gun?

ISOLA. Doesn't it look like one? I know it's old and rusty.

MOROUNKE. Where did you get it?

ISOLA. It belongs to the minister. I'll need it for hunting.

MOROUNKE (*laughing*). For hunting snails?

ISOLA. Perhaps. Anyway there is plenty of game when you go deeper into the bush. I used to follow the minister when he went hunting. Birds mostly. He never would shoot anything on the ground.

MOROUNKE. Why not?

ISOLA. He was afraid it might turn out to be a human being. A friend of his was killed that way in his younger days. He would never stop talking about it.

MOROUNKE. What animals will you hunt?

ISOLA. Well, first there is . . . DON'T TOUCH THAT!

The gun goes off. MOROUNKE *screams.*

Morounke! Morounke!

The shouts merge into song.

> E-e-ya ko se a gbe
> E-e-ya ko se e gbe
> Iba se e gbe ma gbe t'emi
> Asiko ti o ba a se e gbe
> Erin ku l'oko a k'oke wa'le
> Efon ku l'oko a k'oke wa'le,
> Larinka ku n'ile a k'oke ro'ko
> Oju elekun o nru'na
> Iru elekun o njo were
> Ekikan elekun meji abe
> Ba o r'ako'su a f'ewura gun'yan
> Ba o r'eni fe a f'ana eni
> Bo ba ka'ni a kunle wijo
> Bi o si ka'ni a ma sano lo
> Abaja o re keke o opo ona

As the song fades, the church-bell strikes two. MOJI *comes upstairs. She taps on the arm of the chair in which* ERINJOBI *has fallen asleep.*

MOJI. Reverend, Reverend. Won't you come to bed.

ERINJOBI (*wakes up, startled*). Hm, hm? Moji?

MOJI. It's late. Won't you come to bed?

ERINJOBI. What is the time?

MOJI. It has struck two.

ERINJOBI. Two? Past midnight? Do you mean you let me sleep all the time?

MOJI. You were tired. I think it was good that you fell asleep.

ERINJOBI. Isola! Where is he?

He tries the door.

Oho, I suppose he is still at his prayers.

MOJI. I don't know, Reverend, let everything wait till tomorrow. It is middle of night. I'm sure he fell asleep also.

ERINJOBI. He will have to get up. I have sworn that he will not spend another night under my roof.

MOJI. Please, Reverend, I only ask till morning. In spite of your anger you fell asleep. Perhaps it is God's way of postponing judgement.

Pause.

ERINJOBI. I will yield to you in this. But I cannot pass another night under the same roof as he.

MOJI. Where are you going?

ERINJOBI. To the church. I shall sleep in the vestry. But if by sunrise he is still in this house then I will drive him out like a thief and an adulterer.

MOJI. Shall I come too?

ERINJOBI. What for?

MOJI. I need to speak with you. I shall obey you in everything, but first, may I speak with you?

ERINJOBI. There is nothing to talk about.

MOJI. I see the hand of God in these few hours of quiet that we have. Perhaps if we spoke a little . . .?

ERINJOBI. Are you still determined to plead for him?

MOJI. No, no. I merely want to ask for some understanding. They grew up together. Isola and Morounke grew up like children of the same mother.

ERINJOBI. And what lesson must I learn from that?

MOJI. Be patient with me, Reverend. I merely ask for understanding. They played together and they fought together. How often have you sat Morounke on your knees and bought her things?

ERINJOBI. A year ago, in this very house, Olumorin came and complained that Isola was hanging around his daughter far too much for his liking. He said that the two of them were always roaming the woods together. That could only lead to immoral temptations.

MOJI. True, true, but . . .

ERINJOBI. And did I not call him and warn him? Did I not tell him his waywardness must not be taken to another's house to bring shame upon me?

MOJI. It is true, but can one stop the friendship of children by mere word of command?

ERINJOBI. Children? You call him a child? A child, yet guilty of the sin of fornication? How often had I rebuked him? Sternly! I was never one to spare the rod. When further rumours of his dangerous ways came to my ears, I called him and asked him if he remembered my warnings. I made him give me his word never to see Olumorin's daughter. He gave me his word and he broke it. Such a crime . . . from my own house. From my own house!

MOJI. We must rescue him, not drive him out in shame.

ERINJOBI. In my house I must do no less than I would counsel those who look to me for guidance. Must I hold back now when one, not merely of my house but of my blood has transgressed the commandments of God? Will you see my head doubly bowed in shame? (MOJI *is silent.*) Be at peace, woman. Where strength is lacking, God will be provident.

He begins to descend the stairs. Sudden knocks on the front door. ERINJOBI *stops.*

At this time of the night? (*Violent knocking.*) What now? What new mockery of my life is this?

Knocking again, more desperate . . . fade. Pause.

ISOLA (*angry*). You learnt that lesson cheaply. Don't you know you must never do that with guns?

MOROUNKE. I didn't know it was loaded.

ISOLA. Always assume it is. Do you think I brought you here only to have you kill yourself? Now you've gone and used up my only shot.

MOROUNKE. You shouldn't have kept it loaded.

ISOLA. I have to. There is a monster of a snake which lives just across the stream ... over there ... in that clump of bamboos. It's a boa, I think. Really big. Anyway, I'll have to kill it. I cannot live here unless it's dead.

MOROUNKE. Do you mean to live here?

ISOLA. I already live here. From tonight, this is my home.

MOROUNKE. You will sleep here, all by yourself?

ISOLA. I've done it before, from time to time when my father was away visiting some parish in his diocese. Once he was away for a week and I stayed here all that time. But I didn't sleep well. Some nights I didn't sleep at all. Thinking of Erinjobi makes me uncomfortable.

MOROUNKE. Your father? Don't you ever stop thinking of him?

ISOLA. Oh, I didn't mean him. I meant the boa. I call him Erinjobi.

MOROUNKE. Isola, do you want to be a wicked son?

ISOLA. No, but it is a wicked snake. Remember the tortoise eggs? Moji hatched them all and sometimes they would swim across the stream. The snake can't swallow them, so he would pick them up and dash them to pieces against the rock.

MOROUNKE. Can it swim across the stream?

ISOLA. I don't really know. As far as I can see it has never left that bamboo clump. But I feel safer if the gun is here and loaded.

MOROUNKE. All right, I shall get you some powder tomorrow.

ISOLA. No, tell Bimpe to get it. Gunpowder is sold in the same market as she sells the snails. He has to die, that serpent.

MOROUNKE. I'll stay here with you. I shall live here.

ISOLA. No, you won't like it. But you may come when they

make you unhappy.

MOROUNKE. Are you unhappy?

ISOLA. Let's go now. It will be dawn if we stand here talking. And I'm not staying here tonight – not without a loaded gun. I'll take you back and then I'll go and sleep in the church-yard.

MOROUNKE. No, you promised. You promised not to sleep again between the gravestones. Aren't you afraid of spirits?

ISOLA. They are busy people, and so am I. We don't trouble each other.

MOROUNKE. No you mustn't. Anyway, I want to stay here. I have a right to stay. After all we found this place together.

ISOLA. Oh no we didn't. I showed it to you. And anyway, that was a very long time ago. When we were children. Just now you nearly didn't even remember the place.

Pause.

MOROUNKE. Bimpe says we ought to get married. Do you think she's right?

ISOLA. How old are you?

MOROUNKE. The same as you. Nearly fifteen.

ISOLA. No, I'm sixteen and two months. What about you? Do you want to marry me?

MOROUNKE. I haven't thought of it. Do you think we should?

ISOLA. Are you unhappy that you are going to bear my child?

MOROUNKE. No. But it seems to have upset everyone. And it was because of it that your father cursed you.

ISOLA. Are you unhappy?

MOROUNKE. I am not. No, I am not unhappy. But I am a little confused. Until my mother said it this afternoon, I had no idea. She used to ask me lots of questions which I did not understand. And then this afternoon, she called me again and began to ask about you.

ISOLA. Did she tell you that you had done something wrong?

MOROUNKE. No. But she began to abuse you. Father even threatened to see that you were put in prison. And he sent for your father. He said that he would take your family to court.

ISOLA. Your father is a big man. He has friends.

MOROUNKE. Are you afraid of him?

ISOLA. Afraid? Now, do you think I ought to fear him? After all, it was the minister who put me in his power.

MOROUNKE. Your father, Isola, your father.

ISOLA. The minister!

MOROUNKE. Call him your father, Isola. You make me afraid of you when you harden yourself ... Why are you so stubborn? Isola, don't, please ... don't ... don't look at me like that.

A brief silence.

ISOLA. Come here, Morounke. Stand here ... here, under the light.

MOROUNKE. Why? Why do you look at me?

ISOLA. Do you feel different? You are a woman now, do you feel that?

MOROUNKE. I don't know.

ISOLA. Come nearer ... let me listen. That is where the child should be. (*Pause.*) There is no sound.

MOROUNKE. My mother was trying to listen too.

ISOLA (*furious*). Don't ever let her do that again!

MOROUNKE. Why, Isola, what is the matter?

ISOLA. Sorry ... it's nothing ... nothing ...

MOROUNKE. You frightened me.

ISOLA. I'm sorry. It's nothing ... You say you want to stay here?

MOROUNKE. I'm not going tonight. I haven't the strength to leave this place. I must stay with you.

ISOLA. It is my child. You are almost a child yourself, do you know that?

Pause.

MOROUNKE. Isola.

ISOLA. Yes.

MOROUNKE. They are telling lies about you all over the town. Bimpe told me. They say you beat ... your father. All over the town, they've been cursing you.

ISOLA. And *did* I beat him?

MOROUNKE. I don't know.

ISOLA. But you were there, weren't you?

MOROUNKE. I ran away. Your father frightened me, Isola. He was so terrible. When he picked up his walking-stick, I ran away. I was very frightened. I ran away to Bimpe.

ISOLA. I ran away too. I remember he raised the stick against me and I took it from him and broke it. He tried to struggle for it. Then I went home. I still remember the crowd who had gathered together. They made way for me as if I was a leper. They shrank from me, I knew suddenly what it means to be an outcast. Before I reached home, my mother had somehow heard of it. She was wailing and beating her breast as if a great disaster had befallen the family. The children were huddled together. They were clinging to one another in terror.

Silence.

MOROUNKE. Is it cold here at nights?

ISOLA. Yes. But I have a wrapper. You can have it. Come on, you must go to sleep. Are you hungry? There is food.

MOROUNKE. No. But I am sleepy. Come on, let's pray together.

ISOLA. What's that?

MOROUNKE. Pray together.

ISOLA. Yes. I thought that was what you said.

MOROUNKE. Well, don't stand there. Come and kneel beside me.

ISOLA. No, you go ahead if you want to.

MOROUNKE. What is the matter? Don't you all pray together at home?

ISOLA. Yes, we do.

MOROUNKE. But you don't want to pray with me?

ISOLA (*sighs as he lies down*). I'm sleepy. Very soon, you will understand.

MOROUNKE. Understand what?

ISOLA. That I think I do nothing else. Life is one long prayer, but to whom, I don't know exactly.

MOROUNKE. I don't understand you.

ISOLA. No, you don't have to. But if I let you stay long enough, you will.

MOROUNKE. If you let me stay ... Why? Do you want to send me away?

ISOLA. No. It depends on you.

MOROUNKE. If you continue like that you will make me afraid of you.

ISOLA. I thought you were going to pray.

MOROUNKE. Not any more. I won't pray by myself ... Isola.

ISOLA. What now?

MOROUNKE. I asked you this before you refused to answer. Are you unhappy?

Pause.

ISOLA. No. Not unhappy. But I wish I wasn't so sad. Now go to sleep.

ERINJOBI's *house. Violent knocking.*

ERINJOBI. Wait, don't frighten my household, whoever you are. I'm coming. I'm coming! (*He opens and unbars the door.*) Mr Olumorin! And your Mrs too! What brings you here?

OLUMORIN. Where is your son? My daughter has disappeared.

MRS OLUMORIN (*screaming*). Produce him at once! He's at the bottom of this. What has he done with my daughter?

ERINJOBI. My son? He has not left the house since . . .

MRS OLUMORIN. You are in this with him, aren't you? You're protecting him. There is nothing can save your son from prison now.

ERINJOBI. I have disowned him.

OLUMORIN. In public. But what you do in private is another matter. You cannot throw dust in my eyes, Pastor. I have warned you often that I did not want your son near my daughter. But still he managed to take advantage of her and put her in the family way. Now he's absconded with her and still you say you know nothing about it.

ERINJOBI. Before God I swear that none of these deeds is pleasing to me as a father. Isola has brought nothing but shame and disgrace to my name.

MRS OLUMORIN. We are wasting time. Perhaps they are both here and you're giving them time to hide. Call your son, pastor. Why haven't you sent for him? Call him. Call him and tell him to return my daughter before I set the law on him . . .

ERINJOBI. Follow me and see for yourself. God is my witness. I have ordered him out of my house . . . I have denied him my name . . . my whole life is soured by this son of evil . . . But what more can I do?

They climb the stairs.

MRS OLUMORIN. I have heard all the preaching I need. All I

want now is Morounke. What has she ever done to deserve to
fall into the hands of your depraved son? Morounke has
never disobeyed me in all her life ... she has never committed a sin against her parents, until your son came and led
her astray. Now he has stolen her ... What have we done to
your son that he cannot leave my daughter alone. There are
women like him, women who fit into his godforsaken ways,
but it has to be my daughter ...

Steps halt on the landing.

ERINJOBI. Here is my chair. I sat in this chair waiting for him
to come out of his room so that I could chase him out of my
house for ever. That is my wife who will bear witness if I lie.
A moment ago she woke me up. I had betrayed my vigil and
fallen asleep.

He knocks.

I can assure you that your daughter was never here.

He knocks again, heavily.

Open the door, Isola. Open the door or I'll get people to
break it down.

He knocks again.

My patience is at an end. Open this door before a worse fate
overtakes you.

Silence.

MOJI. Isola, how long must I beg you? Open the door.

Silence.

(*Agitated.*) Reverend, I must not say this . . . I must never let evil thoughts into my mind I know, but Reverend (*more and more disturbed*), Isola may be a wayward child, but it is now over six hours since he first locked himself in his room. There hasn't been one sound . . .

ERINJOBI. Nonsense, I heard him when I came in.

He bangs furiously.

Isola, open the door. Open this door. You're deceiving no one.

MOJI. Reverend, if we've killed him. If we've driven him to kill himself.

ERINJOBI (*furious*). Quiet, woman. He is not so lost as to do violence on himself.

MRS OLUMORIN. Break down the door. I want to know where my daughter is. Oh, Morounke, Morounke . . .

She pounds with both fists on the door.

Murderer, open this door. Give me back my Morounke before the Lord curses you for the wickedness you commit. Open the door! I say, open this door! Morounke! Morounke! If you're in there come out to your mother.

OLUMORIN. My dear . . . control yourself . . . please, keep calm. We'll find her. We'll find her and rid this town of the boy once and for all. Reverend, why are you still waiting? We must break down the door. We must break it down if your son won't come out. I'll do it now if you won't.

ERINJOBI. No. I will do it myself. It is still my house, Mr Olumorin. Moji, would you like to try just once again?

MOJI (*with deep resignation*). I can do nothing. He no longer knows me.

ERINJOBI. Then this way it must be. Give me that stand.

Sound of lever against the door, then splitting wood.

Where . . .? No one.

OLUMORIN. Is he gone?

MOJI. Gone where? He has killed himself. Isola! Isola!

ERINJOBI. The window . . . it's open!

MOJI. We've killed him. Isola, my son . . .

ERINJOBI. God forbid that he should so damn his soul.

He strides quickly across the room.

No, he's not below.

OLUMORIN. Of course he's not. There is nobody on the ground. He's run away, that's all. You helped him escape.

MRS OLUMORIN. Morounke . . . oh, what has he done with my daughter. Reverend, at least tell me what he's done with my daughter. Where has he taken her? Morounke . . . Morounke . . . (*Sobs.*)

ERINJOBI. I know nothing. He must have escaped while I slept.

OLUMORIN. There is nothing more to be said. I am going to rouse my men and we will find him before he gets out of town. He cannot have got far. And I will have the law on him – after my men have worked their anger on him. There is no one bears any love for him in this town, and may God have mercy on him when they catch up with him . . .

MOJI. What will you do? Are you going to hunt him now like an animal? What has my son ever done to any of you? You say he stole your daughter. I say that your daughter stole him from us. She led him astray.

OLUMORIN. What did you say! It is just as I thought. You both defend him. And yet only this afternoon he struck you, his own father. Took the stick from your very hands and struck you with it.

ERINJOBI. Those who say so commit a sin against him . . . unless in the eyes of God his act of rebellion meant indeed that he struck me.

MOJI. He did not, Reverend, he did not. Why do they all lie against him . . .?

ERINJOBI. Quiet, Moji!

MOJI. He is only an erring child, why do they make him out to be a monster?

MRS OLUMORIN. An erring child? Has he or has he not seduced and then stolen my child?

MOJI. Mrs Olumorin, you were there. Why do you not tell these people that they lie? You know that he would not so damn himself . . . that he could never totally destroy his soul.

ERINJOBI. He has. Has he not committed fornication?

MOJI. A child's mistake. But he never struck his father. No, he has deserved no curses, only correction.

ERINJOBI. Enough. I have left him in the hands of God. Goodnight. I am going to the church to pray. Oh, cursed be the day when I mistook that child for my son!

Footsteps going down the stairs. The door slams.

OLUMORIN. Let us go, wife. Let us go and rouse the men.

MOJI. If you hurt my son . . . if you hurt my son the Lord will judge you!

MRS OLUMORIN. He's a child stealer. A kidnapper. What has he done to my daughter!

MOJI. I say do not hurt my son! In God's name leave my son alone . . . Don't hurt him. May Heaven judge you if you touch a hair of his head. May Heaven judge you if you stand by and watch him ill-treated . . . may Heaven judge you . . .

She breaks down sobbing. Fade into song.

Mo j'awe gbegbe
Ki won ma gbagbe mi
M'o j'awe oni tete
Ki won ma te mi mo'le
Ojo nlo ko se wa re
Oju i mo r'oko r'oko k'o gbagbe ile
O ma nlo ogerere
O ma nlo ogerere

Fade out.

MOJI (*reprovingly*). Isola.

ISOLA (*a much younger* ISOLA). Ma?

MOJI. You were singing that song again?

ISOLA. Ma?

MOJI. Yes, that's just it. That is the way you behave. Suddenly you find you have gone deaf. Then it's nothing but Ma? Ma? I said you were singing that song again.

ISOLA. What song, Ma?

MOJI. What song! You know very well what song. The one your father told you never to sing again. How often has he punished you for singing songs like that?

ISOLA. But Ma, he isn't here now.

MOJI. That makes it worse! Can't you see that you are a bad child if you will only obey your father when he is around? Suppose he came in unexpectedly, what then? Are you not ashamed to talk like that?

ISOLA. Mama, I haven't disobeyed him. He says he never wants to hear me sing it again, and I try not to sing when he is at home. Anyway, I never feel like singing when he's home.

MOJI. Isola! That was the talk of a wicked child. I don't want to hear you talk like that again. Never, do you hear?

ISOLA. All right, Ma.

MOJI. Oh, Isola, why do you always displease your father? Don't you know how unhappy it makes me to see him angry with you? To see him punish you? But he has to be strict with you — you're his first born. Do you ever remember that? The first-born. You are head of the family. If only you would try to model yourself on him, then those who follow you will look up to you.

ISOLA. Mother . . .

MOJI. Do you want to be a disappointment to him? You, his first-born?

ISOLA. I'll be back soon, Ma, I have to go somewhere now.

MOJI. Wait! You always run away when I try to talk to you.

ISOLA. I must go, Ma. I am nearly late for choir practice.

MOJI. Choir practice? You didn't tell me you had joined up. When was this? Does your father know?

ISOLA. No. Should I tell him?

MOJI. Should you tell him? What an amazing child you are! For months your father has been telling you to join the church choir. Then you decide on your own to obey him but you say nothing to him. You do this one thing to please him and you don't . . . Oh, were you keeping it for a surprise?

ISOLA. But it isn't *his* choir.

MOJI. Is that some new argument you've thought of. I don't want to hear it. You're too fond of arguing. Go on. Hurry or you'll be late.

ISOLA. Mama, I'm not going to church. Don't misunderstand me.

MOJI. Don't be silly now. First you say you're going, then you say you're not going. Now be a good boy and go quickly. Perhaps they'll even let you sing with the choir this Sunday. Oh, wouldn't that please your father! And perhaps that will stop you singing all those pagan songs you're so fond of.

ISOLA. Mama, it is not the same choir we are both thinking of. We only call it choir practice for fun.

MOJI. What is the child talking about?

ISOLA *makes 'egungun' noises.*

Isola, stop that noise. And stop dancing about. Come and tell me what you mean.

He repeats the noises, commences an 'egungun' song.

Isola, come here at once. O-oh, you little devil ... just let me catch you. Oh! Do you want me to fall ... just let me get hold of you ...

ISOLA (*laughing, calls in the same 'egungun' voice*). Aya minister ... Mrs Erinjobi O, Mrs Erinjobi ... o si f'omolomo le ...*

MOJI (*in a horrified whisper*). You wicked child, if it is what I'm thinking ...

ISOLA. Bye-bye, Ma. Tell the minister I've gone to choir practice ...

MOJI. Oh, you wicked child, can't you find more pleasant games to play? ... What! Come here, Isola. Haven't I told you never to call your father minister. Must you always do that to annoy me?

ISOLA. But he is the minister.

MOJI. You only do this to make me unhappy. Why do you refuse to call him father? Isola, when did you begin this new habit? A child like you, and you nurse a grudge inside you like an old man. What will you do when you become a man?

ISOLA. But he is the minister.

MOJI. Don't go anywhere. If you go I'll tell your father where you went. Are you going to promise me or aren't you?

ISOLA. Promise what, Ma?

MOJI. Always to refer to him as father, especially when you are talking to me.

A door is opened roughly.

ERINJOBI. Isola.

*Mrs Erinjobi, wife of the minister, won't you please leave this poor boy alone?

ISOLA. Sir.

ERINJOBI. Come here.

ISOLA. Yes, sir.

ERINJOBI. And bring my stick. Hurry up and don't waste my time.

ISOLA. Sir?

ERINJOBI. Bring yourself over here.

Pulls him roughly and begins to flog him.

You're a child of sorrow, do you hear? A child of sorrow. You are lost, past redemption. I thought this was a Christian house, but you seem determined to turn it into a house of pagans. Don't bring shame to my house! If I have to kill you I will see that you do not shame my house.

He lays the stick down, breathing slightly heavily.

No tears, eh! Look at him. No tears at all. Oh, you've sold yourself to the devil and no mistake. Look at him. His eyes are completely dry ... no sign at all that he had just taken a punishment. (*Shouting.*) Put up your hands! (*Slaps him.*) When next I say put up your hands, raise them properly like a well-trained child. Now, if you do not want worse to happen to you, answer truthfully. What did you tell Morounke? What did you tell her?

ISOLA. I ... I don't know, sir.

ERINJOBI. Are you trying to lie to me? I say, what did you confide in the daughter of Olumorin?

Silence.

Are you trying to be stubborn? What did you tell her? What did you tell her?

He beats him again.

Don't put down your hands. Just keep them up where they are. Now what did you tell her? Are you going to say it yourself or do I have to beat it out of you?

ISOLA. I don't know what particular thing you mean, sir . . .

ERINJOBI. Liar! So early in your life, and you've learnt to hedge like an experienced lawyer! Did you not confess that you went about town yesterday in a masquerade? Did you or did you not?

ISOLA (*nervously*). Yes, sir. I told her so.

ERINJOBI. Well, go on. Tell me now that you only said it in play. That you never at any time appeared in the streets with the masqueraders.

ISOLA. I . . . I am not . . . trying to deny it, sir.

ERINJOBI. And just as well for you! You dressed yourself as an egungun and paraded the town like a pagan. Is this or is this not a Christian house? Have I not brought you up as a Christian . . . Moji! Moji!

MOJI (*off*). Yes, Reverend.

ERINJOBI. Come and hear what latest honour your son has accorded to your house.

MOJI. Reverend, what is the matter?

ERINJOBI. An *egungun* – that's his latest employment. Soon I suppose we shall wake up one morning and find a bestial sacrifice at our door – a dog split in two or some equally revolting mess. Is that what my house must now become on account of you, you child of the devil!

This is accompanied by a blow.

MOJI. Isola, don't you know it is wrong? You're a Christian. Behaviour like this will only bring displeasure to your father?

ERINJOBI. Do you know how I heard about it? Not content with the shameful escapade, he went and boasted of it to Morounke. And she of course told her parents. And you know what the Olumorin family are like. Before the day is

out the whole town will know about it. The pastor's son, eating and drinking sordid pottages with pagans of the town . . .
(*Hitting him.*) Is that the bad name you're bent on giving me
you worthless child? (*He hits him again.*) Is it? Is it?

*'Is it' Is it' is heard over and over again accompanied by a
blow, gaining in intensity with each repitition.* ISOLA *gets
more and more restless, groaning . . .*

MOROUNKE. Isola! What is the matter? Isola. Wake up, wake
up, Isola . . .

ISOLA. Hm? What . . . who is it?

MOROUNKE. It's me. Morounke. Me. Are you awake now,
Isola?

ISOLA. What's the matter? Oh, was I dreaming?

MOROUNKE. Yes, what was it? Why were you so restless?

ISOLA. Sorry. Did I talk in my sleep?

MOROUNKE. No. But you were thrashing about. You were
moaning too. Were you in pain?

ISOLA. No, no. I'm alright. I'm sorry I woke you.

MOROUNKE. Are you sure you're not ill?

ISOLA. Quite sure, Morounke. I was only dreaming. Do go to
sleep again.

MOROUNKE. All right. Goodnight, Isola.

ISOLA. Good night.

Brief pause. Fade forest sounds to household.

ERINJOBI. Isola!

ISOLA (*sleepy*). What is it, Morounke?

ERINJOBI. Morounke? Are you mad? I call you and you answer
me Morounke. What kind of madness is that? Have you got the
girl on your brain?

ISOLA (*the younger* ISOLA). Sir? I . . . I . . .

ERINJOBI. Haven't I warned you about Olumorin's daughter?

Haven't I warned you that I must never see you with her again?

ISOLA. Yes, sir.

ERINJOBI. Then what were you doing with her in the church compound this afternoon? You were seen with her ... and don't lie to me. You were seen with her. What were you doing with her. Haven't I warned you never to see her again?

ISOLA. We were just looking at the gravestones, sir.

ERINJOBI. And did it take the two of you to look at gravestones? Have I not warned you never to linger in the church compound after service is over? All children from decent homes return straight after the service, but you must wander over the churchyard. Looking at gravestones!

He hits him.

Is that the sort of training I gave you?

Repeated blows.

Was that how I brought you up? To disobey every command I give you. How often must I tell you to keep away from her? How often? Go on, how often ... how often ... how often ... HOW OFTEN ...! HOW OFTEN ...! HOW OFTEN! HOW OFTEN!

ISOLA (*groaning uneasily. A sudden stifled cry and he wakes*). Morounke ... Good, didn't wake her.

He strikes a match and lights the lantern.

MOROUNKE (*waking*). Who? Oh, Isola, what are you doing?

ISOLA. Nothing, I merely wanted a light.

MOROUNKE. What for?

ISOLA. I keep having those bad dreams. Go back to sleep.

Maybe I shall sleep better with the light on.

MOROUNKE. I'll keep my hand on your head – like this. Or else a fresh leaf under your armpit. Bimpe says . . .

ISOLA. Oh, yes, Bimpe says . . . now are we going back to sleep or not?

MOROUNKE. It's true. She says if you have a leaf under your armpit or place a . . .

Fade straight into next scene.

ERINJOBI. Isola!

ISOLA. Sir.

ERINJOBI. Moji! Where are you? Moji!

MOJI (*approaching*). Reverend, what is it? What has happened?

ERINJOBI. It is the judgement which the good Lord has seen fit to bestow upon me.

Blows.

You godless child, why do you bring one shame after another on my house? What hatred do you nurse against my good name.

MOJI. Reverend, what has he done?

ERINJOBI. Come here. I will not corrupt the other children by talking of it in my house. Come on with you.

He pulls him so suddenly that ISOLA *falls.*

Get up!

He pulls at him very roughly.

GET . . . UP!

MOJI (*frightened, screams out*). Reverend, please . . . please . . . don't kick him.

ERINJOBI. Get up! Come and look on the face of the girl you

have defiled. Let us see if you can raise your face and look her in the eye . . .

He pulls, half-drags him through the door.

MOJI. Reverend, please . . . gently. Reverend, please . . . OH! You'll kill him. Reverend . . . I must go with him . . . my head-tie, where is my head-tie . . .

Fade out. Fade into ERINJOBI, *half dragging* ISOLA *along the street. Street-noises are mostly people, goats, bicycles, and the occasional motor-horn. Mix with introduction to 'Omo Jowo'.*

> Omo ki o ye jowo o
> Omo jowo
> Mo kunle mo be o o
> Omo jowo
> Mo f'ekuru be o o
> Omo jowo
> Mo f'akara be o o
> Omo jowo
> Ki o ye jowo o
> Omo jowo
> Ki o ye jowo o
> Omo jowo

ERINJOBI. Yours is very clearly the progress of the lost child . . . it has been the true pattern since you were born, and you have followed in it without deviation. I knew you were damned the moment you began to follow the masqueraders. My own son . . . an egungun! You made me the laughing stock of my parish. When I administered the holy Sacrament, every godly person must have been laughing and asking why I wasn't helping my son administer some vile brew in the egungun grove. Oh, you were damned from the start . . . playing with gutter children . . .

singing heathen songs ... slipping out at night and nobody knowing what bestiality you would commit before the break of day! But it is all out now ... the sun has pierced your treasury of sins ... What! What is the meaning of this? Moji. What is the meaning of this?

MOJI. Reverend, I ...

ERINJOBI. Go back at once, Moji. Go back.

MOJI. Reverend, I have a duty to be there.

ERINJOBI. Your duty is where I point it to you, wife. And this is no time for the charitable mother.

MOJI. But Reverend ...

Noise of crowd collecting.

ERINJOBI. If you have any pity, it is the poor girl who deserves it. It is her life that is ruined totally, ruined by your son. Do you now see why it is a sin to show mercy to this fornicator? Go home, Moji. Go back to the children ... (*Angrily, to the crowd.*) What is the matter? Have you no work, all of you? Is this some kind of dance that you think you have been given liberty to stare? Get going and look after your own sins. Get going you hypocrites, go on, get away ... Get away before the Lord reveals your own hidden corruptions and slaps you hard with them.

He goes. Chanting of 'Omo Jowo' is heard as he rails.

I hope you are proud ... it is what you would like, isn't it? After all, why do you go with the masqueraders except to collect crowds after you. Yelling abuses, begging for pennies, cursing, shouting, blaspheming in the face of God. But God strikes you in the end, and be thankful he has not yet struck you dead! (*Bellows suddenly.*) Moji! Why do you stand there? What are you waiting for? Go back, wife. Go back at once. Go and wait for me at home!

ERINJOBI (*going again*). Weak! So weak! One who should be a pillar to me in the hour of trial ... Ah, prepare to look on your handiwork.

They climb some steps. Knock on the door.

We will see now just how hardened you are.

Door opens.

MRS OLUMORIN. Reverend ... my husband is waiting. YOU! What did you do to my daughter? You've ruined her, do you know that? You have ruined her.

OLUMORIN. Isola, this is a sorry day for me. How did my daughter offend you that you picked on her among all the women of the town?

MRS OLUMORIN. Morounke ... Morounke ...

MOROUNKE. Ma.

MRS OLUMORIN. Now go on. Tell us again what you told me this morning.

MOROUNKE. I don't know ... Isola ...

OLUMORIN. Don't talk to him ... answer to your mother.

MRS OLUMORIN. Was it Isola or was it not?

ERINJOBI. Of course it was. I don't think he is so lost that he'll dare deny it.

MRS OLUMORIN. And our daughter did not understand. She was tricked. She said so herself. He tricked you, didn't he? He deceived you. You were too innocent to understand.

ISOLA. Mrs Olumorin ...

ERINJOBI. Quiet! Were you asked to speak?

MRS OLUMORIN. You see, Reverend, the matter is obvious. My daughter is only a child. How could she understand anything? Your son took sinful advantage of her ignorance.

ISOLA. Mrs Olumorin, I think ...

ERINJOBI. Did you not hear me tell you to be quiet.

OLUMORIN. No no. Let us hear what he has to say. Isola, you want to speak to us, don't you? Well, go ahead. Let us hear you deny it if that is what you want to do.

ISOLA. I merely ... I just ... want to ask if ... could I talk to Morounke for some moments?

General pandemonium.

OLUMORIN. You wish to ...?

ERINJOBI. Is the boy mad?

MRS OLUMORIN. Did I hear right? God help me, have you not done enough damage already? He wants to speak to her?

ERINJOBI. Isola, I hope your senses have not deserted you?

ISOLA. Morounke, I wanted to know ... you did not tell me ... are you really with child?

ERINJOBI. Is the boy completely lost? Isola, did you not hear me forbid you to utter a word to the child? Get away from her ...

MRS OLUMORIN. Good God, he has taken hold of her hand! Do you see ... do you see ... I am surely going mad!

OLUMORIN. Get away from my daughter.

ISOLA. Morounke, so you do bear my child, my own child?

MRS OLUMORIN. Help! Help! Don't you dare touch her. Get away, you shameless boy! Get him away from her.

ERINJOBI. Get my stick. Where is my stick?

MOROUNKE. Leave him ... oh, leave him. Don't beat him. Isola, run away.

OLUMORIN. In my presence, holding her hand in my presence. After what he's done to her? The devil's own offspring ... the devil's own misbegotten fruit!

MOROUNKE. I can't ... I can't ...

Footsteps running off.

MRS OLUMORIN. Morounke, come back. Come back here.

Bimpe! BIMPE! Where is that maid? Bimpe ... bring her
back. Bring her back.

ISOLA. Father, I ...

ERINJOBI. Don't call me father ... (*He brings down the
stick.*)

ISOLA. No!

MRS OLUMORIN. Help! Help! He's going to beat his father.
Help! Neighbours! Help!

ERINJOBI (*sternly*). Isola!

ISOLA. No! NO!

> *Sound of brief struggle. A cane snaps.* ISOLA *wakes up,
> leaps up, breathing heavily.*

MOROUNKE. Isola, what is the matter?

ISOLA. Can't he leave me in peace?

MOROUNKE. You were dreaming of him? Isola, can't you forget him?

ISOLA. Why doesn't he leave me alone?

MOROUNKE. Isola. (*Sudden fright.*) Where are you going?

ISOLA. Outside. The moon is out.

MOROUNKE. Wait. Don't leave me alone here.

ISOLA. Well, come on if you like.

MOROUNKE. Oh, it's full moon. Look ... there is Moji,
warming herself in the moon.

ISOLA. She looks peaceful. Now be careful not to scare her off.

MOROUNKE. Isola, look!

ISOLA. What is it?

MOROUNKE. By the bamboo ... there it is again ... Isola, oh
God, it's so huge ... It's so huge.

ISOLA. Get me my gun ... Quickly! It's Erinjobi, I'll get him
tonight. Quickly now before he disappears again. Hurry!

> *Rapid sounds of movement.*

MOROUNKE. Here it is. Isola, suppose you miss or merely

wound it . . . isn't that dangerous?

ISOLA. I won't miss.

MOROUNKE. It looks horrible. Why don't you shoot? Kill it at once, Isola.

ISOLA. I must wait for the head to appear. It's difficult to aim in this light. The moon turns it the same colour as the leaves. And don't shout so much. Just watch for the head, between the leaves.

MOROUNKE. There! There it is. It looks so ugly . . . Isola, I'm frightened.

ISOLA. Don't touch me or I'll miss . . . there it comes again.

He pulls the trigger, only a click.

MOROUNKE. What happened? It didn't go off.

ISOLA (*striking his forehead*). Fool! Fool! Aren't we such fools? We've used up the charge. It went off that time when you took the gun.

MOROUNKE. Oh . . . oh, Isola, I am sorry . . . now I'm really sorry . . . Where are you going?

ISOLA. Home.

MOROUNKE. Home? You mean to your father's?

ISOLA. Yes. I must get some powder. I know where the man keeps his powder and shot.

MOROUNKE. What on earth for? Can't it wait till morning?

The song 'Meta meta l'ore' begins and runs through the rest of the scene.

> Meta meta l'ore o ee
> Meta meta l'ore o ee
> Ikan ni nwa sun l'eni . . . ee
> Ikan ni nwa sun n'ile . . . ee
> Ikan ni nwa sun l'aiya . . . ee
> Mo s'oju were mo ba l'aiya lo

Mo ti lo m'ogun, mo ti lo m'osa
Mo ti lo m'opo bale odo
Ope wewe se'ku pa'pako
Ise nkele se'ku p'okunrin
Ote 'badan m'ogun wa ja'lu
Ondere se'ko yeye
Ye ye o lore o . . . e

ISOLA. No. I must kill it tonight. Tonight. I can't wait any longer.

MOROUNKE. Isola, this is foolish. Let it wait till tomorrow.

ISOLA. No, tonight. This is what gives me the nightmares. Didn't you see it? I must kill it.

MOROUNKE. Wait for me . . . don't leave me . . . Isola, you're always leaving me alone. Wait, please . . .

ISOLA. Well, hurry up.

MOROUNKE. He's gone already. The snake is gone. Why don't you wait till the morning?

ISOLA. If he's gone then I'll have to dig him out. I mean to hunt him down tonight.

MOROUNKE (panting). Isola, you're going too fast. Wait, please . . . wait until tomorrow . . . Isola, you can't go hunting that monster at night . . .

ISOLA. I must . . . I must or I'll never get any sleep . . . Come on, we'll be home soon. I'll creep into the minister's room and get the powder.

MOROUNKE. Now I know it's true. Bimpe says you're quite mad, quite mad. Now I know she told the truth . . . you're mad, Isola . . . you've gone mad.

ISOLA. I can't sleep with that thing crawling around me. You didn't see and I didn't want to show you . . . There was another broken shell on the other side of the stream, and that snake did it . . . smashed against the rocks like the others . . . What is the use if they can't go and come as they please. I'll kill him tonight . . .

Up song fully. Then fade out. A window creaks.

MOJI. Who is that? Who is it? WHO IS THAT? Whoever you are, come out, do you hear? Don't sneak into my house by the backdoor ... my son isn't here and you can search from morning till night. He isn't here so go away and leave me in peace. Go away, do you hear?

Silence.

I know you're in there. I'm not deaf. Come out, whoever sent you. Or you can go back and tell him that I haven't got his daughter, and that I haven't got my son. Go and tell him God will curse him if he touches my son ...

Silence. Slow steps towards the door, which is suddenly flung open.

Isola!

ISOLA. Mother, please ... shut the door.

MOJI. Isola! My son, where have you been? What have you been doing?

He rummages through boxes, working frantically.

Oh, Isola, why do you break me in pieces? Why don't you lift your fist and kill me at once? Am I not your mother? Isola, where is Morounke? Where is the missing girl? Isola, why don't you answer? Her father is looking for her. He's raised the whole town after you. He says you stole her ... Isola, answer your mother ... What are you doing? Isola! Those are your father's things ... my son ... What have we done to you? You're in danger, my son ... you must hide!

ISOLA. Ah ... here it is.

MOJI. What is that?

ISOLA *picks up the gun.*

And that? Put it down. Is that not your father's gun?

The window is opened.

Isola, do you now use the window like a thief? Where are you going? No, you shan't go. You must stay here.

ISOLA. Mother, let me go.

A slight struggle.

MOJI. You will stay here. Have you no fears at all? I say the whole town is after you. They call you kidnapper ... do you not know what that means? A kidnapper. That's the story Olumorin has spread about you.

ISOLA. Mother, let me go ... I mustn't stay here.

MOJI. Have you totally sealed your heart against me? I say your life is the property of the whole town. A kidnapper. They all say you went into the house and abducted the girl.

ISOLA. I did not, so let the matter end there.

MOJI. Will it? Then where is she? Where is she? Isola, where have you been tonight. This hardness belongs to an older man. You fill me with fears, my son. Are you my son at all? I no longer know you.

ISOLA (*more fiercely*). Mother, what are you doing? Let me go!

Struggling.

MOJI (*sobbing*). You will have to kill me. What does the gun mean? And what have you come to find in your father's room? Where is Morounke? Why do you harden yourself against me? What is it in you, Isola? What is it in you that I have nursed from childhood and did not know?

ISOLA. Nothing, nothing, I must go.

MOJI. Go? Go where? Have you any home but this? Do you think you will go out of this house, leaving me with fears and questions? Where is Morounke?

ISOLA. If you must know . . . in her own home.

MOJI. Don't lie to me, son. You have never done that before, don't lie to me now.

ISOLA. I took her there . . . just now. She didn't want to go but I left her there.

MOJI. And Olumorin? Was he at home? Do the parents know their child is back?

ISOLA. That is not for me to worry about. The doors of the house were left open. The place looked empty. Now will you let me go?

MOJI. When they know they have their daughter back, then you may go where you please. But not before then. Here they can only take you over my lifeless corpse.

ISOLA. No, Mother, I shall go now. Leave me now, Mother.

MOJI. When the child is restored, not before!

MOROUNKE (*from outside*). Isola. Isola.

MOJI. Who? Is that not Morounke?

Footsteps running into the house.

MOROUNKE. Isola . . . you didn't come back.

MOJI. What is this? Were you to go back for her?

ISOLA. It was the only way I could get her to stay there. I told her I would come back.

MOROUNKE. The house was empty . . . no one . . . not even Bimpe anywhere. How could I stay? Ma, where did they all go?

MOJI. Looking for you.

MOROUNKE. I saw crowds . . . with torches and weapons . . .

is there trouble?

MOJI. Those were your father's friends ... they say my son kidnapped you. Do you see what troubles you have brought on him?

ISOLA. You look after her, Mother. I'm going.

MOJI. No! I shall keep you both in the house. Let them come and find you here. And daughter, remember they will ask you if Isola abducted you. My son is in trouble on your account. Tell your father he did nothing. Or did he? Are you going to blame him or will you save him from their lust for blood?

MOROUNKE. I don't want to stay here. I never want to go back to my father.

MOJI. Don't talk nonesense, child. Do you know what it is you're saying?

MOROUNKE. I must go with Isola. I must ...

The window is opened suddenly. A surge of crowd noise. ISOLA *leaps out.*

MOJI. Isola! Isola! ... come back. Come back!

VOICES. There he is!

There! Through the window. After him ... After him!

Don't let him get to the woods.

Cut him off! Cut him off! Don't let him take to the bush.

OLUMORIN (*shouting*). Whoever catches him is a free man at my house. Let him ask anything he likes.

VOICES. Don't let him get in the thick grass. Cut him off! Cut him off! Get to the tall grass before he does.

MOJI. Olumorin ... call them off! Olumorin, your daughter is here safe and sound.

MRS OLUMORIN. What's that? Morounke?

OLUMORIN. Where?

MRS OLUMORIN. Morounke ... Morounke ...

MOJI. Call off your human dogs, Olumorin ... your daughter is here, isn't she? Call off your jackals before they harm him. Reverend! Reverend! Oh ... he's in the church. I will have to fetch him myself. You have your daughter now, Olumorin. If my son is harmed, if my son is harmed, may God reward you in like measure.

Her cries die off in the distance.

OLUMORIN. Morounke my girl, you're safe.

MRS OLUMORIN. Come here, let me hold you. Did he harm you?

MOROUNKE. Let me go! Let me go! (*Very fiercely.*) Let me go, you witch!

MRS OLUMORIN. What!

OLUMORIN. What did you say, girl? Come here. COME HERE!

MRS OLUMORIN. Did you hear? Did you hear what she called me?

MOROUNKE. I'm going to him. Leave me alone, I want Isola.

OLUMORIN. Be quiet!

MRS OLUMORIN. He's bewitched her. She's not in her senses. Did you hear her?

OLUMORIN. Just hand her over and I'll cure her once and for all ... Ah! She bit me!

Footsteps running off.

MRS OLUMORIN. Stop her! Stop that girl! For your mother's sake stop her before she is lost again.

OLUMORIN. She bit me. She's gone quite mad. Stop her ... Stop that child!

MAN. We've got him, sir. In that little bush ... we've surrounded it so he can't escape.

OLUMORIN. My daughter ... what about my daughter?

MAN. The men have run after her . . . she won't get far, sir.

OLUMORIN. Why do you merely surround the bush? I don't want to eat the bush. Get the boy. Get him.

MAN. They say he has a gun with him, sir. Some men saw it. That is really why we couldn't cut him off.

OLUMORIN. Then set fire to the bush. Go on . . . are you men or aren't you? Set fire to it and smoke him out.

Footsteps running out.

ANOTHER MAN. Sir . . . your daughter, sir . . .

OLUMORIN. Didn't you catch her?

A steady tread of approaching footsteps.

MAN. No, sir. She ran into the bush.

MRS OLUMORIN. Call yourselves men? What were you look-ing at? Now she's in there with him. What can you do now? What are you going to do?

ERINJOBI (*entering*). Nothing. You are all to do nothing.

In the background, MOJI *sobs.*

OLUMORIN. Rev Erinjobi, you have come in time.

ERINJOBI. I hope so. What is the matter? Can a man get no peace even in the house of the Lord? First the noise of your men deafened me. Then my wife rushed in to say that your daughter was restored to you, but that you still seek ven-geance on my son. Is that true?

OLUMORIN. What daughter? She is in there with him . . . in that bush.

MOJI. She was here. Here in this house. I gave her to you and I begged you to send your men home. But my son is cornered there still, and you are turning him into an animal.

MRS OLUMORIN. That one? He was born an animal. No one is turning him into one.

MOJI. Are you not a mother? What hatred do you nurse against my son?

OLUMORIN. He is a kidnapper.

MOJI. He is not. Morounke will tell you the truth. He did not steal her.

ERINJOBI. Enough. Where is Isola? Where is he now?

MOJI. Over there. Just where the men are gathered.

ERINJOBI. Wait here. I will bring him out. And your daughter.

MOJI (*shouts after him*). Reverend, let him know it is you. He has your gun. Let him know it's his father . . .

Fade into song, softer.

> Omo ki o ye jowo o
> Omo jowo
> Mo kunle mo be o o
> Omo jowo
> Mo f'ekuru be o o
> Omo jowo
> Mo f'akara be o o
> Omo jowo
> Ki o ye jowo o
> Omo jowo
> Ki o ye jowo o
> Omo jowo

ERINJOBI (*distant*). Make way. Have you lost respect? Away with you. Go on, go now. Go down to the house and wait. All of you, I say go! Is this some animal that your tongues drool at the thought of blood? Go now before I bring down the curse of God on your heads. Go!

They slink off, grumbling.

Isola! Isola! It is almost time for our morning prayers. Come home, my son, come home and join the family in prayer.

Song up slightly.

Isola, while I was in church, your mother came and spoke to me. You have sinned, I know . . .

ISOLA. I have not sinned.

ERINJOBI. Be repentant. I have come to you only because I also have sinned. As I opened my heart to God I knew that only He can give up his children, yet he never does. What right had I, his mere servant, to presume so much? What voice had I to damn you before God and men? My sin then became as great as yours. Come home and help me pray for forgiveness.

ISOLA. Erinjobi, leave me in peace.

ERINJOBI. Erinjobi? Son, that is your father's name.

ISOLA. Erinjobi, leave me in peace.

ERINJOBI. Is that a way of shutting me out again? It has been a long night, do not turn your hardened face to me. Repent of your sins, my son . . .

ISOLA. I have not sinned.

ERINJOBI. But you have. We are all sinners in the sight of God; we depend only on his mercy. It is true your mother called me out, she was afraid for your life. But I did not leave my meditation on that account. The good Lord protects his children, and I had no fears for your life. I had left you in His hands . . .

ISOLA. In the hands of Olumorin.

ERINJOBI. My son, I left you in God's hands. When I went into church, it was to pray that the Lord should do his will by you . . .

ISOLA. And Olumorin to do his . . . do not forget that, Erinjobi.

ERINJOBI. My son, is this an egungun grove that you shout your father's name three times in the dark? Send out the girl. Her parents await her.

ISOLA. She is here beside me, unchained. Speak to her yourself. Morounke does as she pleases.

ERINJOBI. Morounke, come home. Your parents are anxious. Come back to them.

Silence, except for the song.

Daughter, return to your parents. You are only a child and you were led astray. Come out and leave me alone with the conscience of my son.

Pause. Just the song.

Son, is it you who hold her back?

ISOLA. Erinjobi, it is you who hold her back.

ERINJOBI. Again? My son, our people say it's an ill moment when a son calls his living father by name. Send out the girl. Tell her to return home.

ISOLA. She comes and goes as she pleases. Talk to her. Ask nothing of me.

ERINJOBI. Morounke.

Pause. 'Omo Jowo' continues.

Then I must come and fetch her.

ISOLA (*barks out the word*). Don't!

Footsteps into the bush.

ERINJOBI. Morounke, I am coming to take you to your parents.

ISOLA. Erinjobi, don't come in here! Go back to your church!

Steady motion through the bushes.

Stay away, Erinjobi, stay away ... if your head appears, Erinjobi, if your head shows once between the leaves. Erinjobi!

He fires, MOROUNKE *screams, begins to cry. Approaching
footsteps running.*

ISOLA. Hush, girl, hush ... why, it is only Erinjobi ... were you
afraid?

Frantic swishing through the bush.

MOJI (*shouting*). Isola! Isola! Reverend! Isola! Where are you?
Where are you? Isola!

Sudden halt.

Ngh? Reverend. REVEREND! REVEREND! (*She breaks down
sobbing.*)

Fade in 'Agbe'.

ISOLA. Moji ... you too? Why, Moji, you mustn't cry ... Hush,
woman, hush now ... hush ... hush ...

Up song fully.

> Agbe t'or'omo re daro o ... Olenle
> Aluko t'or'omo re gosun o ... Olenle
> Baba iyoku t'or'omo re paroko ide o
> Awa o le taro iwon yen
> K'ama a b'olu s'ere imoran ...
>
> > Olenle o.

English Texts of the Songs

Agbe (p 89)

Mourning her child, *agbe* wrapped herself in indigo
Mourning her child, *aluko* ground the camwood dye
The bereaved father forged bells of brass
But we cannot dwell too much on these things
Lest we are caught in a fatal game with the gods.

Mo le j'iyan yo (p 93)

I delight in pounded yam like a man of the farm
I feast on the mealie like a Sango devotee
My back supports the child like a much blessed mother
This child is to you – your own flesh and blood
This twin is to you – your own flesh and blood
And this other of the twins – your own flesh and blood.

E-e-ya ko se a gbe (p 101)

Too heavy, it is too heavy to lift
Too heavy, it is too heavy to lift
Were it only lighter, I too would bear my own
And when it might have proved light enough
The elephant died in the bush, we brought home the mountain
The wild bull died in the bush, we brought home the mountain
The rat died in the house, we took the mountain to the bush
Eyes of the leopard, embers in the dark
Tail of the leopard, a swishing lariat
Claws of the leopard, double-edged razors
If the male yam is scarce, we pound the soft tuber
If a bride eludes us, we marry our in-law
If the matter disturbs us we kneel and complain

But if it does not, we pursue our wooing . . .
Cicatrix on the cheeks, just like the well-blazed route.

Mo j'awe gbegbe (p 114)

I plucked *gbegbe* leaves
Lest I be forgotten
I plucked *tete* leaves
Lest I be trodden under
The day peters out, let it leave us well
Be the eyes so enlightened, they cannot forget home
Thus it goes . . . may it be a good parting
Thus it goes . . . may it be a good parting

Omo ki o ye jowo o (p 122)

Child I implore you
Implore you
Kneeling I implore you
Implore you
With bean curd I implore you
Implore you
With bean cake I implore you
Be appeased I implore you
Implore you
Be appeased I implore you
Implore you

Meta meta l'ore o (p 127-8)

Friends come in threesome
Friends come in threesome
The first offered me a mat to sleep upon
The next offered me the floor to sleep on
The third offered me his breast

Not once did I blink, I accepted the breast offer
I have known the river, I have known the sea
I have known the path of the father of streams
Small fronds may bring death to the thick fibre stalks
A grown man is killed by lackadaisical labour
Conspiracy in Ibadan brought war into town
The parrot makes nonsense of beautiful feathers
Friendship is as fluff, so insubstantial.

THE END

DEATH AND THE
KING'S HORSEMAN

Dedicated
In Affectionate Greeting
to
My Father, Ayodele
who lately danced, and joined the Ancestors.

AUTHOR'S NOTE

This play is based on events which took place in Oyo, ancient Yoruba city of Nigeria, in 1946. That year, the lives of Elesin (Olori Elesin), his son, and the Colonial District Officer intertwined with the disastrous results set out in the play. The changes I have made are in matters of detail, sequence and of course characterisation. The action has also been set back two or three years to while the war was still on, for minor reasons of dramaturgy.

The factual account still exists in the archives of the British Colonial Administration. It has already inspired a fine play in Yoruba (Oba Wàjà) by Duro Ladipo. It has also misbegotten a film by some German television company.

The bane of themes of this genre is that they are no sooner employed creatively than they acquire the facile tag of 'clash of cultures', a prejudicial label which, quite apart from its frequent misapplication, presupposes a potential equality *in every given situation* of the alien culture and the indigenous, on the actual soil of the latter. (In the area of misapplication, the overseas prize for illiteracy and mental conditioning undoubtedly goes to the blurb-writer for the American edition of my novel *Season of Anomy* who unblushingly declares that this work portrays the 'clash between old values and new ways, between western methods and African traditions'!) It is thanks to this kind of perverse mentality that I find it necessary to caution the would-be producer of this play against a sadly familiar reductionist tendency, and to direct his vision instead to the far more difficult and risky task of eliciting the play's threnodic essence.

One of the more obvious alternative structures of the play would be to make the District Officer the victim of a cruel dilemma. This is not to my taste and it is not by chance that I have avoided dialogue or situation which would encourage this. No attempt should be made in production to suggest it. The Colonial Factor is an incident, a catalytic incident merely. The confrontation in the play is largely metaphysical, contained in the human vehicle which is Elesin and the universe of the Yoruba mind – the world of the living, the dead and the unborn, and the numinous passage which links all: transition. *Death and the King's Horseman* can be fully realised only through an evocation of music from the abyss of transition.

W. S.

CAST

PRAISE-SINGER
ELESIN, *Horseman of the King*
IYALOJA, *'Mother' of the market*
SIMON PILKINGS, *District Officer*
JANE PILKINGS, *his wife*
SERJEANT AMUSA
JOSEPH, *houseboy to the Pilkingses*
BRIDE
H.R.H. THE PRINCE
THE RESIDENT
AIDE-DE-CAMP
OLUNDE, *eldest son of Elesin*

Drummers, Women, Young Girls, Dancers at the Ball

The play should run without an interval. For rapid scene changes, one adjustable outline set is very appropriate.

Note to this edition

Certain Yoruba words which appear in italics in the text are explained in a brief glossary on page 220.

SCENE ONE

A passage through a market in its closing stages. The stalls are being emptied, mats folded. A few women pass through on their way home, loaded with baskets. On a cloth-stand, bolts of cloth are taken down, display pieces folded and piled on a tray. ELESIN OBA *enters along a passage before the market, pursued by his drummers and praise-singers. He is a man of enormous vitality, speaks, dances and sings with that infectious enjoyment of life which accompanies all his actions.*

PRAISE-SINGER. Elesin o! Elesin Oba! Howu! What tryst is this the cockerel goes to keep with such haste that he must leave his tail behind?

ELESIN (*slows down a bit, laughing*). A tryst where the cockerel needs no adornment.

PRAISE-SINGER. O-oh, you hear that my companions? That's the way the world goes. Because the man approaches a brand new bride he forgets the long faithful mother of his children.

ELESIN. When the horse sniffs the stable does he not strain at the bridle? The market is the long-suffering home of my spirit and the women are packing up to go. That Esu-harrassed day slipped into the stewpot while we feasted. We ate it up with the rest of the meat. I have neglected my women.

PRAISE-SINGER. We know all that. Still it's no reason for shedding your tail on this day of all days. I know the women will cover you in damask and *alari* but when the wind blows cold from behind, that's when the fowl knows his true friends.

ELESIN. Olohun-iyo!

PRAISE-SINGER. Are you sure there will be one like me on the other side?

ELESIN. Olohun-iyo!

PRAISE-SINGER. Far be it for me to belittle the dwellers of that place but, a man is either born to his art or he isn't. And I don't know for certain that you'll meet my father, so who is going to sing these deeds in accents that will pierce the deafness of the ancient ones. I have prepared my going – just tell me: Olohun-iyo, I need you on this journey and I shall be behind you.

ELESIN. You're like a jealous wife. Stay close to me, but only on this side. My fame, my honour are legacies to the living; stay behind and let the world sip its honey from your lips.

PRAISE-SINGER. Your name will be like the sweet berry a child places under his tongue to sweeten the passage of food. The world will never spit it out.

ELESIN. Come then. This market is my roost. When I come among the women I am a chicken with a hundred mothers. I become a monarch whose palace is built with tenderness and beauty.

PRAISE-SINGER. They love to spoil you but beware. The hands of women also weaken the unwary.

ELESIN. This night I'll lay my head upon their lap and go to sleep. This night I'll touch feet with their feet in a dance that is no longer of this earth. But the smell of their flesh, their sweat, the smell of indigo on their cloth, this is the last air I wish to breathe as I go to meet my great forebears.

PRAISE-SINGER. In their time the world was never tilted from its groove, it shall not be in yours.

ELESIN. The gods have said No.

PRAISE-SINGER. In their time the great wars came and went, the little wars came and went; the white slavers came and went, they took away the heart of our race, they bore away the mind and muscle of our race. The city fell and was rebuilt; the city fell and our people trudged through mountain and forest to find a new home but – Elesin Oba do you year me?

ELESIN. I hear your voice Olohun-iyo.

PRAISE-SINGER. Our world was never wrenched from its true course.

ELESIN. The gods have said No.

PRAISE-SINGER. There is only one home to the life of a river-mussel; there is only one home to the life of a tortoise; there is only one shell to the soul of man; there is only one world to the spirit of our race. If that world leaves its course and smashes on boulders of the great void, whose world will give us shelter?

ELESIN. It did not in the time of my forebears, it shall not in mine.

PRAISE-SINGER. The cockerel must not be seen without his feathers.

ELESIN. Nor will the Not-I bird be much longer without his nest.

PRAISE-SINGER (stopped in his lyric stride). The Not-I bird, Elesin?

ELESIN. I said, the Not-I bird.

PRAISE-SINGER. All respect to our elders but, is there really such a bird?

ELESIN. What! Could it be that he failed to knock on your door?

PRAISE-SINGER (smiling). Elesin's riddles are not merely the nut in the kernel that breaks human teeth; he also buries the kernel in hot embers and dares a man's fingers to draw it out.

ELESIN. I am sure he called on you, Olohun-iyo. Did you hide in the loft and push out the servant to tell him you were out?

ELESIN *executes a brief, half-taunting dance. The* DRUMMER *moves in and draws a rhythm out of his steps.* ELESIN *dances towards the market-place as he chants the story of the Not-I bird, his voice changing dexterously to mimic his characters. He performs like a born raconteur, infecting his retinue with his humour and energy. More* WOMEN *arrive during his recital, including* IYALOJA.

Death came calling
Who does not know his rasp of reeds?
A twilight whisper in the leaves before

The great araba falls? Did you hear it?
Not I! swears the farmer. He snaps
His fingers round his head, abandons
A hard-worn harvest and begins
A rapid dialogue with his legs.

'Not I,' shouts the fearless hunter, 'but –
It's getting dark, and this night-lamp
Has leaked out all its oil. I think
It's best to go home and resume my hunt
Another day.' But now he pauses, suddenly
Lets out a wail: 'Oh foolish mouth, calling
Down a curse on your own head! Your lamp
Has leaked out all its oil, has it?
Forwards or backwards now he dare not move.
To search for leaves and make *etutu*
On that spot? Or race home to the safety
Of his hearth? Ten market-days have passed
My friends, and still he's rooted there
Rigid as the plinth of Orayan.

The mouth of the courtesan barely
Opened wide enough to take a ha'penny *robo*
When she wailed: 'Not I.' All dressed she was
To call upon my friend the Chief Tax Officer.
But now she sends her go-between instead:
'Tell him I'm ill: my period has come suddenly
But not – I hope – my time.'

Why is the pupil crying?
His hapless head was made to taste
The knuckles of my friend the Mallam:
'If you were then reciting the Koran
Would you have ears for idle noises

Darkening the trees, you child of ill omen?'
He shuts down school before its time
Runs home and rings himself with amulets.
And take my good kinsman Ifawomi.
His hands were like a carver's, strong
And true. I saw them
Tremble like wet wings of a fowl.
One day he cast his time-smoothed *opele*
Across the divination board. And all because
The suppliant looked him in the eye and asked,
'Did you hear that whisper in the leaves?'
'Not I,' was his reply; 'perhaps I'm growing deaf –
Good-day.' And Ifa spoke no more that day
The priest locked fast his doors,
Sealed up his leaking roof – but wait!
This sudden care was not for Fawomi
But for Osanyin, a courier-bird of Ifa's
Heart of wisdom. I did not know a kite
Was hovering in the sky
And Ifa now a twittering chicken in
The brood of Fawomi the Mother Hen.

Ah, but I must not forget my evening
Courier from the abundant palm, whose groan
Became Not I, as he constipated down
A wayside bush. He wonders if Elegbara
Has tricked his buttocks to discharge
Against a sacred grove. Hear him
Mutter spells to ward off penalties
For an abomination he did not intend.
If any here
Stumbles on a gourd of wine, fermenting
Near the road, and nearby hears a stream
Of spells issuing from a crouching form.
Brother to a *sigidi*, bring home my wine,

Tell my tapper I have ejected
Fear from home and farm. Assure him,
All is well.

PRAISE-SINGER. In your time we do not doubt the peace of
farmstead and home, the peace of road and hearth, we do not
doubt the peace of the forest.

ELESIN.   There was fear in the forest too.
                       Not-I was lately heard even in the lair
                       Of beasts. The hyena cackled loud. Not I,
                       The civet twitched his fiery tail and glared:
                       Not I. Not-I became the answering-name
                       Of the restless bird, that little one
                       Whom Death found nesting in the leaves
                       When whisper of his coming ran
                       Before him on the wind. Not-I
                       Has long abandoned home. This same dawn
                       I heard him twitter in the gods' abode.
                       Ah, companions of this living world
                       What a thing this is, that even those
                       We call immortal
                       Should fear to die.

IYALOJA.   But you, husband of multitudes?

ELESIN.   I, when that Not-I bird perched
                       Upon my roof, bade him seek his nest again.
                       Safe, without care or fear. I unrolled
                       My welcome mat for him to see. Not-I
                       Flew happily away, you'll hear his voice
                       No more in this lifetime — You all know
                       What I am.

PRAISE-SINGER. That rock which turns its open lodes
                       Into the path of lightning. A gay
                       Thoroughbred whose stride disdains
                       To falter though an adder reared
                       Suddenly in his path.

ELESIN.   My rein is loosened.
                     I am master of my Fate. When the hour comes
                     Watch me dance along the narrowing path
                     Glazed by the soles of my great precursors.
                     My soul is eager. I shall not turn aside.

WOMEN.   You will not delay?

ELESIN.   Where the storm pleases, and when, it directs
                     The giants of the forest. When friendship
                          summons
                     Is when the true comrade goes.

WOMEN.   Nothing will hold you back?

ELESIN.   Nothing. What! Has no one told you yet
                     I go to keep my friend and master company.
                     Who says the mouth does not believe in
                     'No, I have chewed all that before?' I say I
                          have.
                     The world is not a constant honey-pot.
                     Where I found little I made do with little.
                     Where there was plenty I gorged myself.
                     My master's hands and mine have always
                     Dipped together and, home or sacred feast,
                     The bowl was beaten bronze, the meats
                     So succulent our teeth accused us of neglect.
                     We shared the choicest of the season's
                     Harvest of yams. How my friend would read
                     Desire in my eyes before I knew the cause –
                     However rare, however precious, it was mine.

WOMEN.   The town, the very land was yours.

ELESIN.   The world was mine. Our joint hands
                     Raised housepots of trust that withstood
                     The siege of envy and the termites of time.
                     But the twilight hour brings bats and rodents–
                     Shall I yield them cause to foul the rafters?

PRAISE-SINGER.   Elesin Oba! Are you not that man who
                     Looked out of doors that stormy day

	The god of luck limped by, drenched

The god of luck limped by, drenched
To the very lice that held
His rags together? You took pity upon
His sores and wished him fortune.
Fortune was footloose this dawn, he replied,
Till you trapped him in a heartfelt wish
That now returns to you. Elesin Oba!
I say you are that man who
Chanced upon the calabash of honour
You thought it was palm wine and
Drained its contents to the final drop.

ELESIN. Life has an end. A life that will outlive
Fame and friendship begs another name.
What elder takes his tongue to his plate,
Licks it clean of every crumb? He will
encounter
Silence when he calls on children to fulfill
The smallest errand! Life is honour.
It ends when honour ends.

WOMEN. We know you for a man of honour.

ELESIN. Stop! Enough of that!

WOMEN (*puzzled, they whisper among themselves, turning mostly to* IYALOJA). What is it? Did we say something to give offence? Have we slighted him in some way?

ELESIN. Enough of that sound I say. Let me hear no more in that vein. I've heard enough.

IYALOJA. We must have said something wrong. (*Comes forward a little*). Elesin Oba, we ask forgiveness before you speak.

ELESIN. I am bitterly offended.

IYALOJA. Our unworthiness has betrayed us. All we can do is ask your forgiveness. Correct us like a kind father.

ELESIN. This day of all days . . .

IYALOJA. It does not bear thinking. If we offend you now we have mortified the gods. We offend heaven itself. Father of us all, tell us where we went astray. (*She kneels, the other women follow.*)

ELESIN. Are you not ashamed? Even a tear-veiled
Eye preserves its function of sight.
Because my mind was raised to horizons
Even the boldest man lowers his gaze
In thinking of, must my body here
Be taken for a vagrant's?

IYALOJA. Horseman of the King, I am more baffled than ever.

PRAISE-SINGER. The strictest father unbends his brow when the child is penitent, Elesin. When time is short, we do not spend it prolonging the riddle. Their shoulders are bowed with the weight of fear lest they have marred your day beyond repair. Speak now in plain words and let us pursue the ailment to the home of remedies.

ELESIN. Words are cheap. 'We know you for
A man of honour.' Well tell me, is this how
A man of honour should be seen?
Are these not the same clothes in which
I came among you a full half-hour ago?

He roars with laughter and the women, relieved, rise and rush into stalls to fetch rich clothes.

WOMEN. The gods are kind. A fault soon remedied is soon forgiven. Elesin Oba, even as we match our words with deed, let your heart forgive us completely.

ELESIN. You who are breath and giver of my being
How shall I dare refuse you forgiveness
Even if the offence was real.

IYALOJA (*dancing round him. Sings*).
He forgives us. He forgives us.
What a fearful thing it is when
The voyager sets forth
But a curse remains behind.

WOMEN. For a while we truly feared
Our hands had wrenched the world adrift

	In emptiness.
IYALOJA.	Richly, richly, robe him richly
	The cloth of honour is *alari*
	Sanyan is the band of friendship
	Boa-skin makes slippers of esteem.
WOMEN.	For a while we truly feared
	Our hands had wrenched the world adrift
	In emptiness.
PRAISE-SINGER.	He who must, must voyage forth
	The world will not roll backwards
	It is he who must, with one
	Great gesture overtake the world.
WOMEN.	For a while we truly feared
	Our hands had wrenched the world
	In emptiness.
PRAISE-SINGER.	The gourd you bear is not for shirking.
	The gourd is not for setting down
	At the first crossroad or wayside grove.
	Only one river may know its contents.
WOMEN.	We shall all meet at the great market
	We shall all meet at the great market
	He who goes early takes the best bargains
	But we shall meet, and resume our banter.

ELESIN *stands resplendent in rich clothes, cap, shawl, etc. His
sash is of a bright red alari cloth. The* WOMEN *dance round
him. Suddenly, his attention is caught by an object off-stage.*

ELESIN.	The world I know is good.
WOMEN.	We know you'll leave it so.
ELESIN.	The world I know is the bounty
	Of hives after bees have swarmed.
	No goodness teems with such open hands
	Even in the dreams of deities.
WOMEN.	And we know you'll leave it so.

ELESIN.   I was born to keep it so. A hive
                            Is never known to wander. An anthill
                            Does not desert its roots. We cannot see
                            The still great womb of the world –
                            No man beholds his mother's womb –
                            Yet who denies it's there? Coiled
                            To the navel of the world is that
                            Endless cord that links us all
                            To the great origin. If I lose my way
                            The trailing cord will bring me to the roots.

WOMEN.   The world is in your hands.

*The earlier distraction, a beautiful young girl, comes along the
passage through which* ELESIN *first made his entry.*

ELESIN.   I embrace it. And let me tell you, women –
                            I like this farewell that the world designed,
                            Unless my eyes deceive me, unless
                            We are already parted, the world and I,
                            And all that breeds desire is lodged
                            Among our tireless ancestors. Tell me friends,
                            Am I still earthed in that beloved market
                            Of my youth? Or could it be my will
                            Has outleapt the conscious act and I have
                              come
                            Among the great departed?

PRAISE-SINGER. Elesin Oba why do your eyes roll like a bush-
rat who sees his fate like his father's spirit, mirrored in the eye of
a snake? And all those questions! You're standing on the same
earth you've always stood upon. This voice you hear is mine,
Oluhun-iyo, not that of an acolyte in heaven.

ELESIN.   How can that be? In all my life
                            As Horseman of the King, the juiciest
                            Fruit on every tree was mine. I saw,
                            I touched, I wooed, rarely was the answer No.
                            The honour of my place, the veneration I

> Received in the eye of man or woman
> Prospered my suit and
> Played havoc with my sleeping hours.
> And they tell me my eyes were a hawk
> In perpetual hunger. Split an iroko tree
> In two, hide a woman's beauty in its heartwood
> And seal it up again – Elesin, journeying by,
> Would make his camp beside that tree
> Of all the shades in the forest.

PRAISE-SINGER. Who would deny your reputation, snake-on-the-loose in dark passages of the market! Bed-bug who wages war on the mat and receives the thanks of the vanquished! When caught with his bride's own sister he protested – but I was only prostrating myself to her as becomes a grateful in-law. Hunter who carries his powder-horn on the hips and fires crouching or standing! Warrior who never makes that excuse of the whining coward – but how can I go to battle without my trousers? – trouserless or shirtless it's all one to him. Oka-rearing-from-a-camouflage-of-leaves, before he strikes the victim is already prone! Once they told me, Howu, a stallion does not feed on the grass beneath him: he replied, true, but surely he can roll on it!

WOMEN. Ba-a-a-ba O!

PRAISE-SINGER. Ah, but listen yet. You know there is the leaf-knibbling grub and there is the cola-chewing beetle; the leaf-nibbling grub lives on the leaf, the cola-chewing beetle lives in the colanut. Don't we know what our man feeds on when we find him cocooned in a woman's wrapper?

ELESIN.   Enough, enough, you all have cause
> To know me well. But, if you say this earth
> Is still the same as gave birth to those songs,
> Tell me who was that goddess through whose
>   lips
> I saw the ivory pebbles of Oya's river-bed.
> Iyaloja, who is she? I saw her enter

Your stall; all your daughters I know well.
No, not even Ogun-of-the-farm toiling
Dawn till dusk on his tuber patch
Not even Ogun with the finest hoe he ever
Forged at the anvil could have shaped
That rise of buttocks, not though he had
The richest earth between his fingers.
Her wrapper was no disguise
For thighs whose ripples shamed the river's
Coils around the hills of Ilesi. Her eyes
Were new-laid eggs glowing in the dark.
Her skin . . .

IYALOJA. Elesin Oba . . .

ELESIN. What! Where do you all say I am?

IYALOJA. Still among the living.

ELESIN.   And that radiance which so suddenly
                           Lit up this market I could boast
                           I knew so well?

IYALOJA. Has one step already in her husband's home. She is
betrothed.

ELESIN (*irritated*). Why do you tell me that?

   IYALOJA *falls silent. The* WOMEN *shuffle uneasily.*

IYALOJA. Not because we dare give you offence Elesin. Today is
your day and the whole world is yours. Still, even those who
leave town to make a new dwelling elsewhere like to be remembered by what they leave behind.

ELESIN.   Who does not seek to be remembered?
                           Memory is Master of Death, the chink
                           In his armour of conceit. I shall leave
                           That which makes my going the sheerest
                           Dream of an afternoon. Should voyagers
                           Not travel light? Let the considerate traveller
                           Shed, of his excessive load, all
                           That may benefit the living.

WOMEN (*relieved*). Ah Elesin Oba, we knew you for a man of honour.

ELESIN. Then honour me. I deserve a bed of honour to lie upon.

IYALOJA. The best is yours. We know you for a man of honour. You are not one who eats and leaves nothing on his plate for children. Did you not say it yourself? Not one who blights the happiness of others for a moment's pleasure.

ELESIN.   Who speaks of pleasure? O women, listen!
                 Pleasure palls. Our acts should have meaning.
                 The sap of the plantain never dries.
                 You have seen the young shoot swelling
                 Even as the parent stalks begins to wither.
                 Women, let my going be likened to
                 The twilight hour of the plantain.

WOMEN. What does he mean Iyaloja? This language is the language of our elders, we do not fully grasp it.

IYALOJA. I dare not understand you yet Elesin.

ELESIN.   All you who stand before the spirit that dares
                 The opening of the last door of passage,
                 Dare to rid my going of regrets! My wish
                 Transcends the blotting out of thought
                 In one mere moment's tremor of the senses.
                 Do me credit. And do me honour.
                 I am girded for the route beyond
                 Burdens of waste and longing.
                 Then let me travel light. Let
                 Seed that will not serve the stomach
                 On the way remain behind. Let it take root
                 In the earth of my choice, in this earth
                 I leave behind.

IYALOJA (*turns to* WOMEN). The voice I hear is already touched by the waiting fingers of our departed. I dare not refuse.

WOMAN. But Iyaloja . . .

IYALOJA. The matter is no longer in our hands.

WOMAN. But she is betrothed to your own son. Tell him.

IYALOJA. My son's wish is mine. I did the asking for him, the loss can be remedied. But who will remedy the blight of closed hands on the day when all should be openness and light? Tell him, you say! You wish that I burden him with knowledge that will sour his wish and lay regrets on the last moments of his mind. You pray to him who is your intercessor to the world – don't set this world adrift in your own time; would you rather it was my hand whose sacrilege wrenched it loose?

WOMAN. Not many men will brave the curse of a dispossessed husband.

IYALOJA. Only the curses of the departed are to be feared. The claims of one whose foot is on the threshold of their abode surpasses even the claims of blood. It is impiety even to place hindrances in their ways.

ELESIN.   What do my mothers say? Shall I step
            Burdened into the unknown?

IYALOJA. Not we, but the very earth says No. The sap in the plantain does not dry. Let grain that will not feed the voyager at his passage drop here and take root as he steps beyond this earth and us. Oh you who fill the home from hearth to threshold with the voices of children, you who now bestride the hidden gulf and pause to draw the right foot across and into the resting-home of the great forebears, it is good that your loins be drained into the earth we know, that your last strength be ploughed back into the womb that gave you being.

PRAISE-SINGER. Iyaloja, mother of multitudes in the teeming market of the world, how your wisdom transfigures you!

IYALOJA (*smiling broadly, completely reconciled*). Elesin, even at the narrow end of the passage I know you will look back and sigh a last regret for the flesh that flashed past your spirit in flight. You always had a restless eye. Your choice has my blessing. (*To the* WOMEN.) Take the good news to our daughter and make her ready. (*Some* WOMEN *go off.*)

ELESIN. Your eyes were clouded at first.

IYALOJA. Not for long. It is those who stand at the gateway of the great change to whose cry we must pay heed. And then, think of this — it makes the mind tremble. The fruit of such a union is rare. It will be neither of this world nor of the next. Nor of the one behind us. As if the timelessness of the ancestor world and the unborn have joined spirits to wring an issue of the elusive being of passage . . . Elesin!

ELESIN. I am here. What is it?

IYALOJA. Did you hear all I said just now?

ELESIN. Yes.

IYALOJA. The living must eat and drink. When the moment comes, don't turn the food to rodents' droppings in their mouth. Don't let them taste the ashes of the world when they step out at dawn to breathe the morning dew.

ELESIN. This doubt is unworthy of you Iyaloja.

IYALOJA. Eating the awusa nut is not so difficult as drinking water afterwards.

ELESIN.   The waters of the bitter stream are honey to
                         a man
                    Whose tongue has savoured all.

IYALOJA. No one knows when the ants desert their home; they leave the mound intact. The swallow is never seen to peck holes in its nest when it is time to move with the season. There are always throngs of humanity behind the leave-taker. The rain should not come through the roof for them, the wind must not blow through the walls at night.

ELESIN. I refuse to take offence.

IYALOJA. You wish to travel light. Well, the earth is yours. But be sure the seed you leave in it attracts no curse.

ELESIN. You really mistake my person Iyaloja.

IYALOJA. I said nothing. Now we must go prepare your bridal chamber. Then these same hands will lay your shrouds.

ELESIN (exasperated). Must you be so blunt? (Recovers.) Well, weave your shrouds, but let the fingers of my bride seal my eyelids with earth and wash my body.

IYALOJA. Prepare yourself Elesin.

She gets up to leave. At that moment the WOMEN *return, leading the* BRIDE. ELESIN'S *face glows with pleasure. He flicks the sleeves of his agbada with renewed confidence and steps forward to meet the group. As the girl kneels before* IYALOJA, *lights fade out on the scene.*

SCENE TWO

The verandah of the District Officer's bungalow. A tango is playing from an old hand-cranked gramophone and, glimpsed through the wide windows and doors which open onto the forestage verandah are the shapes of SIMON PILKINGS *and his wife,* JANE, *tangoing in and out of shadows in the living-room. They are wearing what is immediately apparent as some form of fancy-dress. The dance goes on for some moments and then the figure of a 'Native Administration'* POLICEMAN *emerges and climbs up the steps onto the verandah. He peeps through and observes the dancing couple, reacting with what is obviously a long-standing bewilderment. He stiffens suddenly, his expression changes to one of disbelief and horror. In his excitement he upsets a flower-pot and attracts the attention of the couple. They stop dancing.*

PILKINGS. Is there anyone out there?

JANE. I'll turn off the gramophone.

PILKINGS (*approaching the verandah*). I'm sure I heard something fall over. (*The* CONSTABLE *retreats slowly, open-mouthed as* PILKINGS *approaches the verandah.*) Oh it's you Amusa. Why didn't you just knock instead of knocking things over?

AMUSA (*stammers badly and points a shaky finger at his dress*).

Mista Pirinkin . . . Mista Pirinkin . . .

PILKINGS. What is the matter with you?

JANE (*emerging*). Who is it dear? Oh, Amusa . . .

PILKINGS. Yes it's Amusa, and acting most strangely.

AMUSA (*his attention now transferred to* MRS PILKINGS).
Mammadam . . . you too!

PILKINGS. What the hell is the matter with you man!

JANE. Your costume darling. Our fancy dress.

PILKINGS. Oh hell, I'd forgotten all about that. (*Lifts the face mask over his head showing his face. His* WIFE *follows suit.*)

JANE. I think you've shocked his big pagan heart bless him.

PILKINGS. Nonsense, he's a Moslem. Come on Amusa, you don't believe in all that nonsense do you? I thought you were a good Moslem.

AMUSA. Mista Pirinkin, I beg you sir, what you think you do with that dress? It belong to dead cult, not for human being.

PILKINGS. Oh Amusa, what a let down you are. I swear by you at the club you know – thank God for Amusa, he doesn't believe in any mumbo-jumbo. And now look at you!

AMUSA. Mista Pirinkin, I beg you, take it off. Is not good for man like you to touch that cloth.

PILKINGS. Well, I've got it on. And what's more Jane and I have bet on it we're taking first prize at the ball. Now, if you can just pull yourself together and tell me what you wanted to see me about . . .

AMUSA. Sir, I cannot talk this matter to you in that dress. I no fit.

PILKINGS. What's that rubbish again?

JANE. He is dead earnest too Simon. I think you'll have to handle this delicately.

PILKINGS. Delicately my . . .! Look here Amusa, I think this little joke has gone far enough hm? Let's have some sense. You seem to forget that you are a police officer in the service of His Majesty's Government. I order you to report your business at once or face disciplinary action.

AMUSA. Sir, it is a matter of death. How can man talk against death to person in uniform of death? Is like talking against government to person in uniform of police. Please sir, I go and come back.

PILKINGS (*roars*). Now! (AMUSA *switches his gaze to the ceiling suddenly, remains mute.*)

JANE. Oh Amusa, what is there to be scared of in the costume? You saw it confiscated last month from those *egungun* men who were creating trouble in town. You helped arrest the cult leaders yourself – if the juju didn't harm you at the time how could it possibly harm you now? And merely by looking at it?

AMUSA (*without looking down*). Madam, I arrest the ringleaders who make trouble but me I no touch *egungun*. That *egungun* inself, I no touch. And I no abuse 'am. I arrest ringleader but I treat *egungun* with respect.

PILKINGS. It's hopeless. We'll merely end up missing the best part of the ball. When they get this way there is nothing you can do. It's simply hammering against a brick wall. Write your report or whatever it is on that pad Amusa and take yourself out of here. Come on Jane. We only upset his delicate sensibilities by remaining here.

AMUSA *waits for them to leave, then writes in the notebook, somewhat laboriously. Drumming from the direction of the town wells up.* AMUSA *listens, makes a movement as if he wants to recall* PILKINGS *but changes his mind. Completes his note and goes. A few moments later* PILKINGS *emerges, picks up the pad and reads.*

Jane!

JANE (*from the bedroom*). Coming darling. Nearly ready.

PILKINGS. Never mind being ready, just listen to this.

JANE. What is it?

PILKINGS. Amusa's report. Listen. 'I have to report that it come to my information that one prominent chief, namely, the Elesin

Oba, is to commit death tonight as a result of native custom. Because this is criminal offence I await further instruction at charge office. Sergeant Amusa.'

JANE *comes out onto the verandah while he is reading.*

JANE. Did I hear you say commit death?

PILKINGS. Obviously he means murder.

JANE. You mean a ritual murder?

PILKINGS. Must be. You think you've stamped it all out but it's always lurking under the surface somewhere.

JANE. Oh. Does it mean we are not getting to the ball at all?

PILKINGS. No-o. I'll have the man arrested. Everyone remotely involved. In any case there may be nothing to it. Just rumours.

JANE. Really? I thought you found Amusa's rumours generally reliable.

PILKINGS. That's true enough. But who knows what may have been giving him the scare lately. Look at his conduct tonight.

JANE (*laughing*). You have to admit he had his own peculiar logic. (*Deepens her voice.*) How can man talk against death to person in uniform of death? (*Laughs.*) Anyway, you can't go into the police station dressed like that.

PILKINGS. I'll send Joseph with instructions. Damn it, what a confounded nuisance!

JANE. But don't you think you should talk first to the man, Simon?

PILKINGS. Do you want to go to the ball or not?

JANE. Darling, why are you getting rattled? I was only trying to be intelligent. It seems hardly fair just to lock up a man – and a chief at that—simply on the er ... what is the legal word again?— uncorroborated word of a sergeant.

PILKINGS. Well, that's easily decided. Joseph!

JOSEPH (*from within*). Yes master.

PILKINGS. You're quite right of course, I am getting rattled. Probably the effect of those bloody drums. Do you hear how they go on and on?

JANE. I wondered when you'd notice. Do you suppose it has something to do with this affair?

PILKINGS. Who knows? They always find an excuse for making a noise . . . (*Thoughtfully.*) Even so . . .

JANE. Yes Simon?

PILKINGS. It's different Jane. I don't think I've heard this particular – sound – before. Something unsettling about it.

JANE. I thought all bush drumming sounded the same.

PILKINGS. Don't tease me now Jane. This may be serious.

JANE. I'm sorry. (*Gets up and throws her arms around his neck. Kisses him. The houseboy enters, retreats and knocks.*)

PILKINGS (*wearily*). Oh, come in Joseph! I don't know where you pick up all these elephantine notions of tact. Come over here.

JOSEPH. Sir?

PILKINGS. Joseph, are you a Christian or not?

JOSEPH. Yessir.

PILKINGS. Does seeing me in this outfit bother you?

JOSEPH. No sir, it has no power.

PILKINGS. Thank God for some sanity at last. Now Joseph, answer me on the honour of a Christian – what is supposed to be going on in town tonight?

JOSEPH. Tonight sir? You mean the chief who is going to kill himself?

PILKINGS. What?

JANE. What do you mean, kill himself?

PILKINGS. You do mean he is going to kill somebody don't you?

JOSEPH. No master. He will not kill anybody and no one will kill him. He will simply die.

JANE. But why Joseph?

JOSEPH. It is native law and custom. The King die last month. Tonight is his burial. But before they can bury him, the Elesin must die so as to accompany him to heaven.

PILKINGS. I seem to be fated to clash more often with that man than with any of the other chiefs.

JOSEPH. He is the King's Chief Horseman.

PILKINGS (*in a resigned way*). I know.

JANE. Simon, what's the matter?

PILKINGS. It would have to be him!

JANE. Who is he?

PILKINGS. Don't you remember? He's that chief with whom I had a scrap some three or four years ago. I helped his son get to a medical school in England, remember? He fought tooth and nail to prevent it.

JANE. Oh now I remember. He was that very sensitive young man. What was his name again?

PILKINGS. Olunde. Haven't replied to his last letter come to think of it. The old pagan wanted him to stay and carry on some family tradition or the other. Honestly I couldn't understand the fuss he made. I literally had to help the boy escape from close confinement and load him onto the next boat. A most intelligent boy, really bright.

JANE. I rather thought he was much too sensitive you know. The kind of person you feel should be a poet munching rose petals in Bloomsbury.

PILKINGS. Well, he's going to make a first-class doctor. His mind is set on that. And as long as he wants my help he is welcome to it.

JANE (*after a pause*). Simon.

PILKINGS. Yes?

JANE. This boy, he was the eldest son wasn't he?

PILKINGS. I'm not sure. Who could tell with that old ram?

JANE. Do you know, Joseph?

JOSEPH. Oh yes madam. He was the eldest son. That's why Elesin cursed master good and proper. The eldest son is not supposed to travel away from the land.

JANE (*giggling*). Is that true Simon? Did he really curse you good and proper?

PILKINGS. By all accounts I should be dead by now.

JOSEPH. Oh no, master is white man. And good Christian. Black man juju can't touch master.

JANE. If he was his eldest, it means that he would be the Elesin to the next king. It's a family thing isn't it Joseph?

JOSEPH. Yes madam. And if this Elesin had died before the King, his eldest son must take his place.

JANE. That would explain why the old chief was so mad you took the boy away.

PILKINGS. Well it makes me all the more happy I did.

JANE. I wonder if he knew.

PILKINGS. Who? Oh, you mean Olunde?

JANE. Yes. Was that why he was so determined to get away? I wouldn't stay if I knew I was trapped in such a horrible custom.

PILKINGS (*thoughtfully*). No, I don't think he knew. At least he gave no indication. But you couldn't really tell with him. He was rather close you know, quite unlike most of them. Didn't give much away, not even to me.

JANE. Aren't they all rather close, Simon?

PILKINGS. These natives here? Good gracious. They'll open their mouths and yap with you about their family secrets before you can stop them. Only the other day . . .

JANE. But Simon, do they really give anything away? I mean, anything that really counts. This affair for instance, we didn't know they still practised that custom did we?

PILKINGS. Ye-e-es, I suppose you're right there. Sly, devious bastards.

JOSEPH (*stiffly*). Can I go now master? I have to clean the kitchen.

PILKINGS. What? Oh, you can go. Forget you were still here.

JOSEPH *goes*.

JANE. Simon, you really must watch your language. Bastard isn't just a simple swear-word in these parts, you know.

PILKINGS. Look, just when did you become a social anthropologist, that's what I'd like to know.

JANE. I'm not claiming to know anything. I just happen to have overheard quarrels among the servants. That's how I know they consider it a smear.

PILKINGS. I thought the extended family system took care of all that. Elastic family, no bastards.

JANE (*shrugs*). Have it your own way.

Awkward silence. The drumming increases in volume. JANE *gets up suddenly, restless.*

That drumming Simon, do you think it might really be connected with this ritual? It's been going on all evening.

PILKINGS. Let's ask our native guide. Joseph! Just a minute Joseph. (JOSEPH *re-enters*.) What's the drumming about?

JOSEPH. I don't know master.

PILKINGS. What do you mean you don't know? It's only two years since your conversion. Don't tell me all that holy water nonsense also wiped out your tribal memory.

JOSEPH (*visibly shocked*). Master!

JANE. Now you've done it.

PILKINGS. What have I done now?

JANE. Never mind. Listen Joseph, just tell me this. Is that drumming connected with dying or anything of that nature?

JOSEPH. Madam, this is what I am trying to say: I am not sure. It sounds like the death of a great chief and then, it sounds like the wedding of a great chief. It really mix me up.

PILKINGS. Oh get back to the kitchen. A fat lot of help you are.

JOSEPH. Yes master. (*Goes.*)

JANE. Simon . . .

PILKINGS. All right, all right. I'm in no mood for preaching.

JANE. It isn't my preaching you have to worry about, it's the preaching of the missionaries who preceded you here. When they make converts they really convert them. Calling holy water nonsense to our Joseph is really like insulting the Virgin Mary before a Roman Catholic. He's going to hand in his notice tomorrow you mark my word.

PILKINGS. Now you're being ridiculous.

JANE. Am I? What are you willing to bet that tomorrow we are going to be without a steward-boy? Did you see his face?

PILKINGS. I am more concerned about whether or not we will be one native chief short by tomorrow. Christ! Just listen to those drums. (*He strides up and down, undecided.*)

JANE (*getting up*). I'll change and make up some supper.

PILKINGS. What's that?

JANE. Simon, it's obvious we have to miss this ball.

PILKINGS. Nonsense. It's the first bit of real fun the European club has managed to organise for over a year, I'm damned if I'm going to miss it. And it is a rather special occasion. Doesn't happen every day.

JANE. You know this business has to be stopped Simon. And you are the only man who can do it.

PILKINGS. I don't have to stop anything. If they want to throw themselves off the top of a cliff or poison themselves for the sake of some barbaric custom what is that to me? If it were ritual murder or something like that I'd be duty-bound to do something. I can't keep an eye on all the potential suicides in this province. And as for that man – believe me it's good riddance.

JANE (*laughs*). I know you better than that Simon. You are going to have to do something to stop it – after you've finished blustering.

PILKINGS (*shouts after her*). And suppose after all it's only a wedding? I'd look a proper fool if I interrupted a chief on his honeymoon, wouldn't I? (*Resumes his angry stride, slows down.*) Ah well, who can tell what those chiefs actually do on their honeymoon anyway? (*He takes up the pad and scribbles rapidly on it.*) Joseph! Joseph! Joseph! (*Some moments later* JOSEPH *puts in a sulky appearance.*) Did you hear me call you? Why the hell didn't you answer?

JOSEPH. I didn't hear master.

PILKINGS. You didn't hear me! How come you are here then?

JOSEPH (*stubbornly*). I didn't hear master.

PILKINGS (*controls himself with an effort*). We'll talk about it in

the morning. I want you to take this note directly to Sergeant
Amusa. You'll find him at the charge office. Get on your bicycle
and race there with it. I expect you back in twenty minutes
exactly. Twenty minutes, is that clear?

JOSEPH. Yes master (*Going.*)

PILKINGS. Oh er . . . Joseph.

JOSEPH. Yes master?

PILKINGS (*between gritted teeth*). Er . . . forget what I said just
now. The holy water is not nonsense. *I* was talking nonsense.

JOSEPH. Yes master (*Goes.*)

JANE (*pokes her head round the door*). Have you found him?

PILKINGS. Found who?

JANE. Joseph. Weren't you shouting for him?

PILKINGS. Oh yes, he turned up finally.

JANE. You sounded desperate. What was it all about?

PILKINGS. Oh nothing. I just wanted to apologise to him. Assure
him that the holy water isn't really nonsense.

JANE. Oh? And how did he take it?

PILKINGS. Who the hell gives a damn! I had a sudden vision of
our Very Reverend Macfarlane drafting another letter of complaint to the Resident about my unchristian language towards his
parishioners.

JANE. Oh I think he's given up on you by now.

PILKINGS. Don't be too sure. And anyway, I wanted to make sure
Joseph didn't 'lose' my note on the way. He looked sufficiently
full of the holy crusade to do some such thing.

JANE. If you've finished exaggerating, come and have something to
eat.

PILKINGS. No, put it all away. We can still get to the ball.

JANE. Simon . . .

PILKINGS. Get your costume back on. Nothing to worry about.
I've instructed Amusa to arrest the man and lock him up.

JANE. But that station is hardly secure Simon. He'll soon get his
friends to help him escape.

PILKINGS. A-ah, that's where I have out-thought you. I'm not having him put in the station cell. Amusa will bring him right here and lock him up in my study. And he'll stay with him till we get back. No one will dare come here to incite him to anything.

JANE. How clever of you darling. I'll get ready.

PILKINGS. Hey.

JANE. Yes darling.

PILKINGS. I have a surprise for you. I was going to keep it until we actually got to the ball.

JANE. What is it?

PILKINGS. You know the Prince is on a tour of the colonies don't you? Well, he docked in the capital only this morning but he is already at the Residency. He is going to grace the ball with his presence later tonight.

JANE. Simon! Not really.

PILKINGS. Yes he is. He's been invited to give away the prizes and he has agreed. You must admit old Engleton is the best Club Secretary we ever had. Quick off the mark that lad.

JANE. But how thrilling.

PILKINGS. The other provincials are going to be damned envious.

JANE. I wonder what he'll come as.

PILKINGS. Oh I don't know. As a coat-of-arms perhaps. Anyway it won't be anything to touch this.

JANE. Well that's lucky. If we are to be presented I won't have to start looking for a pair of gloves. It's all sewn on.

PILKINGS (*laughing*). Quite right. Trust a woman to think of that. Come on, let's get going.

JANE (*rushing off*). Won't be a second. (*Stops.*) Now I see why you've been so edgy all evening. I thought you weren't handling this affair with your usual brilliance — to begin with that is.

PILKINGS (*his mood is much improved*). Shut up woman and get your things on.

JANE. All right boss, coming.

   PILKINGS *suddenly begins to hum the tango to which they were dancing before. Starts to execute a few practice steps. Lights fade.*

SCENE THREE

A swelling, agitated hum of women's voices rises immediately in the background. The lights come on and we see the frontage of a converted cloth stall in the market. The floor leading up to the entrance is covered in rich velvets and woven cloth. The WOMEN *come on stage, borne backwards by the determined progress of Sergeant* AMUSA *and his two* CONSTABLES *who already have their batons out and use them as a pressure against the* WOMEN. *At the edge of the cloth-covered floor however the* WOMEN *take a determined stand and block all further progress of the* MEN. *They begin to tease them mercilessly.*

AMUSA. I am tell you women for last time to commot my road. I am here on official business.

WOMAN. Official business you white man's eunuch? Official business is taking place where you want to go and it's a business you wouldn't understand.

WOMAN (*makes a quick tug at the* CONSTABLE'S *baton*). That doesn't fool anyone you know. It's the one you carry under your government knickers that counts. (*She bends low as if to peep under the baggy shorts. The embarrassed* CONSTABLE *quickly puts his knees together. The* WOMEN *roar.*)

WOMAN. You mean there is nothing there at all?

WOMAN. Oh there was something. You know that handbell which the whiteman uses to summon his servants . . .?

AMUSA (*he manages to preserve some dignity throughout*). I hope you women know that interfering with officer in execution of his duty is criminal offence.

WOMAN. Interfere? He says we're interfering with him. You foolish man we're telling you there's nothing to interfere with.

AMUSA. I am order you now to clear the road.

WOMAN. What road? The one your father built?

WOMAN. You are a policeman not so? Then you know what they call trespassing in court. Or – (*Pointing to the cloth-lined steps.*) – do you think that kind of road is built for every kind of feet.

WOMAN. Go back and tell the white man who sent you to come himself.

AMUSA. If I go I will come back with reinforcement. And we will all return carrying wapons.

WOMAN. Oh, now I understand. Before they can put on those knickers the white man first cuts off their weapons.

WOMAN. What a cheek! You mean you come here to show power to women and you don't even have a weapon.

AMUSA (*shouting above the laughter*). For the last time I warn you women to clear the road.

WOMAN. To where?

AMUSA. To that hut. I know he dey dere.

WOMAN. Who?

AMUSA. The chief who call himself Elesin Oba.

WOMAN. You ignorant man. It is not he who calls himself Elesin Oba, it is his blood that says it. As it called out to his father before him and will to his son after him. And that is in spite of everything your white man can do.

WOMAN. Is it not the same ocean that washes this land and the white man's land? Tell your white man he can hide our son away as long as he likes. When the time comes for him, the same ocean will bring him back.

AMUSA. The government say dat kin' ting must stop.

WOMAN. Who will stop it? You? Tonight our husband and father will prove himself greater than the laws of strangers.

AMUSA. I tell you nobody go prove anyting tonight or anytime. Is ignorant and criminal to prove dat kin' prove.

IYALOJA (*entering from the hut. She is accompanied by a group*

of young girls who have been attending the BRIDE). What is it
Amusa? Why do you come here to disturb the happiness of
others.

AMUSA. Madame Iyaloja, I glad you come. You know me, I no like
trouble but duty is duty. I am here to arrest Elesin for criminal
intent. Tell these women to stop obstructing me in the performance of my duty.

IYALOJA. And you? What gives you the right to obstruct our
leader of men in the performance of his duty.

AMUSA. What kin' duty be dat one Iyaloja.

IYALOJA. What kin' duty? What kin' duty does a man have to his
new bride?

AMUSA (*bewildered, looks at the women and at the entrance to the
hut*). Iyaloja, is it wedding you call dis kin' ting?

IYALOJA. You have wives haven't you? Whatever the white man
has done to you he hasn't stopped you having wives. And if he
has, at least he is married. If you don't know what a marriage is,
go and ask him to tell you.

AMUSA. This no to wedding.

IYALOJA. And ask him at the same time what he would have done
if anyone had come to disturb him on his wedding night.

AMUSA. Iyaloja, I say dis no to wedding.

IYALOJA. You want to look inside the bridal chamber? You want
to see for yourself how a man cuts the virgin knot?

AMUSA. Madam . . .

WOMAN. Perhaps his wives are still waiting for him to learn.

AMUSA. Iyaloja, make you tell dese women make den no insult me
again. If I hear dat kin' insult once more . . .

GIRL (*pushing her way through*). You will do what?

GIRL. He's out of his mind. It's our mothers you're talking to, do
you know that? Not to any illiterate villager you can bully and
terrorise. How dare you intrude here anyway?

GIRL. What a cheek, what impertinence!

GIRL. You've treated them too gently. Now let them see what it is
to tamper with the mothers of this market.

GIRL. Your betters dare not enter the market when the women say no!

GIRL. Haven't you learnt that yet, you jester in khaki and starch?

IYALOJA. Daughters . . .

GIRL. No no Iyaloja, leave us to deal with him. He no longer knows his mother, we'll teach him.

With a sudden movement they snatch the batons of the two CONSTABLES. *They begin to hem them in.*

GIRL. What next? We have your batons? What next? What are you going to do?

With equally swift movements they knock off their hats.

GIRL. Move if you dare. We have your hats, what will you do about it? Didn't the white man teach you to take off your hats before women?

IYALOJA. It's a wedding night. It's a night of joy for us. Peace . . .

GIRL. Not for him. Who asked him here?

GIRL. Does he dare go to the Residency without an invitation?

GIRL. Not even where the servants eat the left-overs.

GIRLS (*in turn. In an 'English' accent*). Well well it's Mister Amusa. Were you invited? (*Play-acting to one another. The older women encourage them with their titters.*)
    – Your invitation card please?
    – Who are you? Have we been introduced?
    – And who did you say you were?
    – Sorry, I didn't quite catch your name.
    – May I take your hat?
    – If you insist. May I take yours? (*Exchanging the* POLICE-MEN'S *hats.*)
    – How very kind of you.
    – Not at all. Won't you sit down?
    – After you.

— Oh no.

— I insist.

— You're most gracious.

— And how do you find the place?

— The natives are all right.

— Friendly?

— Tractable.

— Not a teeny-weeny bit restless?

— Well, a teeny-weeny bit restless.

— One might even say, difficult?

— Indeed one might be tempted to say, difficult.

— But you do manage to cope?

— Yes indeed I do. I have a rather faithful ox called Amusa.

— He's loyal?

— Absolutely.

— Lay down his life for you what?

— Without a moment's thought.

— Had one like that once. Trust him with my life.

— Mostly of course they are liars.

— Never known a native to tell the truth.

— Does it get rather close around here?

— It's mild for this time of the year.

— But the rains may still come.

— They are late this year aren't they?

— They are keeping African time.

— Ha ha ha ha

— Ha ha ha ha

— The humidity is what gets me.

— It used to be whisky

— Ha ha ha ha

— Ha ha ha ha

— What's your handicap old chap?

— Is there racing by golly?

— Splendid golf course, you'll like it.

— I'm beginning to like it already.

– And a European club, exclusive.

– You've kept the flag flying.

– We do our best for the old country.

– It's a pleasure to serve.

– Another whisky old chap?

– You are indeed too too kind.

– Not at all sir. Where is that boy? (*With a sudden bellow.*) Sergeant!

AMUSA (*snaps to attention*). Yessir!

The WOMEN *collapse with laughter.*

GIRL. Take your men out of here.

AMUSA (*realising the trick, he rages from loss of face*). I'm give you warning . . .

GIRL. All right then. Off with his knickers! (*They surge slowly forward.*)

IYALOJA. Daughters, please.

AMUSA (*squaring himself for defence*). The first woman wey touch me . . .

IYALOJA. My children, I beg of you . . .

GIRL. Then tell him to leave this market. This is the home of our mothers. We don't want the eater of white left-overs at the feast their hands have prepared.

IYALOJA. You heard them Amusa. You had better go.

GIRL. Now!

AMUSA (*commencing his retreat*). We dey go now, but make you no say we no warn you.

GIRLS. Now!

GIRL. Before we read the riot act – you should know all about that.

AMUSA. Make we go. (*They depart, more precipitately.*)

The WOMEN *strike their palms across in the gesture of wonder.*

WOMEN. Do they teach you all that at school?

WOMAN. And to think I nearly kept Apinke away from the place.

WOMAN. Did you hear them? Did you see how they mimicked the white man?

WOMAN. The voices exactly. Hey, there are wonders in this world!

IYALOJA. Well, our elders have said it: Dada may be weak, but he has a younger sibling who is truly fearless.

WOMAN. The next time the white man shows his face in this market I will set Wuraola on his tail.

A WOMAN *bursts into song and dance of euphoria — 'Tani l'awa o l'ogbeja? Kayi! A l'ogbeja. Omo Kekere l'ogbeja.'* The rest of the* WOMEN *join in, some placing the* GIRLS *on their back like infants, others dancing round them. The dance becomes general, mounting in excitement.* ELESIN *appears, in wrapper only. In his hands a white velvet cloth folded loosely as if it held some delicate object. He cries out.*

ELESIN. Oh you mothers of beautiful brides! (*The dancing stops. They turn and see him, and the object in his hands.* IYALOJA *approaches and gently takes the cloth from him.*) Take it. It is no mere virgin stain, but the union of life and the seeds of passage. My vital flow, the last from this flesh is intermingled with the promise of future life. All is prepared. Listen! (*A steady drumbeat from the distance.*) Yes. It is nearly time. The King's dog has been killed. The King's favourite horse is about to follow his master. My brother chiefs know their task and perform it well. (*He listens again.*)

The BRIDE *emerges, stands shyly by the door. He turns to her.*

Our marriage is not yet wholly fulfilled. When earth and passage wed, the consummation is complete only when there are grains of

---

**'Who says we haven't a defender? Silence! We have our defenders. Little children are our champions.'*

earth on the eyelids of passage. Stay by me till then. My faithful drummers, do me your last service. This is where I have chosen to do my leave-taking, in this heart of life, this hive which contains the swarm of the world in its small compass. This is where I have known love and laughter away from the palace. Even the richest food cloys when eaten days on end; in the market, nothing ever cloys. Listen. (*They listen to the drums.*) They have begun to seek out the heart of the King's favourite horse. Soon it will ride in its bolt of raffia with the dog at its feet. Together they will ride on the shoulders of the King's grooms through the pulse centres of the town. They know it is here I shall await them. I have told them. (*His eyes appear to cloud. He passes his hand over them as if to clear his sight. He gives a faint smile.*) It promises well; just then I felt my spirit's eagerness. The kite makes for wide spaces and the wind creeps up behind its tail; can the kite say less than – thank you, the quicker the better? But wait a while my spirit. Wait. Wait for the coming of the courier of the King. Do you know friends, the horse is born to this one destiny, to bear the burden that is man upon its back. Except for this night, this night alone when the spotless stallion will ride in triumph on the back of man. In the time of my father I witnessed the strange sight. Perhaps tonight also I shall see it for the last time. If they arrive before the drums beat for me, I shall tell him to let the Alafin know I follow swiftly. If they come after the drums have sounded, why then, all is well for I have gone ahead. Our spirits shall fall in step along the great passage. (*He listens to the drums. He seems again to be falling into a state of semi-hypnosis; his eyes scan the sky but it is in a kind of daze. His voice is a little breathless.*) The moon has fed, a glow from its full stomach fills the sky and air, but I cannot tell where is that gateway through which I must pass. My faithful friends, let our feet touch together this last time, lead me into the other market with sounds that cover my skin with down yet make my limbs strike earth like a thoroughbred. Dear mothers, let me dance into the passage even as I have lived beneath your roofs. (*He comes down progressively among them. They make way for him, the drummers playing. His dance is one of solemn, regal motions, each gesture of the body is made with a solemn finality. The* WOMEN *join him, their steps a somewhat more fluid version of his. Beneath the* PRAISE-SINGER's *exhortations the* WOMEN *dirge 'Ale le le, awo mi lo'.*)

PRAISE-SINGER. Elesin Alafin, can you hear my voice?

ELESIN. Faintly, my friend, faintly.

PRAISE-SINGER. Elesin Alafin, can you hear my call?

ELESIN. Faintly my king, faintly.

PRAISE-SINGER. Is your memory sound Elesin?
Shall my voice be a blade of grass and
Tickle the armpit of the past?

ELESIN. My memory needs no prodding but
What do you wish to say to me?

PRAISE-SINGER. Only what has been spoken. Only what concerns
The dying wish of the father of all.

ELESIN. It is buried like seed-yam in my mind
This is the season of quick rains, the harvest
Is this moment due for gathering.

PRAISE-SINGER. If you cannot come, I said, swear
You'll tell my favourite horse. I shall
Ride on through the gates alone.

ELESIN. Elesin's message will be read
Only when his loyal heart no longer beats.

PRAISE-SINGER. If you cannot come Elesin, tell my dog.
I cannot stay the keeper too long
At the gate.

ELESIN. A dog does not outrun the hand
That feeds it meat. A horse that
throws its rider
Slows down to a stop. Elesin Alafin
Trusts no beasts with messages between
A king and his companion.

PRAISE-SINGER. If you get lost my dog will track
The hidden path to me.

ELESIN. The seven-way crossroads confuses
Only the stranger. The Horseman of the King
Was born in the recesses of the house.

PRAISE-SINGER. I know the wickedness of men. If there is
Weight on the loose end of your sash, such
weight
As no mere man can shift; if your sash is
earthed
By evil minds who mean to part us at the
last . . .

ELESIN. My sash is of the deep purple *alari*;
It is no tethering-rope. The elephant
Trails no tethering-rope; that king
Is not yet crowned who will peg an elephant –
Not even you my friend and King.

PRAISE-SINGER. And yet this fear will not depart from me
The darkness of this new abode is deep –
Will your human eyes suffice?

ELESIN. In a night which falls before our eyes
However deep, we do not miss our way.

PRAISE-SINGER. Shall I now not acknowledge I have stood
Where wonders met their end? The elephant
deserves
Better than that we say 'I have caught
A glimpse of something'. If we see the tamer
Of the forest let us say plainly, we have seen
An elephant.

ELESIN (*his voice is drowsy*).
I have freed myself of earth and now
It's getting dark. Strange voices guide my feet.

PRAISE-SINGER. The river is never so high that the eyes
Of a fish are covered. The night is not so dark
That the albino fails to find his way. A child

> Returning homewards craves no leading by
>   the hand.
> Gracefully does the mask regain his grove at
>   the end of the day . . .
> Gracefully. Gracefully does the mask dance
> Homeward at the end of the day, gracefully . . .

ELESIN's *trance appears to be deepening, his steps heavier.*

IYALOJA.

> It is the death of war that kills the valiant,
> Death of water is how the swimmer goes
> It is the death of markets that kills the
>   trader
> And death of indecision takes the idle away
> The trade of the cutlass blunts its edge
> And the beautiful die the death of beauty.
> It takes an Elesin to die the death of death . . .
> Only Elesin . . . dies the unknowable death
>   of death . . .
> Gracefully, gracefully does the horseman
>   regain
> The stables at the end of day, gracefully . . .

PRAISE-SINGER. How shall I tell what my eyes have seen? The Horseman gallops on before the courier, how shall I tell what my eyes have seen? He says a dog may be confused by new scents of beings he never dreamt of, so he must precede the dog to heaven. He says a horse may stumble on strange boulders and be lamed, so he races on before the horse to heaven. It is best, he says, to trust no messenger who may falter at the outer gate; oh how shall I tell what my ears have heard? But do you hear me still Elesin, do you hear your faithful one?

ELESIN *in his motions appears to feel for a direction of sound, subtly, but he only sinks deeper into his trance-dance.*

Elesin Alafin, I no longer sense your flesh. The drums are changing now but you have gone far ahead of the world. It is not yet noon in heaven; let those who claim it is begin their own journey home. So why must you rush like an impatient bride: why do you race to desert your Olohun-iyo?

ELESIN *is now sunk fully deep in his trance, there is no longer sign of any awareness of his surroundings.*

Does the deep voice of *gbedu* cover you then, like the passage of royal elephants? Those drums that brook no rivals, have they blocked the passage to your ears that my voice passes into wind, a mere leaf floating in the night? Is your flesh lightened Elesin, is that lump of earth I slid between your slippers to keep you longer slowly sifting from your feet? Are the drums on the other side now tuning skin to skin with ours in *osugbo*? Are there sounds there I cannot hear, do footsteps surround you which pound the earth like *gbedu*, roll like thunder round the dome of the world? Is the darkness gathering in your head Elesin? Is there now a streak of light at the end of the passage, a light I dare not look upon? Does it reveal whose voices we often heard, whose touches we often felt, whose wisdoms come suddenly into the mind when the wisest have shaken their heads and murmured; It cannot be done? Elesin Alafin, don't think I do not know why your lips are heavy, why your limbs are drowsy as palm oil in the cold of harmattan. I would call you back but when the elephant heads for the jungle, the tail is too small a handhold for the hunter that would pull him back. The sun that heads for the sea no longer heeds the prayers of the farmer. When the river begins to taste the salt of the ocean, we no longer know what deity to call on, the river-god or Olokun. No arrow flies back to the string, the child does not return through the same passage that gave it birth. Elesin Oba, can you hear me at all? Your eyelids are glazed like a courtesan's, is it that you see the dark groom and master of life? And will you see my father? Will you tell him that I stayed with you to the last? Will my voice

ring in your ears awhile, will you remember Olohun-iyo even if
the music on the other side surpasses his mortal craft? But will
they know you over there? Have they eyes to gauge your worth,
have they the heart to love you, will they know what thoroughbred prances towards them in caparisons of honour? If they do
not Elesin, if any there cuts your yam with a small knife, or
pours you wine in a small calabash, turn back and return to welcoming hands. If the world were not greater than the wishes of
Olohun-iyo, I would not let you go . . .

He appears to break down. ELESIN *dances on, completely in a
trance. The dirge wells up louder and stronger.* ELESIN'S
*dance does not lose its elasticity but his gestures become, if
possible, even more weighty. Lights fade slowly on the scene.*

SCENE FOUR

*A Masque. The front side of the stage is part of a wide corridor
around the great hall of the Residency extending beyond vision into
the rear and wings. It is redolent of the tawdry decadence of a far-
flung but key imperial frontier. The* COUPLES *in a variety of
fancy-dress are ranged around the walls, gazing in the same direction. The guest-of-honour is about to make an appearance. A portion of the local police brass band with its white* CONDUCTOR *is
just visible. At last, the entrance of* ROYALTY. *The band plays
'Rule Britannia', badly, beginning long before he is visible. The
couples bow and curtsey as he passes by them. Both he and his
companions are dressed in seventeenth century European costume.
Following behind are the* RESIDENT *and his* PARTNER *similarly
attired. As they gain the end of the hall where the orchestra dais be-*

gins the music comes to an end. The PRINCE *bows to the guests.
The* BAND *strikes up a Viennese waltz and the* PRINCE *formally
opens the floor. Several bars later the* RESIDENT *and his companion follow suit. Others follow in appropriate pecking order. The
orchestra's waltz rendition is not of the highest musical standard.*

Some time later the PRINCE *dances again into view and is settled
into a corner by the* RESIDENT *who then proceeds to select
COUPLES as they dance past for introduction, sometimes threading
his way through the dancers to tap the lucky* COUPLE *on the
shoulder. Desperate efforts from many to ensure that they are
recognised in spite of perhaps, their costume. The ritual of introductions soon takes in* PILKINGS *and his* WIFE. *The* PRINCE *is
quite fascinated by their costume and they demonstrate the adapta-
tions they have made to it, pulling down the mask to demonstrate
how the* egungun *normally appears, then showing the various
press-button controls they have innovated for the face flaps, the
sleeves, etc. They demonstrate the dance steps and the guttural
sounds made by the* egungun, *harrass other dancers in the hall,
MRS PILKINGS playing the 'restrainer' to* PILKINGS' *manic
darts. Everyone is highly entertained, the Royal Party especially
who lead the applause.*

At this point a liveried FOOTMAN *comes in with a note on a
salver and is intercepted almost absent-mindedly by the* RESIDENT
*who takes the note and reads it. After polite coughs he succeeds in
excusing the* PILKINGS *from the* PRINCE *and takes them aside.
The* PRINCE *considerately offers the* RESIDENT's WIFE *his hand
and dancing is resumed.*

On their way out the RESIDENT *gives an order to his
AIDE-DE-CAMP. They come into the side corridor where the
RESIDENT hands the note to* PILKINGS.

RESIDENT. As you see it says 'emergency' on the outside. I took
the liberty of opening it because His Highness was obviously enjoying the entertainment. I didn't want to interrupt unless really
necessary.

PILKINGS. Yes, yes of course, sir.

RESIDENT. Is it really as bad as it says? What's it all about?

PILKINGS. Some strange custom they have, sir. It seems because the King is dead some important chief has to commit suicide.

RESIDENT. The King? Isn't it the same one who died nearly a month ago?

PILKINGS. Yes, sir.

RESIDENT. Haven't they buried him yet?

PILKINGS. They take their time about these things, sir. The pre-burial ceremonies last nearly thirty days. It seems tonight is the final night.

RESIDENT. But what has it got to do with the market women? Why are they rioting? We've waived that troublesome tax haven't we?

PILKINGS. We don't quite know that they are exactly rioting yet, sir. Sergeant Amusa is sometimes prone to exaggerations.

RESIDENT. He sounds desperate enough. That comes out even in his rather quaint grammar. Where is the man anyway? I asked my aide-de-camp to bring him here.

PILKINGS. They are probably looking in the wrong verandah. I'll fetch him myself.

RESIDENT. No no you stay here. Let your wife go and look for them. Do you mind my dear . . .?

JANE. Certainly not, your Excellency. (*Goes.*)

RESIDENT. You should have kept me informed, Pilkings. You realise how disastrous it would have been if things had erupted while His Highness was here.

PILKINGS. I wasn't aware of the whole business until tonight, sir.

RESIDENT. Nose to the ground Pilkings, nose to the ground. If we all let these little things slip past us where would the empire be eh? Tell me that. Where would we all be?

PILKINGS (*low voice*). Sleeping peacefully at home I bet.

RESIDENT. What did you say, Pilkings?

PILKINGS. It won't happen again, sir.

RESIDENT. It mustn't, Pilkings. It mustn't. Where is that damned sergeant? I ought to get back to His Highness as quickly as possible and offer him some plausible explanation for my rather abrupt conduct. Can you think of one, Pilkings?

PILKINGS. You could tell him the truth, sir.

RESIDENT. I could? No no no no Pilkings, that would never do. What! Go and tell him there is a riot just two miles away from him? This is supposed to be a secure colony of His Majesty, Pilkings.

PILKINGS. Yes, sir.

RESIDENT. Ah, there they are. No, these are not our native police. Are these the ring-leaders of the riot?

PILKINGS. Sir, these are my police officers.

RESIDENT. Oh, I beg your pardon officers. You do look a little . . . I say, isn't there something missing in their uniform? I think they used to have some rather colourful sashes. If I remember rightly I recommended them myself in my young days in the service. A bit of colour always appeals to the natives, yes, I remember putting that in my report. Well well well, where are we? Make your report man.

PILKINGS (*moves close to* AMUSA, *between his teeth*). And let's have no more superstitious nonsense from you Amusa or I'll throw you in the guardroom for a month and feed you pork!

RESIDENT. What's that? What has pork to do with it?

PILKINGS. Sir, I was just warning him to be brief. I'm sure you are most anxious to hear his report.

RESIDENT. Yes yes yes of course. Come on man, speak up. Hey, didn't we give them some colourful fez hats with all those wavy things, yes, pink tassells . . .

PILKINGS. Sir, I think if he was permitted to make his report we might find that he lost his hat in the riot.

RESIDENT. Ah yes indeed. I'd better tell His Highness that. Lost his hat in the riot, ha ha. He'll probably say well, as long as he didn't lose his head. (*Chuckles to himself.*) Don't forget to send me a report first thing in the morning young Pilkings.

PILKINGS. No, sir.

RESIDENT. And whatever you do, don't let things get out of hand. Keep a cool head and — nose to the ground Pilkings. (*Wanders off in the general direction of the hall.*)

PILKINGS. Yes, sir.

AIDE-DE-CAMP. Would you be needing me, sir?

PILKINGS. No thanks, Bob. I think His Excellency's need of you is greater than ours.

AIDE-DE-CAMP. We have a detachment of soldiers from the capital, sir. They accompanied His Highness up here.

PILKINGS. I doubt if it will come to that but, thanks, I'll bear it in mind. Oh, could you send an orderly with my cloak.

AIDE-DE-CAMP. Very good, sir. (*Goes.*)

PILKINGS. Now, sergeant.

AMUSA. Sir . . . (*Makes an effort, stops dead. Eyes to the ceiling.*)

PILKINGS. Oh, not again.

AMUSA. I cannot against death to dead cult. This dress get power of dead.

PILKINGS. All right, let's go. You are relieved of all further duty Amusa. Report to me first thing in the morning.

JANE. Shall I come, Simon?

PILKINGS. No, there's no need for that. If I can get back later I will. Otherwise get Bob to bring you home.

JANE. Be careful Simon . . . I mean, be clever.

PILKINGS. Sure I will. You two, come with me. (*As he turns to go, the clock in the Residency begins to chime.* PILKINGS *looks at his watch then turns, horror-stricken, to stare at his* WIFE. *The same thought clearly occurs to her. He swallows hard. An* ORDERLY *brings his cloak.*) It's midnight. I had no idea it was that late.

JANE. But surely . . . they don't count the hours the way we do. The moon, or something . . .

PILKING'S. I am . . . not so sure.

He turns and breaks into a sudden run. The two CONSTABLES *follow, also at a run.* AMUSA, *who has kept his eyes on the ceiling throughout waits until the last of the footsteps has faded out of hearing. He salutes suddenly, but without once looking in the direction of the* WOMAN.

AMUSA. Goodnight, madam.

JANE. Oh. (*She hesitates.*) Amusa . . . (*He goes off without seeming to have heard.*) Poor Simon . . . (*A figure emerges from the shadows, a young black* MAN *dressed in a sober western suit. He peeps into the hall, trying to make out the figures of the dancers.*

Who is that?

OLUNDE (*emerges into the light*). I didn't mean to startle you madam. I am looking for the District Officer.

JANE. Wait a minute . . . don't I know you? Yes, you are Olunde, the young man who . . .

OLUNDE. Mrs Pilkings! How fortunate. I came here to look for your husband.

JANE. Olunde! Let's look at you. What a fine young man you've become. Grand but solemn. Good God, when did you return? Simon never said a word. But you do look well Olunde. Really!

OLUNDE. You are . . . well, you look quite well yourself Mrs Pilkings. From what little I can see of you.

JANE. Oh, this. It's caused quite a stir I assure you, and not all of it very pleasant. You are not shocked I hope?

OLUNDE. Why should I be? But don't you find it rather hot in there? Your skin must find it difficult to breathe.

JANE. Well, it is a little hot I must confess, but it's all in a good cause.

OLUNDE. What cause Mrs Pilkings?

JANE. All this. The ball. And His Highness being here in person and all that.

OLUNDE (*mildly*). And that is the good cause for which you desecrate an ancestral mask?

JANE. Oh, so you are shocked after all. How disappointing.

OLUNDE. No I am not shocked, Mrs Pilkings. You forget that I have now spent four years among your people. I discovered that you have no respect for what you do not understand.

JANE. Oh. So you've returned with a chip on your shoulder. That's a pity Olunde. I am sorry.

An uncomfortable silence follows.

I take it then that you did not find your stay in England altogether edifying.

OLUNDE. I don't say that. I found your people quite admirable in many ways, their conduct and courage in this war for instance.

JANE. Ah yes, the war. Here of course it is all rather remote. From time to time we have a black-out drill just to remind us that there is a war on. And the rare convoy passes through on its way somewhere or on manoeuvres. Mind you there is the occasional bit of excitement like that ship that was blown up in the harbour.

OLUNDE. Here? Do you mean through enemy action?

JANE. Oh no, the war hasn't come that close. The captain did it himself. I don't quite understand it really. Simon tried to explain. The ship had to be blown up because it had become dangerous to the other ships, even to the city itself. Hundreds of the coastal population would have died.

OLUNDE. Maybe it was loaded with ammunition and had caught fire. Or some of those lethal gases they've been experimenting on.

JANE. Something like that. The captain blew himself up with it. Deliberately. Simon said someone had to remain on board to light the fuse.

OLUNDE. It must have been a very short fuse.

JANE (*shrugs*). I don't know much about it. Only that there was no other way to save lives. No time to devise anything else. The captain took the decision and carried it out.

OLUNDE. Yes ... I quite believe it. I met men like that in England.

JANE. Oh just look at me! Fancy welcoming you back with such morbid news. Stale too. It was at least six months ago.

OLUNDE. I don't find it morbid at all. I find it rather inspiring. It is an affirmative commentary on life.

JANE. What is?

OLUNDE. That captain's self-sacrifice.

JANE. Nonsense. Life should never be thrown deliberately away.

OLUNDE. And the innocent people around the harbour?

JANE. Oh, how does one know? The whole thing was probably exaggerated anyway.

OLUNDE. That was a risk the captain couldn't take. But please Mrs Pilkings, do you think you could find your husband for me? I have to talk to him.

JANE. Simon? (*As she recollects for the first time the full significance of* OLUNDE'S *presence.*) Simon is . . . there is a little problem in town. He was sent for. But . . . when did you arrive? Does Simon know you're here?

OLUNDE (*suddenly earnest*). I need your help Mrs Pilkings. I've always found you somewhat more understanding than your husband. Please find him for me and when you do, you must help me talk to him.

JANE. I'm afraid I don't quite . . . follow you. Have you seen my husband already?

OLUNDE. I went to your house. Your houseboy told me you were here. (*He smiles.*) He even told me how I would recognise you and Mr Pilkings.

JANE. Then you must know what my husband is trying to do for you.

OLUNDE. For me?

JANE. For you. For your people. And to think he didn't even know you were coming back! But how do you happen to be here? Only this evening we were talking about you. We thought you were still four thousand miles away.

OLUNDE. I was sent a cable.

JANE. A cable? Who did? Simon? The business of your father didn't begin till tonight.

OLUNDE. A relation sent it weeks ago, and it said nothing about my father. All it said was, Our King is dead. But I knew I had to return home at once so as to bury my father. I understood that.

JANE. Well, thank God you don't have to go through that agony. Simon is going to stop it.

OLUNDE. That's why I want to see him. He's wasting his time. And since he has been so helpful to me I don't want him to incur the enmity of our people. Especially over nothing.

JANE (sits down open-mouthed). You . . . you Olunde!

OLUNDE. Mrs Pilkings, I came home to bury my father. As soon as I heard the news I booked my passage home. In fact we were fortunate. We travelled in the same convoy as your Prince, so we had excellent protection.

JANE. But you don't think your father is also entitled to whatever protection is available to him?

OLUNDE. How can I make you understand? He *has* protection. No one can undertake what he does tonight without the deepest protection the mind can conceive. What can you offer him in place of his peace of mind, in place of the honour and veneration of his own people? What would you think of your Prince if he refused to accept the risk of losing his life on this voyage? This . . . showing-the-flag tour of colonial possessions.

JANE. I see. So it isn't just medicine you studied in England.

OLUNDE. Yet another error into which your people fall. You believe that everything which appears to make sense was learnt from you.

JANE. Not so fast Olunde. You have learnt to argue I can tell that, but I never said you made sense. However clearly you try to put it, it is still a barbaric custom. It is even worse – it's feudal! The king dies and a chieftan must be buried with him. How feudalistic can you get!

OLUNDE (waves his hand towards the background. The PRINCE is dancing past again – to a different step – and all the guests are bowing and curtseying as he passes). And this? Even in the midst of a devastating war, look at that. What name would you give to that?

JANE. Therapy, British style. The preservation of sanity in the midst of chaos.

OLUNDE. Others would call it decadence. However, it doesn't really interest me. You white races know how to survive; I've seen proof of that. By all logical and natural laws this war should end with all the white races wiping out one another, wiping out their so-called civilisation for all time and reverting to a state of primitivism the like of which has so far only existed in your imagination when you thought of us. I thought all that at the beginning. Then I slowly realised that your greatest art is the art of survival. But at least have the humility to let others survive in their own way.

JANE. Through ritual suicide?

OLUNDE. Is that worse than mass suicide? Mrs Pilkings, what do you call what those young men are sent to do by their generals in this war? Of course you have also mastered the art of calling things by names which don't remotely describe them.

JANE. You talk! You people with your long-winded, roundabout way of making conversation.

OLUNDE. Mrs Pilkings, whatever we do, we never suggest that a thing is the opposite of what it really is. In your newsreels I heard defeats, thorough, murderous defeats described as strategic victories. No wait, it wasn't just on your newsreels. Don't forget I was attached to hospitals all the time. Hordes of your wounded passed through those wards. I spoke to them. I spent long evenings by their bedsides while they spoke terrible truths of the realities of that war. I know now how history is made.

JANE. But surely, in a war of this nature, for the morale of the nation you must expect . . .

OLUNDE. That a disaster beyond human reckoning be spoken of as a triumph? No. I mean, is there no mourning in the home of the bereaved that such blasphemy is permitted?

JANE (after a moment's pause). Perhaps I can understand you now. The time we picked for you was not really one for seeing us at our best.

OLUNDE. Don't think it was just the war. Before that even started I had plenty of time to study your people. I saw nothing, finally, that gave you the right to pass judgement on other peoples and their ways. Nothing at all.

JANE (*hesitantly*). Was it the . . . colour thing? I know there is some discrimination.

OLUNDE. Don't make it so simple, Mrs Pilkings. You make it sound as if when I left, I took nothing at all with me.

JANE. Yes . . . and to tell the truth, only this evening, Simon and I agreed that we never really knew what you left with.

OLUNDE. Neither did I. But I found out over there. I am grateful to your country for that. And I will never give it up.

JANE. Olunde, please . . . promise me something. Whatever you do, don't throw away what you have started to do. You want to be a doctor. My husband and I believe you will make an excellent one, sympathetic and competent. Don't let anything make you throw away your training.

OLUNDE (*genuinely surprised*). Of course not. What a strange idea. I intend to return and complete my training. Once the burial of my father is over.

JANE. Oh, please . . .!

OLUNDE. Listen! Come outside. You can't hear anything against that music.

JANE. What is it?

OLUNDE. The drums. Can you hear the drums? Listen.

> *The drums come over, still distant but more distinct. There is a change of rhythm, it rises to a crescendo and then, suddenly, it is cut off. After a silence, a new beat begins, slow and resonant.*

There it's all over.

JANE. You mean he's . . .

OLUNDE. Yes, Mrs Pilkings, my father is dead. His will-power has always been enormous; I know he is dead.

JANE (*screams*). How can you be so callous! So unfeeling! You announce your father's own death like a surgeon looking down on some strange ... stranger's body! You're just a savage like all the rest.

AIDE-DE-CAMP (*rushing out*). Mrs Pilkings. Mrs Pilkings. (*She breaks down, sobbing.*) Are you all right, Mrs Pilkings?

OLUNDE. She'll be all right. (*Turns to go.*)

AIDE-DE-CAMP. Who are you? And who the hell asked your opinion?

OLUNDE. You're quite right, nobody. (*Going.*)

AIDE-DE-CAMP. What the hell! Did you hear me ask you who you were?

OLUNDE. I have business to attend to.

AIDE-DE-CAMP. I'll give you business in a moment you impudent nigger. Answer my question!

OLUNDE. I have a funeral to arrange. Excuse me. (*Going.*)

AIDE-DE-CAMP. I said stop! Orderly!

JANE. No, no, don't do that. I'm all right. And for heaven's sake don't act so foolishly. He's a family friend.

AIDE-DE-CAMP. Well he'd better learn to answer civil questions when he's asked them. These natives put a suit on and they get high opinions of themselves.

OLUNDE. Can I go now?

JANE. No no don't go. I must talk to you. I'm sorry about what I said.

OLUNDE. It's nothing, Mrs Pilkings. And I'm really anxious to go. I couldn't see my father before, it's forbidden for me, his heir and successor to set eyes on him from the moment of the king's death. But now ... I would like to touch his body while it is still warm.

JANE. You will. I promise I shan't keep you long. Only, I couldn't possibly let you go like that. Bob, please excuse us.

AIDE-DE-CAMP. If you're sure ...

JANE. Of course I'm sure. Something happened to upset me just then, but I'm all right now. Really.

The AIDE-DE-CAMP *goes, somewhat reluctantly.*

OLUNDE. I mustn't stay long.

JANE. Please, I promise not to keep you. It's just that . . . oh you saw yourself what happens to one in this place. The Resident's man thought he was being helpful, that's the way we all react. But I can't go in among that crowd just now and if I stay by myself somebody will come looking for me. Please, just say something for a few moments and then you can go. Just so I can recover myself.

OLUNDE. What do you want me to say?

JANE. Your calm acceptance for instance, can you explain that? It was so unnatural. I don't understand that at all. I feel a need to understand all I can.

OLUNDE. But you explained it yourself. My medical training perhaps. I have seen death too often. And the soldiers who returned from the front, they died on our hands all the time.

JANE. No. It has to be more than that. I feel it has to do with the many things we don't really grasp about your people. At least you can explain.

OLUNDE. All these things are part of it. And anyway, my father has been dead in my mind for nearly a month. Ever since I learnt of the King's death. I've lived with my bereavement so long now that I cannot think of him alive. On that journey on the boat, I kept my mind on my duties as the one who must perform the rites over his body. I went through it all again and again in my mind as he himself had taught me. I didn't want to do anything wrong, something which might jeopardise the welfare of my people.

JANE. But he had disowned you. When you left he swore publicly you were no longer his son.

OLUNDE. I told you, he was a man of tremendous will. Sometimes that's another way of saying stubborn. But among our people, you don't disown a child just like that. Even if I had died before him I would still be buried like his eldest son. But it's time for me to go.

JANE. Thank you. I feel calmer. Don't let me keep you from your duties.

OLUNDE. Goodnight, Mrs Pilkings.

JANE. Welcome home.

She holds out her hand. As he takes it footsteps are heard approaching the drive. A short while later a woman's sobbing is also heard.

PILKINGS (*off*). Keep them here till I get back. (*He strides into view, reacts at the sight of* OLUNDE *but turns to his* WIFE.) Thank goodness you're still here.

JANE. Simon, what happened?

PILKINGS. Later Jane, please. Is Bob still here?

JANE. Yes, I think so. I'm sure he must be.

PILKINGS. Try and get him out here as quickly as you can. Tell him it's urgent.

JANE. Of course. Oh Simon, you remember . . .

PILKINGS. Yes yes. I can see who it is. Get Bob out here. (*She runs off.*) At first I thought I was seeing a ghost.

OLUNDE. Mr Pilkings, I appreciate what you tried to do. I want you to believe that. I can tell you it would have been a terrible calamity if you'd succeeded.

PILKINGS (*opens his mouth several times, shuts it*). You . . . said what?

OLUNDE. A calamity for us, the entire people.

PILKINGS (*sighs*). I see. Hm.

OLUNDE. And now I must go. I must see him before he turns cold.

PILKINGS. Oh ah . . . em . . . but this is a shock to see you. I mean er thinking all this while you were in England and thanking God for that.

OLUNDE. I came on the mail boat. We travelled in the Prince's convoy.

PILKINGS. Ah yes, a-ah, hm . . . er well . . .

OLUNDE. Goodnight. I can see you are shocked by the whole business. But you must know by now there are things you cannot understand — or help.

PILKINGS. Yes. Just a minute. There are armed policemen that way and they have instructions to let no one pass. I suggest you wait a little. I'll er . . . give you an escort.

OLUNDE. That's very kind of you. But do you think it could be quickly arranged.

PILKINGS. Of course. In fact, yes, what I'll do is send Bob over with some men to the er . . . place. You can go with them. Here he comes now. Excuse me a minute.

AIDE-DE-CAMP. Anything wrong sir?

PILKINGS (*takes him to one side*). Listen Bob, that cellar in the disused annexe of the Residency, you know, where the slaves were stored before being taken down to the coast . . .

AIDE-DE-CAMP. Oh yes, we use it as a storeroom for broken furniture.

PILKINGS. But it's still got the bars on it?

AIDE-DE-CAMP. Oh yes, they are quite intact.

PILKINGS. Get the keys please. I'll explain later. And I want a strong guard over the Residency tonight.

AIDE-DE-CAMP. We have that already. The detachment from the coast . . .

PILKINGS. No, I don't want them at the gates of the Residency. I want you to deploy them at the bottom of the hill, a long way from the main hall so they can deal with any situation long before the sound carries to the house.

AIDE-DE-CAMP. Yes of course.

PILKINGS. I don't want His Highness alarmed.

AIDE-DE-CAMP. You think the riot will spread here?

PILKINGS. It's unlikely but I don't want to take a chance. I made them believe I was going to lock the man up in my house, which was what I had planned to do in the first place. They are probably assailing it by now. I took a roundabout route here so I don't think there is any danger at all. At least not before dawn. Nobody is to leave the premises of course – the native employees I mean. They'll soon smell something is up and they can't keep their mouths shut.

AIDE-DE-CAMP. I'll give instructions at once.

PILKINGS. I'll take the prisoner down myself. Two policemen will stay with him throughout the night. Inside the cell.

AIDE-DE-CAMP. Right sir. (*Salutes and goes off at the double.*)

PILKINGS. Jane. Bob is coming back in a moment with a detachment. Until he gets back please stay with Olunde. (*He makes an extra warning gesture with his eyes.*)

OLUNDE. Please, Mr Pilkings . . .

PILKINGS. I hate to be stuffy old son, but we have a crisis on our hands. It has to do with your father's affair if you must know. And it happens also at a time when we have His Highness here. I am responsible for security so you'll simply have to do as I say. I hope that's understood. (*Marches off quickly, in the direction from which he made his first appearance.*)

OLUNDE. What's going on? All this can't be just because he failed to stop my father killing himself.

JANE. I honestly don't know. Could it have sparked off a riot?

OLUNDE. No. If he'd succeeded that would be more likely to start the riot. Perhaps there were other factors involved. Was there a chieftancy dispute?

JANE. None that I know of.

ELESIN (*an animal bellow from off*). Leave me alone! Is it not enough that you have covered me in shame! White man, take your hand from my body!

OLUNDE *stands frozen to the spot.* JANE *understanding at last, tries to move him.*

JANE. Let's go in. It's getting chilly out here.

PILKINGS (*off*). Carry him.

ELESIN. Give me back the name you have taken away from me you ghost from the land of the nameless!

PILKINGS. Carry him! I can't have a disturbance here. Quickly! stuff up his mouth.

JANE. Oh God! Let's go in. Please Olunde.

OLUNDE does not move.

ELESIN. Take your albino's hand from me you . . .

Sounds of a struggle. His voice chokes as he is gagged.

OLUNDE (*quietly*). That was my father's voice.

JANE. Oh you poor orphan, what have you come home to?

There is a sudden explosion of rage from off-stage and power-ful steps come running up the drive.

PILKINGS. You bloody fools, after him!

Immediately ELESIN, *in handcuffs, comes pounding in the direction of* JANE *and* OLUNDE, *followed some moments afterwards by* PILKINGS *and the* CONSTABLES. ELESIN *confronted by the seeming statue of his son, stops dead.* OLUNDE *stares above his head into the distance. The* CONSTABLES *try to grab him.* JANE *screams at them.*

JANE. Leave him alone! Simon, tell them to leave him alone.

PILKINGS. All right, stand aside you. (*Shrugs.*) Maybe just as well. It might help to calm him down.

For several moments they hold the same position. ELESIN *moves a step forward, almost as if he's still in doubt.*

ELESIN. Olunde? (*He moves his head, inspecting him from side to side.*) Olunde! (*He collapses slowly at* OLUNDE'S *feet.*) Oh son, don't let the sight of your father turn you blind!

OLUNDE (*he moves for the first time since he heard his voice, brings his head slowly down to look on him*). I have no father, eater of left-overs.

> *He walks slowly down the way his father had run. Light fades out on* ELESIN, *sobbing into the ground.*

SCENE FIVE

A wide iron-barred gate stretches almost the whole width of the cell in which ELESIN *is imprisoned. His wrists are encased in thick iron bracelets, chained together; he stands against the bars, looking out. Seated on the ground to one side on the outside is his recent* BRIDE, *her eyes bent perpetually to the ground. Figures of the two* GUARDS *can be seen deeper inside the cell, alert to every movement* ELESIN *makes.* PILKINGS *now in a police officer's uniform enters noiselessly, observes him a while. Then he coughs ostentatiously and approaches. Leans against the bars near a corner, his back to* ELESIN. *He is obviously trying to fall in mood with him. Some moments' silence.*

PILKINGS. You seem fascinated by the moon.

ELESIN (*after a pause*). Yes, ghostly one. Your twin-brother up there engages my thoughts.

PILKINGS. It is a beautiful night.

ELESIN. Is that so?

PILKINGS. The light on the leaves, the peace of the night . . .

ELESIN. The night is not at peace, District Officer.

PILKINGS. No? I would have said it was. You know, quiet . .

ELESIN. And does quiet mean peace for you?

PILKINGS. Well, nearly the same thing. Naturally there is a subtle difference . . .

ELESIN. The night is not at peace, ghostly one. The world is not at peace. You have shattered the peace of the world for ever. There is no sleep in the world tonight.

PILKINGS. It is still a good bargain if the world should lose one night's sleep as the price of saving a man's life.

ELESIN. You did not save my life, District Officer. You destroyed it.

PILKINGS. Now come on . . .

ELESIN. And not merely my life but the lives of many. The end of the night's work is not over. Neither this year nor the next will see it. If I wished you well, I would pray that you do not stay long enough on our land to see the disaster you have brought upon us.

PILKINGS. Well, I did my duty as I saw it. I have no regrets.

ELESIN. No. The regrets of life always come later.

Some moments' pause.

You are waiting for dawn, white man. I hear you saying to yourself: only so many hours until dawn and then the danger is over. All I must do is to keep him alive tonight. You don't quite understand it all but you know that tonight is when what ought to be must be brought about. I shall ease your mind even more, ghostly one. It is not an entire night but a moment of the night, and that moment is past. The moon was my messenger and guide. When it reached a certain gateway in the sky, it touched that moment for which my whole life has been spent in blessings. Even I do not know the gateway. I have stood here and scanned the sky for a glimpse of that door but, I cannot see it. Human eyes are useless for a search of this nature. But in the house of *osugbo*, those who keep watch through the spirit recognised the moment, they sent word to me through the voice of our sacred drums to prepare myself. I heard them and I shed all thoughts of earth. I began to follow the moon to the abode of the gods . . . servant of the white king, that was when you entered my chosen place of departure on feet of desecration.

PILKINGS. I'm sorry, but we all see our duty differently.

ELESIN. I no longer blame you. You stole from me my first-born, sent him to your country so you could turn him into something in your own image. Did you plan it all beforehand? There are moments when it seems part of a larger plan. He who must follow my footsteps is taken from me, sent across the ocean. Then, in my turn, I am stopped from fulfilling my destiny. Did you think it all out before, this plan to push our world from its course and sever the cord that links us to the great origin?

PILKINGS. You don't really believe that. Anyway, if that was my intention with your son, I appear to have failed.

ELESIN. You did not fail in the main, ghostly one. We know the roof covers the rafters, the cloth covers blemishes; who would have known that the white skin covered our future, preventing us from seeing the death our enemies had prepared for us. The world is set adrift and its inhabitants are lost. Around them, there is nothing but emptiness.

PILKINGS. Your son does not take so gloomy a view.

ELESIN. Are you dreaming now, white man? Were you not present at my reunion of shame? Did you not see when the world reversed itself and the father fell before his son, asking forgiveness?

PILKINGS. That was in the heat of the moment. I spoke to him and . . . if you want to know, he wishes he could cut out his tongue for uttering the words he did.

ELESIN. No. What he said must never be unsaid. The contempt of my own son rescued something of my shame at your hands. You have stopped me in my duty but I know now that I did give birth to a son. Once I mistrusted him for seeking the companionship of those my spirit knew as enemies of our race. Now I understand. One should seek to obtain the secrets of his enemies. He will avenge my shame, white one. His spirit will destroy you and yours.

PILKINGS. That kind of talk is hardly called for. If you don't want my consolation . . .

ELESIN. No white man, I do not want your consolation.

PILKINGS. As you wish. Your son anyway, sends his consolation. He asks your forgiveness. When I asked him not to despise you his reply was: I cannot judge him, and if I cannot judge him, I cannot despise him. He wants to come to you and say goodbye and to receive your blessing.

ELESIN. Goodbye? Is he returning to your land?

PILKINGS. Don't you think that's the most sensible thing for him to do? I advised him to leave at once, before dawn, and he agrees that is the right course of action.

ELESIN. Yes, it is best. And even if I did not think so, I have lost the father's place of honour. My voice is broken.

PILKINGS. Your son honours you. If he didn't he would not ask your blessing.

ELESIN. No. Even a thoroughbred is not without pity for the turf he strikes with his hoof. When is he coming?

PILKINGS. As soon as the town is a little quieter. I advised it.

ELESIN. Yes, white man, I am sure you advised it. You advise all our lives although on the authority of what gods, I do not know.

PILKINGS (opens his mouth to reply, then appears to change his mind. Turns to go. Hesitates and stops again.) Before I leave you, may I ask just one thing of you?

ELESIN. I am listening.

PILKINGS. I wish to ask you to search the quiet of your heart and tell me – do you not find great contradictions in the wisdom of your own race?

ELESIN. Make yourself clear, white one.

PILKINGS. I have lived among you long enough to learn a saying or two. One came to my mind tonight when I stepped into the market and saw what was going on. You were surrounded by those who egged you on with song and praises. I thought, are these not the same people who say: the elder grimly approaches heaven and you ask him to bear your greetings yonder; do you really think he makes the journey willingly? After that, I did not hesitate.

> *A pause.* ELESIN *sighs. Before he can speak a sound of running feet is heard.*

JANE (*off*). Simon! Simon!
PILKINGS. What on earth . . .! (*Runs off.*)

> ELESIN *turns to his new* WIFE, *gazes on her for some moments.*

ELESIN. My young bride, did you hear the ghostly one? You sit and sob in your silent heart but say nothing to all this. First I blamed the white man, then I blamed my gods for deserting me. Now I feel I want to blame you for the mystery of the sapping of my will. But blame is a strange peace offering for a man to bring a world he has deeply wronged, and to its innocent dwellers. Oh little mother, I have taken countless women in my life but you were more than a desire of the flesh. I needed you as the abyss across which my body must be drawn, I filled it with earth and dropped my seed in it at the moment of preparedness for my crossing. You were the final gift of the living to their emissary to the land of the ancestors, and perhaps your warmth and youth brought new insights of this world to me and turned my feet leaden on this side of the abyss. For I confess to you, daughter, my weakness came not merely from the abomination of the white man who came violently into my fading presence; there was also a weight of longing on my earth-held limbs. I would have shaken it off, already my foot had begun to lift but then, the white ghost entered and all was defiled.

> *Approaching voices of* PILKINGS *and his* WIFE.

JANE. Oh Simon, you will let her in won't you?
PILKINGS. I really wish you'd stop interfering.

They come into view. JANE is in a dressing-gown. PILKINGS *is holding a note to which he refers from time to time.*

JANE. Good gracious, I didn't initiate this. I was sleeping quietly, or trying to anyway, when the servant brought it. It's not my fault if one can't sleep undisturbed even in the Residency.

PILKINGS. He'd have done the same thing if we were sleeping at home so don't sidetrack the issue. He knows he can get round you or he wouldn't send you the petition in the first place.

JANE. Be fair Simon. After all he was thinking of your own interests. He is grateful you know, you seem to forget that. He feels he owes you something.

PILKINGS. I just wish they'd leave this man alone tonight, that's all.

JANE. Trust him Simon. He's pledged his word it will all go peacefully.

PILKINGS. Yes, and that's the other thing. I don't like being threatened.

JANE. Threatened? (*Takes the note.*) I didn't spot any threat.

PILKINGS. It's there. Veiled, but it's there. The only way to prevent serious rioting tomorrow – what a cheek!

JANE. I don't think he's threatening you Simon.

PILKINGS. He's picked up the idiom all right. Wouldn't surprise me if he's been mixing with commies or anarchists over there. The phrasing sounds too good to be true. Damn! If only the Prince hadn't picked this time for his visit.

JANE. Well, even so Simon, what have you got to lose? You don't want a riot on your hands, not with the Prince here.

PILKINGS (*going up to* ELESIN). Let's see what he has to say. Chief Elesin, there is yet another person who wants to see you. As she is not a next-of-kin I don't really feel obliged to let her in. But your son sent a note with her, so it's up to you.

ELESIN. I know who that must be. So she found out your hiding-place. Well, it was not difficult. My stench of shame is so strong, it requires no hunter's dog to follow it.

PILKINGS. If you don't want to see her, just say so and I'll send her packing.

ELESIN. Why should I not want to see her? Let her come. I have no more holes in my rag of shame. All is laid bare.

PILKINGS. I'll bring her in. (*Goes off.*)

JANE (*hesitates, then goes to* ELESIN). Please, try and understand. Everything my husband did was for the best.

ELESIN (*he gives her a long strange stare, as if he is trying to understand who she is*). You are the wife of the District Officer?

JANE. Yes. My name, is Jane.

ELESIN. That is my wife sitting down there. You notice how still and silent she sits? My business is with your husband.

PILKINGS *returns with* IYALOJA.

PILKINGS. Here she is. Now first I want your word of honour that you will try nothing foolish.

ELESIN. Honour? White one, did you say you wanted my word of honour?

PILKINGS. I know you to be an honourable man. Give me your word of honour you will receive nothing from her.

ELESIN. But I am sure you have searched her clothing as you would never dare touch your own mother. And there are these two lizards of yours who roll their eyes even when I scratch.

PILKINGS. And I shall be sitting on that tree trunk watching even how you blink. Just the same I want your word that you will not let her pass anything to you.

ELESIN. You have my honour already. It is locked up in that desk in which you will put away your report of this night's events. Even the honour of my people you have taken already; it is tied together with those papers of treachery which make you masters in this land.

PILKINGS. All right. I am trying to make things easy but if you must bring in politics we'll have to do it the hard way. Madam, I want you to remain along this line and move no nearer to the cell door. Guards! (*They spring to attention.*) If she moves beyond this point, blow your whistle. Come on Jane. (*They go off.*)

IYALOJA. How boldly the lizard struts before the pigeon when it was the eagle itself he promised us he would confront.

ELESIN. I don't ask you to take pity on me Iyaloja. You have a message for me or you would not have come. Even if it is the curses of the world, I shall listen.

IYALOJA. You made so bold with the servant of the white king who took your side against death. I must tell your brother chiefs when I return how bravely you waged war against him. Especially with words.

ELESIN. I more than deserve your scorn.

IYALOJA (*with sudden anger*). I warned you, if you must leave a seed behind, be sure it is not tainted with the curses of the world. Who are you to open a new life when you dared not open the door to a new existence? I say who are you to make so bold? (*The* BRIDE *sobs and* IYALOJA *notices her. Her contempt noticeably increases as she turns back to* ELESIN.) Oh you self-vaunted stem of the plantain, how hollow it all proves. The pith is gone in the parent stem, so how will it prove with the new shoot? How will it go with that earth that bears it? Who are you to bring this abomination on us!

ELESIN. My powers deserted me. My charms, my spells, even my voice lacked strength when I made to summon the powers that would lead me over the last measure of earth into the land of the fleshless. You saw it, Iyaloja. You saw me struggle to retrieve my will from the power of the stranger whose shadow fell across the doorway and left me floundering and blundering in a maze I had never before encountered. My senses were numbed when the touch of cold iron came upon my wrists. I could do nothing to save myself.

IYALOJA. You have betrayed us. We fed you sweetmeats such as we hoped awaited you on the other side. But you said No, I must eat the world's left-overs. We said you were the hunter who brought the quarry down; to you belonged the vital portions of the game. No, you said, I am the hunter's dog and I shall eat the entrails of the game and the faeces of the hunter. We said you were the hunter returning home in triumph, a slain buffalo pressing down on his neck; you said wait, I first must turn up this cricket hole with my toes. We said yours was the doorway at which we first spy the tapper when he comes down from the tree, yours was the blessing of the twilight wine, the purl that brings night spirits out of doors to steal their portion before the light of day. We said yours was the body of wine whose burden shakes the tapper like a sudden gust on his perch. You said, No, I am content to lick the dregs from each calabash when the drinkers are done. We said, the dew on earth's surface was for you to wash your feet along the slopes of honour. You said No, I shall step in the vomit of cats and the droppings of mice; I shall fight them for the left-overs of the world.

ELESIN. Enough Iyaloja, enough.

IYALOJA. We called you leader and oh, how you led us on. What we have no intention of eating should not be held to the nose.

ELESIN. Enough, enough. My shame is heavy enough.

IYALOJA. Wait. I came with a burden.

ELESIN. You have more than discharged it.

IYALOJA. I wish I could pity you.

ELESIN. I need neither pity nor the pity of the world. I need understanding. Even I need to understand. You were present at my defeat. You were part of the beginnings. You brought about the renewal of my tie to earth, you helped in the binding of the cord.

IYALOJA. I gave you warning. The river which fills up before our eyes does not sweep us away in its flood.

ELESIN. What were warnings beside the moist contact of living earth between my fingers? What were warnings beside the renewal of famished embers lodged eternally in the heart of man. But even that, even if it overwhelmed one with a thousandfold temptations to linger a little while, a man could overcome it. It is when the alien hand pollutes the source of will, when a stranger force of violence shatters the mind's calm resolution, this is when a man is made to commit the awful treachery of relief, commit in his thought the unspeakable blasphemy of seeing the hand of the gods in this alien rupture of his world. I know it was this thought that killed me, sapped my powers and turned me into an infant in the hands of unnamable strangers. I made to utter my spells anew but my tongue merely rattled in my mouth. I fingered hidden charms and the contact was damp; there was no spark left to sever the life-strings that should stretch from every finger-tip. My will was squelched in the spittle of an alien race, and all because I had committed this blasphemy of thought – that there might be the hand of the gods in a stranger's intervention.

IYALOJA. Explain it how you will, I hope it brings you peace of mind. The bush-rat fled his rightful cause, reached the market and set up a lamentation. 'Please save me!' – are these fitting words to hear from an ancestral mask? 'There's a wild beast at my heels' is not becoming language from a hunter.

ELESIN. May the world forgive me.

IYALOJA. I came with a burden I said. It approaches the gates which are so well guarded by those jackals whose spittle will from this day be on your food and drink. But first, tell me, you who were once Elesin Oba, tell me, you who know so well the cycle of the plantain: is it the parent shoot which withers to give sap to the younger or, does your wisdom see it running the other way?

ELESIN. I don't see your meaning Iyaloja?

IYALOJA. Did I ask you for a meaning? I asked a question. Whose trunk withers to give sap to the other? The parent shoot or the younger?

ELESIN. The parent.

IYALOJA. Ah. So you do know that. There are sights in this world which say different Elesin. There are some who choose to reverse the cycle of our being. Oh you emptied bark that the world once saluted for a pith-laden being, shall I tell you what the gods have claimed of you?

In her agitation she steps beyond the line indicated by

PILKINGS *and the air is rent by piercing whistles. The two* GUARDS *also leap forward and place safe-guarding hands on* ELESIN. IYALOJA *stops, astonished.* PILKINGS *comes racing in, followed by* JANE.

PILKINGS. What is it? Did they try something?

GUARD. She stepped beyond the line.

ELESIN (*in a broken voice*). Let her alone. She meant no harm.

IYALOJA. Oh Elesin, see what you've become. Once you had no need to open your mouth in explanation because evil-smelling goats, itchy of hand and foot had lost their senses. And it was a brave man indeed who dared lay hands on you because Iyaloja stepped from one side of the earth onto another. Now look at the spectacle of your life. I grieve for you.

PILKINGS. I think you'd better leave. I doubt you have done him much good by coming here. I shall make sure you are not allowed to see him again. In any case we are moving him to a different place before dawn, so don't bother to come back.

IYALOJA. We foresaw that. Hence the burden I trudged here to lay beside your gates.

PILKINGS. What was that you said?

IYALOJA. Didn't our son explain? Ask that one. He knows what it is. At least we hope the man we once knew as Elesin remembers the lesser oaths he need not break.

PILKINGS. Do you know what she is talking about?

ELESIN. Go to the gates, ghostly one. Whatever you find there, bring it to me.

IYALOJA. Not yet. It drags behind me on the slow, weary feet of women. Slow as it is Elesin, it has long overtaken you. It rides ahead of your laggard will.

PILKINGS. What is she saying now? Christ! Must your people forever speak in riddles?

ELESIN. It will come white man, it will come. Tell your men at the gates to let it through.

PILKINGS (*dubiously*). I'll have to see what it is.

IYALOJA. You will. (*Passionately.*) But this is one oath he cannot shirk. White one, you have a king here, a visitor from your land. We know of his presence here. Tell me, were he to die would you leave his spirit roaming restlessly on the surface of earth? Would you bury him here among those you consider less than human? In your land have you no ceremonies of the dead?

PILKINGS. Yes. But we don't make our chiefs commit suicide to keep him company.

IYALOJA. Child, I have not come to help your understanding. (*Points to* ELESIN.) This is the man whose weakened understanding holds us in bondage to you. But ask him if you wish. He knows the meaning of a king's passage; he was not born yesterday. He knows the peril to the race when our dead father, who goes as intermediary, waits and waits and knows he is betrayed. He knows when the narrow gate was opened and he knows it will not stay for laggards who drag their feet in dung and vomit, whose lips are reeking of the left-overs of lesser men. He knows he has condemned our king to wander in the void of evil with beings who are enemies of life.

PILKINGS. Yes er ... but look here ...

IYALOJA. What we ask is little enough. Let him release our King so he can ride on homewards alone. The messenger is on his way on the backs of women. Let him send word through the heart that is folded up within the bolt. It is the least of all his oaths, it is the easiest fulfilled.

   The AIDE-DE-CAMP *runs in.*

PILKINGS. Bob?

AIDE-DE-CAMP. Sir, there's a group of women chanting up the hill.

PILKINGS (*rounding on* IYALOJA). If you people want trouble ...

JANE. Simon, I think that's what Olunde referred to in his letter.

PILKINGS. He knows damned well I can't have a crowd here!

Damn it, I explained the delicacy of my position to him. I think it's about time I got him out of town. Bob, send a car and two or three soldiers to bring him in. I think the sooner he takes his leave of his father and gets out the better.

IYALOJA. Save your labour white one. If it is the father of your prisoner you want, Olunde, he who until this night we knew as Elesin's son, he comes soon himself to take his leave. He has sent the women ahead, so let them in.

PILKINGS *remains undecided.*

AIDE-DE-CAMP. What do we do about the invasion? We can still stop them far from here.

PILKINGS. What do they look like?

AIDE-DE-CAMP. They're not many. And they seem quite peaceful.

PILKINGS. No men?

AIDE-DE-CAMP. Mm, two or three at the most.

JANE. Honestly, Simon, I'd trust Olunde. I don't think he'll deceive you about their intentions.

PILKINGS. He'd better not. All right then, let them in Bob. Warn them to control themselves. Then hurry Olunde here. Make sure he brings his baggage because I'm not returning him into town.

AIDE-DE-CAMP. Very good, sir. (*Goes.*)

PILKINGS (*to* IYALOJA). I hope you understand that if anything goes wrong it will be on your head. My men have orders to shoot at the first sign of trouble.

IYALOJA. To prevent one death you will actually make other deaths? Ah, great is the wisdom of the white race. But have no fear. Your Prince will sleep peacefully. So at long last will ours. We will disturb you no further, servant of the white king. Just let Elesin fulfil his oath and we will retire home and pay homage to our King.

JANE. I believe her Simon, don't you?

PILKINGS. Maybe.

ELESIN. Have no fear ghostly one. I have a message to send my King and then you have nothing more to fear.

IYALOJA. Olunde would have done it. The chiefs asked him to speak the words but he said no, not while you lived.

ELESIN. Even from the depths to which my spirit has sunk, I find some joy that this little has been left to me.

The WOMEN *enter, intoning the dirge 'Ale le le' and swaying from side to side. On their shoulders is borne a longish object roughly like a cylindrical bolt, covered in cloth. They set it down on the spot where* IYALOJA *had stood earlier, and form a semi-circle round it. The* PRAISE-SINGER *and* DRUMMER *stand on the inside of the semi-circle but the drum is not used at all. The* DRUMMER *intones under the* PRAISE-SINGER'S *invocations.*

PILKINGS (*as they enter*). What is *that?*

IYALOJA. The burden you have made white one, but we bring it in peace.

PILKINGS. I said *what* is it?

ELESIN. White man, you must let me out. I have a duty to perform.

PILKINGS. I most certainly will not.

ELESIN. There lies the courier of my King. Let me out so I can perform what is demanded of me.

PILKINGS. You'll do what you need to do from inside there or not at all. I've gone as far as I intend to with this business.

ELESIN. The worshipper who lights a candle in your church to bear a message to his god bows his head and speaks in a whisper to the flame. Have I not seen it ghostly one? His voice does not ring out to the world. Mine are no words for anyone's ears. They are not words even for the bearers of this load. They are words I must speak secretly, even as my father whispered them in my ears and I in the ears of my first-born. I cannot shout them to the wind and the open night-sky.

JANE. Simon . . .

PILKINGS. Don't interfere. Please!

IYALOJA. They have slain the favourite horse of the king and slain his dog. They have borne them from pulse to pulse centre of the land receiving prayers for their king. But the rider has chosen to stay behind. Is it too much to ask that he speak his heart to heart of the waiting courier? (PILKINGS *turns his back on her*.) So be it. Elesin Oba, you see how even the mere leavings are denied you. (*She gestures to the* PRAISE-SINGER.)

PRAISE-SINGER. Elesin Oba! I call you by that name only this last time. Remember when I said, if you cannot come, tell my horse. (*Pause*.) What? I cannot hear you? I said, if you cannot come, whisper in the ears of my horse. Is your tongue severed from the roots? Elesin? I can hear no response. I said, if there are boulders you cannot climb, mount my horse's back, this spotless black stallion, he'll bring you over them. (*Pauses*.) Elesin Oba, once you had a tongue that darted like a drummer's stick. I said, if you get lost my dog will track a path to me. My memory fails me but I think you replied: My feet have found the path, Alafin.

The dirge rises and falls.

I said at the last, if evil hands hold you back, just tell my horse there is weight on the hem of your smock. I dare not wait too long.

The dirge rises and falls.

There lies the swiftest ever messenger of a king, so set me free with the errand of your heart. There lie the head and heart of the favourite of the gods, whisper in his ears. Oh my companion, if you had followed when you should, we would not say that the horse preceded its rider. If you had followed when it was time, we would not say the dog has raced beyond and left his master behind. If you had raised your will to cut the thread of life at the summons of the drums, we would not say your mere shadow fell across the gateway and took its owner's place at the banquet. But the hunter, laden with slain buffalo, stayed to root in the cricket's hole with his toes. What now is left? If there is a dearth of bats, the pigeon must serve us for the offering. Speak the words over your shadow which must now serve in your place.

ELESIN. I cannot approach. Take off the cloth. I shall speak my message from heart to heart of silence.

IYALOJA (*moves forward and removes the covering*). Your courier Elesin, cast your eyes on the favoured companion of the King.

Rolled up in the mat, his head and feet showing at either end, is the body of OLUNDE.

There lies the honour of your household and of our race. Because he could not bear to let honour fly out of doors, he stopped it with his life. The son has proved the father Elesin, and there is nothing left in your mouth to gnash but infant gums.

PRAISE-SINGER. Elesin, we placed the reins of the world in your hands yet you watched it plunge over the edge of the bitter precipice. You sat with folded arms while evil strangers tilted the world from its course and crashed it beyond the edge of emptiness – you muttered, there is little that one man can do, you left us floundering in a blind future. Your heir has taken the burden on himself. What the end will be, we are not gods to tell. But this young shoot has poured its sap into the parent stalk, and we know this is not the way of life. Our world is tumbling in the void of strangers, Elesin.

ELESIN *has stood rock-still, his knuckles taut on the bars, his eyes glued to the body of his son. The stillness seizes and paralyses everyone, including* PILKINGS *who has turned to look. Suddenly* ELESIN *flings one arm round his neck, once, and with the loop of the chain, strangles himself in a swift, decisive pull. The* GUARDS *rush forward to stop him but they are only in time to let his body down.* PILKINGS *has leapt to the door at the same time and struggles with the lock. He rushes within,*

*fumbles with the handcuffs and unlocks them, raises the body
to a sitting position while he tries to give resuscitation. The*
WOMEN *continue their dirge, unmoved by the sudden event.*

IYALOJA. Why do you strain yourself? Why do you labour at tasks
for which no one, not even the man lying there would give you
thanks? He is gone at last into the passage but oh, how late it all
is. His son will feast on the meat and throw him bones. The
passage is clogged with droppings from the King's stallion; he
will arrive all stained in dung.

PILKINGS (*in a tired voice*). Was this what you wanted?

IYALOJA. No child, it is what you brought to be, you who play
with strangers' lives, who even usurp the vestments of our dead,
yet believe that the stain of death will not cling to you. The gods
demanded only the old expired plantain but you cut down the
sap-laden shoot to feed your pride. There is your board, filled to
overflowing. Feast on it. (*She screams at him suddenly, seeing
that* PILKINGS *is about to close* ELESIN's *staring eyes.*) Let
him alone! However sunk he was in debt he is no pauper's
carrion abandoned on the road. Since when have strangers
donned clothes of indigo before the bereaved cries out his loss?

She turns to the BRIDE *who has remained motionless
throughout.*

Child.

*The girl takes up a little earth, walks calmly into the cell and
closes* ELESIN's *eyes. She then pours some earth over each
eyelid and comes out again.*

Now forget the dead, forget even the living. Turn your mind only
to the unborn.

She goes off, accompanied by the BRIDE. *The dirge rises in
volume and the* WOMEN *continue their sway. Lights fade to a
black-out.*

GLOSSARY

alari	a rich, woven cloth, brightly coloured
egungun	ancestral masquerade
etutu	placatory rites or medicine
gbedu	a deep-timbred royal drum
opele	string of beads used in Ifa divination
osugbo	secret 'executive' cult of the Yoruba; its meeting place
robo	a delicacy made from crushed melon seeds, fried in tiny balls
sanyan	a richly valued woven cloth
sigidi	a squat, carved figure, endowed with the powers of an incubus

MADMEN
AND
SPECIALISTS

CAST

The first version of *Madmen and Specialists* was performed at the 1970 Playwrights' Workshop Conference at the Eugene O'Neill Theater Center, Waterford, Connecticutt, U.S.A. The first complete version, printed here, had its première at the University of Ibadan, Nigeria, in March 1971, with the University Theatre Arts Company. The cast was as follows:

AAFAA	} *Mendicants*	Femi Johnson
BLINDMAN		Femi Osofisan
GOYI		Wale Ogunyemi
CRIPPLE		Tunji Oyelana
SI BERO *Sister to Dr Bero*		Deola Adedoyin
IYA AGBA	} *Two old Women*	Nguba Agolia
IYA MATE		Bopo George
DR BERO *Specialist*		Nat Okoro
PRIEST		Gbenga Sonuga
THE OLD MAN *Bero's Father*		Dapo Adelugba

Designed and directed by the author.

The action takes place in and around the home surgery of Dr Bero, lately returned from the wars.

PART ONE

Open space before BERO's *home and surgery. The surgery is down in a cellar. The level ground in the fore and immediate front space serve as drying space for assorted barks and herbs. The higher structure to one side is a form of semi-open hut. Inside it sit* IYA AGBA *and* IYA MATE. IYA AGBA *is smoking a thin pipe.* IYA MATE *stokes a small fire.*

By the roadside is a group of mendicants – CRIPPLE, GOYI, BLINDMAN *and* AAFAA. AAFAA's *St Vitus spasms are designed to rid the wayfarer of his last pennies in a desperate bid to be rid of the sight.* GOYI *is held stiffly in a stooping posture by a contraption which is just visible above his collar. The* CRIPPLE *drags on his knees. They pass the time by throwing dice from the gourd rattle.*

The CRIPPLE *has just thrown the dice.*

AAFAA. Six and four. Good for you.
CRIPPLE. Your turn, Blindman. (*Gives the dice and gourd to* BLINDMAN.)

> BLINDMAN *throws.*

Five and five. Someone is going to give us fivers.
GOYI. Fat chance of that. (*He throws.*)
AAFAA. Three and two, born loser. What did you stake?
GOYI. The stump of the left arm.
CRIPPLE. Your last?
GOYI. No, I've got one left.
BLINDMAN. Your last. You lost the right stump to me yesterday.
GOYI. Do you want it now or later?
BLINDMAN. Keep it for now.
CRIPPLE. When do I get my eye, Aafaa?
AAFAA. Was it the right or the left?

GOYI. Does it matter?

AAFAA. Sure it does. If it's the right one he can take it out now. The left is my evil eye and I need it a while longer.

CRIPPLE. It was the right.

AAFAA. I've just remembered the right is my evil eye.

CRIPPLE. I'll make you an offer. Let me throw against both of you for Goyi's stumps. I'll stake the eye Aafaa lost to me.

GOYI. Why leave me out? I still want to try my luck.

BLINDMAN. You have nothing left to stake.

CRIPPLE. You're just a rubber ball, Goyi. You need a hand to throw with, anyway.

GOYI. I can use my mouth.

AAFAA. To throw dice? You'll eat sand my friend.

BLINDMAN. Sooner or later we all eat sand.

CRIPPLE. Hey, you're beginning to sound like the Old Man.

AAFAA (*voice change*). Did you eat sand, my friend? We'll make you the Ostrich in our touring circus.

BLINDMAN. The limbless acrobat will now perform his wonderful act – how to bite the dust from three classic positions.

GOYI. Upright, take off, and prone.

CRIPPLE. We'll never go on that tour.

AAFAA. Roll up – roll up. Presenting the Creatures of As in the timeless parade.

BLINDMAN. Think we'll ever make that tour?

AAFAA. We will. But until the millions start rolling in, we better not neglect the pennies. (*He nudges them, pointing to* SI BERO.)

> SI BERO *approaches, carrying a small bag from which protrude some twigs with leaves and berries. The* MENDICANTS *begin their performance as soon as they sense her approach.* BLINDMAN *is alms collector,* GOYI *repeats a single acrobatic trick,* AAFAA *is the 'dancer'.* BLINDMAN *shakes the rattles while the* CRIPPLE *drums with his crutches and is lead singer.* BLINDMAN *collects alms in the rattles.*

SI BERO (*as* AAFAA *moves to intercept her*). Don't try that nonsense with me. I live in this neighbourhood, remember?

AAFAA (*his spasms ceasing abruptly. The others also stop playing*). Don't they say charity begins at home?

SI BERO. Your preaching is so good it's a wonder you can't find yourself a congregation.

AAFAA (*stiffening*). What congregation, woman? Who said I was ever a preacher?

SI BERO. You were never anything. Go and find some decent work to do.

AAFAA. With this affliction of mine?

SI BERO. It comes and goes, not so? You can work in between.

AAFAA. And this one? And that? And that? (*Pointing lastly to* GOYI.) If it weren't for the iron rod holding up his spine he would collapse like a toad you step on. Just what sort of work do you want him to do?

GOYI. A penny or two, Si Bero. We haven't eaten today.

BLINDMAN. And that is God's truth. Aafaa, why do you pick a quarrel with her? Just ask her for a few pennies, you know she treats us well.

CRIPPLE. The lane is deserted. Nobody comes and goes any more.

GOYI. Something is driving them away from here. If there isn't something going on, then this isn't an iron I have in my back.

AAFAA. It is your neighbourhood, you say, Si Bero. What are you doing to drive people away?

SI BERO. Perhaps your mother's ghost is haunting the place. Why don't you ask her the next time she visits you?

AAFAA. Why do you always pick on me, old woman? What has my mother done to you?

SI BERO. She gave birth to you for a start. (*She throws a penny to the* CRIPPLE *who tosses it into the gourd.*) If you want more than that, you know where to come. I still need people to sort out my herbs.

AAFAA. Herbs! Herbs! Herbs! Always – come and sort out herbs to earn yourself a decent coin.

SI BERO. And eat. You can have work and eat. The two go together.

She goes out.

CRIPPLE (*throwing the coin in the gourd, calls after her*).
God bless you, Si Bero.

BLINDMAN. He shall, he will, he must.

GOYI. He'd better or I'll know the reason why.

CRIPPLE. Your turn, Aafaa.

AAFAA. What for?

CRIPPLE. A penny is something.

AAFAA. Not for me.

GOYI. Give her a pennyworth, then.

AAFAA. Can't be bothered.

BLINDMAN. Go on. Don't be mean.

CRIPPLE. You're the priest, after all.

AAFAA (*suddenly grinning*). A penny's worth, you say?

CRIPPLE. That's only fair.

AAFAA (*shouting after the now distant woman*). God bless your brother!

They all break out guffawing.

GOYI. More grease to his elbow.

AAFAA. Not forgetting his armpits.

BLINDMAN. More power to his swagger-stick!

CRIPPLE. May light ever shine . . .

AAFAA. From his braids and buttons.

GOYI. May he come home safely . . .

AAFAA. To your loving arms.

CRIPPLE. Not to mention his Daddy's.

GOYI. God help her, that is some brother she has. You may say he is . . . dutiful.

CRIPPLE. Him a dutiful son? You're crazy.

BLINDMAN. I know what he means. (*He points an imaginary gun.*) Bang! All in the line of duty!

GOYI *clutches his chest, slumps over.*

AAFAA. Did we try him?

CRIPPLE. Resurrect, you fool. Nobody tried you yet.

AAFAA (*in a ringing voice*). You are *accused*.

BLINDMAN. Satisfied?

CRIPPLE. Fair enough.

BLINDMAN. Bang!

GOYI *slumps.*

AAFAA (*rinsing his hands*). Nothing to do with me.

BLINDMAN. Fair trial, no?

AAFAA. Decidedly yes.

BLINDMAN. What does he say himself?

GOYI. Very fair, gentlemen. I have no complaints.

BLINDMAN. In that case we permit you to be buried.

GOYI. You are generous, gentlemen. I have a personal aversion to vultures.

BLINDMAN. Oh, come come. Nice birds they are. They clean up after the mess.

CRIPPLE. Not like some bastards we know. (*He spits.*)

AAFAA (*posing*). In a way you may call us vultures. We clean up the mess made by others. The populace should be grateful for our presence. (*He turns slowly round.*) If there is anyone here who does not approve us, just say so and we quit. (*His hand makes the motion of half-drawing out a gun.*) I mean, we are not here because we like it. We stay at immense sacrifice to ourselves, our leisure, our desires, vocation, specialization, etcetera, etcetera. The moment you say, Go, we . . . (*He gives another inspection all round, smiles broadly and turns to the others.*) They insist we stay.

CRIPPLE. I thought they would. Troublesome little insects but . . . they have a sense of gratitude. I mean, after all we did for them.

GOYI. And still do.

BLINDMAN. And will continue to do.

CHORUS. Hear hear hear hear. Very well said, sir.

GOYI. Oh, come on. Shall we follow the woman or yap here all day? Let's get spying.

AAFAA. She's a devil, that's my complaint. She was born with a stone in her stomach.

GOYI. What's wrong? It's the job we are here to do, isn't it?

AAFAA. I still don't like messing about with her herbs.

BLINDMAN. Herbs are herbs, not so? Let's get going.

AAFAA. That woman's herbs are not just herbs. She hoards them and treats them like children. The whole house is full of twigs. If it's a straightforward business, why doesn't she use them? Or sell them or something?

GOYI. But everyone knows she's mad. They get that way after a while living alone. I've known one woman in my village who collects potsherds. Any piece of broken pot would do. Just let an old woman live by herself for a short while and she gets up to all sorts of things. Boxes, cupboards, trunks, every nook and corner. You couldn't walk on the floor without crunching pottery under your foot. Then she would scream curses at you.

CRIPPLE. What are we to do?

GOYI. There must be some way to stay nearer the house most of the day. We can't spend the whole day sorting herbs.

AAFAA. She's a witch. When she spirits out a foetus from the belly of a pregnant woman she pickles it in the herbs and it goes in a bottle for her brother's experiments.

BLINDMAN. For a so-called chaplain you talk plenty of nonsense.

AAFAA. Listen to the blind fool. What do you know about it?

CRIPPLE. Are we going to argue or follow her home?

GOYI. I don't like the whole business. She has been good to us.

AAFAA. With the pennies she throws as if she's feeding a dog? I spit on that kind of goodness!

CRIPPLE. I still don't like it. Why is he doing it? His own family too, what's he up to?

GOYI. He's a specialist.

AAFAA. Amen.

GOYI. What?

AAFAA. Amen. He is a specialist. That takes care of everything, not so?

GOYI. There is bound to be something in it for us.

BLINDMAN. Something like burnt fingers?

GOYI. What do you mean?

BLINDMAN (*shrugs*). When things go wrong it's the lowest who get it first.

AAFAA. There is money at the bottom of it.

CRIPPLE (*places* BLINDMAN'*s hand on his shoulder and starts off in the direction of the house*). And we are at the bottom. So, let's go and make sure the woman doesn't stumble on any official secrets.

AAFAA (*checks*). Rem Acu Tetigisti.

CRIPPLE. What? I don't get you.

AAFAA. R.A.T.! R.A.T.! I smell a rat.

GOYI. Is he having an attack?

CRIPPLE. What's up, Aafaa?

AAFAA. You said it yourself – Official Secrets. Official rat is what I smell. Yessir! We'll get paid something decent. Secret Service funds and all that. Let's celebrate.

GOYI. Nonsense. It's just a simple family vendetta.

AAFAA. Christ! Every one of you freaks will have ideas! And where did you pick up that word, anyway?

GOYI. Where you pick up yours, leave me alone.

AAFAA (*haughtily*). One thing I disapproved of in the Old Man was he didn't discriminate. Talk of casting pearls before swine. Vendetta my foot. I tell you the Cripple has Rem Acu Tetigistied it. Official Secrets that's what's at the bottom of it. Bottomless account. We'll get overtime and risk allowance.

GOYI. It's not going to be risky, is it?

AAFAA. I know you have none, but I'll be risking my conscience. That needs compensation.

CRIPPLE. What do you think, Blindman?

BLINDMAN. Hm. Aafaa may be right. For once.

AAFAA. Never mind the cleverness. You agree.

BLINDMAN. R.A.T. You have touched the matter with a needle.

GOYI. Where? I'm still lost.

AAFAA. Where? I'll soon show you, dumbclod. (*He lunges for* GOYI's *crotch.*)

GOYI (*protecting himself*). No!

AAFAA. Why not? You got any more use for it?

BLINDMAN. Maybe he wants to continue the line.

AAFAA. What! This crooked line? It would be a disservice to humanity.

CRIPPLE. Hey. Think he'll do that to his own father?

BLINDMAN. When the Specialist wants results badly enough...

CRIPPLE. Yes, but what results?

AAFAA. Does it matter? (*Voice change. He points a 'needle' held low, at* GOYI.) Say anything, say anything that comes into your head but SPEAK, MAN! (*Twisting the needle upwards.*)

> GOYI, *hand over crotch, yells.*

BLINDMAN (*solemnly*). Rem Acu Tetigisti.

AAFAA. Believe me, this hurts you more than it hurts me. Or – vice versa. Truth hurts. I am a lover of truth. Do you find you also love truth? Then let's have the truth. THE TRUTH! (*He gives another push.* GOYI *screams.*)

CRIPPLE. ⎫
BLINDMAN. ⎬ Rem Acu Tetigisti.

AAFAA. Think not that I hurt you but that Truth hurts. We are all seekers after truth. I am a Specialist in truth. Now shall we push it up all the way, all the way? Or shall we have all the truth all the truth. (*Another push.* GOYI *screams, then his head slumps.*) Hm, the poor man has fainted.

CRIPPLE. ⎱
BLINDMAN. ⎰ Rem Acu Tetigisti.

AAFAA *makes a motion of slapping his face several times.*
GOYI *revives.*

GOYI. Where am I?

CRIPPLE. Within the moment of truth, dear friend.

AAFAA (*chanting*). Rem Acu . . .

OTHERS. Tetigisti, tetigisti.

ALTOGETHER. Rem Acu Tetigisti.

AAFAA. You have touched it with a . . .

OTHERS. Fine needle, fine fine needle.

ALL. You have touched it with a fine fine.

AAFAA. Rem Acu . . .

They repeat the song, AAFAA *singing Rem Acu Tetigisti in
counterpoint to the others* 'You have touched it with a
needle'.

Hey. (*He taps* GOYI *on the shoulder.*) Are you recovered?
Good. Here we go again.

CRIPPLE. Perhaps he needs a drink of water.

AAFAA. Really? Well, give him one, then. We are no monsters
here. No one will charge me with heartlessness. Give him a
drink of water. A large one.

BLINDMAN *hands* GOYI *a 'bowl' of water.* GOYI *drains it
while they all watch avidly.*

Satisfied? Happy? More? No. (*He takes the bowl and hands it
to* BLINDMAN.) Anything else? Perhaps you would like to
use the conveniences? The toilet? (GOYI *nods.*) Over there.
Be my guest.

GOYI *turns, his hand goes to his fly, he stops, turns round
slowly. A big grin appears on the faces of the other three.*

What's the matter? No wan' pee-pee? Pee-pee pee-pee?
No more pee-pee? I know what it is. (*Chanting.*) Rem Acu . . .

OTHERS. Tetigisti, tetigisti . . .

> *As they go through the chant again* SI BERO *reappears with a small bunch of herbs. They quickly stop singing.*

CRIPPLE. Are we to come now, Si Bero? We need the work.

SI BERO. Wait here. I'll tell you when I'm ready.

> *They watch her pass. She goes into the* OLD WOMEN's *hut and* AAFAA *sneaks near a moment later, to try and eavesdrop. The others pass the time throwing dice.*
> *In the* OLD WOMEN's *hut.*

IYA MATE. A-ah, you have a good eye, daughter.

IYA AGBA. Where did you find it?

SI BERO. Not far from where I went yesterday. Someone had emptied a pile of rubbish near by, that's why I missed it.

> *The two* OLD WOMEN *move nearer the light, examining the berries.*

IYA MATE. The berries are all right too. Birds attack them quite early. You are lucky.

IYA AGBA. I wasn't expecting her to find any berries.

SI BERO (*dipping in the bag*). I brought you some tobacco. And snuff for you, Iya Mate.

IYA MATE. You are a good woman. Some menfolk leave the home and never know whether they will come back to a dung-heap or worse.

IYA AGBA. Weeds growing through the window and bats hanging from the rafters. That is when they find out that some women carry a curse in their breasts.

IYA MATE. Your menfolk are lucky. There will be leaves in their living-room – but not the kind that places the handprint of death on a man's heart. Now, you leave these here.

IYA AGBA (*suddenly*). Let me see that. Let me see it!

IYA MATE. What's the matter?

IYA AGBA. Bring it here. It's not the right one at all.

IYA MATE. Here. Look for yourself. No one can tell me my eyes are failing.

IYA AGBA. Just now I remember what you said – birds haven't attacked it. Usually it's the poison kind they don't go near. (*She breaks the stalk.*) I thought so. This is the twin. Poison.

SI BERO. Poison! But . . .

IYA MATE. It can't be poison.

IYA AGBA. They don't grow much. Haven't seen one in – oh, since I was a child. Farmers destroy them as soon as they see them. But it's the poison twin all right. Except for that red streak along the stalk you wouldn't tell them apart.

IYA MATE. I didn't even know there was the poison kind.

IYA AGBA. You don't see them much. Once in a lifetime. Farmers don't let them live, you know. Burn out the soil where they find it growing, just to kill the seeds. Foolishness. Poison has its uses too. You can cure with poison if you use it right. Or kill.

SI BERO. I'll throw it in the fire.

IYA MATE. Do nothing of the sort. You don't learn good things unless you learn evil.

SI BERO. But it's poison.

IYA MATE. It grows.

IYA AGBA. Rain falls on it.

IYA MATE. It sucks the dew.

IYA AGBA. It lives.

IYA MATE. It dies.

IYA AGBA. Same as any other. An-hn, same as any other.

SI BERO. That means I still have to find the right one.

IYA AGBA. It will be in the same place. They grow together most of the time.

SI BERO. I'll go tomorrow.

IYA MATE. Take some rest. Or . . . is he on his way home?

SI BERO. There is no news at all. I am beginning to . . .

IYA AGBA. Beginning to worry like every foolish woman. He'll come back. He and his father. There is too much binds

them down here. They will take root with their spirit, not
with their bodies on some unblessed soil. Let me see your
hands. (*She scrutinizes the hands carefully, bursts suddenly into
a peal of laughter.*) These hands are not yet ready to wind
shrouds. We shall drink palm wine soon, very soon when
someone returns. (*She takes* SI BERO *by both hands and
begins to shuffle with her, singing.*)
Ofe gbe wa de'le o – Ofe . . .
Ofe gbe wa de'le o – Ofe
Oko epo epa i runa
Gbe wa dele o
Ofe gbe wa de'le

> The MENDICANTS *look at one another, begin to beat time
> with them, then join the singing in a raucous, cynical tone.
> The* WOMEN *stop, amazed and offended. The* OLD WOMEN
> *fold their arms, retire deeper into the hut while* SI BERO
> *dashes out, furious.*

SI BERO. Stop that noise! Did I ask you here for entertainment?

CRIPPLE. No offence, Si Bero, no offence. We only thought you
had forgotten us.

SI BERO. And thought your horrible voices the best way of
reminding me.

GOYI. It's not our fault our voices are no better.

AAFAA. We can't all have voices like choiring angels, you
know.

SI BERO. That's enough from you. Come along if you still
want to work, only keep your voices down and stop frightening the neighbourhood.

> *They follow her to the front of the house.*

CRIPPLE. So here we are, Si Bero. Bring out the herbs and let
us catch the smell of something in your kitchen while we are
about it.

AAFAA. How much are we getting today? Let's decide that first.

SI BERO. Depends how hard you work.

GOYI. Let's start work. It's a hot day and a man may as well stay close to shelter.

SI BERO. I have a whole sack my buyer brought in yesterday.

She takes hold of BLINDMAN's *hand.*

You can give me a hand, the sack is heavy. (AAFAA *immediately positions himself to accompany her.*) Not you, damn your forwardness. Did I talk to you?

AAFAA. He's not much use. He'll trip over and break his neck.

SI BERO. And that's his business not yours.

She leads BLINDMAN *into the house.*

AAFAA. Did you see that?

GOYI. I am sure even the Blindman did.

CRIPPLE. She didn't want any of us three, that was certain, but I . . .

AAFAA. Picks the one who can't see a thing.

CRIPPLE. I saw.

AAFAA. I told you it's funny business.

CRIPPLE. I am trying to tell you I saw. I saw the herbs.

AAFAA. Where? Where?

CRIPPLE. From here. From down here I could see through a gap in the door when she opened it.

AAFAA. What then? What did you see?

CRIPPLE. Herbs. Roots. Nothing but dried plants. The shelves are right up to the ceiling and they were full of leaves. All browned and crinkled.

GOYI. What kind?

CRIPPLE. All kinds.

GOYI. What is she going to do with all that forest?

AAFAA. Perhaps now you will learn to listen to me.

CRIPPLE. She must be slightly crazy. Living all alone, I suppose.

AAFAA. S-sh. They're coming. See if you can sneak another look.

> SI BERO *and* BLINDMAN *enter, carrying a heavy sack between them.*

SI BERO (*entering backwards, she stumbles against the* CRIPPLE *who is trying to see through a crack*). Get out of the way, will you. Are you now the doorstop that I must step on you to get out of my own house?

CRIPPLE (*forced to retreat*). You are in a bad mood today, Si Bero.

SI BERO. Your mother is in a bad mood, not me. Now get working instead of dragging yourself in people's way. Get busy. You know how I like them sorted out.

AAFAA. Yes, we know.

GOYI. First the roots.

CRIPPLE. Then peel the barks.

AAFAA. Slice the stalks.

CRIPPLE. Squeeze out the pulps.

GOYI. Pick the seeds.

AAFAA. Break the pods. Crack the plaster.

CRIPPLE. Probe the wound or it will never heal.

BLINDMAN. Cut off one root to save the other.

AAFAA. Cauterize.

CRIPPLE. Quick-quick-quick-quick, amputate!

> BLINDMAN *lets out a loud groan.*

AAFAA. What do you mean, sir! How dare you lie there and whine?

GOYI. Cut his vocal chords.

AAFAA. 'Before we operate we cut the vocal chords.'

BLINDMAN. That's only for the dogs.

CRIPPLE. Your case is worse. You are an underdog.

GOYI. Rip out his vocal chords.

BLINDMAN *lets out another scream.*

AAFAA. We don't want you in this fraternity.

CRIPPLE. Fool! You should see the others and thank your stars.

BLINDMAN. I can't see them to thank.

AAFAA (*snatches his stick*). Shall I put them on his head? He can have them in all colours.

CRIPPLE. Leave him for now, we'll simply expel him.

BLINDMAN (*screaming again*). Oh God!

GOYI. Who's got the flaming sword?

AAFAA. Right here, Lord, right here.

GOYI. Show him the door.

AAFAA. Out of the garden, bum, don't ever show your face in here again.

BLINDMAN. I appeal.

CRIPPLE. Who to?

BLINDMAN. As.

AAFAA. In the name of As of the beginning, out!

BLINDMAN. No!

AAFAA. Out!

BLINDMAN. No!

AAFAA. One – Two – Three – Four —

BLINDMAN (*druggedly*). Five – Six – Seven – Eight – Nine —

AAFAA. Out!

BLINDMAN (*wearily*). Out! (*His head drops down.* AAFAA *raises the 'sword'.*)

SI BERO. Have you all gone mad?

AAFAA. No. I'm quite good at it, actually. One stroke and – clean through the tendons. Bang through the ball-and-socket, believe me. I never touch the marrow.

GOYI. Heh, stop. The woman.

SI BERO. I said have you gone mad? Are you here to work or fool around?

CRIPPLE. Oh, never mind us. Come on.

> *They settle down quickly. As the sack is emptied on the ground,* SI BERO, *already about to turn into the house, stops, goes over and picks out a bunch of roots which she turns about in her hand, inspecting it. The* MENDICANTS *cannot contain their curiosity, directly observing her action.* BLINDMAN *listens intensely into the silence. Finally she starts towards the* OLD WOMEN's *hut.*

AAFAA. We can sort that bunch if you like. And give it a scraping. It seems dirty enough.

SI BERO (*turns slowly on him*). Not half as dirty as your anus. The day you scrape that you can tell me what needs scraping and what doesn't.

AAFAA (*raising his stick*). You go too far with that mouth of yours!

> SI BERO *looks him up and down contemptuously. She continues on her way.*

I have a mind to set fire to every single herb in that house.

BLINDMAN. Why don't you learn to leave her alone?

AAFAA. What did I do? What did I say? Just because of one stinking root. She has a mouth like a running gutter.

BLINDMAN. Leave the woman alone. She minds her own business, you mind yours.

AAFAA. And that's enough from you, Mr Blind Advocate. I don't have to listen to you take her side all the time. One more word from you . . .

> *He feints a slap across* BLINDMAN's *face.* BLINDMAN, *alert, springs suddenly backwards and grasps his staff.* AAFAA *looks at him a moment, then bursts out laughing.*

Do you see what I see? The man actually wants to fight me. Did you see? Did you see him? He has no eyes but he actually wants to fight. Hm? Is it really a fight you're looking for, Blind One?

He kicks aside his staff but BLINDMAN *immediately closes in on* AAFAA, *reaches for his arms and imprisons them. They strain against each other.*

CRIPPLE. Bloody fools!

GOYI. Look! The specialist.

He points to the spot where they were first seen. Standing there is BERO, *uniformed, carrying a hold-all. He watches. The* CRIPPLE *tugs at the clothes of the struggling men.*

CRIPPLE. Better stop that, he's here.

GOYI. He's waiting for us. Come on.

The two men break apart. AAFAA *is panting heavily. The* CRIPPLE *dashes quickly and brings* BLINDMAN *his stick. Somewhat sheepishly they troop towards* BERO.

BERO (*gives them a long cold stare*). Was that what I sent you to do in that house?

AAFAA. He started it. And the woman.

CRIPPLE. Aafaa hit him first. Knocked off his stick. A blind man too.

He spits.

AAFAA. If people know they have a handicap then they shouldn't open their mouths to provoke their betters.

CRIPPLE. Hits a blind man. (*He spits again.*)

AAFAA. If you think just because you are a cripple you won't get it from me if you go beyond bounds, just try it and see.

CRIPPLE. A blind man. (*He spits again.*)

AAFAA (*raises the rattle threateningly*). Don't think because of him being here I can't . . .

The CRIPPLE *counters immediately by raising his crutch.*

BERO. Shut up! Shut up all of you. I didn't send you to the house to fight. I asked you to keep your eyes open and keep her from going down. (*He looks at them with contempt, then jerks his thumb in the direction of the cellar.*) What about him. Is he staying quiet?

AAFAA (*jerking his thumb at* BLINDMAN). Ask him. He is the only one who got to enter the house. Ask Blindman what he saw.

BERO. I have no time for fooling.

BLINDMAN. He was quiet. I don't think the woman knows anything.

BERO. What room did you enter?

BLINDMAN. The one with the herbs. I don't think there are any bare walls in there; it's all covered with herbs. From the floor to the ceiling, it's all full of herbs very carefully laid and touched and dusted every day of her life. I could tell that as soon as I entered.

CRIPPLE. I saw it. I caught a glimpse.

AAFAA. Last night when we got him into that underground place she was fast asleep. We didn't make a noise.

BLINDMAN. Excuse me, I wish to say something.

BERO. Yes?

BLINDMAN. I can only tell you what I felt – in that room where I stood with her. There is more love in there than you'll find in the arms of a hundred women. I don't know what unhappiness you intend for her but . . .

BERO. That's enough. You don't know a thing about anything, so shut up.

BLINDMAN *shrugs and retires to one side.*

GOYI. My feeling is, I can't help agreeing with him. In any case we are not much use to anyone.

BERO. I said that's enough. You're under orders.

AAFAA. I am not. And I haven't eaten today.

BERO. Very good.

AAFAA. Enh? Say that again. Which of what is very good?

BERO. The fact that you haven't eaten today. If you fall down on the job you know you will go back to being hungry.

AAFAA. Good. I am glad to hear where we stand. We've done one thing already and don't think it was easy getting him in that hole without waking the neighbours or your sister. So what about for now? Have we already fallen down on the job that we see nothing of what you promised?

BERO (*studies him for a while, then turns to the others*). Have you told him who I am exactly?

AAFAA. Oh yes, Dr Bero. I know who you are. The specialist. We all do. So what about it? You say we are under orders but I tell you I am not. I know these three are discharged. As for me, I have never even taken orders from you before.

BERO. These are no longer discharged and you now take orders from me. You either get that into your twisted mind or get out now.

AAFAA. You can't tell me to get out. We teamed together without your help and we are not doing badly as it is. You can't come here and break us up. If we have anybody to thank it's him down there. Not that I care. I always thought he was crazy. But just don't you forget we are a team – one for all and all for one.

BERO. You prefer that? Begging for pennies and getting spat upon?

AAFAA. That's what you think. Ho ho, that's a good one, isn't it? Isn't it? You don't know anything about us, do you? Think we spent all that time with your old man without learning a thing or two? You can't specialize in everything, you know.

GOYI. Shut up, Aafaa.

CRIPPLE. You talk too much, shut your mouth.

BERO. He's saying nothing I don't know already.

AAFAA. You know nothing, Dr Bero. You can't bluff me.

BLINDMAN. You really are a fool, Aafaa.

CRIPPLE (*whining*). Pay no attention to him. We do nothing really bad, just one or two things to eke out the droppings of charity.

BERO. Save that for your customers. I'm not interested in what you've done. But from now on you stop taking any risks. I don't want to have to look for you in every filthy gaol.

CRIPPLE. If you'll make up for our losses, sir . . . we were on our way to greater things.

GOYI. I'll say that for us. We were just beginning.

BERO. To do what?

CRIPPLE. Well, you know . . . your Old Man did come up with some ripe ideas . . .

BERO. You'll be taken care of. That's a promise.

CRIPPLE. Then as I said before, that's all right by me.

GOYI. Me too.

AAFAA. No, it isn't. I don't mind the risks we are taking right now . . .

BERO. I said, no more risks.

AAFAA. That's for us to decide until you say how much. What does he know about risks anyway? Even if I was only a chaplain to the men out there I knew what risk was. I nearly had it once or twice. Quite different from working for Intelligence where all you had to do was sift through papers full of lies and know how to slap people around . . .

BERO cuts him across the face with his swagger stick. AAFAA staggers back, clutching the wound. BERO stands still, watching him. At the sound of pain IYA AGBA looks out of the hut and impassively observes the scene.

BERO. That should remind you I do know how to slap people around. And you'd better remember some other things I know. You weren't just discharged because of your – sickness. Just remember that . . . and other things.

He stands gazing towards the house for a while.

I am due home now. You know when to follow. Just remember to carry out my instructions to the letter.

He walks purposefully to the house. As he passes by the OLD WOMEN's hut IYA AGBA leans back to avoid being seen by him. A moment later SI BERO *emerges, sees* BERO *and shouts, running towards him.* IYA MATE *joins the other women to watch the reunion.*

SI BERO. Bero! Bero! (*She embraces him, then tears herself off and shouts.*)

BERO. Don't do that!

SI BERO (*rushing about, she doesn't hear*). He's home! He's . . .

BERO (*chases after and restrains her*). Be quiet!

SI BERO. What?

BERO. I don't want my return announced.

SI BERO. Why not? (*Suddenly suspicious.*) You're not going back again, are you?

BERO. It isn't that. I want some quiet, that's all.

SI BERO. Oh! how thoughtless I was. But they will be disappointed.

BERO. Who will?

SI BERO. Our neighbours. All your old patients.

BERO. Corpses.

SI BERO. What? I said your old patients.

BERO. I said corpses. Oh, forget it.

SI BERO. I can't. (*She scans his face anxiously.*) They haven't forgotten you.

BERO. They still exist, do they?

SI BERO (*again puzzled*). Who? I don't understand.

BERO. I'm tired. Let's talk of something else.

SI BERO. Oh yes, you must be. Come inside. No, wait. You mustn't come in yet. Be patient now, Bero. (*Hurrying into the house.*) Don't move from there. Stand still.

> BERO *looks slowly round him, he gazes as if he is trying to pierce through walls into neighbouring homes. The expression on his face is contempt.*
>
> SI BERO *reappears with a gourd of palm wine, pours it on the ground in front of the doorstep. Then she moves to unlace his boots.*

BERO. You still keep up these little habits.

SI BERO. I like to keep close to earth.

BERO (*stepping back to prevent her from taking off his boots*). Bare feet, wet earth. We've wetted your good earth with something more potent than that, you know.

SI BERO. Not you. Neither you nor Father. You had nothing to do with it. On the contrary.

BERO. What, on the contrary?

SI BERO. Were you together? Did you manage to work together?

BERO. We were together. For some time.

SI BERO. Is he going to stay with us?

BERO. We'll . . . discuss him later.

SI BERO (*suddenly fearful*). What is it, Bero? Is he . . .?

BERO (*stares back at her, letting the pause hang*). Well, is he – what?

SI BERO (*laughing*). Stop trying to frighten me.

BERO. Who's trying to?

SI BERO. Where are you hiding him? I bet he's waiting round the corner.

BERO. He'll rejoin us in his own time.

SI BERO (*disappointed*). Oh. But he's safe.

BERO (*impatiently*). Of course he is.

SI BERO (*takes his hand*). Come with me. I must show you to the Old Women and tell them also Father is safe.

BERO. What Old Women?

SI BERO. Over there in the hut.

BERO. Who are they?

SI BERO. Herbalists. They helped me with your work.

BERO. But why bring them here? Why camp them on my doorstep?

SI BERO. They were good to me. I couldn't have done a thing without them. Come and talk to them.

> BERO *does not move. Immediately, the* OLD WOMEN *start to speak.* BERO *and* SI BERO *remain still,* BERO *looking towards the* OLD WOMEN'S *hut while* SI BERO *watches him.*

IYA AGBA. Well, has it been worth it, do you think?

IYA MATE. It's good to see her face bubbling like froth on good wine.

IYA AGBA. Not her, him!

IYA MATE. Oh, him. Well, you never can tell with seeds. The plant may be good . . . but we'll know, we'll know.

IYA AGBA. I hope it's a good seed. That was two lives we poured into her hands. Two long lives spent pecking at secrets grain by grain.

IYA MATE. More than two. What she took from us began with others we no longer call by name.

IYA AGBA. She sucked my head dry.

IYA MATE. She is a good woman.

IYA AGBA. Yes, but what about him?

IYA MATE. You sense something wrong in him?

IYA AGBA. It's my life that's gone into his. I haven't burrowed so deep to cast good earth on worthless seeds.

IYA MATE. Nor she. Tramping through all those bushes, finding the desolate spots only we remember.

IYA AGBA. She was stubborn, others would have given up early. (*She giggles.*) I did my best to put her off. Sent her on those fruitless errands, hoping she'd give up. Others would have done.

IYA MATE. Oh, you are wicked.

IYA AGBA. She proved herself, there's no denying it. She proved herself. If she'd wanted it easy or simply out of greed I would have guided her feet into quicksands and left her there.

IYA MATE. You would, I know you, you would.

IYA AGBA. So let him watch it. I haven't come this far to put my whole being in a sieve.

She turns abruptly and returns into the hut. IYA MATE *remains for a while.*

SI BERO. They told me what to look for, where to look for it. How to sort them and preserve them.

BERO (*nods*). You haven't wasted your time. I still need things from my former vocation.

SI BERO. Former vocation?

BERO. A means, not an end.

SI BERO. We heard terrible things. So much evil. Then I would console myself that I earned the balance by carrying on your work. One thing cancels out another. Bero, they're waiting. Go and greet them Bero. They held your life together while you were away.

BERO. What is that supposed to mean?

SI BERO. I never feared for you while they were here.

BERO. You really disappoint me. You are supposed to be intelligent. It was you I asked to do my work, not some stupid old hags. I suppose they filled your hand with all that evil stuff. You've been pretty free with that word.

SI BERO. Not you yourself Bero, but guilt contaminates. And often I was afraid . . . (*Suddenly determined.*) Bero, where is Father!?

BERO. Safe.

SI BERO (*stubbornly*). But you must know when he's coming.

BERO. Sometime.

SI BERO. When? Why didn't you return together?

BERO. He's a sick man. He is coming home to be cured.

SI BERO. Sick? Wounded?

BERO. Mind sickness. We must be kind to him.

SI BERO. How long, Bero? How long had he been sick?

BERO. Ever since he came out. Maybe the . . . suffering around him proved too much for him. His mind broke under the strain.

SI BERO (*quietly*). How bad? Don't hide anything, Bero. How bad is he?

BERO. He started well. But of course we didn't know which way his mind was working. Madmen have such diabolical cunning. It was fortunate I had already proved myself. He was dangerous. Dangerous!

SI BERO. What do you mean? Did he endanger you?

BERO. Did he! He was in a different sector, working among the convalescents. I wouldn't have known what was going on if I had still been with the Medical Corps.

SI BERO. If you had still been?

BERO. I told you. I switched.

SI BERO. But how? You have your training. How does one switch, just like that?

BERO. You are everything once you go out there. In an emergency . . . (*He shrugs.*) The head of the Intelligence Section died rather suddenly. Natural causes.

SI BERO. And that's the new vocation?

BERO. None other, sister, none other. The Big Braids agreed I was born into it. Not that that was any recommendation. They are all submental apes.

SI BERO (*studying him avidly, a slow apprehension beginning to show on her face*). But you have . . . you have given that up now. You are back to your real work. Your practice.

BERO (*turns calmly to meet her gaze*). Practice? Yes, I intend to maintain that side of my practice. A laboratory is important. Everything helps. Control, sister, control. Power comes from bending Nature to your will. The Specialist they called me,

and a specialist is – well – a specialist. You analyse, you diag-
nose, you – (*He aims an imaginary gun.*) – prescribe.

SI BERO (*more to herself*). You should have told me. I have
made pledges I cannot fulfil.

BERO. Pledges? What are you talking about?

SI BERO. I swore I was sure of you, only then would they help
me.

BERO. Who? The Old Women?

SI BERO. They held nothing back from me.

The PRIEST *enters, hails them from a distance.*

PRIEST. A-ah, there you are. Bero, my boy, welcome home. I
caught a glimpse of you from my vestry and I said, No, it's
not him, it can't be. But of course, who else could it be
looking so handsome and imposing. Your prayers are answered, I said to myself, your prayers are answered, you
doubting Thomas. And how is the little lady, the courageous
one who kept the fort in the absence of brother and father?
Overjoyed, I am sure, overjoyed. So are we all.

He observes nothing of BERO's *cold attitude nor the fact
that* BERO *has moved casually away from the patronizing
arm which he tried to place on his shoulder.*

I meant to call on one or two neighbours on the way but
that's just the selfish sinner I am, may God forgive me. No, I
decided, I'll just have him all to myself for a little bit.

BERO. That's rather lucky.

PRIEST. Beg your pardon?

SI BERO. He's tired, Pastor. Don't let it out he's back yet.

PRIEST. Of course not. I wouldn't dream of doing such a
thing. We all have our human failings of course, but I do
know how inconsiderate people can be in their joys. Wouldn't
think a man who's just returned from the seventh outpost of
hell would want a little time to himself. I've suffered from
my old complaint, you know, my boy, but I can suffer a

little longer. Just get settled, son, just get settled and give yourself a well-deserved rest.

SI BERO. Pastor, you know I offered you . . .

PRIEST. Not quite the same thing, young lady, not quite the same thing. The doctor used to make those extracts with his own hand and . . .

SI BERO. It was the same one he made before he left.

PRIEST. No no, I could tell the difference. Oh yes, I could tell.

SI BERO. It was the same.

PRIEST. Good of you to try, but no. You just didn't make it the same. I could tell the difference at once. As soon as you're rested, my boy, as soon as you've rested . . . oh dear me. How shameful. Here I am complaining of my little fits and I haven't even asked news of my good friend. When is your father coming, my lad?

BERO. Soon.

SI BERO. Bero was just telling me . . .

PRIEST. Soon. How soon?

BERO. Soon enough.

PRIEST. Not soon enough for me, boy, not soon enough. I can't wait to take issue with him on all our old debates. Such an argumentative man, your father, such an argumentative man. And he'll have some stories to tell me, I'm sure. Really looking forward to our long evenings together. What an experience he must have had, what an experience! You know, it's strange how these disasters bring out the very best in man – and the worst sometimes. In your father's case, of course, the very best. Truly noble. I couldn't believe my ears when he got up one day and said he was going to join you. At your age, I said, you doddering old thing? I used to call him that, you know, and he would call me the mitred hypocrite. All in play, of course, only in play. So he . . . where was I? Something about your father, I believe. Oh yes, he suddenly got up one evening, right in the midst of our argument and said, I am going to see what's going on.

He was just reading me a letter from you and he got all
worked up. It can't be, he shouted. And then he leapt up
and said – right out of the blue – we've got to legalize cannibalism. Yes, right out of the blue. What do you mean, I
said, thinking he only wanted to start another argument.
But no, he repeats it over and over and of course, I took him
on. Legalize cannibalism? It's a damnable and heathenish
idea. Yes, that's how we started the argument. Warmest
session we ever had together. He wouldn't yield one foot
and I wouldn't budge one inch. Not one fraction of an inch.
My polemical spirit was aroused. Not to talk of Christian
principles. For three hours I fought him foot by foot. Never
been in better form. Nearly all night we argued, if you please,
and then in the morning he was gone. What do you make of
that?

SI BERO. Pastor, I think Bero is a little tired . . .

PRIEST. Had only one letter from him all that time. Told me
he was doing recuperative work among some disabled fel-
lows. No forwarding address, if you please. I couldn't even
continue our old debate by post. Strange man, your father,
very strange. You didn't run into him out there, did you?
I'm really anxious to know if he still intends to legalize
cannibalism.

BERO. He does.

PRIEST. I knew it. A stubborn man, once he gets hold of an
idea. You won't believe it but he actually said to me, I'm
going to try and persuade those fools not to waste all that
meat. Mind you he never could stand wastage, could he?
I remember he used to wade into you both if he caught you
wasting anything. But human flesh, why, that's another
matter altogether.

BERO. But why, Pastor. It's quite delicious, you know.

PRIEST. Just what I say. It's . . . what did you say?

BERO (*reaches out and pulls out the* PRIEST's *cheek*). This.
Delicious.

PRIEST (*struggles free*). You're joking, of course.

BERO. No. Your friend will confirm it when he comes.

PRIEST (*increasingly horrified*). You mean he . . .

BERO. No, not him. He never meant anything. At least, not that way. But we found it delicious just the same.

PRIEST. You?

BERO. I give you the personal word of a scientist. Human flesh is delicious. Of course, not all parts of the body. I prefer the balls myself.

PRIEST (*vehemently*). I don't believe you.

BERO. You don't? Well, then, why don't you stay to dinner?

PRIEST. Dinner? (*Cheering up.*) Of course. I see all you want is an argument like your old man. Delighted, of course. Only too delighted to oblige . . . (*He is stricken by a sudden doubt.*) Er . . . dinner . . . did you say dinner?

BERO. Dinner. I came well-laden with supplies.

The PRIEST *glances at* BERO's *bulging briefcase lying near by, gulps.*

PRIEST. I . . . er . . . I am wondering if I haven't got a little christening to attend to. I . . . er . . . couldn't simply come for drinks afterwards?

BERO. A christening so late in the evening?

PRIEST. Well, you know, the blessing at home and all that. The christening was this morning. (*He is already retreating.*) God bless you, my children both. I shall hurry back as soon as it's all over. Can't get rid of these extra parish duties . . . welcome back once again, my boy . . .

They watch him take flight.

SI BERO (*laughing*). You know, for a moment I nearly believed you.

BERO. Oh? (*Turns and looks at her pityingly.*) You didn't?

Pause. They look each other in the face. Her laughter dies slowly.

SI BERO. Oh God.

BERO. Out of your world, little sister, out of your little world. Stay in it and do only what I tell you. That way you'll be safe.

SI BERO (*vehemently*). Abomination!

BERO. Delicious, you heard me say.

SI BERO. Abomination!

BERO (*deliberate cruelty*). Delicious. The balls, to be exact. I thought I told you to stay in your little world! Go and take tea with the senile pastor or gossip with your old women. Don't come out from where you're safe. (*Quietly.*) Or sane.

SI BERO. But at least tell me why? In God's name why?

BERO. No, not in God's name – in the name of As!

SI BERO. What?

BERO. As. The new god and the old – As.

SI BERO. What are you trying to be, Bero – evil?

BERO. Does it sound that bad? It was no brain-child of mine. We thought it was a joke. I'll bless the meat, he said. And then – As Was the Beginning, As is, Now, As Ever shall be . . . world without. . . . We said amen with a straight face and sat down to eat. Then, afterwards . . .

SI BERO. Yes?

BERO. He told us. (*Pause. He laughs suddenly.*) But why not? Afterwards I said why not? What is one flesh from another? So I tried it again, just to be sure of myself. It was the first step to power you understand. Power in its purest sense. The end of inhibitions. The conquest of the weakness of your too human flesh with all its sentiment. So again, all to myself I said Amen to his grace.

SI BERO. I don't follow you, Bero. Who said grace? Whose words are these?

BERO. Father's part of the liturgy of his bed-ridden audience. Wait a minute. (*Pointing to the* MENDICANTS.) They can tell you more about it.

SI BERO. Who? These? What they have to do with . . .?

BERO. Have you never thought how they came to beg so close to here? At the beginning, that is. Before I found out about them.

SI BERO. Oh, is that it? You mean he sent them? But you know him – Liberty House. It's not a crime. I found them work to do.

BERO (*heatedly*). It's not his charitable propensities I am concerned with. Father's assignment was to help the wounded readjust to the pieces and remnants of their bodies. Physically. Teach them to make baskets if they still had fingers. To use their mouths to ply needles if they had none, or use it to sing if their vocal cords had not been shot away. Teach them to amuse themselves, make something of themselves. Instead he began to teach them to think, think, THINK! Can you picture a more treacherous deed than to place a working mind in a mangled body?

SI BERO. Where is he?

BERO. Where? Here.

SI BERO. Here?

BERO (*pointing to the* MENDICANTS). There. When they open their mouths you can hear him. You! Come here! Tell her. Would you call yourself sane?

The MENDICANTS *have approached,* AAFAA *in the lead.*

AAFAA. Certainly not, sir.

BERO. You got off lightly, Why?

AAFAA. I pleaded insanity.

BERO. Who made you insane?

AAFAA (*by rote, raising his eyes to heaven*). The Old Man, sir. He said things, he said things. My mind . . . I beg your pardon, sir, the thing I call my mind, well, was no longer there. He took advantage of me, sir, in that convalescent home. I was unconscious long stretches at a time. Whatever I saw when I came to was real. Whatever voice I heard was the truth. It was always him. Bending over my bed. I asked him, Who are you? He answered, The one and only truth.

CRIPPLE. Hear hear.

GOYI. Same here.

AAFAA. Always at me, he was, sir. I plead insanity.

CRIPPLE. Hear hear.

GOYI. Same here.

AAFAA (*pointing to* BLINDMAN). Even him.

BLINDMAN. Once I even thought I could see him.

GOYI. Oh, but you did, you did.

BLINDMAN. No, not really.

CRIPPLE. You did, you did. The picture forms in the mind, remember?

GOYI. His very words. But any fool knows they form on the eye.

AAFAA. Lord, he mixed us up.

BLINDMAN. You can see me, he said, you can see me. Look at me with your mind. I swear I began to see him. Then I knew I was insane.

CRIPPLE. Hear hear.

GOYI. Same here.

AAFAA. We all did.

CRIPPLE. And getting me all choosy!

BLINDMAN. Poor you.

CRIPPLE. Beggars can't be choosers, we all knew that.

AAFAA. Yet he got you choosy.

CRIPPLE. I was mad.

BLINDMAN (*changing his voice*). Remember, even if you have nothing left but your vermin, discriminate between one bug and the next.

CRIPPLE. Some bugs are friendly, others wild.

GOYI. The one sucks gently, the other nips.

BLINDMAN. If you must eat a toad . . .

CRIPPLE. . . . pick the fat one, with eggs in its belly.

AAFAA. Listen to the fool. It's you he's calling a toad.

The CRIPPLE *advances on him.*

GOYI. No, it wasn't. Don't listen to him.

AAFAA (*voice change*). You'll listen now or you'll listen later!

SI BERO. Where is Father?

AAFAA. Where is he, where is he? As is everywhere.

CRIPPLE (*picking a flea from his rags*). Got him!

SI BERO (*turning sharply*). What!

CRIPPLE (*throwing it in his mouth*). A fat one.

GOYI. Greedy beggar.

AAFAA. Did you choose it?

CRIPPLE. It chose me.

BLINDMAN. Chose? An enemy of As.

AAFAA. Sure? Not a disciple.

BLINDMAN. An enemy. Subversive agent.

AAFAA. Quite right. As chooses, man accepts. Had it sucked any blood?

CRIPPLE. It tasted bloody.

GOYI. Accept my sympathies.

CRIPPLE. Not needed. The blood is back where it belongs.

AAFAA. The cycle is complete?

CRIPPLE. Definitely.

GOYI. Then you can't complain.

SI BERO. What is this, Bero? Where is Father?

AAFAA. Within the cycle.

BLINDMAN. That's good. The cycle of As. Tell the Old Man that – he'll be pleased.

SI BERO. Where is he?

AAFAA. Where the cycle is complete there will As be found. As of the beginning, we praise thee.

SI BERO (*shutting her ears*). Oh God!

BERO (*pointing to the* MENDICANTS). Do you still want to see him?

AAFAA. As – Was – Is – Now.

SI BERO. Shut up, you loathsome toads!

There is a brief silence. They all look at her.

AAFAA (*grinning*). Toads again. You hear that?

CRIPPLE. She was looking at you.

AAFAA. What! I must say I feel insulted.

CRIPPLE. A man must have some pride.

GOYI. My pride is – As.

AAFAA. And all in the line of duty. Sir, I demand protection.

BERO. That's enough. Open the surgery. (*He turns to* SI BERO.)
You want to see him? You shall.

MENDICANTS (*already moving towards the surgery*). As – Was
– Is – Now – As Ever Shall Be . . .

    Bi o ti wa
    Ni yio se wa
    Bi o ti wa
    Ni yio se wa
    Bi o ti wa l'atete ko se . . .

SI BERO. And what in God's name is that?

BERO. One of their chants. (*He grabs her arm as she tries to run
after the* MENDICANTS.) Now listen, and always remember
this – he is wholly in my charge.

SI BERO. How long? How long has he been home?

BERO. Home? What home? I tell you he is here in my charge. It
was either this or . . . Do not interfere!

*He holds her with his eyes for a few moments, then moves to
follow the* MENDICANTS. *He stops when he sees that she
has made no attempt to follow.*

You want to see him? Come on.

Pause. SI BERO *looks at him with increasing horror and disbelief. She turns and runs towards the* OLD WOMEN *who
receive her at the door of the hut.* BERO *goes on into the clinic
where the light has come on, revealing the* OLD MAN *seated
in the midst of the chanting* MENDICANTS. *Lights fade
slowly.*

PART TWO

The surgery, below the ground floor of the house. An examination couch, assortment of a few instruments and jars in a locked glass case, a chromium sterilizing unit etc. etc., a table, swivel chair etc., a white smock hangs against a shelf, with surgical mask and gloves tucked in the pockets. The MENDICANTS *are crouched, standing, stooping in their normal postures, humming their chant and listlessly throwing dice. The* OLD MAN's *attitude varies from boredom to tolerant amusement.*

AAFAA. A. As is Acceptance, Adjustment. Adjustment of Ego to the Acceptance of As . . . hm. Not bad. B . . . B . . . . (*His eye roams over the room for inspiration, falls on the* BLINDMAN.) Of course. B, Blindness. Blindness in As. I say this unto you, As is all-seeing; All shall see in As who render themselves blind to all else. C . . . C? (*He looks at the others one by one but ends up shaking his head.*) No, nothing from you lot this time. Can't see how I can ask the flock to get crippled for some reward in As. C . . . No, I'll have to skip it for now. D – good – I don't have to go far for that. D, Divinity. That's us. For Destiny too. In fact Destiny first, then Divinity. Destiny is the Duty of Divinity. D-D-D – Destiny in 3-Dimension. We the Divinity shall guide the flock along the path of Destiny. E . . .

BLINDMAN. Epilepsy?

AAFAA (*sharply*). Watch your mouth!

BLINDMAN. For your Divinity to have control, the flock must be without control. Epilepsy seems to be the commonest form – at least, I have witnessed much that is similar.

GOYI. I know what you mean. Taken by the spirit, they call it. It's a good circus turn any day. Aafaa should know.

AAFAA. You are not suggesting I exploited human infirmities, are you?

CRIPPLE. I wish I had the power. Gives a man a sense of power to watch others twitch like so many broken worms. Broken worms, ah, that's a fine thing to come from my mouth.

AAFAA. Before we get to Z I promise you your private and personal consolation. F . . . F . . . F . . .

GOYI. As farts, damn you! (*He turns his rear and gestures obscenely.*)

AAFAA. I was going to suggest Fulfils. As fulfils.

GOYI. And I say Farts.

AAFAA. Are you going to confront your Destiny with a fart?

GOYI. I have done before. I did it in that place where they treated us. Treatment! No doctor. Only nurses who couldn't tell a man's end from their own. Hey, listen, and let me tell you, it was the cleverest thing I ever thought all those sweet times we spent with the Old Man. With him saying this and saying that to us and me on my side – couldn't turn on my back and couldn't turn on my belly – and the sun would come up one day and I wouldn't see it again until it come up the next. One time he told us – remember that day? – he told us the earth goes round and round, which if you remember was just too much for someone like me to swallow. So, the following morning when the sun came round again, I said to myself, well, I suppose the Old Man must be right. I don't know what makes the world go round but I do know what goes round the world. It's wind. And I broke it loudly and felt better.

CRIPPLE. Dirty pig.

GOYI. It's all very well for you to talk. You could get around even then. I sometimes think God made you out of rubber or something.

AAFAA (*who has been thinking his own thoughts, gives a sudden shout*). God, that's it. Godhead! What a real pagan I've become if that took me so long. G, As is Godhead. I is next.

BLINDMAN. I am I, what more do you want?

AAFAA (*chews it over*). I am I, thus sayeth As. No . . . that might cause trouble.

BLINDMAN. What kind of trouble?

AAFAA. Think of it yourself. Sooner or later someone is going to say it and leave out 'so sayeth As'. And that means trouble.

GOYI. I don't follow.

CRIPPLE. Ask the Old Man. He'll settle the question.

> *They turn towards the* OLD MAN, *but he is still motionless, unresponsive.*

AAFAA. Old Man, what do you think of the I matter?

> *Again they wait in vain for his response.*

All right, if that doesn't interest you, at least give us something between I and Z. That is still a long way to go and already I can feel my brain giving out. Not to talk of the others. Anything you like, your forgotten wishes, your deepest cravings, your pet dreams . . .

GOYI. S-sh!

CRIPPLE. Why do you keep making fun of him? Leave him alone.

AAFAA (*looks genuinely surprised*). But I . . .

GOYI. That's what he used to say. You were using his very words just to mock him.

AAFAA. Well, I didn't mean to.

> *His apparent contrition leaves the others a little flat. They steal furtive glances at the* OLD MAN *who does not move.*

CRIPPLE. I have a pet dream.

AAFAA. We know what that is, so shut up!

BLINDMAN. I want to hear his pet dream.

AAFAA. Can't you guess what it is by seeing where he scratches himself at night?

BLINDMAN. No, I cannot see.

A brief pause.

CRIPPLE. I'll tell you. Every night we sleep in this place I have that same dream. It's what makes me stay on. It is what makes me . . . assist . . .

AAFAA. Collaborate.

CRIPPLE. I don't know what the big word means.

BLINDMAN (*gently*). No. Don't bother with it. Continue with your dream.

CRIPPLE. It is what makes me continue to obey the specialist.

Pause.

OLD MAN (*unnoticed, he has turned round to face them*). Go on, your dream.

CRIPPLE (*for a moment he, with the rest, shows confusion*). I . . . dream he tells me to get on that table. He says, I could not attend to you before but there were other things . . . one thing at a time, certain things are more important than others. So he operates on my back and in another moment he's finished, wipes his hands and says . . .

AAFAA. Arise, throw off thy crutches and follow me.

CRIPPLE (*lowering his eyes as if in abashment*). Yes, more or less the same words. But just as I want to get up, I wake up from the blasted dream!

AAFAA (*with explosive disgust*). That's a permanent dream if ever I heard one. You think the specialist has time for your petty little inconvenience? You're getting to be quite important in your mind to afford dreams like that. I wouldn't dare. Would you? (*Turning to* GOYI. *The* CRIPPLE *turns his head in confusion.*) Oh, you too? What have we here? A conspiracy of the élite? I suppose you too have been dreaming you'll get back your sight from him? No, I should have known you better. Just these two. (*Explosively.*) You are just the kind of people who make life impossible for professionals. Miracle, Miracle! That's all we ever get out of your smelly mouths. Because you blackmailed one Christ into showing off once in a while you think all others are suckers for that kind of showmanship. Well, you've met your match this generation. Turn left, turn right, turn right about again, you'll find everyone you meet is more than a match for you.

A short pause.

BLINDMAN. Isn't it time for his food?

AAFAA. The little woman will knock when it's ready. And let him starve a bit anyway, why not? He got us into this mess. If there is one thing I can't stand it's amateurs. Even there I didn't like him all that much. Now the specialist – that's a professional. You only need to remember it's father and son. Human beings both of them. Who is my neighbour, you know – all that stuff and sentiment.

A knock on the door. They all fall silent. The three seeing MENDICANTS *dart a look at the* OLD MAN. *The knock is repeated.*

All right, we heard. Put down the tray and go back to your hole. Go on. Get going.

They listen to the footsteps retreat out of hearing.

(*He chants at the* OLD MAN.) Lord, now lettest thou thy servant depart in peace, according to thy word. (*To* BLINDMAN.) Are you going to open the door?

BLINDMAN *sighs, gets up, followed by* GOYI. *He unbolts the door and* GOYI *exits. He bolts it again,* AAFAA *watching every movement.*

Chop time, Old Man. Your food is on the way.

OLD MAN. Did you take my watch? (*He stirs and feels in his breast pocket.*)

AAFAA. It was broken. I sent it for repairs.

OLD MAN. You have it on your wrist.

AAFAA. Mistaken identity. (*Holding up his wrist.*) Take a look if you like.

OLD MAN. You took my glasses also.

AAFAA (*dips into his pocket*). Try these. No? They might just fit you never can tell. They used to belong to him. (*Pointing to* BLINDMAN.) Are you sure you wouldn't try them? After the blast took off his eyes – that's how we first met – it was my job to go round comforting the poor fools – or burying them. Anyway – and that's the strange thing; the glasses were knocked off all right, but not a scratch on them. So he says, take my glasses from that bedside cupboard in case someone else needs them. I've kept them ever since. Are you sure you won't try them?

OLD MAN. Let me see that watch again.

AAFAA. It won't tell you anything.

OLD MAN. Which of you took my glasses?

AAFAA. What does it matter?

OLD MAN. I want to see what's in the food. What are you giving me to eat?

AAFAA. Leave that to us.

A sudden peremptory knock on the door. Enter BERO, *followed by* GOYI *bearing a tray of food.*

BERO. I thought I would join you for dinner.

OLD MAN (*rounding on him*). Will you tell me just what is going on?

BERO. Nothing Old Man, nothing.

OLD MAN. I wish to write a letter.

BERO. Who to?

OLD MAN. To your superiors.

BERO (*winces, but recovers his poise*). There isn't such a thing.

OLD MAN. Your superiors, I said. I demand the right to send to them at once.

Pause. Finally.

BERO. You shall.

OLD MAN. I wish to write them at once. Now!

BERO (*turns to* AAFAA). Fetch some writing material. Go to the nearest stationers.

OLD MAN. Why all the way to look for a store? Isn't there any in the house?

BERO. None that belongs to you. Perhaps you would give him money for your requirements?

> The OLD MAN *starts to take money from his pockets, slows down in suspicion and looks at* BERO. *Then, slowly, he dips into all his trouser pockets.*

OLD MAN. You know you took my money. Or ordered it removed.

BERO. I don't know anything of the sort.

OLD MAN (*violently*). You know I have no money here!

BERO. I don't know anything. You on the contrary appear to know everything. Isn't that right? You know everything. (*To* AAFAA.) The Old Man appears to have no money. Obviously he can have no writing paper. Perhaps you would like to send a verbal message?

OLD MAN. You can take your verbal message to – (*He looks at him scornfully, then sits down.*)

BERO. I tried to help. You will, of course, be given the best of everything you need. Need. (*Pause.*) Your food will get cold.

OLD MAN. I need my pipe.

BERO (*appears to consider it*). Why not? In this case I raise my idea of your need to coincide with your want.

> He opens a cabinet, gives him his pipe and tobacco.

That gentleman there will offer you a light whenever you – need it.

> The OLD MAN *begins to stuff his pipe, normally at first, then slower and slower. When the pipe is filled he holds it*

by the bowl, waiting. AAFAA *dips his hand in his pocket as if about to pull out matches, pauses, slowly holds out a closed fist then opens it suddenly to reveal the hand empty. He breaks into silent laughter.*

OLD MAN. I need a light.

BERO. And your watch. And glasses. And money. And paper. But do you really? I promised you the best of everything and this will prove to you I mean it. (*He takes a packet of cigarettes from his pocket and offers it.*) They are the best cigarettes on the market.

He takes out a packet of matches, holds out both matches and cigarettes in one hand, holds out the other hand, inviting him to return the pipe and tobacco.

OLD MAN. I prefer . . . my pipe.

BERO *does not move. A long pause. The* OLD MAN *looks round at the* MENDICANTS *avidly watching. Finally he returns the pipe and pouch, accepts the cigarettes and matches, but moves the packet against his face to read the brand name.*

BERO. You can't see to read.

The OLD MAN *snatches the box away from his face, opens the box and takes out a cigarette, lights it, then breaks into a slow smile.*

OLD MAN. You would, wouldn't you? You would try that on me. Me! Shall I teach you what to say? Choice! Particularity! What redundant self-deceptive notions! More? More? Insistence on a floppy old coat, a rickety old chair, a moth-eaten hat which no certified lunatic would ever consider wearing, a car which breaks down twenty times in twenty minutes, an old idea riddled with the pellets of incidence. Enough? More? Are you cramming it up fast for the next victim? A perfect waterproof coat is rejected for a

patched-up heirloom that gives the silly wearer rheuma-
tism. Is this an argument for freedom of choice? Is it sensible
to cling so desperately to bits of the bitter end of a run-down
personality? To the creak in an old chair, the crack in a cup, a
crock of an old servant, the crick in the bottleneck of a
man's declining years . . . (*Pause. His voice changes.*) But it
did come to the test and I asked you all, what is one meat
from another? Oh, your faces then, your faces . . .

BERO. You still boast of that? You go too far, Old Man.

OLD MAN. After all, what's meat for the ranks should be meat
for the officers . . . (*Chuckles.*) It could happen I said, it will
happen. But I never really believed it.

BERO. They would have killed you, you know that? If I hadn't
had you hidden away they would have killed you slowly.

OLD MAN (*still on his own*). No. I've asked myself over and over
again. I said it would happen, I knew it would happen, but
I never really believed it.

BERO. They wanted to kill you, mutilate you, hang you upside
down then stuff your mouth with your own genitals. Did you
know that? (*His explosiveness breaks in on the* OLD MAN.)

OLD MAN. Why do you hesitate?

BERO. To do what?

OLD MAN. I said, why do you hesitate? (*Pause.*) Once you
begin there is no stopping. You say, ah, this is the last step,
the highest step, but there is always one more step. For those
who want to step beyond, there is always one further step.

BERO. Nothing more is needed.

OLD MAN. Oh yes, there is. I am the last proof of the human in
you. The last shadow. Shadows are tough things to be rid of.
(*He chuckles.*) How does one prove he was never born of
man? Of course you could kill me . . .

BERO. Or you might just die . . .

OLD MAN. Quite possible, quite possible.

BERO. You're lucky you've lasted this far.

OLD MAN. I *have* lasted, but the question of being lucky . . .?

BERO. There is a search for you everywhere.

OLD MAN. I thought that was over. Tenacious gods they worship, don't they?

BERO. And you?

OLD MAN. Or maybe they are the tenacious gods.

BERO. And the god you worship?

OLD MAN. Abominates humanity – the fleshy part, that is.

BERO. Why As?

OLD MAN. Because Was – Is – Now . . .

BERO. Don't!

OLD MAN. So you see, I put you all beyond salvation.

BERO. Why As?

OLD MAN. A code. A word.

BERO. Why As?

OLD MAN. It had to be something.

BERO. Why As?

OLD MAN. If millions follow . . . that frightened you all.

BERO. Why As?

OLD MAN. Are you going to reopen the files? The case is closed. Insane, the verdict, thanks to you.

BERO. Why As?

OLD MAN. Why not?

BERO. Why As?

OLD MAN. Who wants to know?

BERO. I. Why As?

OLD MAN. What's in it for you?

BERO. *I* am asking questions! Why As?

OLD MAN. We went through this before.

BERO. I took a chance saving you.

OLD MAN. Risked your neck, yes. Compromised your position.

BERO. I didn't do that for nothing.

OLD MAN. It won't be for nothing. As my next-in-line you are my beneficiary. Legal. These of course are my natural heirs.

BERO. To what?

OLD MAN. As. What else?

BERO. I could turn you out and let them find you.

OLD MAN. The file is closed.

BERO. Is it? They are still looking for you.

OLD MAN. They should be looking for themselves. I robbed them of salvation.

BERO. Oh yes, you are good at quibbling.

OLD MAN. Oh, their faces! That was a picture. All those faces round the table.

BERO. If they hadn't been too surprised they would have shot you on the spot.

OLD MAN. Your faces, gentlemen, your faces. You should see your faces. And your mouths are hanging open. You're drooling but I am not exactly sure why. Is there really much difference? All intelligent animals kill only for food, you know, and you are intelligent animals. Eat-eat-eat-eat-eat-Eat!

BERO (*raises his arm*). Stop it!

OLD MAN (*turns and holds him with his eyes*). Oh yes, you rushed out and vomited. You and the others. But afterwards you said I had done you a favour. Remember? (BERO *slowly lowers his arm.*) I'm glad you remember. Never admit you are a recidivist once you've tasted the favourite food of As.

Pause.

BERO. That's your last meal. Eat.

Going out.

OLD MAN. Because it's *your* last chance? (BERO *stops but doesn't turn round.*) I guessed it. You have to prove you have not yourself been contaminated. But suppose you find no answer to take back, what then? (*Pause, smiling.*) The – choice – is simple. *Be* contaminated!

BERO *exits, slamming the door.*

AAFFA (*dashes towards the food tray, opens the lid and sniffs*). Inspiration! C, Contentment. A full belly. (*He starts to pick at the* OLD MAN's *food. The others join him, wolfing down huge chunks of meat.* AAFAA *gnaws at a huge bone.*) A full belly comes and goes; for half the people I know it never comes. H – Humanity! Humanity the Ultimate Sacrifice to As, the eternal oblation on the altar of As ... I say, I get better all the time!

GOYI (*irritated*). At what? You're just a parrot.

AAFAA. I take exception to that. I'm a good pupil. The Old Man himself admits it. The quickest of the underdogs, he always said.

GOYI. Yes, underdogs. First the Old Man tells us we are the underdogs, then his blasted son makes us his watchdogs!

AAFAA (*shrugs*). Makes life a little more amusing you'll admit...

They continue to eat.

BERO *and* SI BERO *meet in front of the house.*

BERO. What is it? Are you spying on me?

SI BERO. What are you doing to him?

BERO. Keeping him safe. What do you imagine?

SI BERO. I wish to see him.

BERO. I've told you already ...

SI BERO. I wish to see him.

BERO. You had your chance. No one can see him now.

SI BERO. Why not?

BERO. He's dangerous.

SI BERO. I'll risk it.

BERO. Infectious diseases are isolated. Nothing unusual about it, so stop making a fuss. I need to work in peace.

SI BERO. What am I to do? I have time on my hands. What can
   I do but think!

BERO. I've told you, leave the thinking to me. Stay in your
   little world and continue the work I set you.

SI BERO. That's over. And the old women no longer help. They
   sit and fold their arms.

BERO. I have no need of them. And you should never have
   brought them here. Throw them out.

SI BERO. They demand payment.

BERO. Then pay them off.

SI BERO. They won't take money.

BERO. So what do they want?

SI BERO. Nothing. But they refuse to leave until they are paid.

BERO (*looking in that direction*). They are asking for death.

SI BERO. They don't seem to be afraid of you, Bero.

BERO. We shall see.

   He turns to go towards the hut.

SI BERO. Wait, Bero, wait!

BERO. Well?

SI BERO. Don't harm them, Bero.

BERO. Either you throw them out or I will. Whose home is it?
   Theirs? Do they now lay claim to the land?

SI BERO. It belongs to Father.

BERO. Forfeited. Legally, he does not exist. (*He goes into the
   house.*)

   The surgery. The MENDICANTS *are picking at the last
   crumbs of food, licking the last bone of its meat. One or two are
   humming the 'Ballad of the Disabled'. The* OLD MAN *reacts
   to the sound of singing, listens, then turns away in disgust.*

OLD MAN. I should have known better.

AAFAA (*stops*). What, Old Man?

OLD MAN. For a moment I would have sworn I heard singing.

AAFAA. You heard us.

OLD MAN. I said singing, not cursing.

AAFAA. Perhaps you heard my spasms tuning up. It's like a set of wires Old Man. Something touches them, they hum, and off I go.

OLD MAN. It doesn't bother you much these days, I notice.

AAFAA. That's true. They told me up there when it began, that it was something psy-cho-lo-gi-cal. Something to do with all the things happening around me, and the narrow escape I had. It's not so bad now. I still remember the first time. I was standing there just like this, blessing a group of six just about to go off. They were kneeling before me. Then – well, I can't say I heard the noise at all, because I was deaf for the next hour. So, this thing happened, no signal, no nothing. Six men kneeling in front of me, the next moment they were gone. Disappeared, just like that. That was when I began to shake. Nothing I could do to stop it. My back just went on bending over and snapping back again, like the spirit had taken me. God! What a way for the spirit to mount a man.

OLD MAN. But no revelations? No inspired pronouncements?

AAFAA (angrily). What of you! I don't see you saving yourself in the situation you're in. (More to himself.) Or us.

OLD MAN. There is nothing you can do, of course.

GOYI. Be fair Old Man, how does a man cope with a situation like this? It was all right in the other place.

OLD MAN. So you find it different from the other places?

GOYI. It's not the same.

OLD MAN. There was no madness – then? (They react, silently.) You were not maimed then? (He holds up his hand to stop them.) And I mean, not merely in body. You were maimed then as now. You have lost the gift of self-disgust.

AAFAA. So have you, Old Man.

OLD MAN. Meaning?

CRIPPLE. I know what he means. I agree with him.

GOYI. So do I.

OLD MAN (*smiling*). Explain. I do not understand.

CRIPPLE. You took the cigarette.

AAFAA. A man like me is letting himself down to say he is surprised by anything, but . . . I was surprised at you, Old Man. You may say I was a bit let down. We may be on opposite sides of the camp, but I like to see a man stand up for himself.

OLD MAN. Why?

AAFAA. So I can beat him down.

He guffaws but no one joins him. He subsides.

OLD MAN. You were disgusted?

AAFAA (*soberly*). More than.

The OLD MAN *turns silently to each of them in turn.*

CRIPPLE. Disappointed.

GOYI. Crucified.

OLD MAN. Disgust is cheap. I asked for self-disgust.

AAFAA. Yeah? You took the cigarette – what about that?

OLD MAN. Of course I did. Because I saw your faces.

He reaches in his pocket and throws towards them what turns out to be the barely smoked cigarette. All three pounce on it; the CRIPPLE *comes out the winner.*

AAFAA. Only one puff, only one and then you pass it round.

OLD MAN (*watches them with contempt*). We'll go on that world tour yet. I'll take your circus round the world, so help me.

CRIPPLE (*slowly releasing a puff of smoke*). Oh, that feels good. Haven't had such a good puff since that corpulent First Lady visited us and passed round imported cigarettes.

GOYI. The Old Man was mad for days. Suckers, he called us. Quite right too. Good smoke is a good suck. I wasn't going to throw away that superior brand just to please a crackpot.

AAFAA. Hey, remember the song the Old Man wrote to celebrate the occasion? Visit of the First Lady to the Home
for the de-balled.

BLINDMAN. . . . for the Disabled.

AAFAA. Bloody pendant.

BLINDMAN. Pe-dant.

AAFAA (*gives up*). Oh Christ!

CRIPPLE (*singing*).

      He came smelling of wine and roses, wine and roses

MENDICANTS.   . . . wine and roses.

AAFAA *gradually warms up towards his spastic dance.*

CRIPPLE. He came smelling of wine and roses.

      On his arm his wife was gushpillating . . .

BLINDMAN. Palpitating.

AAFAA. Oh, can't you shut up? Don't mind him, start all over
again.

CRIPPLE. He came smelling of wine and roses.

      On his arm his wife was gushpillating, gush-
pillating . . .

MENDICANTS.   . . . gushpillating.

The singing fades out.
BERO *comes out of the house, holstering a revolver. He goes
up to the* OLD WOMEN's *hut quietly and tries to peep inside.*
IYA AGBA *leans out of the hut and speaks almost directly
in his ear.*

IYA AGBA. Does the specialist have time for a word or two?

BERO *is startled, leaps aside.*

  Did I scare you?

BERO (*recovering, looks her over carefully*). What is a thing like
you still doing alive?

IYA AGBA. Can we help you?

BERO. Do what? Just pack up and get out of here before morning.

IYA AGBA. We can help you cure him.

BERO. Who?

IYA AGBA. He's sick, that is what we heard.

BERO. You heard wrong. I am giving you warning to clear out of here. Pick up your lice and rags and get out.

IYA AGBA. Is anyone else sick that we know of?

BERO. By tomorrow I want you out.

IYA AGBA. We want to help him.

BERO. No one needs help from you. Now get out of my way.

IYA AGBA. Maybe you do.

BERO. Do I have to fling you aside!

IYA AGBA (*stands aside*). Pass, then.

She lets him take a few steps, then.

Your sister owes us a debt.

BERO (*stops, turns slowly*). If you know what is good for you, you will never let me hear that again.

IYA AGBA. We took her into the fold – did she tell you that? To teach what we know, a pupil must come into the fold.

BERO. What fold? Some filthy thieving cult?

IYA AGBA. It's no light step for man or woman.

BERO. And what . . . cult is this?

IYA AGBA. Not any cult you can destroy. We move as the Earth moves, nothing more. We age as Earth ages.

BERO. But you're afraid to tell me the name.

IYA AGBA. I try to keep fools from temptation.

BERO (*instantly angry*). Watch it, old woman, your age earns no privileges with me.

IYA AGBA. Nothing does from what we hear. So you want to know what cult, do you?

BERO. I can ask your – pupil.

He turns round to go back to his house.

IYA AGBA. She won't tell you. Take it from me. She won't.

> BERO *stops without turning, waits.*

Your mind has run farther than the truth. I see it searching, going round and round in darkness. Truth is always too simple for a desperate mind.

BERO(*going*). I shall find out.

IYA AGBA. Don't look for the sign of broken bodies or wandering souls. Don't look for the sound of fear or the smell of hate. Don't take a bloodhound with you; we don't mutilate bodies.

BERO. Don't teach me my business.

IYA AGBA. If you do, you may find him circle back to your door.

BERO. Watch your mouth, old hag.

IYA AGBA. You want the name? But how much would it tell you, young man? We put back what we take, in one form or another. Or more than we take. It's the only law. What laws do you obey?

BERO. You are proscribed, whatever you are, you are banned.

IYA AGBA. What can that mean? You'll proscribe Earth itself? How does one do that?

BERO. I offer you a last chance.

IYA AGBA. The fool is still looking for names. How much would it tell you?

BERO. You'll find out when they come for you.

IYA AGBA. What will you step on young fool? Even on the road to damnation a man must rest his foot somewhere.

> BERO *marches furiously back to the surgery. He is stopped at the door by the sound coming from the surgery. He listens.*

CRIPPLE. . . . On his arm his wife was gushpillating, gushpillating . . .

MENDICANTS.   . . . gushpillating . . .

CRIPPLE. You never saw such a gushpillating wife
　　　　　Oh, was it gross and was it ugly, was it ugly . . .

MENDICANTS. 　　　　　　　　　　　. . . was it ugly . . .

CRIPPLE. That thing he had clinging onto his arm
　　　　　And she knew that all the men did think so, men did
　　　　　think so . . .

MENDICANTS. 　　　　　　　　　. . . men did think so . . .

CRIPPLE. Did find their own predicaments much prettier.
　　　　　So she looked them mean and smiled them dirty,
　　　　　smiled them dirty . . .

MENDICANTS. 　　　　　　　　　　. . . smiled them dirty . . .

CRIPPLE. And her mouth formed silent words
　　　　　I may be gross but dears, I'm not beyond it, not
　　　　　beyond it . . .

MENDICANTS. 　　　　　　　　　　　. . . not beyond it . . .

CRIPPLE. I may be old but not beyond it.
　　　　　While you according to diagnosis, diagnosis . . .

MENDICANTS. 　　　　　　　　　　　　. . . diagnosis . . .

CRIPPLE. Will ne . . . ver . . .

*He pauses, splutters as if trying to control his mirth, which
finally breaks out fully. The* MENDICANTS *join in, then at a
rallying signal from* AAFAA, *control themselves long enough
to end —*

ALL. . . . hm-hm-hm . . . no more.

AAFAA. That was the best song you ever wrote for us, Old Man.
　Ballad of the State Visit to the Home of the De-balled.

CRIPPLE. I prefer the second one.

GOYI. Which one?

CRIPPLE. Pro patria mourir.

MENDICANTS. . . . mourir mourir mourir . . .

CRIPPLE. Dulce et decorum . . .

MENDICANTS. . . . quorum quorum quorum . . .

OLD MAN. Corum, stupes, not quorum.

MENDICANTS. Corum corum corum, not quorum.

OLD MAN. Decorum. Dulce et decorum . . .

MENDICANTS. . . . quorum quorum quorum . . .

OLD MAN. God damn you. Can you learn nothing? – corum, not quorum.

GOYI. No quorum, no quorum, that's the damned trouble.

CRIPPLE. Yes sir, you've banged the hammer on the nail.

OLD MAN (*turning to* AAFAA). Will you tell me what these idiots are talking about?

AAFAA. They've lost me.

CRIPPLE. You've gone dense. (*Quoting the* OLD MAN *again.*) In ancient Athens . . .

AAFAA. Damn it, you're right. No damned quorum!

BLINDMAN. In ancient Athens they didn't just have a quorum. Everybody was there! That, children, was democracy.

CRIPPLE (*singing, to the tune of 'When the Saints'*).

Before I join
The saints above
Before I join
The saints above
I want to sit on that damned quorum
Before I join the saints above

Before I bid
This earth adieu
Before I bid
This earth adieu
I want my dues from that damned quorum
Before I bid this earth adieu

> *The others join in, drumming on the floor, table, etc., with their crutches, knuckles, etc., repeating the chorus. 'I want my dues . . . Before adieus' in place of 'Oh when the Saints . . . Go marching in'.*
>
> *As the tempo warms up* BERO *enters.*

BERO (*entering*). So you haven't given up your little tricks.

OLD MAN. Does it bother you?

BERO. No. It is bad for you, though.

OLD MAN. It seems to interest you. Spend more time with us.

BERO. What gives you that idea?

OLD MAN. I could hear you listening outside. You were fascinated.

BERO. My interest in you is strictly . . .

OLD MAN. That of a specialist. Proceed.

BERO. How did you do it?

OLD MAN. Do what?

BERO. No more evasions. How did you do it? What made you do it?

OLD MAN. Prod. Prod. Probe. Probe. Don't you know yet what I am? (*Dramatic whisper.*) Octopus. Plenty of reach but nothing to seize on. I re-create my tentacles, so cut away.

BERO. To me you are simply another organism, another mould or strain under the lens. Sometimes a strain proves malignant and it becomes dangerous to continue with it. In such a case there is only one thing to do.

OLD MAN. Are you equipped for that here?

BERO. Even I have no control over accidents. Just now I came through that room of herbs, I saw something I recognized.

OLD MAN. Something to sap the mind? Or destroy it altogether?

BERO. It depends on the dose. I brought you some. (*He brings some berries from his pockets and drops them gently over the* OLD MAN's *head.*) If you ever get tired and you feel you need a nightcap like a certain ancient Greek you were so fond of quoting, just soak a handful of them in water.

OLD MAN. You've used it before, haven't you? Or something similar. I saw your victims, afterwards.

BERO. They were provided a Creed but they talked heresy. Same as you.

OLD MAN. Creed? Heresy? Bread, pleurisy and what next? Will you try and speak some intelligible language.

BERO. They corrupted unformed minds. That was ba-a-ad.

OLD MAN. Unformed minds in deformed bodies.

BERO. Again you are being evasive.

OLD MAN. I asked to be sent where I would do the most good. I was and I did.

BERO (*smiling*). I also was sent where I would do the most good. I was and I did. (*Pause.*) It would appear that we were both efficient volunteers. (*Again, pause.*) What exactly is As, Old Man?

OLD MAN. As?

BERO. You know As, the playword of your convalescents, the pivot of whatever doctrine you used to confuse their minds, your piffling battering ram at the idealism and purpose of this time and history. What is As, Old Man?

OLD MAN. You seem to have described it to your satisfaction.

BERO (*thundering. Moving suddenly, he passes his swagger-stick across the* OLD MAN's *throat, holding it from behind and pressing*). I'm asking you! What is As? Why As!

OLD MAN (*gasps but tries to smile. He cranes up to look him in the face*). In a way I should be flattered. You want to borrow my magic key. Yours open only one door at a time.

BERO. WHY AS!

OLD MAN. And rusty? Bent? Worn? Poisonous? When you're through the lock is broken? The room empty?

BERO. What is As?

OLD MAN. But why? Do you want to set up shop against me? Or against . . . others? (*He rolls his eyes towards the* MENDICANTS.) I think we have a conspiracy.

BERO. What is As?

OLD MAN. As Was, Is, Now, As Ever Shall be . . .

BERO (*quiet menace*). Don't play with me, Old Man.

OLD MAN. As doesn't change.

BERO (*increases pressure*). From what? To what?

OLD MAN (*choking, tugs at the swagger-stick.* BERO *lets go. The* OLD MAN *gets up, chafing his neck*). Do you know what one of

those men once said? Let's send our gangrenous dressings
by post to those sweet-smelling As agencies and homes. He
sat down to compile a mailing list.

BERO. Yes?

OLD MAN. I understood.

BERO. What did you understand?

OLD MAN. As.

BERO (*violent reaction. Controls himself*). You are certified insane. Your fate creates no anxiety in anyone. Take a look at
your companions – your humanity.

OLD MAN. I recognized it. A part of me identifies with every
human being.

BERO. You'll be disillusioned soon enough.

OLD MAN. I do not harbour illusions. You do.

BERO (*genuinely astonished*). I? You say that of me. I, of all
people?

OLD MAN. Oh, you are in good company. Even the cripple
who is down-to-earth harbours illusions. Now, that's strange.
I would have thought you would find that funny.

BERO. I do not need illusions. I control lives.

OLD MAN. Control – lives? What does that mean? Tell me
what is the experience of it. Is it a taste? A smell? A feel?
Do you have a testament that vindicates?

BERO. We have nothing that a petty mind can grasp. (*Pause.*)
Try if you can, Old Man, to avoid twitching. Control belongs
only to a few with the aptitude.

OLD MAN. One should always expect something new from
the specialist. (*Contemptuously.*) Control!

BERO. Your old games won't help you. Forget that line.

OLD MAN. Throw me a new line then. Feed the drowning
man a line.

BERO. You can swim.

OLD MAN (*turning to the others*). See? He's getting good. Swim?
How?

BERO (*viciously*). We'll flood the place for you.

OLD MAN (*pleased*). You're getting very good, very good. It catches, you see. How do I swim? We'll flood the place. Or . . . is it merely in character? Is that it? Your peculiar little specialization. Perhaps that's it. So. When do you start?

BERO. Perhaps not at all. It would take too long.

OLD MAN (*nodding*). Y-e-s. And the place is not waterproof. I noticed rats. That means holes. You should see the rats.

BERO. They'll desert.

OLD MAN (*gazing round at the* MENDICANTS). I suppose so.

BERO. Or smoke you out. You will suffocate, slowly.

OLD MAN. Smoke. Smoke-screen. That's what it all is.

BERO. What?

OLD MAN. The pious pronouncements. Manifestos. Charades. At the bottom of it all humanity choking in silence.

BERO. You think a lot of yourself, don't you?

OLD MAN. Who else shall I think much of? You?

BERO. I control . . .

OLD MAN (*waves it aside*). Tell me something new. Or if you won't, these ones will. Aafaa!

AAFAA. What now?

OLD MAN. We are done with the flood. It never came. These midgets try to re-create the Flood but they lack the power. At least God had a reason. A damnable reason but at least he had a reason. And a good pump to clean up the mess. Not like these. What do you offer in place of the Flood?

AAFAA (*challenging*). Running water.

OLD MAN (*disgusted tone*). Nothing better?

AAFAA. You're dodging.

OLD MAN. Running water! (*He turns to the* CRIPPLE.) You deal with that. It's beneath my intellect.

CRIPPLE. Muddy. How do I get across it?

OLD MAN. God, they're all so self-centred. He means running progress. Faucets, pipes.

CRIPPLE. Can't reach the tap. Too high.

AAFAA. And who cares about you? Just who the hell do you think you are?

CRIPPLE (*stubbornly*). Too high.

OLD MAN (*smiles*). Like the price. See? Blindman?

BLINDMAN. Running water? Running mouths. Election promises.

OLD MAN (*to* BERO). See? Let's have a new one.

AAFAA. Electricity. (*Seeing* BLINDMAN *about to speak.*) And don't you tell me it's no good to you.

BLINDMAN. And whose fault is that? I wasn't born blind, you know.

CRIPPLE. Ho ho, remember that story of the blind man with a lamp?

GOYI. Don't tell me you went to school too?

AAFAA. What! Same old primer? Reader II or ... was it Reader III?

CRIPPLE (*complacently*). Reader III, Elementary. Lamb and Wool Reader for Schools – well, something like that.

AAFAA. I bet you stopped at III.

CRIPPLE. No. Went up to four. Then I got the call of the road.

GOYI. I'll tell the story. A blind man went walking one day, carrying a lamp. Thereupon he met a neighbour. The neighbour stared, amazed ...

AAFAA. A born fool.

CRIPPLE. I bet you would have found it queer too.

AAFAA. You forget I am a student of human peculiarities. Human peculiarities.

GOYI. Shut up, let me continue.

AAFAA. The neighbour said, Good blind neighbour, what good on earth is a lamp to you?

GOYI. Whereupon the blind man replied ...

ALL TOGETHER (*in kindergarten voice*). I carry this lamp, good fellow, not that I may see but ... (*Pause.*)

AAFAA. So that the whole world can see you when you try to

rob me. (*He bursts into his maniacal laughter, joined by the others.*)

OLD MAN (*reflectively*). A lamp has its uses.

AAFAA. So, electricity.

GOYI. Bleeah! Election promises.

CRIPPLE. What we want is individual manifestos.

AAFAA. Manifesto for every freak? General Electric!

OLD MAN. Electrocutes. Electric chair. Electrodes on the nerve-centres – your favourite pastime, I believe? Tell me something new. What hasn't been abused?

BERO (*has taken out his gun, weighs it significantly*). And lightning strikes. What about it?

OLD MAN. The boy learns. The boy learns.

BERO. Don't you dare patronize me. Answer me, what about it?

OLD MAN. That lightning strikes? It could strike you, no?

BERO. Yes.

OLD MAN (*quiet triumphant smile*). Then you're not omnipotent. You can't do a flood and you – (*Pause.*) – can't always dodge lightning. Why do you ape the non-existent one who can? Why do you ape nothing?

BERO. You tax my patience. Better watch out in future.

OLD MAN (*quietly*). The future?

BERO. The future, yes. The End . . .

OLD MAN. Justifies the meanness.

BERO (*again, angry reaction. He controls himself*). Just think of this – you have none.

OLD MAN (*calls after him*). Tell me something new. Tell me what is happening in the future. (*They all listen to* BERO's *footsteps receding.*) If he'd waited, I would have told him what's happening in the future. A faithful woman picking herbs for a smoke-screen on abuse.

Lights up sharply in the OLD WOMEN's *hut. No break in action.*

IYA AGBA (*screaming*). Abuse! Abuse! What do we do? Close
our eyes and see nothing?

IYA MATE. Patience now. Patience.

IYA AGBA. What is it then! I see abominations. What do you
see?

IYA MATE. The same, but . . .

IYA AGBA. Then what are we waiting for? Get ready the pot of
fire.

IYA MATE. Do you think a little more time . . .?

IYA AGBA. To do worse? To do more? It's a good night for
settling accounts.

IYA MATE. She's a good woman.

IYA AGBA. Get it ready. Get it ready. I'll not be a tool in their
hands, not in this ripe state – No! Too much has fallen in
their hands already, it's time to take it back. They spat on
my hands when I held them out bearing gifts. Have you
ever known it different?

IYA MATE. We hoped this might be.

IYA AGBA. Hope is dead, I must defend what is mine. Or let it
die also. Let it be destroyed.

IYA MATE. Everything?

IYA AGBA. Everything. Everything they took from me.

IYA MATE. I think only of her.

IYA AGBA. She's a good woman and her heart is strong. And
it is that kind who tire suddenly in their sleep and pass on to
join their ancestors. What happens then?

IYA MATE. We can wait till then.

IYA AGBA. And I? Have you spoken to the ones below and did
they tell you I shall still be among the living when her bones
are rested.

IYA MATE. You leave me nothing to say.

IYA AGBA. There is nothing more to say. We pay our dues to
earth in time, I also take back what is mine.

The clinic as last seen. Instant transition as before.

CRIPPLE (*singing*).
I want my dues
Not promises
I want my dues
Not promises . . .

AAFAA (*singing*). I want my dues. (*Stops.*) How about it, Old Man? I want my world tour. Old Man, you promised. I want that world tour you promised.

CRIPPLE. Promises. What else have we ever got from him?

GOYI. He got us the cigarettes anyway.

AAFAA. Raises a man's hopes for nothing. So where is this world tour you kept promising?

CRIPPLE. A Travelling Exhibition of As Grotesques, I remember.

AAFAA. You should, you illiterate reptile. You flung your crutches at his head because you thought it was an insult didn't you? Said he was making fun of you.

CRIPPLE. Why bring it up? The Blindman explained it. He said Grotesque only meant Greatest and I said I was sorry.

GOYI. He did too, I remember. And the Old Man also promised me top billing. (*Pause.*) I didn't want to ask at the time, but what is top billing, Blindman?

AAFAA. It means the Old Man would see that you got to the top of the ladder.

Pause.

CRIPPLE. How do *I* get there, Aafaa?

AAFAA. Why ask me foolish questions you persistent little egotist? When the specialist told you you'd soon be doing better than you were when you had both legs, did you come to Aafaa for explanations?

GOYI. So? Are we getting the world tour or not?

CRIPPLE. Nitwit! As if he could even do anything about that now. Better forget it.

AAFAA. Old Man, you shouldn't have promised the travelling

show. (*Changing voice.*) Beat all known circuses hollow. I'll take the wrappings off you and leave the world gasping. What else . . .?

CRIPPLE. You've been pushed in the background too often.

GOYI. Always hidden away.

CRIPPLE (*coyly*). Not that we're shy.

GOYI. Always hidden away.

CRIPPLE. We're more decent than most. Hn-hn, than most.

AAFAA. Hidden under pension schemes you are.

GOYI. Tail-of-the-parade outings.

AAFAA. Behind the big drum.

CRIPPLE. Under royalty visits.

AAFAA (*graciously proffering his hand*). You may.

GOYI *kisses his hand.*

CRIPPLE. Imperial commendations.

AAFAA *unfurls the scrolls, slaps his tongue up and down.*

CRIPPLE. Unveiling of the plaque . . .

GOYI. Commemoration occasion . . .

AAFAA. Certificates of merit . . .

GOYI. Long-service medals . . .

The CRIPPLE *dashes forward to the feet of* AAFAA *who takes medals from an invisible aide. His eyes roll from side to side, seeing no one.* GOYI *goes to him, taps him and points to the* CRIPPLE. AAFAA *tries but cannot make it. Finally he kisses* GOYI *on both cheeks, who then kisses the* CRIPPLE *on both cheeks. He pins the medal on* GOYI'S *left shoulder, who then pins medal on the* CRIPPLE'S *chest. All three cry: 'Speech' 'Speech' 'We want Him' 'We want Him' 'We want Him' rising to a crescendo. Finally* BLINDMAN *gets up, walks slowly downstage.*

BLINDMAN (*the speech should be varied with the topicality and locale of the time*). It was our duty and a historical necessity. It is our duty and a historical beauty. It shall always be. What we have, we hold. What though the wind of change is blowing over this entire continent, our principles and traditions – yes, must be maintained. For we are threatened, yes, we are indeed threatened. Excuse me, please, but we are entitled to match you history for history to the nearest half-million souls. Look at the hordes, I implore you. They stink. They eat garlic. What on earth have we in common with *them*? Understand me, please, understand me and do not misinterpret my intentions. The copper is quite incidental. Manganese? I don't know what it means. I always thought it was female for Kantagese. As for oil, I can't tell which is the margarine. If we don't stop them now, who knows but it may be our turn next moment. I ask you, do you want to wake up murdered in your beds? (*The others laugh.*) I assure you it's quite possible. No, please, it's no laughing matter. I mean . . . oh, I beg your pardon. You know what I mean, of course, do you want to wake up and find you've been . . . no I suppose that is also unlikely; better simply say . . . oh, well, look, strictly between you and me, all it boils down to is – would you want your daughter married to one of them? . . . It may happen, believe me, it may happen – if we're lucky. Rape is more natural to them than marriage. Even Confucius said it – if it must be, lie back and enjoy it. That coming from their greatest – er – er – atomic scientist is not a statement to be taken lightly. The black menace is no figment of my father's imagination. Look here . . . have you had the experience of watching them – breed? No no, I mean . . . I don't mean being actually *there* . . . please please please, I was referring to statistics, statistics. We feed those statistics into a computer and here is what they say . . . What we have, we hold. What though the wind of change is blowing over this entire continent, our principles and traditions – yes, must be maintained. For we are threatened. Yes, we are indeed threatened. Excuse me, but we are entitled to match you

history for history to the nearest half-million souls. Look at
the hordes, I implore you. They stink. They eat garlic . . .

As BLINDMAN *begins the re-run, the other* MENDICANTS
commence their chant, AAFAA *taking the lead. The song goes
faster and faster and louder and they clap him down until*
BLINDMAN *gives up and bows.*

As Is Was Now
As Ever Shall Be

Bi o ti wa   etc. etc.
Ni yi o se wa
Bi o ti wa
Ni yi o se wa

They give BLINDMAN *a round of applause while he feels
his way towards the* OLD MAN.

BLINDMAN. I hope I didn't do too badly.

OLD MAN (*sighs, turns to face him*). No. It was quite a good
effort.

BLINDMAN. It was rather like old times.

OLD MAN. Very much like old times.

CRIPPLE. Hey, listen. The Old Man was pleased.

AAFAA. I should bloody well hope so. It was just like old
times.

CRIPPLE. My feelings exactly. Just like old times.

GOYI. It . . . was . . . just . . . like old times.

AAFAA. Yes. So why risk putting us here together?

OLD MAN. Because . . . we are together in As. (*He rises slowly.*)
As Is, and the System is its mainstay though it wear a
hundred masks and a thousand outward forms. And because
you are within the System, the cyst in the System that irri-
tates, the foul gurgle of the cistern, the expiring function of
a faulty cistern and are part of the material for re-formulat-
ing the mind of a man into the necessity of the moment's

political As, the moment's scientific As, metaphysic As, sociologic As, economic, recreative ethical As, you-cannot-es-cape! There is but one constant in the life of the System and that constant is AS. And what can you pit against the priesthood of that constant deity, its gospellers, its enforcement agency. And even if you say unto them, do I not know you, did I not know you in rompers, with leaky nose and smutty face? Did I not know you thereafter, know you in the haunt of cat-houses, did I not know you rifling the poor-boxes in the local church, did I not know you dissolving the night in fumes of human self-indulgence simply simply simply did I not know you, do you not defecate, fornicate, prevaricate when heaven and earth implore you to abdicate and are you not prey to headaches, indigestion, colds, disc displacement, ingrowing toe-nail, dysentery, malaria, flat-foot, corns and chilblains. Simply simply, do I not know you Man like me? Then shall they say unto you, I am chosen, restored, re-designated and re-destined and further further shall they say unto you, you heresiarchs of the System arguing questioning querying weighing puzzling insisting rejecting upon you all shall we practise, without passion –

MENDICANTS. Practise . . .

OLD MAN. With no ill-will . . .

MENDICANTS. Practise . . .

OLD MAN. With good conscience . . .

MENDICANTS. Practise . . .

OLD MAN. That the end shall . . .

MENDICANTS. Practise . . .

OLD MAN. Justify the meanness . . .

MENDICANTS. Practise . . .

OLD MAN. Without emotion . . .

MENDICANTS. Practise . . .

OLD MAN. Without human ties . . .

MENDICANTS. Practise . . .

OLD MAN. Without – no – Lest there be self-doubting . . .

MENDICANTS. Practise . . . As Was the Beginning, As Is, Now, As Ever Shall Be, World Without.

As the OLD MAN *slowly resumes his seat,* AAFAA *rises, speaking.*

AAFAA. In the beginning was the Priesthood, and the Priesthood was one. Then came schism after schism by a parcel of schismatic ticks in the One Body of Priesthood, the political priesthood went right the spiritual priesthood went left or vice versa the political priesthood went back the spiritual priesthood went fore and vice versa the political priesthood went down the spiritual priesthood went up or vice versa the loyalty of homo sapiens was never divided for two parts of a division make a whole and there was no hole in the monolithic solidarity of two halves of the priesthood. No, there was no division. The loyalty of homo sapiens regressed into himself, himself his little tick-tock self, self-ticking, self-tickling, self-tackling problems that belonged to the priesthood spiritual and political while they remained the sole and indivisible one. Oh, look at him, Monsieur l'homme sapiens, look at the lone usurper of the ancient rights and privileges of the priesthood, (*The* CRIPPLE *makes an obscene gesture.* AAFAA *registers shock.*) look at the dog in dogma raising his hindquarters to cast the scent of his individuality on the lamp-post of Destiny! On him practise Practise! Practise! As was the Beginning –

MENDICANTS. Practise . . .

AAFAA. As Is . . .

MENDICANTS. Practise . . .

AAFAA. Now . . .

MENDICANTS. Practise . . .

AAFAA. As Ever Shall Be . . .

MENDICANTS. Practise. . .

AAFAA. World without . . .

MENDICANTS. Practise! Practise! Practise!

From the chorus of 'Practise' they slip into their chant, softly.

OLD MAN (*rising again*). On the cyst in the system, you cysts, you damnable warts . . . (*He freezes with his arm raised towards the next scene as if in benediction.*)

> *The 'Bi o ti wa' chant continues underneath and* AAFAA *continues with his spastic dance somewhat muted all through the next scene.*
> IYA AGBA *and* IYA MATE *have arrived in front of* SI BERO'S *house, the latter carrying the pot of glowing coals. She places it on the ground.*

IYA AGBA. Call her name.
IYA MATE. Si Bero!

> SI BERO *comes out a few moments later, obviously roused from sleep. She notices first the pot of coals, then makes out figures of the two women in the dark. She shrinks back.*

Don't be afraid, daughter. No harm will come to you.
IYA AGBA. We thought it was time for a visit. Bid us welcome so we can go about our business.
SI BERO. It's . . . it's an unusual time for earth-mothers to visit their daughters.
IYA AGBA. Not if they have debts to collect. Say how you want it done, woman.
SI BERO. Debts! No, not him. Don't touch him, my mothers.
IYA AGBA. I waste no strength on carrion. I leave him to earth's rejection.
SI BERO. Give me more time. I have the power of a mother with him.
IYA MATE (*gently*). We waited as long as we could, daughter.
IYA AGBA. Time has run out. Do you think time favours us? Can I sleep easy when my head is gathering mould on your shelves?

SI BERO. You said yourself nothing goes to waste.

IYA AGBA. What is used for evil is also put to use. Have I not
sat with the knowledge of abuse these many days and kept the
eyes of my mind open?

IYA MATE. It cannot wait, daughter. Evil hands soon find a use
for the best of things.

SI BERO. Let it wait my mothers, let it wait.

IYA AGBA (*angrily*). Rain falls and seasons turn. Night comes
and goes – do you think they wait for the likes of you? I
warned you when we took you in the fold . . .

SI BERO. I'll repay it all I promise . . .

IYA AGBA. I said this gift is not one you gather in one hand. If
your other hand is fouled the first withers also.

IYA MATE. That is how we met it. No one can change that.

SI BERO (*clutching* IYA MATE *around the knees*). Not you too.
You were never as hard as she.

IYA MATE. Nothing we can do, daughter, nothing but follow
the way as we met it.

SI BERO. And the good that is here? Does that count for
nothing?

IYA AGBA. We'll put that into the test. Let us see how it takes
to fire.

SI BERO. Fire?

IYA AGBA. It is only the dying embers of an old woman's life.
The dying embers of earth as we knew it. Is. that anything
to fear?

SI BERO. We laboured hard together.

IYA AGBA. So does the earth on which I stand. And on which
your house stands, woman. If you want the droppings of
rodents on your mat I can only look on. But my head still
fills your room from wall to wall and dirty hands touch
it . . .

SI BERO. No, no, nobody but myself . . .

IYA AGBA. I need to sleep in peace . . .

She raises the pot suddenly to throw the embers into the store. BERO *steps out at that moment, gun in hand, bearing down on* IYA AGBA.

OLD MAN (*his voice has risen to a frenzy*). Practise, Practise, Practise . . . on the cyst in the system . . .

BERO *is checked in stride by the voice. He now hesitates between the two distractions.*

. . . you cyst, you cyst, you splint in the arrow of arrogance, the dog in doma, tick of a heretic, the tick in politics, the mock of democracy, the mar of marxism, a tic of the fanatic, the boo in buddhism, the ham in Mohammed, the dash in the criss-cross of Christ, a dot on the i of ego an ass in the mass, the ash in ashram, a boot in kibbutz, the pee of priesthood, the peepee of perfect priesthood, oh how dare you raise your hindquarters you dog of dogma and cast the scent of your existence on the lamp-post of Destiny you HOLE IN THE ZERO of NOTHING!

CRIPPLE. I have a question.

OLD MAN (*turns slowly towards the interruption*). It's the dreamer.

CRIPPLE. I have a question.

OLD MAN. Black that Zero! (AAFAA, GOYI *and* BLINDMAN *begin to converge on the* CRIPPLE.)

CRIPPLE. I have a question.

OLD MAN. Shut that gaping hole or we fall through it.

CRIPPLE. I have a question.

The MENDICANTS' *chorus 'Practise' as they beat him.*

OLD MAN. Stop him cold, stop him dead! Let me hear the expiring suction of an imperfect system.

CRIPPLE. My question is . . .

AAFAA *snatches one of* GOYI's *crutches. In the background the sound of* BERO *breaking down the door.* AAFAA *brings down crutch on the* CRIPPLE's *head.*

OLD MAN. Stop him! Fire! Fire! Riot! Hot line! Armageddon!

As he shouts, the OLD MAN *snatches the* SURGEON'S *coat from where it is hanging, puts it on, dons cap, pulls on the gloves and picks up a scalpel.*

OLD MAN (*at the top of his voice*). Bring him over here. (*He dons mask.*) Bring him over here. Lay him out. Stretch him flat. Strip him bare. Bare! Bare! Bare his soul! Light the stove!

They heave him onto the table and hold him down while the OLD MAN *rips the shirt open to bare the* CRIPPLE'S *chest.* BERO *rushes in and takes in the scene, raises his pistol and aims at the* OLD MAN.

OLD MAN. Let us taste just what makes a heretic tick.

He raises the scalpel in a motion for incision. BERO *fires. The* OLD MAN *spins, falls face upwards on the table as the* CRIPPLE *slides to the ground from under him. A momentary freeze on stage. Then* SI BERO *rushes from the* OLD WOMEN *towards the surgery. Instantly* IYA AGBA *hurls the embers into the store and thick smoke belches out from the doorway gradually filling out the stage. Both women walk calmly away as* SI BERO *reappears in the doorway of the surgery. The* MENDICANTS *turn to look at her, break gleefully into their favourite song. The* OLD WOMEN *walk past their hut, stop at the spot where the* MENDICANTS *were first seen and look back towards the surgery. The song stops in mid-word and the lights snap out simultaneously.*

Bi o ti wa
Ni yio se wa

         Bi o ti wa

Ni yio se wa
Bi o ti wa l'atete ko.

THE END

OPERA WONYOSI

FOREWORD

Since Opera Wonyosi was written and performed (December 1977), the *African* continent has been rid of the two singularly repellent and vicious dictators who feature in the play: 'President-for-Life' Idi Amin and 'Emperor-for-Life' Jean-Bedel Bokassa. A third, no less odious and bloodthirsty, 'President-for-Keeps' Macias Nguema of Equatorial Guinea has not only been removed from power; he came to a well-deserved end on a hangman's rope. 1979 proved a very bad year for the continent's spawn of political and moral mutants, and a warning for those who have managed to survive that unprecedented Year of the Purge.

But how did (and do) they succeed in retaining power so long?

Primarily by the active connivance and mutual protection games of other equally guilty (or nearly so) incumbents of seats of power on the continent. In some cases there was genuine ignorance, carefully nurtured by the falsified reports of their national diplomatic representatives in the various countries, expatriate élites motivated by personal self-interest. Assiduously courted by agents of repressive power in such countries as Uganda, flattered, pampered, privileged and sealed with their own acquiescence from the realities of the nation upon whose miseries they feasted, these panders fed their governments with glowing reports of the monsters to whom they were assigned, and dismissed the outcries of the peoples as Western-orchestrated noises designed to discredit the true heroes of African nationalism.

I recall, with shame and disgust, the bland dismissals of a highly placed official of the OAU, whom I encountered in Addis Ababa early in 1977. To every demand that he, and others like him, accept the duty to make known to his masters and his people the truth of the Ugandan situation, he had only one reply: Idi Amin was a genial, witty and unpretentious African whose generosity could not be faulted. He had just returned from a three-day visit to Uganda, at Amin's own invitation where, he insisted, he was literally given the freedom of the country. Beyond this personal, *privileged* experience, his horizons did not extend. Let us take note of the existence of these moulders of 'informed' public opinion.

Let us take note also of another type, whose sophistry so readily overwhelms, deadens or excuses all obligation towards even a vocal commitment to the victims of such inhuman malformations. For such 'dispassionate' observers of society, the Bokassas, Nguemas of this world do not exist except as the products of specific socio-economic causes. This malformation of the critical intellect of African neo-Marxists will require fuller attention in its proper place; for now it is only necessary to affirm that a distinction is recognized between the mouthers and opportunists on the one hand; and the genuine but theoretically obsessed on the other. The medium of such literary genre as *Opera Wonyosi* will be reserved for the former while we will attempt to 'dialogue' with the latter in brief and at length whenever occasion demands it. At the foundation of our rejoinders will be found an uncompromising concern for the social values of literature, a recognition of the limitations and its potential, and an assertion of the writer's rôle as being merely complementary to that of the politician, sociologist, technocrat, worker, ideologue, priest, student, teacher etc., not one which can usurp one or all of these roles in entirety without forfeiting its own claim to a distinctive vocation.

A quite favourable review in the University of Ifé based journal *Positive Review* nevertheless laments the lack of a 'solid class perspective' in *Opera Wonyosi*. Translated in practical, dramaturgical terms, the reviewer desires an adaptation which would latch a class exegesis on to my parade of clowns, fools, villains, mass-murderers etc. in their arbitrary setting of a Nigerian expatriate colony in the (then) Central African Empire. Let us make it wearisomely clear that the province of the artist, while it does not exclude a direct

interest in the class, socio-economic, psychological, and other
possible promoters of his characters' being, on stage or on paper, is
not such as cannot validly manifest itself in any given work without
taking into its immediate provenance all or more of these various
contributors to the *history* of that character, or his fate at curtain-
time.

A play, a novel, a poem, a painting or any other creative
composition is *not a thesis on the ultimate condition of man*. Even
Marxism recognizes that revolutionary theory is incomplete in
itself; the praxis, the operation of that theory when power is seized
by a revolutionary party that professes the theory is what constitutes the infallible test of that theory. *Opera Wonyosi* is an expo-
sition of levels of power in practice – by a satirist's pen. To ask for a
'solid class perspective' in such a work curtails creative and critical
options and tries to dodge labour which properly belongs to the
socio-political analyst. The Nigerian society which is *portrayed*,
without one redeeming feature, is that oil-boom society of the
seventies which every child knows only too well. The crimes committed by a power-drunk soldiery against a cowed and defenceless
people, resulting in a further mutual brutalization down the scale
of power – these are the hard realities that hit every man, woman
and child, *irrespective of class* as they stepped out into the street for
work, school or other acts of daily amnesia.

Indeed, I am definitely in agreement: 'Art can and should reflect,
with the "dominant" temper of the age, those vital, positive points
which, even in the darkest times, are never totally absent.' Equally
is it necessary that art should expose, reflect, indeed magnify the
decadent, rotted underbelly of a society that has lost its direction,
jettisoned all sense of values and is careering down a precipice as
fast as the latest artificial boom can take it. Was, or was this not a
period of public executions which provided outing occasions for
families, complete with cool drinks, ice-cream, akara, sandwiches
and other picnickers' delights? We must demand if the class and
socio-economic analysts of society found, or indeed attempted to find
a way to end this coarsening assault on the sensibilities of the

populace, and most unforgivably, the development of children? Or was it perhaps dialectically correct? A nauseating spectacle that could, by a suitable election of historical conditions, be programmed into the *scientific* surrender of our 'irrational' impulses that simply insist through the medium of art: a child should not be manipulated into a tacit acceptance of the public slaughter of his kind.

What does the class conflict have to say – or even more relevantly, what did the class conflict have to say about the epidemic of ritual murder for the magical attainment of wealth? Of those syndicates which kidnapped and murdered victims *of all classes* in order to convert their vital organs to wealth talismans? We know of course that this latent ailment developed into an outright epidemic in the wake of the oil boom and Udoji Wages Commission increments – that is obvious. The course is easily traced. What the writer will not accept is the irrational claim that a work of social criticism must submerge its expression of moral disgust for the anodyne of 'correct' class analysis. At the very least, the former takes the subject away from the escapist rhetoric, from conveniently remote and 'scientific' causes and rubs the faces of the collaborators – the audience – in social shame, in the sewer of their material existence. We do not intend to give any 'intellectual' audience the comfort of seeing their material situation as the *inevitable* consequence of their socio-historical condition. We pronounce; 'Guilty' on all counts, then we leave the rest to the potential re-shaping force of society – among which we, the writers, consider ourselves – to work upon.

The dangers posed to society by those who, on the one hand, paint a bleak, unrelieving picture of an amoral, uncaring society and on the other, the ideologues who batten on the supposed 'class-perspective' short-comings of the former but cannot evolve an effective idiom for their own active social alternatives would, I am certain, constitute a relevant comparative study for yet another class of neo-praxists. Those of us who see no reason to present a utopian counter to the preponderant obscenities that daily assail our lives and, whose temporary relief is often one of 'sick humour', will continue to press this line of confrontation by accurate and negative reflection, in the confidence that sooner or later, society will recognize itself in the projection and, with or without the benefit of 'scientific' explications, be moved to act in its own overall self-interest. Any serious student of the sociology of theatre who witnessed *Opera Wonyosi*, and the reactions of audiences would not dare deny the social impact of that experience on a truly wide spectrum of the audience, across all class divisions – from the 'lace' madams to Oduduwa Hall kitchen-hands; from the Military Governor to the victim (or victim acquaintance) of his soldiers' code of anti-civilian conduct; from the university down to the parks attendant. ... theatre is rooted in the responses of such audiences for whom it is meant, not in the theoretic speculations of even genuinely committed ideologues. To suggest that the turning up of the maggot-infested underside of the compost heap is not a prerequisite of the land's transformation is the ultimate in dogmatic mind-closure. All evidence in the material world of theatre and society asserts the opposite.

Wole Soyinka
(Ile-Ife, March 1980)

CAST

Opera Wonyosi was first performed on the occasion of the University of Ife Convocation, 16 December 1977 in the University main theatre, Oduduwa Hall. The cast, with the University of Ife Theatre, and students was as follows:

DEE-JAY	Hamed Yerimah
ANIKURA	Gbemi Sodipe
AHMED	Akin Akinyanju
DE MADAM	Bola Popoola
CAPT MACHEATH	Segun Bankole
MATAR	Sola Soile
POLLY	Gaynor Bassey
HOOKFINGER JAKE	Peace Wakama
DAN DARE	Kola Oyewo
BABA	Laide Adewale
JIMMY/LOOKOUT/VENDOR/VERY	
RICH GENTLEMAN	Uko Atai
JERUBABEL	Yomi Fawole
INSPECTOR BROWN	Dolu Segun
EMPEROR BOKY	Gbola Sokoya
AIDE/PATIENT	Kola Oyewo
SUKIE	Shade Agbaje
JENNY/NURSE	Yemi Adebayo
OLD SUGAR	Gboyega Ajayi
LUCY/NEIGHBOUR	Buchi Chukwuogor
COLONEL MOSES	Femi Euba
PROFESSOR BAMGBAPO	Kole Omotoso
DOGO/ALATAKO/OFFICER	Ayo Lijadu

PRIEST, BEGGARS, GANGSTERS,
LAYABOUTS, WHORES, GOON- SQUAD:

Caroline Agbowoerin, Mosun Falode, Florence Oni, Olu
Okekanye, Muyiwa Dipeolu, Peter Fatomilola, Ola Awofade,
Andrew Akaenzue, Stella Obioha, Oyilade Igbekele, Tunji
Ojeyemi and the Company.

The orchestra, under the direction of Tunji Vidal:

CLARINET	Karen Barber
	Felix Olaniyonu
VIOLIN	Ajibola Mesida
DRUMS	Muraina Oyelami
	Thomas Adefisan
TUBA	Frank Olude
PIANO	Tunji Vidal

PART ONE

Scene One

The orchestra plays 'Mack the Knife' in the background.

DEE-JAY. I'll just introduce myself. I'm your MCDJ – Master of Ceremonies Disc-Jockey. Or Master of Ceremonies or Disc Jockey. Or simply dee-jay. Take your choice. I'm hosting this show. One time we called it the *Way-Out Opera* – for short, *Opera Wayo*. Call it the *Beggars' Opera* if you insist – that's what the whole nation is doing – begging for a slice of the action.

And don't think it's the kind of begging you're used to. Here the beggars say 'Give me a slice of action, or – (*Demonstrating.*) – give me a slice off your throat. Man, some beggars! You know what, why don't you just make up your own title as we go along because, I tell you brother, I'm yet to decide whether such a way-out opera should be named after the beggars, the army, the bandits, the police, the cash-madams, the students, the trades-unionists, the Alhajis and Alhajas, the Aladura, the Academicas, the Holy Radicals, Holy Patriachs and Unholy Heresiarchs – I mean man, in this way-out country everyone acts way out. Including the traffic. Maybe we should call it, the *Trafficking Opera*. Which just complicates things with trafficking in foreign exchange. Nice topical touch. Man, this country whips you right out on cloud nine! I'd better bring you back to earth with a song about that universal species of humanity – and if you haven't heard Louis Armstrong do his own thing with good old Mack, man, just where you been? One-a-two-a-three-take it from there baby. Let's go.

The Company stroll in, in character, and in their various

*groups — Beggars, Good-Squad, Mackie's gang etc — prome-
nade about the stage while they sing the song 'Mack the
Knife.'*

> Now the shark has teeth like razors
> And he shows them in a fight
> All Mackie has is a flick-knife
> And he keeps it out of sight
>
> Where the night flows dark and silent
> There you'll find men lying dead
> Was it plague that really killed them
> Or a fee to Mackie paid?
>
> You'll recall that Lagos doctor
> In Ikoyi slashed to death
> The report lies in a Closed File
> Mackie vanished like a wraith
>
> Was Mackie seen in Badagry
> Where another seemed to drown?
> Did our expert of convenience
> Fix the man who won't pipe down?
>
> Would you like a marble headstone
> And be martyred in a cause?
> Go and meddle in Igbeti[2]
> And a slab for free is yours
>
> For it takes more than the darkness
> To protect one beast of prey
> When there's interest joined to interest
> All we can do is pray.

DEE-JAY. Now you know where we're at. If you're still uncertain, let me tell you that your dee-jay isn't feeling all that cocksure himself. But there is to be a coronation. An imperial coronation, first in Africa – at least in the last few decades or so. Emperor Boky, Boky the Cocky, no less – and if you think that's mere boasting, ask him how many daughters presented their credentials when he advertised for his long-lost daughter from Indochina. He confirmed the claims of one and married the others. Man, he's wa-a-a-ay – out. Also known as Folksy Boksy on account of he likes to meet with the folks. You dig? The common folks, like vagrants, felons and – dig this – school children. Actually rubs feet with them – well, on them sort of – he's gone beyond shaking hands – wow, he's ahead man! But so am I on the story. And this is your MC dee-jay turning the scene to introduce to you Chief Anikura King of Beggars. A professional artist who belongs to the school known all through the ages as Con Art. In short, a master of the psychology of charity.

ANIKURA *emerges. Kicks awake the bundles of rags and cloth which have been strewn all over the floor. Human forms emerge, slink off, taking their rags with them.*

Anikura's Song

Christians smooth and sleek, wake up
Moslems in gold turbans, fake up
Now tell me you pieties
Is there one jot, bar niceties
To choose from your cozening make-up?

You bankrupt your neighbour every day
And smother good consciences with pay
Then on Sundays and Fridays
You deny all your fun-days
And the next week resume your dirty play.

Pray do not change your con technique

For to many, life isn't a picnic
And outside the church
Or the mosque is a wretch
Who depends on your mood philanthropic.

But look out, one day you will find
That pus-covered mask hides a mind
And then – boom! – oga sah[3]
What's that blur? – oga sa?
With a red flame fanning his behind.

ANIKURA. What a cushy job Moses had – what with God on his side and all. Simply hit his staff on a rock and all that water came gushing out. I have to do what I can without that kind of help. And getting money out of people is rather like that magic of Moses. Well, those who have no powers of miracle must make do with psychology. I understand human nature. Maybe Moses understood God but I doubt it just the same. I also understand my society – which is more than could be said for him. He was always getting caught out, surprised. Me, no. That's where science triumphs over magic. The only problem I have is novelty – something new to clutch the heart-strings and loosen the purse-strings. Every model is soon *déjà vu*. But I forget, you don't speak French do you? I'm a first-generation Nigerian exile here. Came here during that Civil War we had over there. This used to be Central African Republic – still is, but I hear it's going to become something grander very soon. So what with one thing and another, I parlay vous fransay. But we try to keep us the old home culture around here, so not to worry, I know you're going to feel at home. You know what they say of us Nigerians don't you? We know how to take care of business. We are always getting thrown out of one country or another but, while we last, well – we do know how to take care of business. So, with your permission, I beg leave to make hay while the sun shines through the imperial arse-hole. (*Knock on the door.*) Enter.

AHMED. Ranka dede.[4] 'You are Chief Anikura.

ANIKURA. I am thus addressed.

AHMED. You own the business 'Home from Home for the Homeless'?

ANIKURA. Indeed

AHMED. I was recommended to you.

ANIKURA (*takes out a notebook, puts on his glasses*). Name?

AHMED. Chief Anikura, I am totally destitute, my parents' house was burnt over our head during the Civil War. My father lost his life and my mother is still missing . . .

ANIKURA (*writing furiously*). It's a good story. A variation on the old line. They've heard too many tales of that problem here. I may as well tell you that every other Nigerian who comes here is a victim of the war. Still, there was that little extra touch you added – mother still missing. Oh there are lots of missing mothers but you see, you could add that you came looking for her here and got stranded. You were duped. Defrauded. Gave your money to a fellow Nigerian to change and he disappeared. Yes, they'll believe you. They know that any Nigerian will rob his starving grandmother and push her in the swamp. You'll do.

AHMED. Oh no chief. I would hate to libel my fellow countrymen.

ANIKURA. If only you knew how much your countrymen libel their mothers! But you take that story and stick to it. Memorize it, avoid unnecessary embellishments and you are well away.

AHMED. Perhaps you're right. I was telling it straight only yesterday, on the corner of Avenue Charles de Gaulle and the Place de la Republique . . .

ANIKURA (*rising in a fury*). Place de la Republique? Oh, so you were the scab. Poacher. Trespasser. Illegal entrant. Were you well flogged?

AHMED. I don't understand it, chief. Two gentlemen suddenly appeared and set on me. They flogged me nearly senseless, then gave me your card.

ANIKURA. You were lucky. Or maybe they had just lunched.

(Turns to a map on the wall.) Take a good look at that. This shaded area is entirely within my jurisdiction. We call it New Ikoyi.[5] There we try to retain all the living styles we had at home, down to the naming of the streets. The rest of Bangui is shared with the foreigners – the natives that is – a rather unsophisticated lot if I may say so. We had to help them with certain details of organization, so in effect, we have a *laissez passer* – passport to you – to work in their own territory. You want to work across the border or in New Ikoyi?

AHMED. I think I prefer to feel at home. I'm not likely to get lost there.

ANIKURA. Don't be so stupid. Our sector is marked by sign-posts of up to ten feet of garbage, so you can't miss your way. Now choose your sector within our national boundaries divided into 19 districts. Which do you prefer? Different rates of course. Central areas more expensive than the suburbs . . .

AHMED. Chief. I think I must let you know that I have only . . .

ANIKURA. The prices are listed on the board. And considering the fact that I've provided you with a story . . .

AHMED. But I came with my real story.

ANIKURA. Useless. I wouldn't even sell you a union card with that tale. It's the variation I added which turned it viable. A thousand CFA. Three naira if you like. We accept our national currency here. And so – *(makes a rude noise)* – to that Foreign Exchange Decree you've just passed.

AHMED. Please Chief Anikura, one naira.

ANIKURA. Two. And only because of the beating you had yesterday. Our job is to induce charity in others, not practise it ourselves.

AHMED. One naira fifty please, Chief Anikura. It's all I have. *(Holds it out.)*

ANIKURA. Plus 50 per cent of your weekly takings. Don't think you are not constantly watched. Some of your donors may be among my auditors. It is strictly forbidden to keep a closed bowl or use your pockets. You will be issued standard bowls – different shapes but with identical mechanism. You deposit the money, press a button and the false bottom opens and the coins fall in. It opens only one way. Don't try to tamper with it.

AHMED. As if I would dream of such a thing.

ANIKURA. You will. But don't try to make your dreams come true. Or you'll find yourself doing the Cripple — and that won't be make-up either. Name.

AHMED. Ahmed, chief.

ANIKURA (looks him up and down). Hm. You'll need a costume all right. That brings it to 70 per cent of takings. (Begins to inspect costumes.)

AHMED. Chief . . .!

ANIKURA. Oh you do the strangled-voice anguish all right. (Mimics.) Chief. (Laughs.) Just remember it doesn't move me. Give and it shall be given unto you. I know my Bible. Do you?

AHMED. Actually I am a Moslem.

ANIKURA. Oh? Of course with a name like that you would be. That makes you something of an interesting proposition. We don't get too many of you coming to me. There's a marabout among the natives who takes care of people like you. We expatriates are mostly Christians if you get what I mean. We practise Charity Begins at Home. Your faith isn't against that is it?

AHMED. Oh, not in the least.

ANIKURA. I'll tell you why I don't seem to mind you at all. Indeed, if for once I may be emotional, why I seem even to heartily welcome your presence in our establishment. (Raising his voice.) My dear . . .

DE MADAM (from inside). Are you calling me chief dear?

ANIKURA. Tell me, our fellow the Life President, what's he these days?

DE MADAM. I think he's back to the Christian fold.

ANIKURA. Are you sure?

DE MADAM (emerging). Well, he returned from Libya a fortnight ago didn't he?

ANIKURA. But that's when he became converted.

DE MADAM. That was the first trip when Gadafy promised him 20 million dollars. He got converted on the spot. Then he went back last week to ask for contribution for his coming coronation and the Arab man told him to go home. So he changed back to Christianity.

ANIKURA (to AHMED). You see, the power of money. Oh, may I present — my consort and right-hand man-and-woman rolled in one — Madam Cecilia Anikura, better known in these parts as — De Madam.

AHMED. Your servant, ma'am.

DE MADAM. Delighted, I'm sure.

ANIKURA. He is a Moslem he says. Not a bad thing to have on our books if the Life President Emperor-to-be should change back to Islam again. Fashions change with the leader you know. In the two weeks Emperor Boky was a Moslem you had more civil servants and professors coming in and out of mosques than there was population in the country. Not to talk of businessmen. Everyday the personal column of the papers, you know, the Change of Name Section . . . I, formerly known as Fidelis Desirée Michel Charlemagne now wish to be known as Mohammed Idris Suleiman etc. etc. (He seems to find a satisfactory one among the costumes. Changes his mind. Looks him up and down.) Can't really find one to go with our story. Mind you, you're starting at the right time, being on the eve of coronation and all. (Hauls them all up.) Look, you pick one. My consort will adjust as necessary.

AHMED (recoiling). What's that?

ANIKURA (in formal lecturing voice). These represent the five types of misery most likely to touch people's hearts. The sight of them brings about that unnatural state of mind in which people are actually willing to give money away. (Selects one.) That's the Cheerful Cripple — victim of modern road traffic. We call it the Nigerian special. The next model — War Casualty. Can't stop twitching you see. Now that first puts off the public. But the sight of the war medals he's wearing softens them. The third model – we call it the Taphy-Psychotic.[6] It's got a whip you see. He rushes around in a frenzy as if he's going to flog you. But that's where we put in the variation. He doesn't actually flog you. He stops with his hands raised and breaks into an idiot's grin – and you realize he's only soft in the head. You are so relieved you give him money. Number four. Victim of Modern Industry. Collapsed chest. That sits down well with the business tycoons. Remember the Cement Bonanza? Well, to clear those ports they had the hungry sods moving the cement bags round the clock. Pay was – good to decent, and every labourer earned all the overtime he could. What no one bothered to tell them was the effect of breathing in cement dust 12 to 18 hours a day. It's called Fibrositosis. Same as in asbestos factories. Wait, I'll tell you all about it in a song. *(Looking up at the* DEE-JAY.*)* Accompaniment please.

DEE-JAY. Ladies and Gentlemen, Chief Anikura and present Company will now sing a song entitled: Big Man Chop Cement; Cement Chop Small Man.

Big Man Chop Cement; Cement Chop Small Man

A labourer's life is a healthy one
It's fresh air from dawn till the sun goes down
Clean exercise; see how those muscles bulge
Power beyond you my bookish don
And what if a man does himself indulge
At night when the bloody labour is done
Every cloud has its silver lining
Clouds of cement ensure my dining
A mound of eba washed down in palm wine
And overtime pay brings the suzies[7] in line

Chorus:

> I know now it's true – life is a wheeze
> The proof's in my lungs when I sneeze
> Well, my chest is congested
> But the port's decongested
> While I breathe like a dying accordion
> Seven more years says the surgeon
> And you end on a slab of cement
> It ends on a slab of cement.
>
> No thought for tomorrow, this Jack's all right
> Grind all day long and grind all night
> Udoji[8] will come when things grow dull
> Then watch me jump on a Saturday night
> I tell you this cat's right on the ball
> Like a sailor in town, high as a kite
> Twelve-inches platform, dig the sky-scraping geezer
> Superfly dandy, sharper than razor
> Easy come, easy go, God bless Udoji
> And the season of ships and cement orgy.
>
> From port to horizon the ships lay spent,
> Cement in the holds, on the decks, cement
> And I gave up my nights of leisure and fun
> For overtime pay makes the worker content
> Right round the clock I had a good run
> The money came handy, now I repent
> A man's lungs for clean air is meant
> Not for breathing in clouds of cement
> And overtime pay comes to mere chicken feed
> When the cement tycoon has filled out his greed

Chorus.

ANIKURA. Well now to the next model. (*Turning round suddenly with the costume before him.* AHMED *recoils in horror.*) A Blind

Man, heart-breaking very effective. *(He notices* AHMED's *reaction for the first time. Bawls.)* He feels pity! My God, look at you. He actually feels pity. You feel the same way as the passers-by should feel. You're only fit to be begged from. Lead him away — give him the Bleeding-Heart outfit. And we'll have to change your story. You won't get far with the original one. Your new story is that of the Good Man Ruined by Kindness. Successful man run to seed. Grace to grass. Show him the costume my dear. Follow her and come out for inspection. *(Exit* DE MADAM.*)*

AHMED. Where do I keep my own things?

ANIKURA. *I* keep them. Property of the firm.

AHMED. Ah, Allah, these clothes are the very last things belonging to me. They were the last things bought me by my mother before she vanished.*(*ANIKURA *fixes him with a long look.)* I'm sorry, chief, I'm very sorry.

ANIKURA. Be off before I change my mind. And don't forget to leave your shoes.

AHMED. Chief!

ANIKURA. Don't you take off your shoes in the mosque? Allah, what airs!

MADAM ANIKURA *returns with an outfit which she throws at* AHMED *pointing to the changing room.*

Where's our daughter?

DE MADAM. Polly? Upstairs, of course.

ANIKURA. Was that man here? The fellow who always sneaks in when I'm out.

DE MADAM. Don't be so suspicious, Jonathan. There isn't a finer gentleman alive than the captain. I think he's taken a real fancy to our Polly.

ANIKURA. Hm!

DE MADAM. If my eyes aren't deceiving me, Polly has taken a fancy to him, too. I see a match.

ANIKURA. Use your head, Cecilia. If Polly had a husband he'd soon have us in his grip. No doubt about it. Do you think she can keep her mouth shut in bed any better than you can?

DE MADAM. It's a fine opinion of our daughter you have.

ANIKURA. The worst, the very worst. She's hot for anyone.

DE MADAM. Well, she certainly never got that from you.

ANIKURA. I'm a mastermind, not a superstud. And whatever else he is he is first and foremost a gold-digger. It's my money he's after. It can't just be her virtue because I'm sure she disposed of that a long time ago.

DE MADAM. What a thing to say! Jonathan, you're just an ignorant brute.

ANIKURA. Ignorant? Well you tell me this gentleman's name then.

DE MADAM. He was always simply called 'The Captain'.

ANIKURA. You haven't even asked him his name. Did she meet him on a blind date?

DE MADAM. You'd hardly expect us to ask him for his birth certificate – and him kind enough to ask us to a dance at the Octopus Disco.

ANIKURA. Where do you say?

DE MADAM. At the Octopus Disco. We stopped there for a drink.

ANIKURA. At the Octopus Disco? That's where to get picked up all right.

DE MADAM. It's a respectable place! And the gentleman never laid a hand on me or Polly except with his lace gloves on.

ANIKURA. Lace gloves . . .

DE MADAM. Yes, he always wears lace gloves.

ANIKURA. And a stick with an ivory handle? And gold chain on patent leather shoes.

DE MADAM (hopefully). Real gold?

ANIKURA. Pure gold. Smuggled from Lebanon specially for him by his Alhaja, one of many. At least before their Civil War. Those Lebanese you know, the Jews of the Arab world. Hm. I still don't understand how everybody is the something of somewhere else, not just something in his own right.

DE MADAM (*thoughtfully*). We have no Middle East contacts you know. And they say there is plenty of lace and gold coming in from there.

ANIKURA. What's this now? You want to go into the smuggling business? Don't be so common.

AHMED *comes out from the fitting room.*

AHMED. Chief Anikura, will you please give me a few hints.

DE MADAM (*sighs*). They all want to know what to do. As if begging isn't an instinct where he comes from.

ANIKURA. He's an idiot. (*To* AHMED.) Come back at six o'clock tonight and you'll be given all you need. Now get out. I want to think. (*He strikes his thinking pose.*)

AHMED. Thank you, chief, thank you so much.

Exit AHMED.

ANIKURA (*short pause*). Now I'll tell you who this fine gentleman with the lace gloves is. It's Macheath — Mack the Knife. (*He rushes out and is heard shouting.*) Polly! Polly!

DE MADAM. Good God! Mack the Knife! Holy Virgin! Polly! Polly! Oh what has she got herself into! I always said that daughter of mine would come to no good. Polly!

ANIKURA *comes back.*

ANIKURA. Polly hasn't been home. Her bed's not been touched.

DE MADAM. She's been out to supper with the lace merchant. I'm sure of it, Jonathan.

ANIKURA. I hope to God she is with the lace merchant. I hope she aims no higher than the lace merchant. But will she?

The Song of Ngh-ngh-ngh

(Sung by CHIEF ANIKURA *and* DE MADAM.*)*

DE MADAM. Oti o. Ngh-ngh-ngh.[9]

Rather than spend all her nights with her love
She chases class, she chases class
And who's got the class? Who's got the class?
It's khaki and brass. It's khaki and brass
So rather than spend all the nights with her love
She's planting the seeds of a brass-khaki class
And taking the salute of the Army as they pass.
(Obscene gesture by ANIKURA *on 'Salute')*

ANIKURA. Oti o. Ngh-ngh-ngh.

Once his white collar was as high as she gazed
Oh how she adored the ink on his cuff
And how she would swear, how she would swear
Ever to cherish the smooth with the rough
But fashion and time all her oaths have erased
His clerical sweat is the worst social smear
Which even a Honda makes no easier to bear.

DE MADAM. Oti o. Ngh-ngh-ngh.

But who will deny that love is no match
For contracts galore, for foreign exchange.
And who's got the clout? Who's got the clout?
Who *can* swear to me, I shall ne'er do without?
The ex-politician who's not worth a scratch?
Or Mr Professor? The Perm-Sec? A Chief?
Well, time anyway has proved each one a thief.

BOTH. Oti o. Ngh-ngh-ngh.

You think I regret love's obvious demise?
Not on your life! Do I look mad?
But why pick a loser? Why pick a loser?
A petty-cash crook? Now isn't that sad?
We know it's the big fish the net's sure to miss
While your small-time bandit earns lead perforations
But come, we must act. Enough perorations.

Scene Two

DEE-JAY. Deep in the Bidonville of Bangui known as the Nigerian Quarter by the natives but christened New Ikoyi by the expatriates, the bandit Mack the Knife celebrates his marriage to Polly, daughter of Chief Jonathan Anikura, Friend of the Poor, Proprietor of Home from Home for the Homeless.

Enter MATAR, *with torchlight and pistol.*

MATAR. Hands up, if anyone's in here.

MACK. Well, is anyone here?

MATAR. No, empty. Perfectly safe for a wedding. *(Pointing his torch everywhere.* MACK *goes out and returns with* POLLY *wearing a wedding dress.)*

POLLY. But – it's a stable.

MACK. No, it's the Polo Club.

POLLY. It *is* a stable.

MACK. Don't let's start the day with arguments my dear. A stable is where Jesus Christ was born. I don't aim that high, all I want is a quiet wedding to my own sweetest, dearest Polly. *(Kisses her.)* I assure you it's the Army Polo Club. We've been loaned their lounge – the horses' lounge of course. I asked for the roomiest.

MATAR. A lot of our people will reckon this a very chancy thing you're doing Mack. Pinching Anikura's only daughter right under his nose.

MACK. Who *is* Anikura?

MATAR. He'll call himself the poorest man in Bangui.

POLLY. But Mack, you can't be thinking of having our wedding here. Polo Club or not, it's nothing but a stable. How could a minister come here? This is supposed to be the happiest day in a girl's life.

MACK. My dear little girl, if Christ could consent to be born in a stable, one of his own ministers can administer communion in the same place. The furnishings will be here in just a moment or two.

MATAR. Furniture this way!

Enter BABA, HADJI, DAN DARE *and* HOOK-FINGER JAKE *carrying furniture, crockery etc. The stable is quickly made to look like a loud, over-furnished drawing-room.*

MACK. Rubbish!

JAKE. Wish you the best of luck. (*Brings in a big painting of the once fashionable Nigerian 'naive' style.*) Now, you'll never guess it, but ten years ago, we'd have called this rubbish. But there were tourists looking for local culture kicks, so . . . there you are. Oh, talking of kicks, the old American collector who owned this thought culture was dearer than survival — we had to put in a few kicks to persuade him otherwise. Nothing serious . . .

MACK. I said no bloodshed!

DARE. Nor was there. A broken rib or two I think, maybe a case of heart attack — cardiac arrest I think it's called these days — but definitely no blood.

MACK. I feel sick when that happens. It's bad business. You'll never make good businessmen. Cannibals maybe, but businessmen, never!

DARE. Wish you the best of luck. This quadraphonic set, dear madam, belonged only half-an-hour ago to Mrs Professor of Physiotherapy, University of Bangui. You'll probably hear some complaint from that direction about her person. (*Giggles dirtily.*)

MACK. Animal! Do you mean you molested her?

DARE. I didn't. That's her complaint.

POLLY. What's all this furniture?

MACK. Do you like it Polly?

POLLY (*crying*). But . . . killing all these poor people, just for a bit of furniture.

MACK. And such rubbishy stuff! I *am* ashamed. And you are right to be upset. Quadraphonic set, none phonier. Naive painting — what do you think we are ? Collectors? And of course you had to be so cheap as to bring a black-and-white television set? Black and white! Just what throw-backs are you ? What age do you think you're living in? Even radio is coloured these days, if you ever listen to the news. I suppose none of you even thought of bringing a table.

BABA. A table!

A big covered object is brought down. Uncovered, it reveals a fully equipped banquet table.

POLLY. Oh Mack, I'm so unhappy. I just hope the minister doesn't come.

MACK. My wife is completely upset. How often does it happen I get married? Yet you've got to upset my wife right from the beginning.

JAKE. Dearest Polly . . .

MACK (*knocks off his hat*). Dearest Polly! Dearest Polly! I'll shove your head down your guts you cheeky sod! Dearest Polly! Since when did you get so familiar? I suppose you've even slept with her.

POLLY. Mackie!

JAKE. I swear to you . . .

BABA. Madame, if there's a few odds and ends you need, we'll go out again . . .

POLLY. No. Except we have nothing to sit on.

MACK. Unscrew the legs off the quadraphonic.

DARE. Done. Plus the speakers we have another six seats. Are we expecting a large company?

MACK. Christ, look at them! Apart from Baba, none of you even thought of getting properly dressed. After all, this isn't the wedding of a nobody. And Polly, do get busy with that spread of eatables.

POLLY. Is it all stolen, Mackie?

MACK. Polly you disappoint me. All this stuff has been merely liberated.

POLLY. And if the police come in?

MACK. That's no problem. I'll take care of it.

BABA. Besides, today all the police are lining the streets. The emperor is making a tour of inspection for his coronation arrangements.

POLLY. Fourteen forks but only one knife.

MACK. What a mess! That's the trouble with beginners. No style. But you'll manage won't you, dearest Polly?

DARE. We concentrated on bringing only the classy stuff. Look at the finish on that television set for instance. You don't miss the colour with wood like that.

MATAR. Sssh! Permit me captain ... (*Opening the magnum of champagne.*)

MACK. Come here, Polly. (*They pose for congratulations.*)

MATAR. Permit me, captain, on behalf of everyone here, to offer you, on the happiest day of your life, at the zenith of your career ... its turning point, as it were ... to offer you our heartiest congratulations. (*Shakes* MACKIE's *hand.*) Chin up boys!

MACK. Thank you. That was very nice of you, Matar-boy.

MATAR (*shakes* POLLY's *hand, pats* MACKIE *on the back*). And it was spoken from the heart. Well, keep your head up, old chap. I mean — so to speak. And may the old ... never go (*demonstrating*) limp.

Roars of laughter from the MEN. MACKIE *suddenly grabs* MATAR's *hand and gently forces him to the floor.*

MACK. Shut your trap. Keep your smutty jokes for Kitty — she's the right slut for them.

POLLY. Mackie, don't be so common.

MATAR. You're a fine one to complain. Lucy has told me some of the ones you've told her. Mine are lavender water in comparison.

POLLY. Lucy!

MACKIE *slowly draws his sword-stick.*

JAKE. This is a wedding, Mack.

MACK. A fine wedding, eh Polly? Putting up with all this vermin. You'd never think your friends would let you down like this.

POLLY *(uncertainly).* I think it's a very nice wedding.

BABA. Of course it is. No one's letting you down. *(To* MATAR.*)* Your Kitty is as good as anyone else. There's no finer whore between Bangui and Kano I swear. Come on now with the present my lad.

MATAR *(a little mollified. Offers* POLLY *the gift).* Here you are then.

POLLY. Oh, a wedding present. That's very kind of you Mr Matar. Oh look Mack, a night-gown. Isn't it lovely.

MATAR *(eyeing* MACK*).* Another dirty joke I suppose?

MACK. It's all right. I don't want to press a point on this happy occasion.

MATAR. Very big of you, captain.

POLLY. Oh, it is so wonderful. I am so happy. I haven't any words for it. You are all so kind.

DARE. Well wait till you see this *(uncovers a slim futuristic object).* Latest in grandfather clocks. A genuine Seiko.

POLLY. A Seiko?

DARE. Those Japanese will make anything. This grandfather clock is the first of the kind. No hands. *(Presses a button.)* See? Pure quartz, computerized and fully automatic. Not many countries have any use for it but our people tell me it sells by the hundred at home. Only Nigerians fancy culture you know. This one had been sitting in Monoprix downtown; thought it was time it came where it would be appreciated.

POLLY. But it's so . . . so conspicuous.

DARE. The only one in town, in the empire in fact. It's a fashion-setter.

POLLY. I mean, it will be easily traced.

DARE. You let the captain worry about that ma'am.

POLLY. Ah well. Thank you for taking so much trouble for me.

DARE. No trouble ma'am.

POLLY (*tearful*). It's a pity we have no house to put it in.

MACK. Think of it as just the beginning, Polly. All beginnings are difficult. Now clear some of the stuff away so we'll have room to eat.

They start boxing some of the presents.

This is the best food to be had anywhere today. And that is no idle boast Polly. The best. Shall we start?

BABA. Splendid plates. From Hotel Intercontinental. Same firm as makes the emperor's cutlery.

DARE. To tell you the truth, ma'am. Everything is the same as the emperor will have on his coronation. The salmon is from La-fayette, by special appointment Fishmongers to His Imperial Majesty. Specially flown from France last night. No problem slipping in among the crates at the airport. Came through the VIP lounge – a Right Royal Salmon I tell you.

MACK. I promised you a royal banquet.

JAKE. *Imperial* banquet if you don't mind, captain.

MACK. Have some caviar. (*Reads.*) Guaranteed one-hundred per cent caviar from the Caspian Sea.

BABA. That must set back the Treasury a quid or two.

DARE. Don't gobble up your eggs like that Jake. The mayon-naise is dripping all over your chin.

JAKE. There is nothing wrong with my way of eating eggs.

MACK. There is plenty wrong with the table manners of all of you!

BABA. Nothing wrong with the food though. A little too rich for

my tastes mind you, but then our captain only gets married once
in his life.

A titter from MATAR. *He chokes on his food.*

MACK. Are you also finding the food too rich, Matar-boy?

MATAR. Oh no, just something someone said. That was rich all
right.

MACK. I cannot say I appreciate your sense of humour on an occasion like this.

JAKE. I'll bet you've never had truffles like that, Polly. Mack has it
every day. Has it delivered at his mobile address every morning
with the newspaper. You've landed all right. I've always said
Mack'll make a fine match for a girl with refined feelings. Said so
to Lucy yesterday.

POLLY. Lucy? Mack, who is Lucy?

JAKE (*embarassed*). Lucy? Now you mustn't start getting the
wrong ideas about that.

DARE *is making frantic gestures behind* POLLY *to silence*
JAKE.

POLLY (*seeing him*). Is there something you want Mr Dan Dare?
Well, what were you going to say, Mr Jake.

JAKE. Nothing, nothing. If I'm not careful I'll be biting my tongue.

MACK. Slicing it off you mean? What have you got on your plate
Jake?

JAKE. Well, I think . . . yes, I think it's that stuff you called caviar.

MACK. I see. And what have you got in your hand?

JAKE. My pocket-knife captain.

MACK. I could have sworn it was. And you were going to eat caviar
with your knife. And not just a knife but a pocket-knife. Not to
mention the fact that it looks rusty from here.

JAKE. That isn't rust captain. It's blood.

MACK. Blood. You hear that my dear. He eats caviar with a knife.
With a blood-stained knife. Oh Polly, you'll have a heartbreaking

job before you can teach these ruffians to act like gentlemen.

BABA. By the way whose blood was it?

POLLY. O-oh. *(Bursts into tears.)*

MACK. Now look what you've done, you silly old man.

BABA. I am sorry. I was just wondering if it was anyone we knew.

MACK. Shut up! Can't you all understand my wife is very sensitive?

JIMMY *(bursting in)*. Captain, I think we've got visitors.

BABA *(looking round the door)*. Nonsense, it's the Prophet Jerubabel. *(Enter* JERU *pronounced Jèrú.)*

MACK *(smoothly)*. Good evening Prophet Jeru.

JERU *(looking round)*. A stable. I like that touch. Captain Macheath, my dear erring brother, my proverbial lost sheep whom I consider it my duty to return to the fold . . .

BABA. I knew he could account for his sponging around.

JERU. Let me assure you how much I consider it a veritable act of Divine Providence that he has guided your feet to this significant abode that is – to put it literally – the very cradle of our religion.

JAKE *(offering the plate)*. The salmon is good prophet.

JERU. Ah, fish. A veritable sacrament. Was our good lord not himself the Divine Fisherman?

MATAR *(to* DARE*)*. I thought you said the fish came from Paris.

MACK. Do make yourself comfortable Prophet Jeru. I am deeply honoured that you took the great trouble of finding your way here.

POLLY. Oh thank you, thank you prophet. Now I know that my marriage is truly blessed.

JERU *(mouthful of fish)*. Blessed? I'll say it is. I have here the special bottle of Holy Water which has just come from the Holy City, Jerusalem . . .

BABA. Prophet, a little of this champagne?

JERU. I accept it in the name of the Miracle at Cana. It was a wedding too if I may remind you.

JAKE. I give up.

MACK. You are uneducated Jake. Don't take on better men than yourself.

POLLY. Why not a hymn now please, Mack. Now that the prophet is here, it would make everything so nice if we could have a hymn.

MACK. A hymn it is. A hymn in honour of Prophet Jeru.

DARE. Oh, captain . . . *(He stops, a little embarrassed.)*

BABA. Go on, don't be so bashful.

MACK. What is it?

DARE. Oh well . . .

JAKE. He has a song. Composed by his very self.

MACK. Well well, in my honour?

DARE. In honour of our good captain and his wife.

POLLY. Oh, they are all so nice to me, Mack. Really nice. And you say such rude things about them.

MACK. I *know* them. They have a heart of gold I know, but I can't cut them up just so we can see it more often. All right, let's have the song.

Wedding Song for Polly and Mack
(Sung by the Entire Company)

> Hail, pair of turtle-doves
> Perfect of earthly loves
> All hearts go out to you
> Envious of love so true
> Live every happily
> Raising your family
> Both long to cherish
> This our very wish.
>
> Daughter of House of Fame
> With mind as clear as flame
> No Ph.D. degree
> Can match your pedigree
> Base be that rank or file

Who thinks to match your style
Dear Belle of our Delight
Belle of true Delight.

To you our Captain brave
Terror of King or knave
Long life, prosperity
Free from asperity
Nay, never shall you bow
Low at the Bar Beach show[10]
Though if that must be so
Bravely, bravely go.

During the singing MACK *exhibits signs of torture.* POLLY *is however radiant with delight.* JERU *is blandly beaming. On the last lines however, he explodes.*

MACK Less of the graveyard humour if you don't mind.

JIMMY *(bursts in).* The cops! This time it is the cops! The Commissioner himself.

BABA. Yes, it's Tiger Brown and no mistake. Security expert from Nigeria on loan to the emperor since the old civilian days. *(Sighs.)* Why doesn't he go back home?

MATAR. How could he? Don't you know why he was loaned in the first place? Glad to get rid of him.

JAKE. Add to that, he feels at home from home, among us.

MACK *(as* BROWN *enters).* Make yourself at home, Commissioner.

BROWN *(offended).* Commissioner!

MACK. All right. Make yourself at home you old scoundrel.

BROWN. Is that the young lady?

MACK. It gives me great pleasure to introduce my old friend and brother, known in popular parlance as Tiger Brown. And this is my own beloved fiancée soon to be my wife, Polly Anikura.

(BROWN *is startled, stares at* POLLY.)

The wedding party is complete at last since we now have what
amounts to official sanction ...

BROWN. Official sanction! Oh Mack, did you have to pick on the
Army Polo Club? Breaking and entering, and ... oh Christ, I
recognise that salmon.

MACK. Have some, Commissioner.

BROWN *(accepting it)*. I was detailed to protect that right through
the VIP lounge. It came from Paris ...

DARE. See?

BROWN. How did it get here? Oh my god ...

MACK. Does it taste all right?

BROWN *(unhappily nibbling)*. I suppose so ...

DARE. Then there's no harm done, I left enough for the imperial
banquet.

MATAR. What's going on here anyway? Why is he here? Why is he
always snooping? I don't trust him.

MACK. *I* do.

MATAR. Why doesn't he go back home?

MACK. Sit down! Shut up and listen. Polly my dear, I want you to
understand tonight, our wedding night why you need never
worry about Commissioner Inspector Brown, Officer of the
Nigeria Police on Loan to the Centrafrique Empire – then
Republic – in the bad old days, and stayed on ever since out of
deference to the worse new days. You see in his person the individual in whom the present ruler of Centrafrique reposed his
trust – his absolute trust in the bad old days, and has learnt to
increase that absolute trust in the worse new days. You see before
you one in whom the president, then life president, then emperor
has never ceased to rely and who, despite this precarious honour,
has never failed to remain my friend through the various vicissi-
tudes of status that have beset his patron, and consequently, himself. This friendship is mutual. Never, never have I in my humble
capacity as safe-breaker and multiple murderer failed to share
the proceeds of my adventures with Tiger Brown. And never,
never, well, almost never – has he organized a raid without

giving me just that little hint in advance. Give and take, give and take is what it takes, is how to live. To Tiger Brown!

Excepting MATAR, *they all toast: Tiger Brown.*

BROWN (*he's been examining the table-cloth*). Unusual in these parts . . .

MACK. Persian damask. I had hoped to drape, not just the table but the very walls in that latest Nigerian favourite called Wonyosi. But the ban . . .

BROWN. Surely you don't allow trifles like bans to bother you.

MACK. It bothers the suppliers from home. The shops here are still waiting for their orders to arrive. We can't rob them of what they haven't got, can we?

BROWN. Mack, the camaraderie! It's what I find so irresistible . . .

MACK. You remember those good old days?

BROWN. Old soldiers never die.

MACK. You and I together . . .

BROWN. What can others understand of this?

MACK. Last crumb . . . last drop of blood . . .

BROWN. Even if we finally went different ways, but isn't that life?

Khaki is a Man's Best Friend

(*by* MACKIE *and* BROWN)

> Khaki is a man's best friend
> The girls seem to favour the trend
> So one fine day I upped and enrolled
> With patriots and others, mean and bold
> And I dreamed of the deeds I would do
> And I glowed with the glory of me
> For what is a man but the sum of his power
> To kill or to spare, to make the world cower
> So one fine day, I upped and enrolled
> With patriots and others, mean and bold.

Chorus:

'Secession' cried one; the other – 'One Nation'
For oil is sweet, awoof[11] no get bone
The task was done, the nation is one
We know who won and who got undone
No thought of keeping his body one
It's scattered from Bendel to Bonny Town.

Now I was one of the frisky trio
Who staked out the night-spots, *con brio*.
There was Johnny the Soak, and Pele the Dandy
Loathe they were to leave their pal Randy
For they dreamed of the deeds we would do
And they glowed with the glory of us Three
And they pictured in 3-D the power of man
To spare or to kill, to approve or to ban
So one fine day, they upped and enrolled
With patriots and others, mean and bold.

Now Pele, named for his footballing hero
Found war, as a game, was – Zero.
He was blown up in Uyo, while wine-loving Johnny
Lies drinking his fill of the marsh of Bonny
And I dream of the deeds they could do
And I sigh with the waste of all three.
Randy's the name sir, just the name, only in name
And that, you'll excuse me, is a damn bloody shame
For a man who one fine day upped and enrolled
With patriots and others, mean and bold.

Well, power is power whatever the name
The Khaki sure makes up for the shame
Civilians are sheep, just hear them bleat
When my good Taphy whip clears the street

And to think of the things they could do
Yet they take all this bullying shit from me
Well one can't distinguish in matters of vengeance
Some made the loot while we took the chance
When one fine day we upped and enrolled
With patriots and others, mean and bold.

Scene Three

DEE-JAY. But you must be dying to know what's going on in the imperial cranies of Emperor Boky, otherwise known as Folksy Boksy. What preparation is he making towards his coronation? What is it that the Nigerian population in Centrafrique have not been booted out as undesirable aliens? Well, we can't answer that latter question all at once, but we can provide a link in the geographic situations. Hi Boksy, come on out, man. Stepping high if you dig the beat. Yeah – a-one, a-two, a-three, a-four; a- . . .

Enter EMPEROR BOKY *and* SQUAD *in formation. Like a seasoned Sergeant-Major, he brings the* SQUAD *to a co-ordinated halt.*

BOKY. Listen you fools. I am a revolutionary. You know the motto of my mother country – *(Lifts hat as he does each time he mentions France or 'mother country'.)* – France. *Liberté. Egalité. Fraternité.* I am an egalitarian. If I were not an egalitarian I would not be among you dregs, you scum, you *residue de bidet!* But I'm an egalitarian. I have the common touch. I am a commoner. But I am not common. Get that clear. You are clearly common. I am not. Better let that distinction sink into your head and seep always onto your tongue. I don't believe in slips. Slips of the tongue and things like that. It may cost you your tongue or worse.

For instance, Napoleon. Emperor Napoleon was a commoner. He was not even French you know. Just a Corsican. Even at that time they didn't just hand round French citizenship for every pirate or Mafia-type. You had to earn it. So Napoleon was not even a Frenchman to begin with. Took him quite some scheming to become one but he finally made it, so there it is.

And he was a revolutionary. You may not remember, but France is the cradle of revolution. Every revolution in the world began in France. And Napoleon it was who eventually placed our mother country on the map. We have to emulate him. Enough.

I have condescended to be with you today not to talk politics but culture. You must know that our mother country, not content with being the cradle of revolution is also the cradle of culture. So understand this – in this empire . . . em, nation, culture is on our priority list.

And that, cretins, is why we are going to participate in Festac Seventy Whenever. To demonstrate our culture. African culture. Revolutionary culture. Our presentation must be revolutionary. South Africa is in the throes of revolution. Therefore, I shall teach you something of South African culture. It takes the form of a dance to which we can give the appropriate title, 'Putting in the Boot'. Never mind what they call it down there. Now, a revolutionary dance must possess what we Marxists call social reality. So we are going to adapt this dance to the social reality of our progressive Centrafrique Social Experiment. Boots!

AIDE *(rushing in, gives him a pair of Wellington boots.* BOKY *examines the soles)*. Fool! Cochon! Serf! Rebel! Where are the hob-nails?

AIDE. But these are just for rehearsals your Imperial Majesty.

BOKY *(freezes)*. That is not yet official. You are guilty of gross indiscretion. You are not to be trusted. Take him away and cut out his tongue.

AIDE *(prostrating)*. Comrade Life President!

BOKY. Drag him out. Out! Wait. Stop. Cut out his tongue and send that silenced item to my friend Idi Amin, with my compliments. No. Stop. Send Amin the entire wretch and add that his tongue is not to be trusted. He'll know what to do. Take him out. *(Exit* AIDE *screaming, dragged out by* GUARDS.*)* Hm. Strictly between you and me, that Amin gives himself airs. Not satisfied with being a windbag he gives himself airs. *(Pause with deliberate emphasis.)* Not a windbag but gives himself *airs. (He turns slowly to the parade.)* Wind. Airs. *I* think that was witty. *(They roll on the ground laughing. He watches for some time, then turns to the* BODYGUARDS.*)* I want an example. Just one. *(He covers his eyes with one hand and, with the other, blindly gropes for a victim. Two men drag him off, screaming.)* Wit is culture. If you are not cultured you are not French. Tention! At ease! *(He turns back to the audience.)* I was saying . . . oh yes, that windbag. But he's also an ape. You know, he apes. He apes me. I appear in a uniform – an official uniform understand – Amin sees me, and straightway he orders a duplicate, complete with medals, plus a few more he's dreamt up. I earned my medals fair and square – in action. Indo-china. North Africa. I've travelled and seen action. And then to make it worse he carries his own much better. Got the size for it you know. I didn't like that photo of him and me together. It was as if it was taken on a tossing ship – actually, it was my medals weighing me down on one side, but he didn't feel his own at all. Of course mine are pure gold – trust him to resort to a trick like gold-plated aluminium. No class. Anyway, what does he do, gives himself Victoria Cross, Long Service Medal, Medal from the Crimean War, Order of Florence Nightingale – oh it's really too embarassing. And then he's a pig. Yes, a pig. You know what a pig is don't you? And you know what a pig does with graves. Well, it's on account of Idi Amin – Moslem though he calls himself – that real Moslems don't eat pork.

Turns slowly to the SQUAD. *They fling themselves down with forced mirth.*

Enough! Where was I? Yes, I was about to dilate on the tactics of one-upmanship.

Right. So there was I, constantly embarassed by this apishness. I made myself life president, he followed suit. I thought maybe I'd beautify my person and become a saint. But I knew him. He'd simply add another title to his court list – Field-Marshal and Dr Saint Alhaji Idi Amin, DSO, VC, VD ... oh I mean ... VC etc. Well, that's how confused the man is – Saint Alhaji. Like wearing Israeli paratroop wings to confer with Arafat on Zionist aggression. Typical Aminian idiocy – oh he makes me blush for poor Africa that pig does.

Oh, does that surprise you? We Frenchmen blush easily you know. It's a sign of French sensitivity. We are emotional, sensitive, much too *raffiné* when compared to the English. You should have seen me crying at the graveside of Daddy – you know that great Immortal – General Charles de Gaulle, father of modern France. Yes, I wept buckets. *(Raises his hat for a moment's silence.)* It was the French in me coming out. All emotion you see, we the French. But I was saying – Amin forced on me my coming elevation you know. He'd become a gross caricature of everything I represent, so the only choice left was to aim far above his horizon – nothing less than a black Napoleon. Now you must admit that was original thinking – that was really outclassing that nigger – I mean, how do you top the Imperial crown? No way baby, no way. Enough! I hope you all came with recording machines, because this is the last time you will be privileged to enjoy my condescension. After the imperial crowning, protocol will be so strictly observed that only God will be granted the occasional interview – and even then, strictly by appointment. *(Examines his watch.)* Time for culture. I know I should sing for you, but you can't do much with the voice in the way of social reality. With boots on the other hand, with or without hob-nails ... Ready!

Rhythm Section! Ready ... Two – go! One-two-three-a-four! One-two-three-a'four! Come on! One-two-three-a'four! One-two-three-a'four! One-two-three-dig! In! One-two-three-heels In! I said Stomp! Stomp! See their eyes – Dig In! Skulls! Imperial Stomp! Stomp! Stomp! Studs In! Toe-caps! Grind! Grind! Crotch movement! Crotch! Dig In! Dig In! Spinal Column! Aim for the pelvic junction! Pelvic junction! Grind! Grind! you bastards, I said Grind! Where's the expert from Nigeria? Inspector Brown! There you are – take over while I put some life into them.

BROWN. Certainly your Imperial Majesty, but er ... could I quickly make a report sir? A slight unrest in the city ...

BOKY. Unrest Inspector Brown? Did I hear unrest?

BROWN. Hardly even that your Highness ... just a minor disturbance, and already contained.

BOKY. No unrest or – disturbance – is to be considered minor on the eve of my coronation Inspector Brown.

BROWN. Your Imperial Majesty may himself condescend to consider it minor sir, when I inform him that the disturbance involved only minors. Schoolchildren to be precise, Your Highness.

BOKY. Schoolchildren? *Mes petits enfants?*

BROWN. Nothing but the usual high spirits Your Excellency. We were able to gather that it had something to do with their new school uniforms.

BOKY. School uniforms? And what, Inspector Brown, did school uniforms have to do with schoolchildren? These – pupils were required to wear them, nothing more.

BROWN. Well er ... Your Imperial Highness is er ... as our Intelligence reports have already suggested to Your Majesty ... er ... there has been a degree of disquiet over the er ... I mean since the ... er Your Imperial Highness's decree on the uniforms. A demonstration took place – only school pupils involved Your

Highness. They have all been locked up for their own protection.

BOKY (*stands still for some moments, then clutches his head which he shakes dolefully*). Les pauvres. Mes enfants. Les petits. Oh they break the heart of their loving papa emperor. I open a clothes shop, especially for them. To make sure no one cheats the little ones, I permit no one else to sell the material for their school uniform. They know that their papa cannot cheat them in his own imperial boutique. I, with my cultured tastes, I condescend to design the uniform myself. My own brothers and nephews operate the only tailors' shops at which the uniforms may be sewn. I have, as you will admit Inspector Brown, taken all paternal measures to protect the little ones.

BROWN. Indeed indeed Your Imperial Majesty. No parent could have done more.

BOKY. But how do they respond Inspector Brown? With gratitude? No. They demonstrate. They march. They protest. They carry placards. Perhaps they sing songs. Inspector Brown, did my children sing songs?

BROWN. Er . . . we . . . that is, there was report of some singing . . .

BOKY. Loyal songs to their Emperor Papa or bad songs Inspector Brown? Did they sing patriotic songs Inspector?

BROWN. Difficult to say sir . . . er . . . the words were mostly inaudible . . . out of tune sir as . . . er . . . with most children's singing . . .

BOKY. Liar! They sing bad songs about me, their Imperial Papa. Ingrates! Parricides! Bring them to me Inspector. Round them up!

BROWN. They have been arrested already sir.

BOKY. Right here Inspector Brown, right here! At once! (BROWN *turns to go.*) No, wait. You! (*Points at random to one of the* GOONS.) Fetch me the criminals! Bring them to their papa at the double. Brown, take over the drill. This is a family affair, a — minor — misunderstanding between Emperor Papa and his misguided children. It is my fatherly duty to take the lead in my own person in administering the necessary corrective measures. (*He takes off his jacket and flings it down. Leaps among the squad and does a rapid limbering-up.)* King Herod was right Inspector Brown. We shall emulate his worthy example. Come on Inspector Brown – give us that Lagosian lynch-mob rallying rhythm.

BROWN *(snaps into action from a confused state).* Yes Your Imperial Majesty. One-two-three –

> O nse mi ki-ki-ki-
> O nse me ki-ki-ki-
> O nse mi mon-ron-yi
> O nse mi mon-ron-yi
> O nse mi ki-ki-ki

BOKY *(alternating between himself stopping and exhorting the* SQUAD *to greater action).* Those are ingrates at your feet. Juvenile delinquents. Future criminals. Little ingrates! Putative parricides! Pulp me their little brains! Wastrels! Prodigal sons! Future beggars! Suspects! Vagabonds! Rascals. Unemployed. Subversives. Bohemians. Liberals. Daily paid labour. Social menaces. Habeas corpusites. Democrats. Emotional parasites. Human Rightist Vagabonds. Society is well rid of them. They disgrace Imperial dignity. Louts. Layabouts. Now their heads are under your feet. Your chance to clean up the nation once for all. Protect property. Protect decency. Protect dignity. Scum. Parasites. What do you do with parasites? What do you do with fleas! Bugs! Leeches! Even a dog is useful. But leeches on a dog? Ticks? Lice! Lice! Lice! Crab-louse! Stomp! Imperial Stomp! Studs In. Grind! Prefrontal lobotomy – the Imperial way! Give your Emperor a clean empire. Sanitate. Fumigate, Renovate. *(He clubs the* SQUAD *right and left to give them encouragement, decimating them until the very last one keels over. Finally realises he's alone.)* Hey, what's this? A mutiny?

BROWN. Your Imperial Majesty, I think they are not quite as strong as you.

BOKY. Ah yes? Of course. Brown, I want to talk to you.

BROWN. At your service sir.

BOKY. I have my own lines to the people, and I don't like what I hear. And now these schoolchildren . . .

BROWN. Everything is under control Your Excellency.

BOKY. The poor. The poor mustn't go hungry on my coronation day. I hear the hungry have plans.

BROWN. So have we Your Excellency.

BOKY. Even during your Civil War in Nigeria, your chief had a wedding[12] that was, from accounts right princely. Straight out of the Arabian Nights. And there were no riots! It's peacetime here, so we've no excuse. And it is an imperial coronation. We are paying good money for your services. Apart from the good relations that naturally accrue to both our sister nations.

BROWN. You are noble and generous Your Excellency.

BOKY. If there is a disturbance, we would of course expel all your countrymen – without notice, without compensation, and without – you.

BROWN. I don't quite understand.

BOKY. *You* would not be expelled. You, Inspector Brown, Special Security Officer loaned to us on special duties, you would remain here with us – well, your remains anyway. *(Chuckles.)* Yes your remains – will remain.

BROWN. Your Excellency, my government would make enquiries.

BOKY *(smiles).* Our records will show that you left with the rest of your countrymen. Any international commission would be free to examine our papers and interrogate witnesses. Now send me a fresh squad – to deal with the children. I'll go and change these boots.

Exit. BROWN *stares after him, open-mouthed. The* SQUAD *drag themselves out, groaning.*

Scene Four

ANIKURA's *establishment 'Home from Home for the Homeless'.*

ANIKURA *(he is seated at a table, making up his accounts).* Come in Commissioner, I've been expecting you.

BROWN *(enters and signals over his shoulders. His* MEN *enter, disappear in every direction).* So you've been expecting me have you?

ANIKURA. Indeed I have. Everyone gets here sooner or later.

BROWN. I see. And apart from that general observation, I suppose that you have done nothing, and you are planning nothing which might lead you to expect a visit from the Law.

ANIKURA. Maybe you can tell me. *(A scream from inside is followed by one of* BROWN'S MEN *backing into the room, fending off blows from a broom wielded by* MRS ANIKURA.)

DE MADAM. I'll teach you to burst into a lady's bedroom. I'll charge you with assault you piss-pot flat-footed baboon.

The OFFICER *turns and runs for protection behind* BROWN.

BROWN. All right Madame, that's quite enough. We do have a search-warrant you know.

DE MADAM. And I know my rights I'll have you know. Nothing gives you the right to burst into my bedroom without knocking.

ANIKURA. All right, my dear, I'll handle it. What do you want Inspector Brown?

The rest of the OFFICERS *come out one by one, shaking their heads negatively.*

BROWN. I see. A leakage as usual eh?

ANIKURA. A leakage? What leakage? (*Looks up at the ceiling.*)

BROWN. Kindly stop beating around the bush. Where are the habituees of this place? They are usually to be found here at this hour. Let's see ... (*He marches on the table, turns the book round.*) That's right. They've just been in to render accounts. We watched them come in. The place was surrounded and we saw no one leave.

ANIKURA. Great detective. Good reasoning Sherlock Holmes.

BROWN (*to his* MEN). Search the place for secret passages.

ANIKURA. Save yourself the trouble. Boys ...

What looked like a large stand for clothes and hats suddenly comes alive, like a rotten tree shedding obscenities in human form. The BEGGARS *emerge in all forms of deformity.*

BROWN. Good God! What a nightmare.

ANIKURA. Take your pick.

BROWN. Arrest them all. March them into the Black Maria.

ANIKURA. On what charges, pray?

BROWN. Coronation preventive measures. We had a hint.

ANIKURA. Your good brother Captain Macheath of course.

BROWN. That's neither here nor there. Good night. And as for you, chief, better keep your nose clean.

ANIKURA. Just a minute Commissioner. (*He gets up from the table, confronts him.*) Are you sure you have enough here.

BROWN. Enough? I don't get you.

ANIKURA. I mean, these look to me a pitiful small number. A raid should yield something more numerous. Think how the papers will report it. Now, tell me, how many would you really like for a netful. A hundred? Two hundred? Three? I tell you what, I could manage five to six hundred and yet be able to field a thousand mendicants for the Emperor's coronation.

BROWN. What are you planning to do chief?

ANIKURA. Inspector Brown, you annoy me. Really you annoy me.

On the word of a thief, arsonist, drug-peddlar, murderer etc. etc., you rush here to arrest a few loyal citizens who were gathered here to discuss plans for their own modest participation in the national occasion. They cannot afford Wonyosi, even though, if you'll excuse my saying so, that is a costume for lunatics; nor can they afford champagne – yes, champagne Inspector Brown. Unlike some officers of the law, they can neither afford champagne nor do they have *friends*, friends Commissioner Brown, who fill the corrupt bellies of government officials with champagne. Nevertheless, they have pieced the finest of their rags together. They will join the great throng of jubilating subjects. They will wave their little national flags which, as your man may have observed, my dear loyal consort was preparing for them before she was so rudely interrupted.

DE MADAM. I'll sue you for damages too. I believe my sewing machine was damaged.

BROWN. Look chief . . .

ANIKURA *(brusquely)*. Where is Captain Macheath?

BROWN. How am I expected to answer that question?

ANIKURA *(resuming his seat)*. All right. Go with him all of you. On your way you will find another hundred or two already hobbling to join you in prison. Then, on coronation day itself, thousands of the army of the poor will march. Right in the path of the imperial chariot Inspector Brown! Right on to the concourse of princes, presidents, kings and queens, dictators, chairmen, generals and life presidents. The papal nuncio will be there, so will the grand bishops and imams of the world's great superstitions. The event will be covered on world-wide television, transmitted to the corners of the globe by satellite . . . Emperor Boky will be very pleased.

Throughout the BEGGARS *stand in a huddle, silent.* BROWN *looks at them, shuts his eyes and shudders.*

BROWN. What do you want?

ANIKURA. Macheath. Arrested tonight. Tried in the morning. Shot by noon. Or else!

BROWN. But I don't know where to find him.

ANIKURA. Too bad. *(Resumes his accounts.)*

BROWN. Well, I can't just manufacture him can I?

DE MADAM. You can't be a very good copper if you don't know where to find a notorious public figure like Macheath.

BROWN. This is blackmail.

DE MADAM. Gambling and women. There aren't so many of those haunts that you can't cover in one night.

BROWN. Be reasonable. I just can't go round *hunting* him. I mean, actually *hunting* him! It's bad enough having to arrange his arrest, but to actually hunt him. Be fair Madame!

DE MADAM *(eyes him scornfully)*. All right. *If* I find him for you . . .

BROWN *(wearily)*. I'll do the rest.

ANIKURA. And that's letting you off very lightly. Very lightly indeed. Bursting on the humble dwelling of law-abiding citizens just to do the bidding of nefarious gangsters. There are corpses lying everywhere, you don't busy yourself tracking down their killers, oh no. The streets are no longer safe for a poor man, Commissioner Brown. It's a rough world when even the beggar has something to fear.

BROWN. What corpses. I never see any corpses.

DE MADAM *(sniffs)*. I bet you don't. Your friend Macheath always tells you where they are so you can look the other way. Take that doctor . . .

ANIKURA. And the lawyer . . .

BEGGAR. What of the musician . . .

ANOTHER. There was that schoolboy . . .

ANOTHER. Even a copper . . .

ANOTHER. And the pastor . . .

OFFICER. My own sister . . .

OFFICER. Entire family wiped out . . .

OFFICER. The trade unionist . . .

ANIKURA. Civil Servants . . .
DE MADAM. That Alhaja . . .
BEGGAR. The pretty trader . . .
ANIKURA. It's a dog's life.

Who Killed Neo-Niga?

Each chorus is performed to a parody of drill formations by
BOKY'S GOON SQUAD *while the various social stock*
characters — the CASH-MADAMS, ACADEMICS,
PROPHETS, BEARDED RADICALS, POLICE
DETECTIVES *etc. etc. mince, snoop, bless, rant, strut*
in between the drill lines.

BEGGAR.   Who killed Neo-Niga?
BIGSHOT.   I, said Sir Bigger
                 Puffing on his cigar
                 I killed Neo-Niga

                 Chorus
                     All the Army and the Police
                     Went a-drilling and saluting
                     When they heard of the death of Di Neo-Niga
                     When they heard of the death of Di Nu-Neo-Niga
                     Tra-la-la-la-la-la-la etc.

BEGGAR.   Who caught Neo-Niga?
HIT-MAN.   I, said Chief Free-lance
                 Payment in advance
                 I caught Neo-Niga
                 Chorus
BEGGAR.   Who heard Neo-Niga?
ACADEMIC.   I, said Professor
                 He screamed outside my door
                 I heard Neo-Niga

Chorus.

BEGGAR. Who sold Neo-Niga?

CASH-MADAM. I, said Ma Trader
I'm the Market Leader
I sold Neo-Niga
Chorus.

BEGGAR. Who carved Neo-Niga?

MEDICO. I, said Doc Morgans
For his vital organs
I carved Neo-Niga
Chorus.

BEGGAR. Who dumped Neo-Niga?

OFFICER. I, said the Inspector
On the A2 Sector
I dumped Neo-Niga
Chorus.

BEGGAR. Who saw Corpse Niga?

ALL. I, said the Public
I'm the New Republic
I saw Corpse Niga
Chorus.

During this chorus, two MEN *cross stage bearing a plain box-coffin inscribed on one side: BODY OF 1001st UN-KNOWN VICTIM. They re-cross the stage revealing other side of coffin inscribed: GIFT OF TAI SOLARIN[13] TO A CONSCIENCELESS RACE.*

ANIKURA. Who'll solve Case Niga?

Silence. Bigger puffs his cigar, Army salutes, Police drills assiduously, Doctor sheathes stethoscope, several variations of the 'three brass monkeys'.

Chorus
Poor Neo-Niga is a-rotting on the Route A2

And a stream of people passing – including you
And a long stream of cars of the New Republic
Tra-la-la-la-la-la-la etc.

*The rhythm changes to a Conga. All join up in a snake-line
and exit dancing to the beat of the Conga.*

Scene Five

*The stable. The banqueting-table is still there, bare. Seated around
it are the members of* MACKIE's *gang,* MACK *at the head,* POLLY *on
his right,* BABA *to his left. The solemnity of the scene suggests a
parody of a board meeting. A thin file and a heavy ledger, with
lock, are tidily placed in front of* POLLY.

MACKIE. The meeting is declared open. We will dispense with the
  reading of the minutes of the last board meeting and proceed
  straight to business. My dearest wife Polly has brought me the
  kind of news for which we have devised that contingency plan
  known under the codename Hideaway ... *(Exclamations of
  shock and disbelief all round.)* It is all too true. My own brother
  and comrade Commissioner Brown has ratted on me, blackmailed into his perfidy by the rotten devices of Jonathan
  Anikura ...

MATAR. You were warned. Messing around with his daughter ...

MACK. That, is neither here nor there.

MATAR. Isn't it? I knew it would come to no good.

POLLY. Why are you so much against me? After all, I brought him
  the warning. Would anyone else have done that?

MATAR. Listen to her! If he hadn't gone and meddled with you
  there would be no warning to give.

DAN DARE. Hm. I always said Matar should have been a lawyer.

MACK. He's more likely to be a corpse if he doesn't shut up soon.

MATAR. You don't frighten me Captain Mack. You've gone and lost us the protection of the law simply because you kept thinking of your own pleasure. *We* are the ones affected. You go into hiding, nice and comfy, you receive your regular cut while we continue to take the risks – without protection!

BABA. Matar, you have a point. Only, don't belabour it so much. The question is what to do?

JAKE. Hear hear. Let's get into Operation Hideaway. Spell it out.

MACK. It's not difficult. You all continue as you are. Simply continue doing what you are doing all along the line.

MATAR *(looking from one to the other)*. What's this? I don't get it. If Baba takes over the chairmanship from you, that's got to affect his own functions, and so on all down the line . . .

MACK. That's what I want to announce, a slight change in Operation Hideaway . . .

JAKE. All right captain, let's have it.

MACK. You all forget, we have acquired a new partner . . .*(He ignores the exclamations that spring up all around him.)* . . . in the person of my dear wife, Polly. She is the new chairman.

A stunned silence, then MATAR *breaks into a guffaw, followed by all the others except* BABA, *who remains impassive.*

DARE. All right captain, now you've had your little joke . . .

MACK. It is not a joke. Polly takes over.

They all turn to stare at POLLY, *then at* BABA.

JAKE. Well, what does Baba say about that?

BABA *(after a pause)*. Well, it seems to me she is better at figures than I am. This is not the old days you know. We are not just hoodlums, we have investments in banks and cooperatives. All those things are rather complicated.

MATAR. I don't care. *I* am not taking orders from any woman.

MACK. Perhaps you wouldn't even take orders from Baba if I wasn't around. Maybe you are even thinking you should run the outfit in my absence?

MATAR. I wasn't thinking that but, now you mention it, why not? At least I wouldn't do such a dumb thing as go into matrimonial alliances which endanger the firm.

MACK *(half-rising)*. Shut up!

BABA *(restraining him)*. Let's all be calm. Matar, look, the trouble with you is that you simply don't understand how complex our operations have become lately. We no longer bury our proceeds in the wall you know, sneaking through some smelly latrine to go and take out a wad or two for the week's pocket-money. We invest them. We buy shares in businesses. We follow the rise and fall of stocks and shares on the market. We have a cut in the lucrative foreign exchange racket, that is, our partners are some of the most respectable men around. Now, Mack could handle a lot of that himself. You'd be surprised how much of that business is conducted over the table at the casino, or in the exclusive Club of Top-Twenty, of which Mack was made a special visiting member. You have to have class to get into that kind of company.

MATAR *(sneering)*. And she's got class?

POLLY. You're right I haven't. *(She has picked up the ledger and, swinging it spine first, catches him forcefully at the base of the head.)* Take that you insolent bastard! *(MATAR pitches forward, stunned.)*

MACK *(looking around)*. Any other objections?

JAKE. Not me.

MACK. Dan?

DARE. I see we've got a real chief.

BABA. I always knew she had spirit. Let's get on with business, captain.

MACK. Take over my dear.

They change places.

POLLY (*jerking her head at* MATAR). Somebody wake him up.

JAKE. Allow me chief. (*He gets a glass of water, lifts up* MATAR's *head and dashes the water at his face.* MATAR *splutters and revives.*)

MATAR. What . . . what . . .

POLLY. Now sit up. Pay attention and listen. Before we get to real business there are one or two things which must change around here. First, your comportment.

JAKE. Go easy chief! Comportment, what's that?

POLLY. The way you bear yourselves, your manner of dressing, of addressing people, your general appearance. Right now it's disgusting. I noticed it first on my wedding day. You have to improve.

DARE (*groans*). I don't understand. What's wrong with us as we are?

POLLY. Nothing when you were merely hoodlums. From now on, think of yourselves as businessmen. You must change with your new status.

DARE. Do you mean we are not going to be able to do the odd job here and there, knocking off this and that . . .

JAKE. Just to keep in training you know. Businesses go bust all the time and then we'll need to fall back on the old pickings.

POLLY. That brings us to the next point. We have to do some recruiting . . .

MACK. Polly, are you sure you aren't moving too fast?

POLLY. Mack my dear, if you'd moved this fast before now, my father would not have been in a position to run you out of town. I want you to be walking the streets again soon, with your head held high and no one daring to touch you.

MACK. Sweetheart, I knew I was making the right choice. Go ahead.

POLLY. I've picked up a few tips here and there from my father's way of running his business. We could use them here.

MACK (*gesture of surrender*). As you please, my dear.

POLLY. Tomorrow, you'll all go to the tailor and get measured for new clothes. Lace of course. In a week's time I don't want to see any of you appear in public in anything but lace. Blue lace.

MACK. Wait a minute, wait a minute . . .

POLLY. Don't worry dear, I know what I'm doing. You Mack, when you come out of hibernation, you'll re-enter society in a new outfit no one in these parts has ever seen.

MACK. Well, won't you tell me what it is?

POLLY. I'll do better than that. I'll show you. *(Takes out a parcel from her briefcase.)* It's the latest craze from home. The very latest. No one has ever seen it in this country.

(She unwraps the parcel, unfolds the dress in it to reveal an outfit which closely resembles some form of lace 'agbada' stuck together in bits and pieces.)

MACK. What on earth is that!

DARE. Christalmighty!

POLLY. Watch your language Dannyboy! Don't swear before me.

DARE. I beg your pardon ma'am. But seriously, what is it?

POLLY. It's the one and only – Wonyosi. The only fashion in the right circles. This one costs some five hundred dollars a yard.

DARE. Five hundred dol . . .!

BABA. So that's the famous Wonyosi.

POLLY. When you wear this at home, it's a sign that you've arrived.

MATAR. Or going places? Like our captain.

POLLY. Oh, you are now with us are you?

MACK. My dear, I'll do most things for you but . . .

POLLY. Try it on please.

JAKE. Yeah, go on captain, let's see if it suits you.

MACK. But Polly, you wouldn't really foist on me some cast-off from your father's wardrobe would you now? Not even the most desperate beggar would wear this.

DARE. Oh come on captain, put it on.

MACK *(sniffing it)*. Well, it smells brand-new . . .

POLLY. As if I would dream of putting you in second-hand clothing.

BABA. Captain, wear it. I know the stuff, honest, I mean, I've heard of it. The best people wear it at home. The very best.

MACK. Yes, but . . .

BABA. You've got a right sharpish missus here captain. The more she gets into things, the more I see what a sharp business mind she's got.

MATAR. Now what are you talking about?

BABA. I think I see what she's up to. We are expanding all the time right? And we've got all those business associates at home. Well, what happens when one of our home partners comes here ? He meets our group chairman here, our Captain Mack, all togged up in Wonyosi. Well, what is that visitor going to be, you tell me that?

DARE. Impressed. Baba's right.

MACK. Is that the idea, Polly?

POLLY. Of course. You in Wonyosi, your business advisers here in blue lace, seated at a table like this. Our partners will start talking in millions . . .

MACK. All right. I recognize business logic when I hear it. I'll go and try it on.

DARE. Good captain.

POLLY. And now gentlemen, while Mack is changing, let me bring you up to date on the way business has been shaping lately. Acting on my advice, we have bought a thousand shares of Igbeti Screwall Investments Ltd.

JAKE. Never heard of them.

POLLY. A new multinational corporation with special holdings in developing countries. Launched from Nigeria of course, after the discovery of a rich lode of marble in some obscure villge. Today it is personally, repeat, personally backed by at least fifteen African Heads of State.

MATAR (straining to read the ledger). How much did that set us back?

POLLY. Practically all we have in fluid cash. And there is no need to twist your neck trying to sneak a look at the accounts. *(Pushes the ledger at him.)* All you have to do is to ask to read it.

MATAR *(hotly)*. I wasn't trying to sneak any look . . .

POLLY. Read it. All members of the firm are free to inspect the books anytime.

MATAR *(pointing)*. Is that it?

POLLY. That's it. Any questions? You may pass it round the table.

MATAR. Pretty steep eh? Though I must say the profits are equally high.

POLLY. In three months, higher than you all ever made in three years of robbing and smuggling and killing and pimping.

MATAR *(pushing the ledger back)*. I've no questions.

POLLY. Are you sure? Take another look. Nothing there strikes you as rather funny?

MATAR. Oh ease off on me, lady. Did I make any imputations? I say I'm satisfied.

POLLY. Then let that be a lesson to you. Listen very carefully, and I mean all of you. The figure against those thousand shares is inflated four times.

MATAR. What!

POLLY. Yes, four times. Because you see, although there are only one thousand shares written down, we actually paid for four thousand shares. Five hundred went to Commissioner Brown. Five hundred went to a mistress of Emperor Boky, another five hundred were bought in the name of one of his latest bastards. Five hundred went to the Director of Prisons and the final thousand were personally handed to the Deputy Chief Justice of the Empire for re-distribution if and as how he thinks fit. Any questions?

JAKE. Ma'am, you mean we distribute three-quarters of everything we get?

POLLY. You are learning fast Jake. And the lesson of it for you all is that, while the books are always open for inspection, only I *know* the book. I distribute as I think fit and I report back to the firm when I think it necessary. And I want no silly questions from any ignorant sods who don't know their left from right in the new business.

DARE. Ma'am, if we are going into high finance, I am quite happy to leave it all to you. Especially with profits shooting up as high as that.

JAKE. I call it as-tro-no-mi-cal!

BABA. I told you all.

JAKE. A financial genius!

MATAR (*protesting*). I still think we ought to know something of . . .

DARE (*singing*). For she's a jolly good fellow . . . (*The others join in, excepting* MATAR. *The singing is interrupted suddenly by a loud whistle. They freeze.*)

POLLY. Commissioner Brown?

JIMMY (*dashing in*). They are practically on the doorstep. Tiger Brown and the emperor's elite raiders.

JAKE. The Y Squad?

JIMMY. No less.

MATAR (*disappearing*). See you all!

POLLY. Mack! Mack!

MACK (*putting out his head*). What's going on?

JAKE *and* DAN DARE *also vanish.*

POLLY. Tiger Brown, and the Y Squad.

MACK. Already?

POLLY. Hurry Mack, hurry!

MACK *emerges, with only one leg in his new trousers. Stumbles and falls.* POLLY *hauls him up. He struggles to find the other leg with his foot as a crash is heard.*

POLLY. Mack!

MACK *abandons the effort to complete his dressing, hops out on one leg.*

BROWN *(followed by* SQUAD*)*. Fan out! Find him!

POLLY. Were you looking for someone, Commissioner?

BROWN. Don't imagine I didn't see you behind the clothes-rack in your father's place. But fair's fair. It was only reasonable I should allow Mackie his fair warning. Or . . . was I thinking that it would make it easier to find him by simply following you? *(Sententiously, with a sigh.)* Oh the complexity of human motives!

POLLY. And I thought you were his friend.

BROWN. I still am. But your father drives a hard bargain. Blame yourself and Mackie for getting me into this mess. *(Looks around.)* Yes, board meeting I suppose? *(He stands expectant.)*

POLLY *(pushing the ledger to him)*. There are the accounts.

BROWN. I don't need to read that. I trust you. *(Pause.)* Well?

POLLY *(still pretending to misunderstand)*. Oh, of course. *(Brings out a piece of paper.)* Sawleg Dudu – you can have him for that murder on rue St Augustine. Mack says we can provide three witnesses who caught him in the act. And Shoo-Be-Show – he's getting too showy. Our boys have got to keep a low profile in the new line of operation. Shop him for that rape of the nun behind the Sacred Hearts' Hospital. Pasco Kid had the nerve to do some intimidating on his own account – remember that manager of the Supermarket Chain Stores who wouldn't lodge a complaint? Well, that's Pasco Kid. He's running a protective racket on the side and letting people think he's boss. Well, Mack *is* the boss. Out of sight or actively engaged, he's going to remain the No. 1. Take Pasco Kid for the burglaries at St Lazarin. We'll give you some merchandise from there decorated with his full set of fingerprints . . .

BROWN. I bet you will. *(Pulling out a piece of paper in turn.)* And when do you propose to give me the felon whose charge sheet includes *(Reading.)* murder of two shopkeepers and four tourists,

30 burglaries, 23 street robberies, arsons, attempted murders, forgeries, perjuries etc etc not to mention the seductions of two sisters under the age of consent . . .

POLLY *(heatedly)*. That's a lie!

BROWN. Which one?

POLLY. Mack never seduced anyone

BROWN. A-ah, so you do know who did all the other things. Got you. Now skip all that business of the fall-guys. *(Holding out his hand.)* We were actually discussing book-keeping before we got — sidetracked.

POLLY. Not while Mack is in danger.

BROWN. Business is business. The rest of the firm still need protection.

POLLY. I'll discuss that after Mack is out of danger.

BROWN. My dear girl, I run a lot of expenses.

POLLY. Oh you are really heartless. To think that you and Mack were once comrades-in-arms.

BROWN. *I* am heartless? Oh, that's rich. Just look at you, taking over the business as if you were born into it. Calm as a cucumber. Where is that sweet innocent girl whose wedding I attended it seems only yesterday?

POLLY. Where is the palm-wine that frothed so sweetly yesterday?

BROWN. Drunk. Imbibed.

POLLY. Drained. Soured. Turning vinegary.

BROWN. But stronger in spirit content, right?

POLLY. That's nature for you.

The Song of Lost Innocence

In case you're trying to puzzle out my transformation
I'll let you all into some secret information
Once I was one like the wilting lily of the valley
Who didn't have to sweat to fill her little belly
Then something else began to fill my little belly
A fruit of love or, say, of frolics in the alley

And to teach what life is all about
There's nothing like a new life hereabouts
And your breadwinner on the fast way out
Soon ends your period of self-doubts
If women seem weak, it's because they prefer to avoid too much
bother.
You know of my father; you've yet to learn of De Madam, my
mother.
Heard of 'Attack Trade'?[14] While Mackie and Brown were
ripping the insides
Of foes; Mother was dodging the bullets and ripping off both
sides.

Enter Chorus of WOMEN, *led by* DE MADAM

WOMEN. Forward Ever! Backward Never
   Attack! Attack! Attack! Attack!
   Trade is the stuff of life
   War is the stuff of trade
   Cash has no after-life
   Shuns company of the dead
   Come, your scruples sever
   Act a little clever
   When you've no friend or foe
   Business is never slow
   You don't believe me?
   Ask your masters the Big Powers
   While the poor wretch counts his last hours
   Trade is boom-time in Megalopolis
   London. New York. Moscow. Paris.
   How to sell to Left and Right
   Yet prove you're doing right
   Weapons for each bloody fight
   Man, I tell you it's out-of-sight!
   So why condemn me? So why condemn me?

I'm just a pretty-trading, high-risk, low-profit, quick turnover,
one-act, Mother Courage, troop-comfort,
friend-and-foeing sunshine-rainshine Attack Trader!

POLLY. If men are beasts, shan't we ensure they cannot eat us?
One day it's love, the next they raise their fists to beat us
They throw you over when beauty goes and strength is sapped
And you stare at the shreds of eternal love you had mapped
When, eager to bear his seed, to spawn and raise his heir,
The future filled with music, roses and eternal care.
But to teach you what life is all about
There's nothing like a new life hereabouts
And your breadwinner on the fast way out
Soon ends your period of self-doubts
Whatever the male can do, the female can do even better
Don't rely on your tears, when push comes to shove from the
rotter
Mackie is different I swear, but a girl must protect her future
If a girl doesn't learn from her mother, experience will prove a
harsh teacher.

The chorus of Attack Trade *is repeated, with* BROWN'S
OFFICER'S *returning and joining in, feigning shot and
dying. The* WOMEN *march over them, stop to empty their
pockets, take off their watches and carry on business throughout the chorus. Curtains close and lights come on in the audi-
torium with the* WOMEN *offering those wares among the
audience along the aisles.*

PART TWO

Scene one

A whore-house in Bangui, also known as Play-Boy Club.

MACK *(entering through a window).* Verily verily is it spoken, Hell hath no fury like an aggrieved father-in-law. I escaped the clutches of the law by seconds only, driven from the promise of a honeymoon bed, yet grateful for the warning of my faithful, ever-loving wife concerning the desperate machinations of her father. Well, I must seek solace for momentary deprivation. *(Whistles.)* Though I must say, it's pretty hard on a newly-wedded bridegroom to be separated from his beloved. *(Places two fingers in his mouth and whistles.)* One thing about Sukie, even if she is with her millionaire sugar-daddy, she'll find a way to dodge him for old Mackie. For a few minutes anyway . . . I don't believe in pressing my claims unduly.

A door opens slightly and a face peeps out, followed soon by the rest of the body.

SUKIE *(coldly).* What do you want?

MACK *(looks round, unbelieving).* Who?

SUKIE. Do you see any other skunk in the corridor?

MACK. Why Sukie, it's me Mack, your Mack.

SUKIE. I can see it's you Mack. Smooth Mack. Dandy Mack. Wonyosi Mack. *Polly's Mack. (Turns round and slams the door.)*

MACK. Oh dear, I do believe she's heard about Polly. *(Suddenly he listens. Sure enough, sounds of sobbing are heard from behind the same door.)* Ah, I couldn't quite believe that such a sweet-natured girl would turn heartless tigress because of a simple marriage. *(He goes to the door, opens it cautiously, looks inside.)*

SUKIE *(from within)*. Oh Mackie, how could you break a poor girl's heart so.

MACK. I can explain everything . . .

The door is shut on the rest. Enter DE MADAM. *Looks up and down. Enter a* VERY RICH GENTLEMAN.

VERY RICH GENTLEMAN. Oh there you are. You must be the madam.

DE MADAM *(instantly suspicious)*. How come you know me?

VERY RICH GENTLEMAN. Well, it's a simple matter of deduction. You are a little . . . er . . . if I may say so, a little too old to be one of the girls, so you must be the madam.

DE MADAM. And who gave you the right to mistake me for a common brothel-keeper? I'll ask you to keep your distance and maintain respect for the wife of Chief Jonathan Anikura, chairman of highly successful groups of companies.

VERY RICH GENTLEMAN. Oh, I most awfully beg your pardon. But you yourself, I thought you said . . .

DE MADAM. I am known as De Madam. A very different and respectable kettle of fish from the *madam* with whom, if I may so presume, your business lies. And now if you'll excuse me . . . *(Goes off.)*

VERY RICH GENTLEMAN. Oh dear, oh dear, very touchy lady. Ah, that looks more like it. *(He sees* JENNY *who has entered with bucket and mop, broom etc. going to do the rooms.)* Excuse me young lady.

JENNY. You want the office don't you? Straight along the corridor, turn right, first room on the left. The madam is always there.

VERY RICH GENTLEMAN *(tips her with a note and chucks her on the chin)*. Most obliged my dear child. *(*JENNY *lets the note hang in her hand, looks after him as he goes off. Bitterly.)*

JENNY. Do have fun!

VERY RICH GENTLEMAN *(turns round, a leer and a wink)*. I was assured this is the place for it. *(Waggles his fingers and goes off.)*

JENNY *puts down her pail and mop, sings the 'Song of Jenny Leveller'.*

Jenny Leveller

Sodom and Gomorrah
Will seem quite paradisial
When this whorehouse comes to trial
On that soon-to-be tomorrow
You in your golden villa
Will know this life for real
In that cup of no denial
As I shout Hip-hip-Hurrah!

But the hand that passes sentence
Will not descend from heaven
There's a girl who cleans the linen
Smeared in spunk of moneyed wantons
It's the girl you tip the tuppence
Who scrubs from nine to seven
She'll watch you slowly riven
On the rack named DECADENCE.

Your hat sir, your umbrella
Hope you had a very good time
Mind the stairs now as you climb
Lest you break your bloody neck sir
There's a horde who've marched from far
Just to fill your mouth with grime
And roll you in your slime
As I shout Hip-Hip-Hurrah!

Nor Sodom nor Gomorrah
Did ever see such panic
As when I end the picnic

> Yes, this shabby Cinderella
> Would have lit your last cigar
> For it's time to face the music
> Of the crowd you've driven frantic
> Hear them shout Hip-hip-Hurrah!

DE MADAM (*re-entering*). I'm not getting the right cooperation. (*Sees* JENNY.) A-ah. As a student of human nature, admittedly not in the same league with my husband the chief, I think I know an ally when I see one.

JENNY (*pointing to the door through which* MACK *disappeared*). In there. Her patron millionaire is due any moment now so you won't have long to wait.

DE MADAM. Oh Jenny my dear . . . (*Feeling inside her purse.*)

JENNY (*showing her the note*). No need to bribe me. Someone else has paid me for doing my job, so take your account as settled. (*She takes out her key, opens the door into another room and shuts it behind her.*)

DE MADAM. Well, well, the cheeky hussy.

> *Sounds from* SUKIE*'s room brings her back to caution. She sprints down the corridor and hides.* MACK *re-emerges, buttoning up.*

SUKIE. Hurry now, he'll soon be here.

MACK. Later tonight then.

SUKIE. Make it before one in the morning. He usually leaves at twelve.

MACK. Okay, okay.

SUKIE. Oh Mack dear do be careful. Are you sure you wouldn't rather hide in the wardrobe? At least with me I know you're safe.

MACK. I might fall asleep and start snoring.

SUKIE. But he's deaf and half-blind I tell you. If you fall in through the door he'd still think it was a rat or something.

MACK (*appears to consider it*). No. Anything could happen. He might detect me and then I'd be forced to kill him.

SUKIE. Well, that's never bothered you much has it?

MACK. This one would. Against my principles – killing the goose that lays the golden egg.

SUKIE (*chuckling*). Oh Mackie you are a one. You know how to make a girl laugh. Where will you hide meanwhile?

MACK. I might visit the casino . . . oh, which reminds me . . . I am rather short. Can you . . .?

SUKIE. But the casino Mack! Everybody will see you there.

MACK. Only the rich. And they don't read the *WANTED* column of newspapers.

SUKIE. Are you sure . . .?

MACK. Oh shut up and give me what you have. You want your sugar to come in while we stand here yapping?

SUKIE (*sulkily*). Oh all right. You always get in a temper when you set off to gamble. (*Reaching inside her bra.*) Which do you love more Mackie? Me or gambling?

MACK. Both, silly. See you first thing after midnight. (*Saunters off.*)

SUKIE. Bye Mackie. Do be careful.

She watches him disappear. Immediately DE MADAM *appears.*

DE MADAM. Well, Sukie?

SUKIE. I haven't seen him.

DE MADAM. I know you haven't seen him dearie. But when is he coming back?

SUKIE. How do I know, when I haven't seen him?

DE MADAM. Sukie, think of what he's done to you. Think of what he's done to us. That's our only daughter. We bring her up, treat her right, we plan great things for her and see what happens. He's going to take her to the gutter with him.

SUKIE. My Mackie is a fine gentleman, he's not taking anyone to the gutter 'cause he ain't there himself.

DE MADAM. You still aren't using your head. Polly's a minor.
But, all right, she's also a wife . . .

SUKIE. Wife! Liar. He never married her.

DE MADAM. Oh, is that what he told you?

SUKIE. He swore to me. Oh I admit he's fond of her. He's fond of
every woman and I can't say I blame him. He is quite good-
looking you know.

DE MADAM. Stop being so scatter-brained. He married her.
MARRIED! And if you don't believe me, ask Commissioner
Brown. He was present at the banquet.

SUKIE *(beginning to break down)*. And he swore to me . . .

DE MADAM. Don't snivel. Just listen carefully. If Macheath cops
it, that makes her a widow, right? But she's also a junior. So that
means she really couldn't get married without our consent —
Chief Anikura's that is. With Mack gone, we become her legal
guardians. Don't worry, the chief has some nifty lawyers among
his lot and they've worked it out. Now you know that Mack is
not a poor man . . .

SUKIE. Mack not poor! Business has been bad for him. His associates rob him blind! He has to borrow money from me to keep
going.

DE MADAM. Exploitation! That's what it is — exploitation. He ex-
ploits you, you soft-headed ninny. Next to the chief my husband
in person, your poor Mack represents the largest shareholder in
all the businesses of New Ikoyi. Don't take my word for it — ask
Commissioner Brown. Mack pays him 25 per cent of everything
he gets, you ask Brown how much he gets and work it all out
from that.

SUKIE *(discomfited)*. He's just taken every last penny I had on me.
He's going to spend it gambling.

DE MADAM. Gambling! See? That's what he does with the money
you earn the hard way. Putting up with that toothless, hairless,
sightless, spunkless old goat. When are you going to grow up?
Now let me finish what I set out to say. With Mack gone, his
properties revert to his widow, which means that as her legal

guardians we control them. You know Chief Anikura, he never breaks his word. And he says one-quarter of that is for whoever helps us nab him.

SUKIE. Oh Mack . . .

DE MADAM. When does he come back?

SUKIE. I couldn't betray him. Never. Oh, here comes Old Sugar now.

DE MADAM. Sukie . . .

SUKIE. I won't betray Mack. (*Going, pauses.*) Well, just the same, for whoever is interested, Old Sugar always leaves at midnight. Goodnight. (*Sniffs.*) Poor Mack. (*Enters room.*)

DE MADAM (*grinning*). In this world of treachery, it is good to meet such loyalty in a working girl.

A wizened old MAN, *nearly bent double, taps with his stick along the corridor, peering closely at each door.*

This way Romeo. (*Pulls at him sharply so that he is almost catapulted through the door.*) And be sure you're out of here by midnight.

Scene Two

PRISON. MACKIE'*s cell.*

DEE-JAY. It's done. The great bandit Macheath is in gaol, betrayed by one love too many. The law has taken its course, proving most vibrantly that no one is above it – Hear, hear! – except of course you happen to wear the right kind of uniform – Three hearty stripes – or – Pip! Pip! Pip! Hurray! – Oh man I'm flipping again – let's get back to the great man. What are his thoughts as he stares at the broad back of his gaoler through the thick bars of his cell?

MACK. Do you fancy my clothes?

DOGO (*turns round and studies him for a few moments*). Well sir, now that you bring the matter up, I've been meaning to ask you sir, were you trying to climb through barbed wire when they caught you?

MACK. Ha ha very funny. Very very funny. You don't understand how ignorant that makes you.

DOGO (*he comes closer*). No, seriously sir, when they brought you in I thought what a pity you had to ruin such good lace. I like lace you know. But this one looks as if the police dogs and barbed wire had been fighting over it.

MACK. Well, take a closer look. That's the latest fashion back home. This one cost over five hundred dollars a yard.

DOGO. Is that god's truth? (*Puts his hand through the bars and feels the cloth.*) You may be right sir. It feels expensive.

MACK. Of course I'm bloody right.

DOGO. It will never catch on here mind you. The Faranse[15] prefer that business-like two-piece thing they wear – except for the been-tos[16] of course. You can't separate those ones from their three-piece collar and tie affair.

MACK. Would you like it?

DOGO. Which one? Me wear a three piece?

MACK. No, this one. My Wonyosi.

DOGO. Oh, is that what it's called?

MACK. That's right.

DOGO. Hm, well, I must say one might get used to it. But right now . . .

MACK (*impatiently*). Use your imagination man. Christ, that's why people like you never get on. Get used to it . . . who asked you to get used to it! Didn't you hear what I said? This dress cost over five hundred dollars a yard.

DOGO. Well, I still don't see what you are getting at. Even that price takes some getting used to wouldn't you say sir?

MACK *(holding his head)*. You'll never make it! You're only fit to be a prison warder.

DOGO. Maybe. I thank you for the insults. It's the privilege of a man who is at the point of death to speak his mind.

MACK. Don't! Don't use that word.

DOGO. Oh, I'm sorry sir. I wasn't trying to say anything painful. I'm a religious man you know. I never hurt a man when he is down.

MACK. Nor help him up I suppose. Well then, listen again. How many yards do you think have gone to make me this thing.

DOGO. You mean the whole complete?

MACK. Everything. There is even a cap – I lost it while trying to escape.

DOGO. Hm, I think there are some 10 yards involved in all of that.

MACK. All right, we'll say 10 yards. Multiply 500 by 10.

DOGO *(gives a slow long whistle)*. Five . . . thousand dollars!

MACK. Now convert that to CFA and work out for yourself how many thousand francs I am wearing on my person right at this moment.

DOGO *(pop-eyed now)*. The things a man could do with that amount!

MACK. You have a family?

DOGO. Two wives, seven children.

MACK. And of course they are well-fed, they wear good clothes, they lack for nothing . . . in short, you don't need money.

DOGO. Who doesn't need money!

MACK. Maybe you even have debts.

DOGO. How did you guess?

MACK. Now, answer, do you want this wonyosi or don't you?

DOGO. Well . . . it seems hardly fair to er . . . I mean, it's like robbing a corpse – oh, I am sorry.

MACK. Never mind. Let's get down to business. If – what we have agreed not to mention again were to happen, I would have no use for it, right? So, take it. Now!

DOGO. But what will you wear?

MACK (*snapping*). Yours yours! Don't you understand? We change clothes. For that you get five thousand dollars in Wonyosi convertible currency. You can sell it in the Nigerian quarter – you know it don't you? – New Ikoyi. It's even worth your while to take a special trip to Nigeria – ask for sick leave or something. The latest news is that the stuff has been banned, so it will cost even twice as much. You are not above a little smuggling are you? I'll give you a note to those who will show you the ropes . . .

DOGO (*who has finally taken it in*). I am beginning to see your little game sir . . .

MACK. And about time too. What do you say?

DOGO. It's a big risk for a man, a family man like me, to take.

Noise off, like a steel gate opening.

MACK. Someone's coming. Think quickly man!

DOGO. I'll go and see who it is. (*Goes off.*)

MACK. That one is a dead loss. A born pauper. All timber up here. You can't bribe a man like that. To be bribable you've got to be imaginative. That's why the cleverest men are the most corruptible.

DOGO (*runs in*). It's Inspector Brown. A thousand dollars down.

MACK (*puzzled*). What?

DOGO. A thousand dollars down. I prefer cash to Wonyosi, or whatever you call it.

MACK. Where could I find such a sum?

DOGO. Not where but when. Not would but must. Before midnight. (*Dashes off.*)

MACK. I could have sworn . . . just shows how wrong you can be. No doubt about it, my countrymen have inherited the earth.

BROWN (*off*). At ease Dogo. And out! Stay out of earshot. (*As he enters,* MACK *turns his back.*) Oh Mack, don't do this to me. You are breaking my heart.

MACK (*not turning*). It is generally accepted that a man, in his last hours on earth, should be afforded the privilege of choosing his company.

BROWN. I did all I could Mack. You know that. And you had warning . . .

MACK. Warning? Not from you. You never had the slightest intention of warning me.

BROWN. Polly warned you. I saw her behind the clothes-stand. I saw her run out and, even after trailing her to your meeting-place I went through the motions of gathering up the Elite Squad just to give you time.

MACK. Very impressive Commissioner Brown, very very impressive. In that case, I am not here at all. I am not in prison. I was never captured by you, taken to court, tried on the evidence you provided. I have never been condemned to death, oh no. I am enjoying the pleasure of my normal haunts, not held here at the pleasure of His Imperial arsehole, awaiting execution.

BROWN. That's it Mackie. That's exactly what did it. Why did you not leave town altogether? Why go to the brothels where you are so well known. Whose fault is that?

MACK (turning round, draws himself up proudly). That question, Commissioner Brown, illustrates all too clearly, if at all any illustration were needed, what a mundane, pedestrian, low-born, hoi-poloi soul inhabits your carcass. You actually expected that I Captain Macheath would give up my normal routine of pleasures because some flat-footed rookies were after me? You have never yet – and there have been times when I have wondered at the inequality of our friendship, times when you have sunk so low that I have hesitated to acknowledge you in public – but never till now have you achieved such an all-time low. I see you now on a par with the sewer-rat in a skunk-hole and implore you to remove your obnoxious presence from my sight . . .

BROWN (dabbing at his eyes). Oh Mack please . . .

MACK. . . . unless of course you have come here with some practical suggestions about getting me out of here!

BROWN. No Mack, I cannot.

MACK. I thought not. Go. No, stay. Have you thought out every possible way?

BROWN. I haven't slept a wink or eaten a bite for thinking.

MACK. For God's sake man! You couldn't get up any good ideas even on a full belly and a good night's sleep, yet here you are starving your stomach of food and drink and your brain of rest, and you imagine you can think straight? I am well and truly lost!

BROWN. Oh don't say that Mackie.

MACK. Why not? You have some rescue plan?

BROWN. Mackie, Polly your wife is outside. She wants to see you.

MACK. Fine. Very Fine. I ask you for a rescue plan you tell me my wife wants to see me. If that's the best you can do, send her in. Go on, go and fetch her. At least she can muster ten times your intelligence.

BROWN (going). Oh Mack, you simply enjoy torturing me.

DOGO (dashing in). A thousand dollars, before midnight. What do you say?

MACK. You're an expatriate aren't you?

DOGO. Of course. Same as you, from Nigeria. That's why I'm doing it. I wouldn't take such a risk for anyone. But blood is thicker than water.

MACK. Or cash eh? The money has nothing to do with it.

DOGO. I have to take risks. The money must be in my hand by midnight.

MACK. We swop clothes and I get out?

DOGO. That's the idea isn't it?

MACK. My wife is coming in. She'll arrange it. (DOGO dashes off.) Amazing how animated his face has become in the past few minutes. Maybe it's the other way round. The smell of money endows the dumbest Nigerian with instant intelligence.

Enter POLLY, *followed by* BROWN.

POLLY. Oh Mack!

MACK. Leave us copper. I need some private discussion with my wife.

BROWN. I can't do that Mack. You are not even allowed visitors – officially you know.

POLLY. The rest of the firm are outside too Mack. They said they have come to pay their last respects.

MACK. Don't! Don't say such thing. Christ! People only say that of a corpse already lying in state.

POLLY. Forgive me Mack, I am so sorry.

MACK. How could you be so insensitive!

POLLY. I wasn't thinking, I'm sorry. I just blurted out what they said.

MACK. Oh, that's what they said was it? It goes to show you. Positive thinking is not for that lot, oh no. Are they thinking of how to get me out? Not on your life. They are concerned only with paying their last respects. Brown, I want to see those bastards.

BROWN. Oh no, oh no no no, you can't hold a convention here.

MACK. I want to see them I said. You're getting very obstructive aren't you Brown? Just remember there are papers and things which could be released to make things a little uncomfortable for you.

BROWN. You wouldn't blackmail an old comrade, Mack.

MACK. I can and I will, if you don't let those men in. Is it asking too much of you? If you can't help me out of here at least you can help me put my affairs in order. I propose to hold a board meeting. Here!

BROWN. All right, but you must promise to . . .

LUCY (off). Get out of my way you mutton-headed bum. I'm his wife and I demand to see him . . .

MACK. Christ, Lucy!

POLLY. Lucy?

BROWN. What's going on? (Runs off.)

LUCY (still off). I saw that bitch come in here. If she can go in so can I.

POLLY. Who is Lucy, Mack?

MACK. Oh er, you mean Lucy. Well, er, you have to er . . .

> *Enter* LUCY *heavily pregnant, followed by the* GANG, *in uniform lace. They carry neat portfolios.* BROWN *pants in behind them.*

MACK (*quickly to* POLLY). She's a bit mad, I remember her now. You'll see for yourself.

LUCY (*pulls up short at the sight of* POLLY. *She circles her scornfully, then makes a spitting noise*). So that's the Lady of the grand airs she gives herself. They tell me you think you are married to Mack. I hear it all over town, now let me hear it from your own mouth.

POLLY. Who is this cow Mack?

LUCY. Ah good. That's very good. I knew all that varnish would soon come off when it came to the point. Not quite the fancy bitch you try to pass off on those who don't know better eh? Get her out of here Mack, tell her you want to talk to your wife. Alone.

POLLY. His wife!

THE GANG. His wife.

POLLY. Mack, is this woman your wife?

MACK. I was going to tell you; she is actually the daughter of the prison governor.

POLLY. Well well Mack, you certainly move in the best circles.

MACK. Polly, let me talk to her a little. She's mad, quite mad, but I can calm her down. I know about her through her father you understand?

POLLY. Well you can talk to her in the presence of your wife I hope. You have no secrets from me have you Mack?

MACK. No no, but listen. Don't you understand? She is the daughter of the prison governor, the *prison governor* Polly! Now you see why we've got to humour her.

LUCY. Is she going or not Mack?

MACK. Yes dear, of course she's going. Brown, talk to Polly outside for a moment will you.

POLLY *allows herself to be led off by* BROWN, *protesting.*

POLLY. Mack ...

MACK. Trust me. *(She goes. The* GANG *is about to follow.)* As for you lot, start thinking about how to get a thousand dollars together.

MATAR. What for captain?

MACK. What for, you frog-face? Maybe to paste all over the walls of my cell. Maybe to wipe my arse with since prisoners don't get supplied with toilet paper. Maybe just to stuff down your greasy throat you double-crossing bastard. I said start working out how to get a thousand dollars raw cash together, so get started. I want it within the hour.

BABA. Right boss, leave it to us.

JAKE. But we don't have that sum.

DANDARE. The time is too short.

BABA. Come on boys. let's go and think it over. We may come up with something.

MACK. You'd better. Unless you want to see me full of holes by to-morrow night.

MATAR. Oh come on boss, who would wish a thing like that on you? *(Grins evilly.)*

They troop off.

LUCY. Oh Mackie, look at the mess you've got yourself into. You promised you would lay off those whorehouses didn't you? Now you've gone and got yourself betrayed by some cross-eyed bitch who can only capture to herself a half-blind scaly lizard that can't even get it up any longer.

MACK. I am really surprised at myself you know Lucy. But you know, old habits die hard. Anyway, it's you and you alone I've ever loved. That I still nurse a passion for the old slap-and-tickle doesn't mean a thing. After all, what's a man without his ruling passion?

LUCY. I couldn't love you without one.

MACK. You understand me Lucy, for once a man can truly say I have a wife who understands me.

Song of 'The Ruling Passion'
(MACK *and* LUCY.)

What is your ruling passion?
Being without's not in fashion
Since Alexander Pope observed it
Discriminating men have served it.
It will save you and me a lot of time
To know how to please you in your prime
So come out with it
Let's get on with it
Tell me your ruling passion.

Don't pledge yourself to ration.
Is it lace that brings you elation?
Was it on your account they banned champagne?
Tell the truth and we'll counter-campaign
Man should indulge in what he pleases
Who cares who calls them social diseases
Don't sit on the fence
You'll go all tense
Tell me your ruling passion.

I tell you this bloody nation
Is getting above its station
It turns on you its voice of prudery
If you get an orgasm from bribery
Corruption's the oil that greases
The national wheels and smoothes the creases

Of the body politic
So don't be romantic
Tell me your ruling passion.

Now sex always stays in fashion
An egalitarian passion
When question papers succumb to leakage
And the student is foaming with rage
When the dumbest suzie obtains a first-class
Remember that sex transcends all class
So hitch up your star
And hitch down that bra
Tell me your Ruling Passion.

Is it Wealth that makes you bash on?
And throw to the winds all caution?
If the Money Ritual demands your wife
Why hesitate – it's only a life
And think of the parties you can give
When money flows all hearts forgive
So don't be so squeamish
Serve her to your Fetish
Tell me your Ruling Passion
Lay down your Rules of Pash!

LUCY. But Mack, what about that bitch who was here? It's all over town she is your wife.

MACK. I won't lie to you, Lucy. You know me too well and you understand me. Of course I had something to do with her. She's attractive and I am always seducable.

LUCY. I knew her type the moment I set eyes on her. She's the seducing type all right.

MACK. Yes, she went straight for me. Threw herself at me. I didn't resist. How was I to know she would go round town saying I'd promised to marry her? From there it was only one short step to actually claiming I've married her.

LUCY. The trollop! I knew you couldn't commit bigamy.

MACK. I wouldn't dream of it. But Lucy, let's not talk of her. The problem is getting me out of here tonight. Otherwise . . .

(He makes a firing noise.)

LUCY. You mean they will actually shoot you.

MACK. Unless you help me, Lucy.

LUCY. But what can I do?

MACK. I think I can get out of the building itself. The guard is open to ideas. It's the outer gates that may give a little trouble. Can you get the key to the warders' entrance from your father's room?

LUCY. It isn't possible Mack. He carries the whole bunch around with him.

BABA *(re-entering with* POLLY*)*. Captain, we've sent the others away so we can tell you what we've been up to. They might raise objections − that Matar especially − over the expenditure. You needn't worry about that thousand dollars you see . . .

MACK *(excitedly)*. You hear that Lucy? Can't you do your own part.

LUCY *(shaking your head)*. You know you wouldn't need to ask me twice if I could. I know it can't be done.

POLLY. Hm. A broken reed.

LUCY. And just what is that supposed to mean madam?

POLLY. Just what it said. A broken reed. Obviously Mack finds he cannot lean on you.

LUCY *(patting her stomach)*. Can't he? If he wasn't doing more than leaning on me, how do you think that got there?

POLLY. Mack, is what she is saying true? Is that really yours?

LUCY. You think I put it there myself?

MACK. Er Polly . . . listen . . .

POLLY. Is this woman carrying your child, Mack?

MACK. Is this a time to worry about details like that? Go after the thousand dollars and get me out of here!

DOGO (*strolls past as if on patrol*). Time is running out sir.

MACK. You heard him.

BABA. Is it past visiting time?

MACK (*wildly*). No, no. He's talking about the deadline for his bribe.

POLLY. When you come out Mack, where will you go? I mean, who is your wife?

LUCY. What a foolish question!

MACK. When I get out of here Polly, I leave town, not so?

POLLY (*persistent*). Who will you send for? Who will you rely on? Who do you call wife Mack?

LUCY. Stop pestering him with silly questions.

POLLY. Well, it's simple. The firm has taken in hand arrangements for your escape. I stuck out for you Mack. I rushed to give you warning, yet you left me Mack, and went straight into the arms of that whore Sukie, when you should have been fleeing town. She betrayed you. Now we're trying to get you out again. If we succeed, are you going to get trapped again in the dugs of some other cow like that?

LUCY (*leaping at her*). Are you referring to me you shit-face?

> They fight. BABA *tries to separate them and gets flung aside. In the struggle,* LUCY's 'pregnancy' slips down, POLLY *gains the upper hand, kneeling over her.*

POLLY. Well well, what's this then?

> She slips a hand under LUCY's skirt and brings out a bundle. Just then BROWN comes running in.

BROWN. What's going on? Oh. Is it a boy or girl?

MACK (*chuckling*). The prettiest baby bundle I ever saw.

BROWN. Come on you trouble-maker, out you go. (*Seizes her under the arms.*)

LUCY. Let me alone.

BROWN. Come on. And I don't care whose daughter you are. I'm responsible for the well-being of this prisoner. (*He drags her out, assisted by* DOGO.)

MACK. Now you see for yourself Polly. Are you now convinced? She is quite mad.

POLLY. Well, I am not convinced Mack. (*Presses gently on her stomach.*) And mine is for real.

MACK. What! Already?

POLLY. So you've got to come out. I don't want my child's father to end up shot in public like a common criminal.

MACK. Now that's the kind of talk I like, Polly. The thousand dollars is assured then I take it.

POLLY. Better than that Mack. It's been put to use already. And more than a mere thousand.

BABA. We've been doing some hard work captain. That's what we really came to tell you. You are almost as good as free.

MACK. Hey, that's not good enough. I don't like the sound of that word, almost.

POLLY. Don't worry Mackie. First, we've got a stay of execution. Signed by the Deputy Chief Justice in person. (*Hands him the paper.*)

MACK. Hot dog! I knew those Igbeti Screwall shares were worth a tidy sum on the international market.

POLLY. And you've won a re-trial. Or appeal. He'll decide what to call it when you appear before him tomorrow.

MACK. I can't take it all in yet. To have miracles pouring down among prison walls, with a veritable angel, my own Polly dishing them out right and left ... it's too much. Give me your hand to kiss. (*Pulls her hand inside the bars and kisses it all the way up to the shoulders.*)

POLLY. By noon tomorrow, you'll be a free man.

BABA. But ten thousand dollars poorer.

MACK. A sound investment Baba. (*He is studying the document.*) But tell me Polly, who thought up this loophole, this secret society business?

POLLY. The Justice himself of course.

MACK. It's genius. Pure genius.

DOGO *(patrolling)*. Time is running out sir.

MACK. Hey you. Come here.

DOGO. Sir? You called me sir?

MACK. Yes, you beanpole, come here. What did you say just now?

DOGO. You haven't forgotten the thousand dollars have you sir? You've less than 30 minutes to deliver.

MACK. Does your mother yet know what a blubber-bottomed pin-head-brain orang-utan of a son she delivered? Back on your beat, loser!

POLLY. Oh Mack, isn't it nice to see you have lost none of your spirit.

BABA. Yeah, the captain is always the captain no matter the circumstances.

MACK. Well, I'll tell you something, I can't say I've been very fond of these particular circumstances. I'll be glad when I'm far from them.

POLLY. Don't worry my dear, it won't be very long now. If you knew how much I've worried.

BABA. The prospect was revolting captain. And you in that new get-up. I mean, there are already enough holes in it ... oh I'm sorry.

MACK. No, I don't mind references now that it's all over. Too much of a good thing is bad – aesthetically speaking.

POLLY. Only one more night my dear and then ...

MACK. Back to the life of ease ... I can't wait. God, what a hole!

POLLY. And oh Mack, promise me, promise me you won't do any foolish thing that would bring you back in here. No treacherous women, no dangerous adventures. Let's go legitimate like the bigger crooks.

MACK. Of course my dear. Trust your Mack. One thought of my near escape, even the very thought of prison ... *(Shudders.)* Ugh, words cannot express the sense of degradation, humiliation etcetera etcetera. No, words are most inadequate, so why don't I just sing you the song I've composed here to pass the time. I've given it the title 'It's the Easy Life For Me' because, looking from the inside to the world outside, that's what everybody seems to be after – a life of ease – at the expense of somebody else of course.

POLLY. Naturally.

BABA. Quite so.

It's the Easy Life for Me
(Sung by MACKIE.)

Have you seen those workers daily jostling
To catch a bus to beat the factory deadline?
And the pregnant mother wedged with elbows
Barely dodging those haphazard blows
You'll claim the boss is also on the breadline
The 'go-slow' has wrecked his daily hustling
Well, a whole day in an air-conditioned car
Is sweeter than one hour in over-heated air

Chorus.

Explain the smugness on the face of the chauffeur?
He knows that at the bus stop life is even rougher.

Have you been to the hospital lately
And seen despair on faces in the line
Insolence from clerks lolling on the table
A waiting-room that smells worse than a stable
You'll say the rich are also laid supine
Diseases fell them though their life is stately
Well the rich can telephone for private cure
While for an aspirin the poor must long endure

Chorus.

Explain the joy-on-the-face of the Medical Apprentice?
The Medical Council has voted for Private Practice.
Did you go to the cathedral the other Sunday
And hear the bishop on the theme of pain?
Suffering is sent to make a fellow great
Fighting with rats for gari[17] in a garret.
Bullshit! Let riches fall on me like rain
And keep your starving greatness any day.
A life of ease is what a rich man knows
Glory is cold when the wind of hunger blows

Chorus.

Explain the beggar's rapture hustling by the mosque
He's chewing fleshy nuts while the prisoner gets the
husk.

Scene Three

DEE-JAY. And now, fellow expatriates, we proceed to show you
that even the greatest men have their moments of doubt. True
greatness comes however from the methods applied to resolve
doubts, and if such doubts prove impossible to resolve, from an
ability to transfer such doubts unto others. Once again, the scene
is the headquarters of Home from Home for the Homeless.

ANIKURA *(he has been standing still, chewing his lower lip)*. A
dirty trick. Just the kind of low-down skunk-stunk trick to expect
from a so-called captain who does not even understand what it

means to talk of *(Palm over his heart.)* 'my honour as an officer and a gentleman'.

DE MADAM. It only worked because he has the police on his side.

ANIKURA. The police hm? Well, maybe we can rake up something higher than the police.

DE MADAM. But dearie, the police are in charge of the law.

ANIKURA. The question is not who's in charge but who makes the law. The question is always – who's the law-giver? *(A knock on the door.)* That will be Colonel Moses now. Right, let him in.

JIMMY. Enter the Capo di Capi. He's all yours chief.

ANIKURA. Stay! And bring in the others. I asked them all to stay around. Colonel Moses has to see us for himself.

> JIMMY *gives a piercing whistle. From every direction the* BEGGARS *begin to limp, crawl and otherways ingratiate their way in.*

Stop! Stop it! Do you think you can milk one centime out of the colonel here? He'd as soon shoot out your empty sockets as give you money for a false eye. Sit down, act normal. I brought you here as evidence, as witnesses. Get up! Get up! Where's your manners? Have you found the colonel a seat yet? Telling you to cut out the beggar-stuff isn't the same as asking you to lose your sense of precedence. Can't I ever teach you anything? If you can't act servile before the military you haven't yet learnt the art of begging without seeming to beg, right?

BEGGARS *(as they scramble to find* MOSES *a chair)*. How to beg without seeming to. Lesson nine.

ANIKURA. Now that's better. Squat where you are and occupy as small a space as possible – the army's here.

MOSES. Oh please chief . . .

ANIKURA. No, if *you* please Colonel, only if you please. Now please, I want you to take a look. Take a good look.

DE MADAM *(stage whisper)*. Do you think he might like a drink?

ANIKURA. Of course. Colonel, may I present . . . my consort. De

Madam is how she is known among ours.

MOSES. I am honoured, madam.

DE MADAM. *We* are Colonel, *we* are. Now what shall I offer you as refreshment?

ANIKURA. Open that champagne we've been saving for the emperor's coronation . . .

MOSES. Oh no, it's banned. Oh, of course I'm away from home. No, no matter what, I'm still an ambassador for the nation.

ANIKURA. The champagne my dear. (MADAM ANIKURA *goes off.*) Captain Macheath had six magnum at his wedding and Commissioner Inspector of Police Brown didn't say no. Now what's Brown but a mere law enforcer? You by contrast, Colonel Moses are a law-giver. If champagne is okay for a mere enforcer, and a bent one at that . . . ah there you are my Colonel. (MADAM ANIKURA *enters with three glasses of champagne which are taken by* MOSES, ANIKURA *and herself.*) Your health Colonel.

MOSES. Yours chief. (*He looks round uneasily as he drinks. The* BEGGARS *are staring unblinkingly at him.*)

ANIKURA. Gazes down rookies! (*All eyes are immediately lowered.*) You must forgive them my colonel. It isn't so much that they are ill-mannered for staring, as that they can't forget what they were, or what they hope is in store for them. Too impatient you see. And yet, the sight of this champagne, drunk so fraternally by you, me and my consort, serves to stimulate them along the path of dilligence in scholarship. Take a look at them Colonel. Take a good look at them.

MOSES (*clearly embarrassed*). I er . . . I . . .

ANIKURA. Naturally, with their guards dropped, with their play-acting suspended you cannot believe your eyes. Well, your eyes do not deceive you. Stand up Professor Bamgbapo.

BAMGBAPO (*suavely*). Colonel Moses, surely you remember me.

MOSES. What! Not Professor . . . I mean, our chairman of the Mining Corporation.

BAMGBAPO. At your service.

MOSES. But what are you doing here? I mean, you were not retired. I . . . I . . . yes, you were even commended for . . .

BAMGBAPO. Yes, I am still on active service Colonel, both at the university and in the Ministry of Mines and Power. But right now I am on sabbatical from the university and on study leave from the Ministry.

MOSES. But surely, I mean, why . . .

BAMGBAPO. Sabbatical, *and* study leave. As you observe, I am undergoing a refresher course. All perfectly in order.

MOSES. A refresher course in what, Professor?

ANIKURA. Do sit down Professor, I'll take it from there. Now Colonel, how do you think our good friend here bagged his professorship? And how do you think he went on to bag the chairmanship of one corporation after another? And how, let me ask you, am I prepared to bet you 500 naira to the entire day's takings of Anikura's Army of Beggars that, shortly after his refresher course, he will also bag the chairmanship of the National Haulage, Air-Freight and Shipping Lines? Now you tell me that.

MOSES (*shaking his head*). I think I'm going crazy.

ANIKURA. Not at all. Boys, read him the First Commandment.

ALL. He who begs, bags.

ANIKURA. He who begs, bags. (*They all burst out laughing.*)

BAMGBAPO. Colonel Moses, how do you think I developed such a persuasive style of sucking up to the army boys. Well, I suppose to some it comes naturally. At first I fooled myself I was a natural beggar. Fortunately, one of chief's talent scouts spotted me in time. I was invited for special training.

DE MADAM (*pouring*). A little more champagne, Colonel.

BAMGBAPO (*self-assured*). I haven't done too badly have I master?

ANIKURA. Down! Gazes down! Right down! Crawl! (*They all obey.* DE MADAM *refills the champagne glasses.*) Boots, boots! (*They begin to lick* MOSES' *boots, noisily. He flees.*) Now take a good look Colonel. Take a damned good look. Does that bunch look like a secret society?

MOSES. What!

ANIKURA. Well, decide for yourself. Does that look like a dangerous, secret society?

MOSES. I'm afraid I don't . . .

ANIKURA. Understand? I'll explain. This establishment, this high institution of learning, of research, this beneficient society for the relief of burdened consciences, this . . . oh, it's too much! It's too much captain.

MOSES. What is it chief? Tell me.

ANIKURA (goes nearer, booting the BEGGARS out of his way. They crawl back to their positions). Did you not follow the appeal session of the case of Macheath? We were denounced. An enemy of state, in prison for multiple murders, arson, forgery, fraud, bawdry, blasphemy, rape and seduction and other unmentionable acts, this social fiend, deservedly condemned to public execution tomorrow got some traitors to swear to an affidavit denouncing my Home from Home for the Homeless as a secret society – just to escape hot perforations.

MOSES. But why? What has it to do with you?

ANIKURA (puffing his chest). We did it. He was convicted on our evidence. But the appeal court has now decided that evidence was worthless. Macheath's appeal was granted and he was set free to roam the streets an hour ago.

MOSES (getting up recites). Since I came to Centrafrique as Legal and Security Adviser, whose brief, apart from matters of internal security, embraced the reform of the present reactionary and colonial legal system inherited from the French, the formulation of new statutes in consonance with the forward-looking spirit of a modern imperial age, I have done my best to ensure the independence of the judiciary at all stages. I have been gratified to find that the emperor himself – we might as well give him his full title now (Looking at his watch.), it's less than 15 hours to go – I was saying, I have been very gratified that the emperor has accepted this principle of the independence of the judiciary. I cannot now go back and recommend any interference in the carefully laid-out judicial processes.

ANIKURA. It does you credit Colonel. Still, he who makes can

break – that's an even older adage. You made the law. Even if
you won't exactly break it you can bend it a little.

MOSES. And how do you recommend one does that?

ANIKURA. A tiny decree, back-dated of course, abolishing the
right of appeal from your special tribunals.

MOSES *(going)*. Excuse me.

ANIKURA. You think that's fair do you? You advised the Imperial
Decree on secret societies didn't you?

MOSES. A short cut for dealing with subversives. All subversive
movements are by nature secret. The stability of the regime had
to be protected.

ANIKURA. But you've gone and given a convenient weapon, not
just to our enemy, but to the Public Enemy Number One. He's
escaping the local Bar Beach Show thanks to you. Mr Law-giver,
do you call that justice?

MOSES. The law is ineffectual unless it guarantees the security of
the ruler. In the process, it is not unthinkable that a minor
criminal or two might escape the noose.

ALL. Minor criminal!

MOSES. Well, good night. Stay out of sight tomorrow. The streets
must be free of any unsightly appearance.

> As he exits, a scream is heard from outside. COLONEL
> MOSES *backs inside while* JIMMY *dashes out in the direc-*
> *tion of the noise.*

ANIKURA. What the hell . . .!

> JIMMY *returns dragging a squirming prophet* JERU *with*
> *him.*

JIMMY. Look what I found.

ANIKURA. Well, well well, fancy meeting you here. Spying as
usual I suppose?

JERU. Changing sides if you want to know. *(He keeps his*

frightened eyes on COLONEL MOSES.)

ANIKURA *(a big guffaw)*. Changing sides. That's rich. And from which side to which?

JERU. It's simple really. One of my er . . . little flock came to inform me that a uniformed man was seen entering your headquarters. Counting by the stars and pips and whatever, it was my informant's opinion that the officer was of no less a rank than that of a brigadier.

ANIKURA. Colonel actually. Well, what about it?

JERU. What difference does it make? Even a corporal would do for Captain Macheath. All he's got is the police. If you've got the army on your side . . . well, at the very least it puts his fate in the balance. I don't like hanging there with him.

ANIKURA *(to* MOSES). See? What a friend. What a holiness. Still you haven't told us why you had to yell out like that.

JERU. Oh, I recognized him that's all. He took the skin off my back the other day. Well, night to be more accurate. But I recognize him all right.

ANIKURA. What's all this about? He's a legal adviser; he's not a Commissioner Brown prowling the streets you know.

JERU *(stubbornly)*. It's him all right.

The BEGGARS *have become more alert, begun to take interest.*

BAMGBAPO. Did you say at night?

AHMED. Allah, it's him!

MOSES. I . . . er . . . I think there's some mistake.

JERU. Mistake! His men held me down on the bonnet of my car — you know my Volvo 264 of course, bought for me by my grateful congregation. My driver overtook his car and that annoyed him, so they chased me, held me down on the bonnet while he applied a koboko to my back. Twelve strokes in all.

AHMED. Yes, it's him. Chief, you know that culvert under the bridge where we sometimes pass the night. They came in one night and dragged us all out. I remember him saying he was getting rusty and needed to keep in shape. Eighteen strokes apiece!

BAMGBAPO. I wouldn't have believed it of you Colonel Moses. So it was you at the Night-Club Bistingo! Chief, look! *(He shows him his back.)* I had just come out from the Bistingo – I go there to relax after the day's practicals, you know. I began negotiations with this . . . er . . . prostitute. All work and no play you know . . . Well, he sat in his car . . . I didn't see his face you see. But he sent his driver to go and bring the same girl. I told the driver to go to hell. The next moment I was down in the gutter. The driver took my neck at the back and pressed my face into the muck. He came out of the car and lay into me with his swagger-stick. I fainted, chief.

MOSES *(coldly).* It was someone else. If you fainted, how could you say it was me?

BAMGBAPO. Because of what you said. They were the last thing I heard before I passed out. You said, Ha, that's cured a little of my nostalgia for good old Lagos.

MOSES. I tell you, you are all mistaken. I who have shaken hands with the emperor-to-be, could I descend to such a level?

AHMED. It's sheer profanity Chief. The Koran approves begging.

ANIKURA. My beggars. My boys. My prize pupil. *(He collapses in a chair.)*

DE MADAM. Mind your heart dearie.

ANIKURA. My prize pupil! The humiliation.

JERU. And a holy man in my prophet's habit. Laid out on the red-hot bonnet of my Volvo 264, flaggellated like the two thieves on either side of the cross . . .

ANIKURA. Shut up you double-dealing profaner! *(Sips from the glass offered him by* DE MADAM. *)* Law-giver Moses did you really get back into your old habits at the expense of my boys?

MOSES. A mistake. It can happen to anyone.

ANIKURA. *You* laid a hand on my boys! Do you know how much I pay your counterparts here for protection? Do you?

MOSES. Please, don't make such an issue of it.

BAMGBAPO. You bet *I* will. I'll make a report of your conduct when I return home. I can reach ears higher than yours you know. You'll be recalled and court-martialled. A disgrace to your uniform.

MOSES *smiles smugly.*

ANIKURA. He'll like that. Ho ho, he'll like that. Look at him! He knows nothing will happen to him from that direction. I could report him to Folksy Boksy who likes to have a monopoly in the matter of stamping the life out of vagrants and children but, Boksy might actually give him a medal. He's getting no younger you know, so he doesn't mind a little help from specialists. No, what we'll do is . . . Let me think! *(He strikes his thinking pose.)*

JERU. If I may make a suggestion.

ANIKURA. Shut up! *(A few seconds silence.)* I have thought. Where is Tako the Law?

ALATAKO. Chief?

CHIEF. Boky is our target. Think of a way of getting him bad with Emperor Boky in person. Frame him or something. Some act of *lese majeste* – that's French for imperial infra dig. Maybe Commissioner Brown can come into it . . .

MOSES *(frightened).* Look here . . . perhaps I can explain. You have to remember I was not properly briefed.

ANIKURA. Not properly briefed . . . that's the black man for you. He arrives in a strange country and starts skinning his own countrymen . . .

AHMED. The Koran says it's blessed to give.

ANIKURA. Colonel, meet a fellow professional of yours, A. G. Alatako, whom I've assured will beg his way to the rank of attorney-general in less than three years. He will prove such a beautiful beggar that the Sharia[18] Courts will compete for him to be their president. Relax Moses. Alatako here is going to devise a beautiful frame-up for you. Maybe he will furnish proof that the Nigerian government actually sent you here to sabotage his coronation. He'll believe us – our people have been making radical noises lately.

ALATAKO. The notice is short Your Worship. Could one plead for an adjournment?

ANIKURA. Not much time, if he is to get the emperor to sign that Retroactive Repeal of Right of Appeal, track down and recapture Captain Macheath, tie him to a stake and execute him before tomorrow's coronation pageant . . .

ALATAKO. I'll need the latest newspapers from home. And a few moments er . . . Your Lordship . . . yes, just a short adjournment to prepare my brief.

ANIKURA. Court adjourned! Jimmy, fetch that bundle of papers which came with the consignment of second-hand velvet from Alhaja Bosikona. Class, while we are waiting for the court to re-convene, what about a little song on the noble art of begging. Dee-jay?

DEE-JAY. Why not the anthem itself chief. It's a high point in the *deroulement* of events I think. I would recommend 'The Beggars' Anthem' at this point.

ANIKURA. I bow to your professional judgement.

The Beggars Anthem

> To beg is to bag
> Not, is to lag
> Behind most successful men
> Is a history of fulsome mien
> It's not such a shame
> If you wish to make a name
> To learn how to butter up
> How to be a sucker-up
>
> I know a famous type
> Who seeks for favours ripe
> When a Big Shot calls him on the phone

He would fling down his body prone
He turns lizard clown
His head up and down
And recites his favourite formula:
Idobale ni mo wa.[19]

When a soldier sets on you
And beats you black and blue
Don't bother to protest
It's no worse than Soro manhood test
And the louder you can beg
The less your knees will sag
And remember to say Thank you sah
Lest he show you yet more power.

Pride has a price
Too heavy for the wise
The excess weight of opulence
Is balanced by benevolence
We fill a social need
Take the stigma out of greed
Have you money, power or place to spend?
The beggar is your friend.

ALATAKO. Chief, we have him! *(Flourishing a newspaper.)*

ANIKURA. Are you sure?

ALATAKO. Try me, chief. I propose to hoist him on his own petard.

ANIKURA. The court is now in session!

ALATAKO. With your permission your Lordship, I wish to present this document in evidence!

ANIKURA. Is it admissible? Speak, law-giver. (MOSES *remains silent.)* Silence means consent. The document[20] is admitted in evidence. The document is headed Ref. No. B.63214 / Vol 11/258 Federal Ministry of Establishments dated 15th August,

1970. It is hereby admitted.

ALATAKO. I shall now proceed to cross-examination.

ANIKURA. Stand by Jimmy. This is not the United States, Colonel Moses, where you can get away from speaking the truth by pleading the Fifth Commandment.

BAMGBAPO. Amendment, chief.

ANIKURA. What?

BAMGBAPO. Amendment, amendment. Not commandment.

ANIKURA. Are you sure?

BAMGBAPO. My CV boasts some five solid papers on the subject.

ANIKURA. Are you suggesting they made up ten Amendments to the Ten Commandments?

BAMGBAPO. Chief, we are talking about the Fifth Amendment.

ANIKURA. Thank you. Which is what you Moses, are not allowed to take. If he does Jimmy, you know what to do. This is not a savage country where people pretend to obey the Ten Commandments but make one Amendment so they can frustrate all ten. Proceed.

ALATAKO. Colonel Moses, do you admit that you are the army legal adviser to the current regime in the old homeland etc. etc. (MOSES *remains stubborn.* JIMMY *moves to a position directly behind him.*)

MOSES. I am not the legal anything.

JIMMY *(arm poised for a blow).* Do I . . .?

ALATAKO. No, not needed. Colonel Moses, do you understand legal arguments?

MOSES. I was trained as a lawyer.

ALATAKO. Good, good, we make progress. Would you say, Colonel Moses, that you are the most senior member of your profession who holds an army rank?

MOSES. What does that prove?

ALATAKO *(indulgently).* You have to answer the question.

MOSES *(shrugs).* I suppose so.

ALATAKO. I am satisfied with your answer. And now Colonel Moses, pay strict attention please, Do the following names and dates mean anything to you? Mushin Riots 1970; Ugep Village, 1975; Epe Riots, 1975; orile-Agege, January 1976; Kalakuta Feb. 1977; Shendan, Plateau State, June 1977; Enugu, September 1977. . . . I could go on for ever your Worship . . .

ANIKURA. No please don't go on for ever. He is the one who would like to hang on for ever. Terminate his agony.

ALATAKO. As Your Lordship pleases. I have yet another question for the accused. Did you have a hand in the drafting of the Secret Society Decree for Centrafrique?

MOSES. Don't you agree that secret societies are an evil menace, a cankerworm in the fragile solidarity of the nation, a danger to national security.

ALATAKO. Absolutely, absolutely. I implore the court to take special note of the loyal sentiments of the accused. Condemned or not by this court, they should be passed on to his bosses.

ANIKURA. Pray proceed.

ALATAKO. With your permission your Lordship, I would like to offer the already tendered document B.63214/Vol 11/258 to the accused. Do you recognize it?

MOSES. Yes that's the government directive to . . .

ALATAKO. Kindly limit yourself to the simple answers Yes and No. Yes-no?

MOSES. Yes.

ALATAKO. Do you admit to having a hand in these definitions of a secret society?

MOSES. I certainly will not deny it. If you had any idea the harm which secret societies . . .

ALATAKO. I assure you Colonel Moses, this document does you credit. I congratulate you. It is one of the most inspiring and cleansing documents of our time. Now be good enough to read your first definition of a secret society.

MOSES (reading). A secret society is defined to include any society 'whose membership is not known or made public'.

ALATAKO. I am grateful to the witness. Not known. Not made public. Now Colonel Moses, kindly tell me what the organization which you represent had to report about the identity of the culprits in the military-civilian riots which we have had the displeasure of enumerating before this court. Of the criminal gang involved in the burning down of villages, assault, rape, murder etc. etc. your organization blamed, in 1970 . . .

ALL. Unknown soldiers.

ALATAKO. In 1971?

ALL. Unknown soldiers

ALATAKO. 1972?

ALL. Unknown soldiers.

ALATAKO. 1973?

ALL. Unknown soldiers.

ALATAKO. 1974?

ALL. Unknown soldiers.

ALATAKO. 1975?

ALL. Unknown soldiers.

ALATAKO. 1976?

ALL. Unknown soldiers.

ALATAKO. 1977?

ALL. Unknown soldiers.

ALATAKO..1978?

ALL. Unknown soldiers.

ALATAKO. 1979?

ALL. Unknown soldiers.

ALATAKO. 1980? Oh, wait a minute. Are we ahead of time?

ANIKURA. While you are getting back in time, let's have the 'Ballad of the Unknown Soldier'.

DEE-JAY. Gee, I'm sorry, haven't got all the sound-effects for that yet. We tried to get the real thing you know, the sound of smashed windscreens, bones crunching, koboko descending, violated daughters, screaming students, you know, the usual stuff. But the recording machine got smashed.

ANIKURA. What! Who dared?

ALL. Unknown soldiers.

The BEGGARS *break into the 'Unknown Soldiers' dance, full of contortions, limping and groaning.*

ANIKURA. Ha! All right, let the law take its course.

ALATAKO. Unknown soldiers. Not known. Not made public. Major Moses, I put it to you you are part of a secret society.

MOSES. Nonsense, you can't persuade the emperor with that. All soldiers have their names on the government payroll. What's so secret about that?

ALATAKO. Colonel Moses, I must impose upon you once more. Kindly read the last paragraph of definitions of a secret society in Document B.63214 /Vol 11/258. Loud please.

MOSES *(reads with emphasis)*. . . . whose members are under oath, obligation or other threat to promote the interests (legitimate or illegitimate) of one another and come to one another's aid *under all* circumstances, without due regard to merit, fair play and justice, to the detriment of the legitimate expectation of non-members.'

ALATAKO. Thank you Colonel Moses. Your Worship, I refer you to the widely-reported details of the burning down of the Kalakuta Relpublic. I refer you to the even more recent incident in Kano where a whole batallion of soldiers, because one of them was knocked down, barricaded the streets, violated all passers-by, totally innocent passers-by, maimed, looted, burnt and intimidated all and sundry without a consideration of the *merits or demerits* of their grievance. And I quote again portions of the definitions of a secret society . . . formulated by Colonel Moses, law-giver extraordinary in person – I quote . . . 'whose members are under oath, obligation, repeat, obligation, or other threat to promote the interests (legitimate or illegitimate) of one another and to come to one another's aid *under all* circumstances.' . . . 'Under all', Your Worship, being a qualification actually underlined by Colonel Moses and his brink-tank . . . I continue, quote . . . 'without due regard to merit, fair play and justice, to detriment of the legitimate expectation of non-members.' Non-members. That's us, Your Worship. Us. I beg to rest my case.

Applause from all the BEGGARS, *they crowd round him, slap him on the back, shake his hand. Cries of 'Tako the Law' etc. create a din.*

ANIKURA *(banging a bottle on the table).* Order! Order in my court damn you! Order! *(Silence is gradually restored. Some seconds after silence* ANIKURA *still sits, pondering.)* Hm. Class, certain issues of constitutional dimensions have been raised. Such as – are we, or are we not being run by a secret society? Colonel Moses, be a friend of the court and come to our aid. What say you?

MOSES. Well, I don't know. What do you want me to say?

ANIKURA. Oh nothing, nothing. But you are an officer and a gentleman, that means, a man of honour. If you find . . . and as an enlightened man you are not one to refuse the validity of arguments . . . If you discover how easy it is to be accused of being that which you are not, and you happen to know also of others who are being victimized through the accusation of being what they are not – and with even less reason! Damn it! 'Come to one another's aid?' Look at them! These rats would take the last morsel from each other's mouth if they could get away with it. No Colonel, there is nothing secret about this society. Can you say the same of yours? If we were to contact Commissioner Brown with our evidence – you represent rival organizations and Emperor Boky is a very hasty man, very hasty indeed. For him *any* secret society represents a personal threat. What say you, sir?

MOSES *(suddenly resolved).* Enough! *(All eyes turn towards him.)* Macheath . . . shall die. *(He marches off as one who means business.)*

DEE-JAY *(commentator's excited voice).* . . . And it's Civil Guard, Civil Guard ridden by Baba Yaro heading once again for a winner – a full length ahead of Kijipa his nearest rival and only other real contender worth bothering about. Boy, what a horse!

That's not to say he's having it easy all the way. Sunny Boy on Kijipa is making it quite a race. Trying everything to get the last ounce out of that horse, really laying on the whip. No, no question about it, Sunny Boy isn't a quitter, he's using the whip more and more in desperation but no, he really isn't in the same class as Baba Yaro. That game little jockey has ridden Civil Guard with beautiful teamsmanship. He seems to have that uncanny horse intelligence, knows just when to give Civil Guard a second wind, when to restrain him a little, knows when to take him all out. They are coming round the final bend now and the position is exactly the same, Civil Guard one length ahead. No doubt about it, what Baba Yaro has is strategy. Sunny Boy seems to depend entirely on the whip to bring the best out of Kijipa. Only some ten lengths away from the tape, Baba Yaro really coaxing the last effort out of his mount, pulling away a further head and . . . that's it! Civil Guard the winner by nearly a length and a half. And what a superb finish. What a pair! What a team! Baba Yaro on Civil Guard, winner of the Imperial Stakes . . . *(Volume trails off.)*

ANIKURA. Of course! Coronation races. The Imperial Stakes. After him Jimmy! After Colonel Moses. That's where he'll find Macheath. Hurry up the lot of you. You should be at the races begging. Find Macheath and keep him under close watch until Colonel Moses gets there. Better not fail!

DEE-JAY. . . .and the moral of that astonishing contrast of styles is this – You can whip a horse to water, but it takes the know-how to make him drink. *(Winks broadly.)* End of message. Oh, you don't mind do you? You have to get it in whenever you can. One of these days it might actually sink in – Fat chance!

Scene Four

Directly after the DEE-JAY's *comment, the* BAND *strikes up the tune of 'Who Killed Neo-Niga', this time in a brisk, 'Putting-in-the-boot' tempo. The* DEE-JAY *follows them in, doing a yet inaudible commentary into a hand-mike. Balloons float down from every direction and streamers fly through the air. Shouts of 'Hail Boky!' 'Long live the emperor', 'Long live the imperial family', 'Long live the dukes, the duchesses, the earls and marquises' 'Long live Africa', 'Hail the dawn of a new age'. Then to the steady beat of 'Neo-Niga', Boky's goon-squad enter chanting 'Vive, vive, vive L'empereur', 'Vive, vive, vive L'empereur ...' They are nearly across the stage when a voice sings out:*

VOICE. Who *crowned* de-Niga?

> *Dead silence. The squad-leader brings them to an on-the-spot movement, looks round him, searching for the singer. Suddenly he sees the culprit, screams 'There!', warms up the squad for action with the first steps of the Boot Stomp and launches them after the victim. They disappear off-stage.* DEE-JAY *comes on stage.*

DEE-JAY. Yea-eah man, go get him! Yeah folks, on this beautiful dawn in Bangui, it's fun-and-games as usual, only more of the same, more colour more splendour, more pageantry. And Captain Macheath is going to lend his own bit of colour to the occasion by bleeding through several holes to the delectation of the populace – men, women and children, the aged and crippled, from all walks of life ... oh here they come! They've come from distant parts of the country and – oh yes, the scramble has begun for ringside seats.

An ice-cream vendor cycles past.

VENDOR. Ice-cream! Keep cool with your favourite ice-cream. Special coronation flavours. Imperial vanilla. Caramel Bonarparte. Gateau Imperatrice . . .

DEE-JAY *(holding out a mike)*. Hey brother, how many ice-creams you hope to sell today?

VENDOR. Are you kidding? Do you know how many schools have declared a holiday so they can watch the execution? Man, I'm already sold out!

DEE-JAY. There it is. It makes your heart glow to see such a crimebusting, righteous people. They HATE sin, and they are going to see that the criminal gets his right royal deserts.

Enter a PATIENT, swathed in bandages, on crutches. A NURSE follows him with a drip-bottle still attached to his arm

PATIENT. Stop nagging me! I tell you I'm going to watch this one even if it kills me.

DEE-JAY *(holding out mike)*. Excuse me sir . . .

PATIENT. Of course I believe in public executions.

DEE-JAY. Well, that wasn't really what I was going to ask you sir.

PATIENT. Then it ought to be young man. I see you don't know your job. And I tell you something else, before they shoot them, they should drain their blood and put it in a blood-bank.[21] Then upright lawabiding citizens like me can gain something as least from their worthless existence.

DEE-JAY. Thank you very much sir. Now I wonder if you would mind telling the listeners how you . . .

PATIENT. Correction! I wasn't thinking. If they drained their blood in advance then there'll be no blood spattering around when the bullets land would there?

DEE-JAY. I imagine not sir.

PATIENT. So there you are. What's an execution without letting blood eh? Hm. I suppose they could always hang them. No. That's no use either. There's got to be blood. It's shooting. Nothing else would do.

DEE-JAY. Well, thank you sir, I hope you enjoy the show.

PATIENT. Wait a minute. Am I still on the air?

DEE-JAY. Certainly sir.

PATIENT. In that case . . . (He clears his throat, sings:)

> Blood, blood, glorious blood
> Nothing quite like it for offering to God
> Banish the gallows
> So I can wallow
> In the crimson juice of the criminal sod!
>
> Blood, blood, copious blood
> I'd happily drown if this earth it would flood
> It's blood I can feel well on
> So puncture the felon
> Give glory to God and make gory your god.

He breaks into a fit of coughing, followed by spasms and expires.

NURSE (feels for his pulse, finding none, closes his eyes and picks up his feet). I think he died happy. (Drags him out by the feet.)

DEE-JAY. Oh dear. A-ah . . . here comes a familiar face. A neighbour of mine to be precise. (Enter a WOMAN, angry-looking, herding five children.) Neighbour! You look angry. What's the matter?

NEIGHBOUR. What's the matter? I've divorced that foolish man that's all. Packed out of his house. He had the nerve to say we would stay at home and watch the shooting on television. The children said they wanted to see it live and I agreed with them. Television is not the same thing. We spent so much time arguing

I'm sure we have missed all the best seats. God punish him! *(Exit, with brood.)*

DEE-JAY *(using his binoculars).* The moment approaches. Macheath is on the way. From this distance I can say that he looks calm, unruffled, ready to meet his Maker. He has gambled his last, bedded his last and butchered his last. When the moment comes, there shall pass over this city a great gust of wind. That sound which you may or may not hear at home, those of you who are watching the scene on your television, will be the sigh of relief from the entire populace. And here comes . . . if my eyes do not deceive me . . .

Enter CHIEF ANIKURA *and* DE MADAM. BROWN *follows, sneaks in and hides in a corner.*

DEE-JAY. Chief Anikura, would you like to say a word to . . .

Chief ANIKURA *makes a rude noise.* DEE-JAY *recoils.*

DE MADAM. Good for him, the cheeky sod!
DEE-JAY. I think what the chief was trying to say is, No Comment.

Enter POLLY *and the syndicate. They stand on the opposite side.* POLLY *is uncomfortable, undecided. Suddenly she breaks into a run to their side, sobbing.*

DE MADAM *(comforting her).* There there, dearie. Blood will out. I always said it, blood's thicker than water. *(*POLLY *bursts into louder sobbing.)*
ANIKURA. Now you've gone and done it Cecilia.
DE MADAM. What did I do?
ANIKURA. Don't mention blood to her!
DE MADAM. Oh dear, and she such a sensitive child. Got that from me you know. Maybe you'd better not watch, Polly. What do you think? Shall I take you home?

POLLY *(recovers suddenly)*. Oh no, I'll be alright. I ought to stand by him to the last. It wouldn't be right for me to miss it would it?

ANIKURA. Quite right. Loyalty. That, she got from me.

Strains of 'Just a closer walk with thee', increasing in volume. Enter the bevy of WHORES, *led by* SUKIE, *doing a single-line dance to the tune.*

DEE-JAY. Do my eyes deceive me? There's your answer. For those bleeding-heart *cynics* and *liberals* who say that public execution is bad for public morale, behold the perfect answer. The entire female habituees of Playboy Club, the famous whorehouse of Madame Gbafe have been converted. To the last tit they have joined the CSU and here they come singing a different tune from that which we used to hear. Oh the age of miracles! Nothing like a public execution to melt the hardiest heart of stone. It's a sight to touch the most depraved heart. *(Wipes a tear.)* I am saved! I too am saved! Wash me clean in the blood of Mackie. Sorry – I mean in the blood of the Lord, Amen! I am saved sister, come round the corner and I'll show you.

He dashes to the front, partners SUKIE *and dances out. He later re-appears in his booth with his arms round* SUKIE, *during* MACKIE's *farewell song. Enter* MACHEATH, *in a contraption not unlike a tumbril. He is wheeled to the execution spot.* PROPHET JERU, a ROMAN CATHOLIC PRIEST, *an* ANGLICAN, *an* IMAM, *and a* SANGO PRIEST *detach themselves from the crowd and move towards* MACHEATH.

CATHOLIC. He's mine. He's taken Mass with us.

ANGLICAN. He's mine. I baptized him.

JERU. He's mine. I officiated at his wedding.

IMAN. He's mine. We celebrated Ileya[22] together.

SANGO PRIEST. Lightning is about to strike him. He's mine. Plus his property.[23]

OFFICER. Which of them do you acknowledge, prisoner?

MACK (*points to the* SANGO PRIEST). I like his style. (*The others protest.*) After all, property is what it's all about, not so?

The SANGO PRIEST *grins.*

Also, as it happens, I have none left. Nothing.

All the PRIESTS *retire, disgusted.*

Vultures!

POLLY (*moving towards him*). Oh Mackie you defiant soul. I knew you'd remain the same whatever happens.

MACK. Don't talk such nonsense. Have you ever seen anyone remain the same after he's been pierced by several bullets?

OFFICER. Have you any last pronouncements to make sir before we perform our side of the business?

MACK. Thank you officer. Your subtlety, your finesse is most impressive.

OFFICER (*looking at his watch*). Make it brief.

MACK. I shall be brief. Tell your men to take positions and take aim. When I have finished I shall raise my lace handkerchief like this and say 'So long'. They are to fire immediately. Speed and accuracy shall be greatly appreciated.

OFFICER. The army will oblige. (*He returns to squad.*) Positions! Aim! Hold your fire until I signal. Proceed Mr Macheath.

Mackie's Farewell

I hate to see the morning sun come up
I hate to see the morning sun come up
For it reminds me that my hour is up
Feeling tomorrow is not a thing I'll know

Feeling tomorrow is not a thing I'll know
Instead I'll be filling a hole down below

I'd like to tell you that I forgive you all
Who have done things to bring about my fall
You rotten policemen who double-crossed Mackie
At least I know I'm not the emperor's lackey
You venal women who betrayed your man
That's the way you've been since the world began
So if I tell you that I forgive you all
That's the same as saying, I hope you roast in he-e-ell!

Chorus:

I've got the imperial blues
I'm as blue as I can be
But not as blue as I'll be
In the face as the bullets hit me
Or grey or blue-black or whatever niggers are when they quench
I love my Emperor
I'm crazy 'bout the little terror
I think he's crazy too
He really belongs in the zoo

MACK. And who knows when he'll send you to join me in the cold, cold trench.

CHORUS. And who knows when he'll send us to join you in the cold cold trench.

MACK. So please forgive me if I have done you wrong And mind you kiss the emperor's arse if your life you would prolong
Mackie is going now who's been with you . . . so long.

As the song reaches the very end and MACK*'s hand raised half-way up, a siren is heard fast approaching.*

DEE-JAY. What's this? The emperor's extraordinary courier!

CROWD. The emperor! Long live the emperor! Long live the emperor! Vive vive vive l'empereur! Vive vive vive l'empereur! Vive vive vive l'empereur!

Preceded by a trumpeter blowing a fanfare, the COURIER *races towards the* DEE-JAY *with a scroll.*

COURIER *(lifts his hand. Silence)*. Read the proclamation.

DEE-JAY. 'We, Our Serene Highness, newly reincarnated, and crowned Emperor Charlemagne Desiree Boky the First, Lion of Bangui, Tiger of the Tropics, Elect of God, First among Kings and Emperors, the Pulsing Nugget of Life, and Radiating Sun of Africa hereby pronounce, in honour of our coronation on this day, a general Amnesty for all common criminals. Take heed however, that this great condescension shall not, repeat shall not extend to anyone accused or convicted of crimes of a political nature. Long live the emperor!'

COURIER. Long live the emperor!

CROWD. Long live the emperor! Long live the imperial family! Mackie's saved. He's saved. Saved! Three hearty cheers for the emperor. Hip Hip Hip Hurray! Hip Hip Hip Hurray! Hip Hip Hip Hurray!.

ANIKURA *(steps forward and addresses audience)*. Well, does that surprise you? It shouldn't. We men of influence – of power if you like – respect one another. We speak the same language, so we usually work things out. As for you lot,

> Remember, it's not everyday
> The emperor's courier timely arrives
> Repairing wrongs, sustaining rights
> And neatly installing the back-to-square-one.
> And watch out! Beware certain well-tuned voices
> That clamour loudest: 'Justice-for-all'!
> A ragged coat does not virtue make

— Here I stand as your prime example —
Nor is the predator a champion of rights,
A brave Robin Hood equalizing the loot
It's too easy to declare society fair game —
For proof, my son-in-law is more than ample.
What we must look for is the real beneficiary
Who does it profit? That question soon
Overtakes all your slogans — who gains?
Who really accumulates and exercises
Power over others. The currency of that power
Though it forms the bone of contention
Soon proves secondary. I tell you —
Power is delicious *(Turns sharply.)* Heel!

Immediately the BEGGARS *shuffle towards him.* MACKIE
next snaps his fingers. POLLY *followed by the gang, gather
round him. The band strikes up the tune of* 'Mack the Knife'.

Enter BOKY *in his Imperial robes, drawn in a chariot by four
stalwarts. He drives across, and a procession forms behind him
in the following order: The* PRIESTS; *the* UNIFORMED
SERVICES; CHIEF ANIKURA *and* MACHEATH *who
first go through a dumb-play of* 'After-you' *courtesies; then fall
in step with each other, followed by their* WOMEN; *the*
GANGS; *the* WHORES; *the* GENERAL RABBLE.

THE END

Appendix

DEE-JAY. We've taken over. It's as simple as that. In case it has escaped your notice, I'm laying it on you man, we've taken over. I mean, man, get wise, when did you last see a *live* band back home, I mean live man? A *real live* band with living musicians? Okay Okay, so when some society fatso wants to spray, he gets a band together someplace and gets some sweaty foreheads to stick Murtalas[1] on. But that's special man, that's *occasion*. We're talking about real life, dig? So I'll just introduce myself. I'm your MCDJ – Master of Ceremonies Disc-Jockey. Or Master of Ceremonies or Disc Jockey. Or simply Dee-jay. Take your choice. See what I mean? You got a choice. You don't get a choice with a live band. And you don't get much choice between live-band or dee-jays, cause the home country is broke see? And when that country goes broke you know what goes first. If you don't, ask the Universities. Well, dee-jays come cheap, that's why I'm hosting this show. One time we called it the *Way-Out Opera* – for short, *Opera Wayo*. Call it the *Beggars' Opera* if you insist – that's what the whole nation is doing – begging for a slice of the action.

And don't think it's the kind of begging you're used to. Here the beggars say 'Give me a slice of the action or – *(Demonstrating.)* – give me a slice off your throat. Man, some beggars! You know what, why don't you just make up your own title as we go along because, I tell you brother, I'm yet to decide whether such a way-out opera should be named after the beggars, the army, the bandits, the police, the cash-madams, the students, the trade-unionists, the Alhajis and Alhajas, the Aladura, the Academicas, the Holy Patriarchs and Unholy Heresiarchs – I mean man, in

this way-out country everyone acts way out. Including the traffic.
Maybe we should call it, the *Trafficking Opera*. Which just complicates things with trafficking in foreign exchange. Nice topical
touch. Man, this country whips you right out on cloud nine! I'd
better bring you back to earth with a song about that universal
species of humanity — and if you haven't heard Louis Armstrong
do his own thing with good old Mack, man, just where you been?
One a-two-a-three — take it from there baby. Let's go.

Textual Notes

[1]MURTALAS: Local slang for 20 naira notes.
[2]IGBETI: A village in Western Nigeria whose rich marble resources
have become the monopoly of a private group. Several mysterious
deaths have overtaken the champions of public rights to the marble.
(This deposit has since been taken over by the Civilian government
in Oyo State: 1979.)
[3]OGAH SAH: Big Chief Sir.
OGA SA: Big Chief turn tail.
[4]RANKA DEDE: A very respectful salutation of feudal origin.
[5]IKOYI: A Lagos elite suburbia.
[6]TAPHY: A by-word now for the authorized flogging of Nigerian
citizens by soldiers for alleged traffic infractions etc. Neither women
nor the elderly were spared this experience of public humiliation.
[7]SUZIES: Local for dashing young women.
[8]UDOJI: Named for the 1975 wages review commission which
created Nigeria's record inflation.
[9]OTIO: Never Never!
[10]BAR BEACH SHOW: The Bar Beach became the public execution arena in Lagos for Nigeria's armed robbers.

[11]AWOOF: Booty.

[12]A reference to General Gowon's wedding during the Nigerian Civil War. Commemoratory stamps were printed and launched throughout Nigerian embassies while this then Head of State claimed the (late) capture of a Biafran stronghold as his wedding present.

[13]An actual incident. Fed up with the public obscenity of corpses in public places, Tai Solarin, a tireless reformer and former Public Complaints Commissioner obtained a plain coffin and, with some helpers, personally scooped the decomposed remains of a 35-day old corpse on a public highway into the coffin and presented it to the Lagos City Council.

[14]ATTACK TRADE: Named for the brisk across-the-lines business during the Civil War.

[15]FARANSE: The French, or black francophones.

[16]BEEN-TOS: Been to Europe and 'abroad'.

[17]GARI: A West African staple food. A farina.

[18]SHARIA: The Moslem religious law. There was then strong agitation for its elevation to the Federal Appeal level in Nigeria. (The Iranian example may yet resurrect such piety.)

[19]IDOBALE NI MO WA: Respectfully prostrated am I.

[20]SECRET SOCIETIES: The quotes are from a government directive on the subject, a typical overkill response to the sudden wave of sanctimonious denunciations by the Nigerian public. There are of course *evil* secret societies.

[21]Actual suggestions in Readers' Letters to newspapers.

[22]ILEYA: Moslem Festival.

[23]SANGO: God of Thunder and Lightning. Kills his victims, and his priests claim their property.

Methuen World Classics

Aeschylus (two volumes)
Jean Anouilh
John Arden
Arden & D'Arcy
Aristophanes (two volumes)
Aristophanes & Menander
Peter Barnes (two volumes)
Brendan Behan
Aphra Behn
Edward Bond (four volumes)
Bertolt Brecht
  (four volumes)
Howard Brenton
  (two volumes)
Büchner
Bulgakov
Calderón
Anton Chekhov
Caryl Churchill
  (two volumes)
Noël Coward (five volumes)
Sarah Daniels
Eduardo De Filippo
David Edgar
  (three volumes)
Euripides (three volumes)
Dario Fo (two volumes)
Michael Frayn
  (two volumes)
Max Frisch
Gorky
Harley Granville Barker
  (two volumes)

Henrik Ibsen (six volumes)
Lorca (three volumes)
David Mamet
Marivaux
Mustapha Matura
David Mercer
  (two volumes)
Arthur Miller
  (four volumes)
Anthony Minghella
Molière
Tom Murphy (three volumes)
Peter Nichols
  (two volumes)
Clifford Odets
Joe Orton
Louise Page
A. W. Pinero
Luigi Pirandello
Stephen Poliakoff
Terence Rattigan
Ntozake Shange
Sophocles (two volumes)
Wole Soyinka
David Storey
August Strindberg
  (three volumes)
J. M. Synge
Ramón del Valle-Inclán
Frank Wedekind
Oscar Wilde

Methuen Modern Plays

include work by